RODEO HEARTS

JOYCE LIVINGSTON

ISBN 978-1-60260-797-2

Scripture quotations are taken from the King James Version of the Bible.

Scripture quotations are taken from The Living Bible © 1971. Used by permission of Tyndale House Publishers, Inc. Wheaton, Illinois 60189. All rights reserved.

This book is a work of fiction. Names, characters, places, and incidents are either products of the author's imagination or used fictitiously. Any similarity to actual people, organizations, and/or events is purely coincidental.

Cover design: Kirk Douponce, DogEared Design

Published by Barbour Publishing, Inc., P.O. Box 719, Uhrichsville, Ohio 44683, www.barbourbooks.com

Our mission is to publish and distribute inspirational products offering exceptional value and biblical encouragement to the masses.

Printed in the United States of America.

Dear Readers,

How can I thank you for deciding to read *Rodeo Hearts*? I had so much fun writing these three stories. Being a City Gal I had never been exposed to the world of rodeo until it was my privilege to attend one held in the Dallas, Texas, area. Fortunately, a lovely couple who sat directly behind me took the time and effort to explain to me what was going on in each event. From then on, I was hooked! If you love rodeo I know you will enjoy these stories. Even if you aren't a rodeo fan, I think you will love the characters and their trials. The setting of each story is unique. And best of all—each one is a love story. Oh how I adore love stories! So, pick up your copy of *Rodeo Hearts*, curl up in your favorite chair, and vicariously join my heroines—Rose, Dina, and Tassie—as they search for that perfect love we all seek.

I, personally, have found that love. After losing my precious, godly husband to a cancerous brain tumor five years ago, I vowed I would never marry again—sure I would never find another man who could even begin to equal him and his totally committed love for me. But God had a plan, and in His infinite wisdom, sent Pastor Dale Lewis into my life. Like me, Dale had lost his precious spouse of many years. Within a matter of days (after our first evening of spending time with one another—just to talk) we knew, without a shadow of a doubt, our God had brought us together. Three months later, we were married.

Dale (who has been one of the pastors of our church for over thirty years) is still serving the Lord in a full-time capacity, and I praise God for allowing me to serve beside my wonderful husband. He is an example of a true man of God. Our life is so full. Each day is an amazing adventure. I never expected to be a Pastor's Wife, but I am loving every minute of it! The love we share is so precious. Our goal in life is to serve the Lord as long as we have breath.

Do I plan to continue to write inspirational romance books? I've been asking God that same question. I love to write. So if God wants me to continue, I know He will lay it on my heart and give me the stories He wants me to write. In the meantime, may the Lord bless you and yours!

Joyce Livingston Lewis

THE BRIDE WORE BOOTS

Dedication

I dedicate this book to my wonderful husband, Pastor Dale Lewis—a true hero. He is a constant inspiration to me; an example of what every husband should be. Showered each day by his amazing, totally committed love, I am truly blessed to be his wife! Thank you, Dale, for all you do for me. But mostly I thank you for just being you! Mere words cannot express how much I love you!

God, in His infinite wisdom, saw fit to bring Dale and me together as husband and wife September 13, 2008. So I also want to dedicate this book to my six precious children: Dawn Lee Johnson; Don Livingston, Jr; Mark Livingston; Dari Lynn Leyba; Matthew; and Luke Livingston—and to Dale's three precious children: Dalene Hutson, Larry Lewis, and Randy Lewis. May our love for one another continue to grow!

Chapter 1

Rose Kinsey looked around the lawyer's cluttered office as she waited for him. She tried to compose her thoughts as she shifted nervously in the hard chair.

"Miss Kinsey? Sorry to be a few minutes late."

Her thoughts were interrupted by the voice of a beady-eyed little man in an out-of-date, double-breasted suit and string tie. As he entered the room, he was followed by a second man, who looked as though he belonged on the cover of a Sheplers Western Catalog. His look said *cowboy* from the hammered silver hatband on his jet-black Stetson, to his silver and turquoise belt buckle, to his expensive hand-tooled, black leather cowboy boots.

"It's all right," Rose said. "I think I'm a bit early."

The first man extended his birdlike hand. "I'm Ben Horner, your father's attorney. Sorry about your father's untimely death."

Rose swallowed hard and tried to blink back the tears that were pushing their way past her lids. Being here, doing this, was harder than she'd imagined it would be. "Thank you, Mr. Horner. I—ah, miss him so much. He was always there for me. Being back home now, thinking of going to the ranch—without him being there—" She attempted to regain her composure. "I'm sure you understand, if you've ever lost a loved one."

"Yes, indeed." The little man stood awkwardly, his hand still extended.

"But it is nice to meet you, Mr. Horner." She shook his hand. "I'm just sorry it has to be under these circumstances."

Why had her father chosen this scrawny little man to represent him? Surely there were other capable lawyers in the area, if not in Rock City. As her glance skittered past the skeletal man, apparently the little attorney noticed. He turned away from her and reached up to rest his hand on the taller man's shoulder.

"Bane is here." He gestured toward the second man. No explanation, no last name. Just *Bane*.

She gave a slight obligatory nod.

"Oh, sorry. I forgot. You two probably haven't met." For the first time, he smiled as he circled his desk and seated himself. "Rose Kinsey, this is your father's friend. Bane Jacob."

The handsome cowboy lifted his black Stetson, revealing a full head of curly, black hair. He gave her a slight bow and a warm, broad smile.

What is he doing here? She watched the stranger move toward her, his big hand extended.

"Hello, Miss Kinsey." Strong fingers pressed hers as the man shook her hand vigorously. "Or may I call you Rose?"

Although his smile was captivating and his greeting more than cordial, he had no right to be there at such a difficult time. "Rose will be fine," she said coolly.

He tilted his chin and lifted a dark brow. "Pretty name."

She ignored his compliment and shot a questioning glance toward the attorney.

"I think you'll understand why Bane is here when you read your father's will, Rose." He motioned Bane to the empty chair opposite the young woman.

Ben Horner rummaged through a pile of folders stacked haphazardly on a corner of the massive pine desk. "Ah, here it is. Your father's will."

She watched as the little man sorted through the vast amount of papers in the file before he pulled out a single sheet and handed it to her.

"I'll give you the entire will later, if you like. But, as per your father's instructions, I am to present you with this letter first. He laughingly called it his *Reader's Digest* version, and said it better explained his wishes than the legal mumbo jumbo of his actual will. I'll read it to you if you like, or you may read it for yourself, it's up to you." He leaned across the desk, the single sheet in his hand as he waited for her response.

"Thank you." She cast a sideways look at the stranger as she took the paper and began to read, eager to see the message her father had left her. It was so like him to leave her a letter like this, to spare her the agony of the confusing legal words she'd never understand, and she loved him for it.

> *To you, Rose, my beloved daughter, I leave all my worldly goods, everything I own, providing you meet the following stipulations:*

Stipulations? The word jumped off the paper. *Stipulations?* Why would her father put stipulations in his will? She was his only child. What stipulations could there be? She read on.

> *This is what I expect of you, my dear child. You must live on Sweet Water Ranch for one full year following my death and learn every phase of the ranch's day-to-day operations. I want you to actually take a hands-on part in each of the daily tasks, chores, and functions. You also need a workable knowledge of its book work.*

Her face flushed with exasperation as she considered the complications his requests would bring. How could he do this to her? True, she hadn't made an effort to be home like he'd wanted her to—but he'd visited her in New York, and they'd been together quite often. She bit her lip and blinked furiously, determined to hold back the tears of anguish she felt rising within her as she considered her father's conditions. She wiped at her eyes with the back of her hand and continued reading:

You must attend Mill Creek Community Church regularly while you are here. This is my most important request.

Her eyes widened. Attend church? What a strange request, coming from her father, of all people. Although she'd attended church regularly with her friend's family when she was a child, her father had never attended the services. He was always too busy, even when she had begged him to come with her.

With pursed lips and a heavy heart, she read on.

All of these requirements will be under the supervision of my trusted friend and neighbor, Bane. . .

Aghast, Rose stood quickly to her feet and pointed an accusing finger at the man who was sitting quietly, his big hands folded in his lap. "Bane? You?"

He nodded.

"Why would he give you this power? Who are you?" Her voice shook. All her life she'd known she was to be her father's heir. There had never been any question as to who would inherit his estate; she would. Rose Kinsey, her father's only child.

Very simply, without expression or emotion, the man answered, his deep voice seeming to echo off the walls and ceiling. "I was your father's closest friend."

Her heart sank. A complete stranger? Why? Why would her father demand such a thing?

She continued to read. Surely her questions would be answered.

If, at the end of the year, he agrees you have adequately lived up to my requests and he signs the release form my attorney has prepared, the ranch, along with everything I own, will be signed over to you, my daughter, to do with whatever you choose. You will be able to stay on the ranch and continue to run it, or you may dispose of it in any way you see fit. It is my hope you will choose the ranch.

A look of horror crossed her face as she turned toward the stranger. "My life is in *your* hands? I don't even know you." The paper dropped to the floor as she lowered her head into her hands.

Bane rose, picked up the paper, and placed a hand on her shoulder, his voice soft and reassuring. "I'm sorry. If you hadn't been in such a hurry to leave when you came for your father's funeral, I would have introduced myself and perhaps we would have become friends."

She pushed his hand aside and faced him with tear-filled eyes, her mascara damp and smeared. "Who are you to judge me? You don't even know me. There were reasons I could only be here for such a short time. Reasons my father would have understood!" Now she was glaring at him, this complete stranger who could make her a princess or a pauper with the twist of a pen.

Again, he responded with gentleness as he placed the paper in her lap. "Your father may have said he understood when you couldn't find time to come home and visit him, but it hurt him deeply. He loved you and wanted to spend time with you. Time here—on Sweet Water Ranch."

She couldn't deny his words. She'd wanted to come home more often, but with her career and other obligations, she hadn't had a choice. No, she concluded, as she eyed the man standing before her, she hadn't purposely hurt her father. He knew and understood why she hadn't come back to Rock City more often, no matter what this Bane man said.

Through bleary eyes she found her place and read:

Rose,

I'm sure at this point you're furious with me. But, my darling daughter, as much as you disliked living on Sweet Water Ranch, you have never given it a chance. It is my hope and prayer that by living on the ranch and learning how to run it, you will come to love it as much as I did. Sweet Water Ranch has been in our family for generations. Think carefully before you allow it to escape from you.

Her father was wrong. She loved the ranch. Hadn't she grown up there? Hadn't she been active in 4-H? Learned to ride? But there was no future for her in Rock City. To achieve her dreams, she had to leave, she hadn't had a choice; western Kansas offered her nothing. Moving to New York had been her only option. Of course, her father didn't want her to leave; she was the only family he had. But hadn't he agreed? Wasn't he the one who had sent her to college, paid for everything, and encouraged her career? Surely he didn't expect her to come back to the ranch to live, after working so hard for her degree. He'd done with his life what he wanted, hadn't he? And, hadn't he encouraged her to find her own niche? Rose leaned back into the uncomfortable chair with a look of defeat. "There's no other way? I can't let the hired hands run the ranch for a year and then decide what to do with it?"

"Please be assured, Miss Kinsey," the little lawyer warned, posturing himself for whatever response she might offer. "It was not your father's intention to cheat you out of anything. Quite the contrary. But he was afraid you might make a hasty decision and sell the ranch. As he said, you are the final descendent in a long line of Kinseys."

Without looking up, she reached for a tissue, but before she was able to negotiate her purse's clasp, a pristine white handkerchief was pressed into her hand, the initial B in its corner. She noisily blew her nose, then continued reading without a glance toward either man in the room.

If, for any reason, you decide not to accept or fulfill my stipulations, the ranch and everything I own will go to my friend, Bane Jacob.

She gasped and glared at the well-dressed cowboy, mystified by her father's statement. His gentle expression never wavered, and she read on.

> *No, my darling, I have not lost my mind. I am perfectly sane. Bane is a good man, fair, honest, and the best rancher I know. He has agreed to do this one last thing for me, at his own great personal sacrifice. Listen to him. Heed his words. Follow his instructions, for your inheritance is in his hands. Trust him, Rose. And, trust my judgment. It is for your good. I love you.*
>
> *Dad*

I love you? Her thoughts moved from clouded love to confused anger. There was nothing more to be said. Her father had spoken through this letter, and apparently, legally, nothing could be changed.

"Miss Kinsey?" Mr. Horner adjusted his thick horn-rimmed glasses and locked his hands behind his head as he leaned back in his black vinyl chair. "Do you have any questions?"

With a tired expression on her face, she rose to face him and tossed the page onto his desk. "Oh yes, Mr. Horner. I have questions, but apparently you and my father and Mr. Jacob have all the answers. If you'll excuse me, I'll be on my way now. I've had a long flight. I'm tired, and I need to think."

Bane Jacob, obviously a gentleman, rose quickly to his feet. "No, Rose. It's not what you suspect. I never even knew of your father's decision until just before his death—when he asked me to—well, you know. To oversee—"

"My life, Mr. Jacob? To oversee my life?"

His voice remained gentle as the man faced the beautiful, frustrated woman before him. "If that's the way you see it, then—yes. To oversee your life. Your father wanted you to have a chance to love the land his great-great-grandfather homesteaded many years ago. Is that asking too much?"

There was no easy answer to his question. Arguing with these strangers would accomplish nothing. She squared her shoulders, whipped the strap of her handbag over one arm, and resolutely faced them.

The grim-faced little man shook his head. "I'm sorry you feel this way, Miss Kinsey. Before you make any decisions, you may want to take these back to the ranch and read them." He lifted a thick folder from the top of his desk and thrust it toward her. "I'm confident your father had far more wealth than you were aware of, young lady. Stocks, bonds, certificates of deposit, commercial property in Denver, among other things. It's all in here. He was a very prosperous man. I'd certainly think twice before turning it all down, if I were you."

She made no attempt to take the hefty folder as he extended it toward her.

His chair grated on the uneven flooring as the frail man lifted himself and walked around the desk.

"It's up to you, Miss Kinsey. The papers, along with another copy of the letter and the will, are in here. I suggest you take them with you and read them thoroughly." He thrust the folder toward her once again and waited until she took it from him. "I have another appointment elsewhere and must go. If you have any questions, call me." He pulled a weathered Stetson from the coatrack by the door and tipped it to her before stuffing it onto his head.

"Bane, see you later." He nodded to the other man, and then he was gone.

She lifted her chin and forced a slight, mocking smile for the man who stood silently before her, hat in hand. "And, Mr. Jacob. You will give me a few days to consider my options, I hope. Before you evict me from my family's home." With that, she shifted the heavy folder, moved to the door, and closed it firmly behind her.

Outside, the fresh country air filled her lungs, but feelings of defeat filled her heart. *Daddy. Oh, Daddy. I am so sorry. I knew you loved me, but I didn't realize how much you missed me. What a disappointment I must have been to you. I know it's too late, but please, oh please, if you can hear me from heaven, forgive me.*

Rose curled up in the corner of the massive sofa in front of the fireplace in the ranch's living room, with the file folder in her lap. She had pretty well decided that if that's the way her father wanted it, old Bane Jacob could have it all. The ranch, her father's investments, the property, everything. She deserved nothing. Apparently, her father had thought she had turned her back on all of it when she decided to become a fashion illustrator and left home. Yet as she sat in the comfortable living room and warmed herself before the open fire, she realized for the first time since she'd returned home how nice it was here at the ranch and how much she had missed it. Other than her recent trip to Rock City for the funeral, it had been nearly two years since she'd been home, and then only for a quick overnighter. *Two years? Has it been that long?* She had intended to get home more often, but it had been so easy to put off her visits. Her father had always managed to visit her in New York, so she had never felt the need to return to Kansas and Sweet Water Ranch.

"Need anything before I close up the kitchen for the night, Rose?" Nel stood before her, dish towel in hand. Nel had been her father's housekeeper since Rose's mother had left so suddenly, when the girl was only two. While Nel had remained in the position of a servant, she was the nearest thing to a mother the young girl had ever had.

Rose smiled at the portly woman. Nel never changed. Sometimes Rose wondered if that little bun of hair on top of Nel's head had been glued there; she had never seen her wear it any other way. "No thanks, Nel. I'm fine. But, thanks for asking."

"I've turned down your bed," Nel said. "Just like I used to when ya was little. And I put some of that rose bath oil on the tub. It's nice to have ya home. Kinda like having your old dad with us. We've missed ya."

Rose rubbed her forehead wearily. "Thanks, Nel. I've missed you, too."

As she turned back to the documents, she realized the attorney was right: She had had no idea her father's holdings were so large. A person would have to be crazy to turn it all over to a stranger. Her desire for her career battled with her good sense. The career could bring her satisfaction, but would it bring her fortune, the fortune she held in her hands? But if she put her career on hold for one year, would she be able to reclaim it? Or would she have to start all over again?

It was all too confusing. Four hours earlier, when she had read her father's letter, she'd been ready to chuck it all, go back to New York, and forget Sweet Water Ranch ever existed. But now that she was home on the ranch again, basking in the soothing warmth of the open fire, she found herself having second thoughts. One year. Twelve short months. Then she'd be able to sell the ranch, take her father's assets as her own, and her future would be secure for life. That scenario was pretty hard to turn down. And no doubt her father had known that when he'd written his letter.

She rubbed her head again, trying to ease the beginnings of the headache she felt coming on.

"Want me to tell the boys to check out them fences first thing in the mornin', Rose?" Nel's husband, Bitty, stood before her, hat in hand, waiting for her direction.

"What, Bitty?" She hadn't heard him come into the room and was startled by his craggy voice.

"The fences, Rose. We found some of the cattle down by Dry Creek. Don't know how they got there, must be a break in them fences somewhere. Want me to have the men check 'em out before they start brandin' them new cattle?"

She shrugged. "How should I know? Why are you asking me, Bitty?"

He twisted the top button on his plaid flannel shirt. "Ain't ya the new boss around here? Now that your pop is gone? Who else would I ask?"

The truth hit her: He was right. Who else would he ask? At least for now, she was in charge.

"Sure. That'd be fine." She tried to appear authoritative, although she hadn't the faintest idea, nor did she care, why it would hurt if the cattle did get down by Dry Creek. "Do whatever Dad would've done."

She slipped the papers back into the folder for safekeeping. Her mind might be whizzing with the decisions that confronted her, but her body was tired. It had been an overwhelming day, a day for which she'd been totally unprepared. She had expected the will to leave her the ranch, and she had planned to immediately put it on the market. Then she would have gone back to New York, back to her normal everyday routine of fashion illustrating until the ranch was sold. Later, she would have come back and signed the papers, removing any little mementos she might decide to keep. Perhaps she would have held onto a few acres, just enough to keep the Kinsey name and Sweet Water Ranch in the bloodline, and leased them to a nearby rancher. If she ever married and had children, she could have passed it on to them. Maybe the area down by the creek. She could even have built a cabin there, a retreat, where she could have come to relax when she had time off.

But thanks to her father, that hadn't happened. Instead, he'd blessed her with his bombshell stipulations. She could almost feel him looking down at her from heaven, laughing.

"Well, dear old Dad." She glanced upward with a smile as she gathered her robe about her and headed for her old bedroom. "Wouldn't you be surprised if I decided to play your game? Or did you know what my decision would be? I know I disappointed you when I wasn't the son you'd hoped for. And, I know you never wanted my career to take me away from Sweet Water. Is this your sneaky way of trying to bring me home for good?"

A clap of thunder sounded overhead, and scattered raindrops began to ping against the large overhead skylight. She laughed. "Okay, Daddy. You don't have to go to all that trouble. I get the message. I'm thinking. I'm thinking!"

When she entered the country kitchen at ten the next morning, she was surprised to find Nel standing before the sink, peeling potatoes and crying as though her heart would break. Rose put her arm around the little woman's shoulder and gave her a slight squeeze. "Nel, what's wrong? Aren't you feeling well?" In all the years she'd known their housekeeper, she had never seen her cry.

Nel wiped her tear-stained cheeks with the hem of her calico apron. "I'm sorry, Rose. I didn't know ya was up." The woman seemed embarrassed that she'd been caught weeping.

"What's wrong, Nel? You can tell me."

Nel sniffled and touched the hem to her cheeks again. "Me and Bitty talked most of the night about the ranch. Ben Horner told him he didn't think ya was gonna take over here. We've worked for your papa ever since we got married. Where will we go? What will we do if the ranch is sold? We're too old to start over." The paring knife dropped alongside the unpeeled potatoes as Nel clutched her apron to her face and hurried from the room.

Rose stood in the sudden silence of the kitchen. She'd never thought about the security of all the people who had worked for her father most of their lives. People who depended on him, who had devoted their lives to the running of the ranch. What if the new owner decided he didn't need them, that he had his own people who could do their jobs? It was a heavy thought, filled with awesome responsibility. Now, not only her own future lay in her decision, but the future of dozens of others did, too.

She picked up the paring knife and absentmindedly began peeling the remaining potatoes, dropping them into the big stainless steel pot. Maybe a sure thing like the ranch would be a better choice for her life than her blossoming career. It would certainly be more secure.

Nel returned, smiling, all traces of the telltale tears gone from her friendly face. "Sorry, Rose. You got your own troubles. Bitty said your dad's will didn't deal too kindly with ya." She lifted the big pot and placed it on the stove. "Thanks for peeling the rest of them potatoes; you shouldn't have done it, that's my job. Your poor old daddy would have had my head if he could've knowed you was peeling potatoes." She gave the young woman a wink of her eye, then added, "By the way, what can I fix you for breakfast?"

Rose selected a banana from the wicker basket on the kitchen's island and began to peel it thoughtfully. "How did you know about my father's will, Nel?"

Nel pulled a large package of pork chops from the refrigerator and began pulling them apart. "Your father told the men. About his conditions, I mean. Bitty told me." The woman seemed uncomfortable talking about it, like she'd been privy to something that wasn't her business.

"I see," Rose said slowly as she dropped the banana's peel into the garbage with the potato peelings. "Then you know if I don't stay on the ranch a year, I'll lose it?"

"Yes, I know," the woman admitted sadly as she placed the lid on the pot. "I told Bitty there's no way you'd live here again. Even for a year. That's why we're so worried."

Rose suddenly felt manipulated by what her father was doing to her. He had tried to manipulate her all her life, making her decisions for her, from what projects she chose in 4-H, to where she went to summer camp, to what dress she wore for her high school graduation. He'd kept her from dating as long as he could and only allowed her to date boys of whom he approved. Oh, he'd said it was because he loved her, and she could understand his feelings, since he was both mother and father to her, but she felt he'd gone way overboard. None of her friends' parents was so domineering. No, domineering wasn't the right word to describe his actions. Overprotective. Yes, that was the word for it. Overprotective.

Was he doing the same thing from the grave? Protecting her from life? When did he devise this foolish plan? Or had he gotten senile and she'd been too busy to notice?

Nel was dredging the thick pork chops with flour and dropping them into hot grease in the giant iron skillet. The delicious aroma filled the kitchen as the chops sizzled and browned in the long-handled pan. The marvelous scent brought back memories of childhood and Nel's wonderful cooking. How she'd loved Nel's cooking. Nel's cooking had been famous among the teenage set, and Rose's friends all tried to wangle dinner invitations to her house.

"Nel, did my father tell Bitty what'll happen to the ranch if I decide not to stay?"

Nel stopped poking at the chops with her fork. "He never said. We all guessed Mr. Horner would be the one to put the place on the market, to settle your father's estate. What else was in that will, we never heard." She scooted a pork chop to one side with the meat fork and gazed at the bubbling liquid.

"He didn't tell you the part about Bane Jacob?"

The stirring stopped as the women locked eyes. "Nope. Don't rightly think so, or Bitty'd told me. What's Bane got to do with it?"

Rose dropped into a chair at the big round table and nibbled on the banana. "Tell me about this Bane Jacob. Who is he? I may have heard Dad mention his name a time or two, I'm not sure. But I never met that man before. I'm sure I'd remember him." She watched as Nel flipped more pork chops over in the pan, her mouth watering for just one small bite of the delicious meat.

Nel quit flipping and turned to face her. "Well, let's see. He's a nice man, been a good friend to your father. He's probably the smartest rancher in the state. Anytime your papa had a problem with the animals or the hired help, he'd give Bane a call and he'd come a-runnin' and stay until they got things worked out."

"But, doesn't he have a ranch of his own to tend to?" Rose pushed the last bite of the banana into her mouth as she watched Nel go back to flipping chops.

"Sure does. I'd say he's got the biggest spread in this area. Maybe the whole state. But, the man runs it like one of them Fortune 500 companies. Bitty says even though the guy's a slave driver, he works right alongside the men and doesn't ask 'em to do nothin' he don't do himself. And he pays well, even better'n your dad did. Some of your dad's hands have tried to leave him and go to work for Bane. He won't have 'em. Says loyalty is too important. Unless they have good reason to leave a job, they should stay. And your dad never gave 'em no reason to leave."

Rose's mouth compressed into a tight line of frustration. "Sounds like a tyrant to me. He must have had some kind of hold on my dad for him to write a stupid will like that. There has to be more to this story than what I've heard so far."

Nel placed the spatula on the ceramic spoon rest, checked the fire under the iron skillet, and turned to Rose. "Look, like I said, Bane is a fair man. If your father trusted him, then I trust him. He's a fine Christian man. I've never heard of him taking advantage of anyone and I'm sure he's not going to start with you. He has a good reputation. His handshake is as binding as a signed contract. That's the way he does his business. With a handshake."

Rose pondered the housekeeper's words. No man could be that trustworthy, not in this day and age. "I've decided to go into town, Nel. I need to buy a few things. Need me to pick up anything for you?"

"Land sakes no, child. Bitty'll drive in and get anything I need. Don't forget, for now this place is yours and you don't need to be runnin' no errands for your housekeeper."

Not realizing her trip to Kansas would take so long, Rose hadn't planned to spend more than one night in Rock City and she hadn't brought along any casual clothes. All she had with her was the suit she'd worn on the flight and the sheath and jacket she planned to wear on the plane trip back to New York.

Now she slipped into the bright, very red, very chic, fitted sheath dress with the slit up the side of the skirt and topped it with the trendy, red mohair jacket. She hadn't brought any shoes other than the pair she'd worn on the plane, skinny black leather straps with spike heels. Not a good choice for the tip of northwestern Kansas. Well, that was no problem; she would buy jeans and a pair of boots at Adams's Mercantile in town. Rock City didn't offer much in the way of high-fashion wear, but you could always count on an abundance of jeans, shirts, and boots, anything you'd need for ranch living. From the looks of things, she might be there for a few more days than she'd anticipated. At least, until she'd made her decision.

The rental car seemed to suck in the dust from the roads as she aimed it toward town; she could feel the grittiness on the steering wheel. The prior evening's thunderstorm had only amounted to a few drops of rain and a lot of noise, and now the car seemed to be as disgruntled about the dust as she was. It sputtered several times before the engine died and the car came to a dead stop.

Now what? She had gone only a few miles; it had to be at least eight more to town. Her cellular phone was still in her apartment in New York City, and she'd forgotten to bring Nel's along. She drummed the curve of the steering wheel with long, red nails, then glanced at her shoes. They were definitely not the walking kind, at least not on Kansas's dirt roads.

There were only two choices: walk or wait. And who was there to wait for? It could be hours before Nel told Bitty she was missing and he'd come looking for her. If only she'd taken the main road instead of the rarely used cutoff. No, *wait* was out of the question. So walk it was.

Turning up the mohair jacket collar about her neck, she took off down the road toward Sweet Water Ranch, which was closer than town, although it hadn't been her intended destination. The tall, spike heels twisted and turned with each stride, and she was cold in the early spring winds. Each step reminded her why she shouldn't give a year of her life to Kansas.

"Need a ride, ma'am?" The voice startled her; she hadn't heard a car approaching. Turning quickly, she gasped. Not a car was in sight—but on the most beautiful horse she'd ever seen sat a dark-eyed cowboy in a black Stetson.

Chapter 2

She eyed the man from head to toe as he grinned at her with teeth too perfect for any man's mouth. With the black Stetson pulled low on his brow, his eyes were nearly invisible, but she recognized him immediately.

"Well, do you want a ride?"

She looked first at the cowboy, then at the horse. "On that?"

He chuckled in response to her question, and deep crescent-shaped dimples sprang out on both sides of his strong mouth. Even with his well-trimmed black mustache, she could see the indentations, and she wondered how any man could be so good-looking and be a working rancher at the same time. He looked as if he'd just stepped from the shower, all clean-shaven and debonair. He extended a leather-gloved hand and waited for her response.

Although she hadn't ridden a horse since she'd left the ranch, she was tempted to ride this one with Bane Jacob, despite the power he had over her future. Unfortunately, her tightly fitted sheath made that impossible.

"I can't. I'm not dressed for it," she groaned, wishing she'd brought her jeans and tennies with her. But then again, if she had brought them, she wouldn't be stranded on the road right now, headed for Adams's Mercantile.

"No," he replied with a lifted brow, "I'd say you're not dressed for anything that goes on around these parts. You look like a city gal who took a wrong turn somewhere around I-70." He smiled, relaxed the reins a bit, and leaned both hands on the saddle horn as the big stallion pawed the ground impatiently. "Do you or don't you want a ride? Last chance."

Again, she evaluated her slim dress and strappy sandals, then turned to the man grinning from his lofty perch high above her. He was her only hope. Without him, she might be stranded on this road for hours, and who knew who might come by? "Could you call a mechanic or a wrecker for me?"

He yanked the black felt hat from his head and gave it an impatient swat against his jeaned leg, exposing a head of black hair. "Sorry, guess I left my cell phone on my other horse. It's sure not on this one. Sit tight, little lady. Since you won't accept my offer of a ride, I'll send Clem out with either my Mercedes or my BMW to pick you up and take you to town. Don't you go anywhere now, ya hear?" He slapped the giant animal on its flanks, and they took off down the road in a gallop, leaving her in a puff of dust.

She tried to hobble toward the ranch, then gave up and returned to her incapacitated car to wait, hoping he'd been serious about sending help. After all, she'd been anything but friendly in the lawyer's office. Why should he be nice to her now?

A half hour later, a rusty pickup pulled up behind her and stopped. A small, leathery-looking man approached and peered in through the dusty windshield. She cracked the window a bit.

He removed his hat from his balding head and smiled with crooked teeth that would be any dentist's nightmare. "Howdy, ma'am. I'm Clem. The boss sent me over to see if I could help ya. Would you pull the latch on the hood, so's I can check the motor?"

Clem must have known what he was doing, for in a matter of minutes the car roared to attention and the motor hummed evenly. Rose tried to pay the man, but he wouldn't accept the money she extended through the open window. "You must be a city gal. Round these parts, we help each other. Someday, somebody'll stop and do me a good deed when I need it, and we'll be even." He tipped his hat and was gone in that familiar cloud of Kansas dust.

By the time she reached the Mercantile, Mr. Adams was hanging the CLOSED sign on the front door. When he saw the beautiful, young woman park in front of his store, he flipped the sign back to the OPEN side. What man in his right mind would close his store when a lovely woman was heading for his door?

She hurried inside and went directly to the jeans counter and found a pair that didn't fit like her Calvin Kleins but were acceptable for Rock City. She had her choice of black or brown boots, and she settled for the brown ones; for some reason, since her acquaintance with Bane Jacob, she had a sudden aversion to black. For good measure, she purchased three long-sleeved flannel shirts and a corduroy jacket, along with three pairs of socks. If she had to stay at Sweet Water Ranch for a few days, at least she'd be dressed for it.

On the way back home, she passed the spot where she had been stranded and was reminded of the handsome rider and his horse. He had sent help after all, hadn't he? Those cracks about the Mercedes and the BMW were uncalled for, but he couldn't be all bad.

Nel met her at the door when she pulled her rental car up in front of the massive farmhouse. "Where have you been, Rose? I've been worried sick. I told Bitty if you weren't here in fifteen minutes I was gonna call the sheriff."

"Just a little car trouble, Nel. A knight in tarnished armor sent someone out to rescue me. No big deal. Just delayed my shopping trip an hour or so." She was in no mood to explain her adventure, and she was glad when Nel accepted her skimpy explanation without further questions.

Without the traffic noises she was used to in New York, the night was deafeningly still as Rose lay in her bed mulling over the demanding options that suddenly confronted her. Only an occasional mournful cry of a coyote broke the stillness, and she remembered how that same silence had frightened her when she was a child, sleeping in this very bed. Even the creaking of a floorboard would waken her, and she'd lie quietly with her head under the covers, holding onto her teddy bear, envisioning ghosts and goblins hovering over her. She'd wished for a mother to run to, instead of her father; he'd only make fun of her for being silly and send her back to the darkness of her bedroom, claiming night-lights were for sissies, and no daughter of his was ever going to be a sissy. That man should have had a son; obviously, a daughter had not been his first choice. But he'd done the best he could, she was sure of that, and he'd always been good to her. He just didn't know how to be as gentle with her as he should have been.

Later, when she was a teenager, the nighttime silence had irritated her. No one was around for miles, except for the people who worked for her father. She'd felt isolated from her friends and the world; the silence seemed like a thick prison wall that held her captive in the vast plains of northwestern Kansas. She would lie awake in her bed for hours, planning her future and dreaming of becoming a well-paid illustrator. Everyone, including her high school art teacher, had encouraged her, telling her she had a natural-born talent that shouldn't be wasted.

It wasn't that she hated the ranch. She didn't. She loved it. The horses, the sweet little calves, the picnics in the woods with her dad on the rare occasions when he had time. She loved the smell of newly mown hay, the sight of bright green fields in the early spring. The stream that ran through the east meadow where she fished with old Bitty. But the ranch had held no future, and her eyes were set on other sights, lofty sights available only in a city like New York.

Most of her friends had also left Rock City to pursue their careers, at least the ones who were in the in-group, like she was. Except RuAnn, her best friend. On most things, the two saw eye-to-eye. But when it came to leaving home territory, their goals separated; RuAnn would never leave the Kansas prairie she loved. She was more at home on her horse than Rose had been in her little Corvette convertible, the one her father had given her for her sixteenth birthday.

And when it came to clothing, RuAnn wouldn't have traded her Acme boots and Levi's for all the Gucci shoes and Guess jeans Rodeo Drive could offer. Rose was going to New York to make her mark as an illustrator—and RuAnn was going to have her veterinary clinic in Kansas.

RuAnn. Rose smiled as she thought about her old friend. She hadn't seen RuAnn for several years, and she wondered if her old chum had opened her clinic yet—and if she had, had she come back to this chunk of Kansas to do it? Rose would phone RuAnn's parents in the morning and find out.

Eventually, sleep overtook her weary brain. She dreamed about a man on a black horse, scooping her up in his strong arms and riding off toward his castle somewhere on the Kansas prairie. . . .

Bane Jacob slipped from the saddle and tied the stallion's reins to a low branch on the willow tree behind the Kinsey farmhouse. Carefully, as stealthily as a minesweeper, he made his way through the bushes and toward the kitchen door. Through the brightly lit window, he could see Bitty dipping some of Nel's cookies into a glass of milk. He tapped lightly on the door several times, until finally Bitty saw him and motioned him to come in. "Whatcha doin' here this time of night, Bane? Somethin' wrong?"

Bane put a finger to his lips. "No, just checking on your houseguest. I saw her car out front. . .guess she made it back okay. Not that I was concerned, of course."

Bitty smiled. "Okay. If you say so, Bane."

Bane punched the old-timer in the arm. "Watch it, Bitty, you old codger you."

Bitty passed the plate of cookies and Bane took two. "Want some milk to go with those?"

Bane nodded and Bitty filled a glass and handed it to him. "Think she'll stay?"

The late-night visitor paused thoughtfully, a cookie dipped halfway into the milk. "Don't know, Bitty. I hope so. But if she does, I'll have my work cut out for me. She's a city gal now."

The older man laughed. "Yep, that she is. But she hasn't always been that way. That kid was a good one. Nel and me loved her like she was our daughter. Give her some slack, Bane. Give her some slack."

Bane gulped down the last swallow of milk and tipped his hat. "Good night, Bitty. Thanks for the advice."

As he made his way toward the willow tree, he thought about the beautiful young woman who had come into his life through this quirk of fate. Before he met Rose, Charlie Kinsey's request had sounded difficult but possible. The old man had had no doubt his daughter would choose the ranch if he made her a deal she couldn't refuse. But now Bane wasn't so sure. Maybe she'd choose to return to New York and refuse to stay on the ranch. Now that he'd met her, he hadn't a clue. Bitty was right about one thing, though: She was a city gal now. But, surely, no person in her right mind would give up Sweet Water Ranch.

No one had mentioned a third alternative: She could contest the will, take it to court, and try to break it. That could be a long and ugly ordeal, and he'd be right in the middle of it. He hoped that option would never be considered.

Snowflakes began to fall softly as he untied the reins and headed his horse toward home. The weatherman had predicted heavy snow by morning. That could make everyday tasks more difficult for the ranch hands. Could Rose handle the difficult times she'd face on the ranch? He prayed she'd make the right decision, for all of their sakes.

Rose awoke early to a winter wonderland. She'd forgotten how quickly a spring snowstorm could strike the flatlands of western Kansas and eastern Colorado. The radio said I-70 had been closed from Hays west to Limon, with travelers stranded in every little cranny along the way. The snow was wet and heavy, clinging to every twig, branch, and tree it touched. It clothed the terrain in a puffy blanket of white, camouflaging all traces of the previous day's dust.

She dressed quickly and hurried toward the kitchen. Surely it wasn't her imagination; she smelled bacon and pancakes. She hadn't told Nel she'd be having breakfast this morning, but when she bounded into the kitchen, there was Nel flipping big, lacy-edged pancakes, and the table was set—for two? Surely not for her and Nel. The housekeeper had never eaten at the table with her and her father, not even on her birthday.

But if not Nel, then who?

"Did ya hear the phone ring earlier?" Nel asked as she filled a little pitcher with warm syrup. "It was Bane. I invited him for pancakes. He should be here any minute."

Rose turned to glare at the older woman. "Nel! Why'd you do that? Just because Daddy liked the man doesn't mean I have to."

"Now, Rose. . ."

Rose had heard just about enough of this man who was being forced into her life. "Nel, I don't mean to be unkind, but you should've told me before you invited company for breakfast." She grabbed her glass and whirled around, leaving Nel standing alone in the kitchen with the table set for two and only one person planning to eat.

As Rose sat cross-legged in the center of her bed, watching the snow blow across the open field, she heard the sound of a truck in the driveway, then a man's voice and the door closing. Only an idiot would drive the distance between their houses in this storm just to eat breakfast. Why didn't Bane stay home and tend his cattle or whatever he did on his ranch? Was he so anxious to take over Sweet Water Ranch even on a day like this?

Eventually, the sounds of talking stopped, and she assumed he'd finished his pancakes and gone. She had been so anxious to get out of the kitchen earlier, she'd left with an empty glass. Maybe now she could go back and fill it with juice. Deciding the coast was clear, she headed down the hall and into the warm, cozy kitchen. Much to her surprise, the man was still seated at the table with his back to her, munching pancakes, and Nel was nowhere in sight. The back of his head looked all too familiar with its curly, black hair, and so did his long, lean body. And, if that wasn't enough, he was clothed from head to toe, including his boots, in black.

The cowboy in the chair spun around and eyed her without a word, only a sideways smile as he surveyed her standing in the doorway in her new jeans, shirt, and boots.

"Did you come here so I could thank you for sending Clem, or to criticize my clothing?" she asked with a hand on one hip and a challenge in her flashing eyes.

He rose quickly, reared back his head, and laughed. "Criticize? Not me. I like you in jeans and boots. Much better than that red job. Which reminds me, I brought you something." He pulled a box from under the table and handed it to her. "Bought you some new boots." He shoved the box into her hands.

She shoved it back.

"Aw, come on. They're my welcome gift. Take them. Every cowgirl should have a good pair of boots."

With a mocking grin, she lifted her booted foot and plopped it onto the chair. "I have boots, or hadn't you noticed?"

He removed the lid and reached the box toward her. "Those are workin' boots. These are Sunday boots, real fancy ones, to be worn on special occasions. I asked Nel for your size." He pushed the box toward her, smiling that dimpled grin.

She smiled in spite of herself as she took the box and lifted the tissue paper. The beautiful boots were flame red with heavy white stitching, and very feminine. She lifted one of the red boots into the air as if it were a crystal goblet and she were toasting him. "Thanks, I'll save them to wear at my wedding."

"Oh? And how soon do you think that might be?"

As Nel came into the kitchen carrying a load of clean dish towels, she saved Rose from having to come up with a retort she might be sorry for later. "I heard the buzzer go off on the dryer and had to go get these before they wrinkled," Nel said. "I'm sure glad you decided to come back in for breakfast, Rose." She put a hand on Rose's shoulder. "I take it you two have met?"

"Yes, we've met." Rose continued to stand.

"Honey, Bane was your daddy's best friend."

"So he says," she answered coolly.

"He was, we all knowed that. Your papa thought Bane was the best rancher in these parts."

Rose shot Nel a quick stay-out-of-this look that chilled the air. "He offered me a ride when I had car trouble yesterday. On his horse."

The cowboy lifted a brow mockingly. "And being Charlie's daughter, I would have expected you to be smart enough not to be running around this country dressed like you were going to lunch at the Ritz."

Her steel glare pierced him like an arrow.

"Ouch! I'm kidding. Can't you take a joke?"

"Thank you for pointing out my inappropriate attire, Mr. Jacob," she countered with a slight smile. She was finding it difficult to harbor a grudge against the handsome man.

"You're welcome, and if it's any consolation, you look great this morning. Now that's the way a rancher should dress, especially a pretty rancher."

She blushed.

"If you aren't going to eat breakfast I hope you'll forgive me if I do." He lowered himself into the chair and turned to Nel. "If Miss Rose decides to get rid of the ranch, you and Bitty can come and work for me, providing you'll make pancakes like these every morning. I'd never let you two get away, Nelly-girl."

Rose stared in amazement, appalled at his audacity. He was trying to hire her housekeeper right out from under her nose, after all Nel had said about his precious ethics. She tilted her head and lifted a belligerent chin. "Don't even think it, Mr. Jacob. Nel and Bitty are part of this ranch. I have no intention of losing them."

He lifted dark eyes shadowed by thick lashes. "Does that mean you've decided to stay?"

She grabbed her glass of juice and turned away, avoiding his stare.

"When I make my decision, you'll hear about it from my daddy's lawyer."

Bane stabbed a big bite with his fork, three pancakes deep, and twisted it in the thick, sticky syrup. "Well, Miss Rose, now that you're dressed for the occasion, would you like to see your ranch? I understand from the hands that it's been years since you've seen this place. Your father made a lot of changes for the better, new outbuildings and barns. He built a new bunkhouse and some other things you haven't seen. How about taking a ride with me? I'll show them to you." He stuffed the last of the pancakes into his mouth, then wiped his black mustache with his napkin.

She couldn't believe her ears. "Today? Now? In this storm?" A glance out the kitchen window confirmed the snow hadn't let up one bit, with northerly winds pasting it to the house's cedar siding.

"Yep. Good a time as any." He turned to Nel as though he already owned the place. "Fix a thermos full of that good hot coffee to warm the lady's innards."

"Hey," Rose protested as she grabbed his arm. "Who said I was going with you?"

"Don't you want to see your ranch?" he countered. "Now, eat your pancakes, then run along and get your jacket—and make it a warm one. And don't forget some gloves." Bane took his dirty dishes to the sink and rinsed them out before loading them in the dishwasher.

When she didn't move, he turned to Nel. "Get her a warm jacket and loan her some gloves. The jeep'll heat up pretty quick, but I don't want Miss Petunia catchin' cold."

Rose glared at him again. "Rose. I'm Rose."

He took her chin into his gloved palm and looked into her eyes. "Oh? Well, I'm Bane, and I'll be waiting in the jeep." His words were soft and gentle. He raked his hand through his hair before lowering the black Stetson onto his brow, then pulled on his long leather coat. "And, I don't like to waste gas."

She crossed her arms over her chest in a snit, as if to say, *Oh yeah?* He moved toward the door, straight and tall and handsome, too handsome. He tipped the Stetson, then backed out and closed the door firmly behind him, but not before a cold wind whipped in and wrapped itself around her.

"Better get a move on, honey." Nel placed a lone pancake in the center of her plate and shoved the syrup in her direction. "I think he means it."

Bane tugged his collar up about his neck and hunkered down in his coat. The jeep was still cold, although ten minutes had passed since he'd started warming it up. Was she coming, or was she going to call his bluff? He smiled. *That woman is a real looker. . .too bad she's such a city gal. But she was raised on the ranch; maybe, eventually—it'd all come back to her.*

He drummed his fingers in time to the music and reluctantly settled back to wait. Five more minutes. If she wasn't out in five more minutes, he'd leave. He had better things to do with his life than wait for a woman who might not show up.

The snowflakes continued to fall as he watched the kitchen door. Exactly four minutes later, according to the broken-faced clock in the jeep's dash, Rose emerged, bundled up from head to toe in her father's full-length coat and stocking cap, a muffler around her neck. Without a word, she climbed into the black four-wheel-drive vehicle and stared straight ahead.

"Not what you expected, huh?" He sped up the wiper setting and the blades began to struggle even faster against the falling snow. When he'd said jeep, he wondered if she'd expected something like the big, plush Jeep Cherokee touted by television ads. He watched her eyes as they surveyed their surroundings, and guessed she had. Yep. It was obvious this was not what she had expected.

"Not exactly," she replied uneasily. "I thought maybe. . . Well, never mind what I thought."

His eyes twinkled at her statement. Not what she'd expected was an understatement. This jeep was old. And tiny. And had a canvas top. And as much as the heater tried, it couldn't compete with the frigid air creeping in around the flimsy top. "Glad to see you dressed for it."

Squinted eyes gave him a sideward glance over the top of the muffler, but her head remained rigid.

"Better buckle up," he cautioned as he shifted into reverse and the little jeep lunged backward with a leap.

She tugged at the seat belt and strapped it across her lap. "Didn't realize they had seat belts in these old jeeps," she commented, with an emphasis on the word *old*.

Bane chuckled aloud. "This old jeep's got a name."

"Dare I ask?"

"Marilyn Monroe."

Now her head turned toward him, her bright eyes peering through the slit between her upturned collar and the stocking cap. "Marilyn Monroe? You're kidding me."

"Yep. Marilyn Monroe. Don't know why the hands named her that, but that's her name."

"Well, would you turn Marilyn's heat up a bit? I'm freezing."

"Sorry, she's a doin' all she can right now."

They bumped and bounced along silently. He knew she felt awkward. She was out of her element, yet he respected her for making the effort to see the improvements her father had made to Sweet Water Ranch. Maybe he was pushing it a bit to invite her to take the tour during one of the winter's heaviest snowstorms. But so far she was being a good sport about the whole thing. He hoped she didn't think he'd taken her out on a day like this to discourage her from staying on the ranch. That was the very opposite of what he wanted to do. For Charlie's sake, he'd promised to do all he could to encourage her to stay. Yes, he'd made a promise to her father and he intended to keep it.

With snow covering the ground, the narrow roads that wound themselves around the windswept pines were nearly invisible. Rose's great-great-grandfather had planted the pines to separate the buildings from the house. As they rounded the big barn and pulled to a stop, Bitty appeared in the doorway. Bane opened his door and leaned out into the blowing snow. "How's she doing?"

"Okay so far. Be awhile yet." Bitty held onto his hat and braced himself against the wind.

Bane slammed his door. Then without taking his eyes off the road, he reached behind the seat and pulled up a black plastic trash bag. He placed it in her lap.

"What's this for?"

He shoved the gear into low, and they resumed their journey around the ranch. "Warmth. Put it over you."

She drew a deep breath, rolled her eyes, opened the bag, and took out a blanket. "Thanks. Bet you think I'm a real sissy." She spread the blanket across her lap.

He cast a *no-you're-not* smile in her direction. He could tell she was grateful for the blanket, and he wished he'd thought of it earlier, before she got chilled.

Marilyn made a sharp right, then a sharp left, and pulled to a stop in front of a narrow, well-kept building. Bane tugged the black Stetson lower on his brow and exited the jeep, then flung open the door for her.

Once inside, two men looked up from a game of cards and nodded as the two entered. "Mornin', Miss Rose. What brings you to Sweet Water on a day like this, Bane?"

Bane removed his Stetson and brushed the snow off with his gloved hand. "Bitty said he might need some help getting the new calf. And I thought it would be a good day to show Miss Rose how the place looks covered with snow."

"How long ya here for?" the taller man asked. "We've heard rumors your daddy wanted ya to stay on the ranch and run it. Any truth to that?"

"Come on, men," Bane said. "Give the little lady a break, okay? She just arrived yesterday. She hasn't had time to catch her breath, let alone make a major decision."

"Sure. Sorry. Guess you can understand why we're all anxious to know—with your daddy gone." The cowboy nudged the other man with his elbow.

"Yeah. Sorry we asked," the other man chimed in awkwardly as they resumed their card game.

Bane strode across the bare wooden plank floor to the coffee pot, poured himself a cup, and took a sip before turning to Rose. "It's pretty good—want a cup?"

She watched as the steam rose from his cup. "Sure."

He poured a second cup, then crossed the room and handed it to her. "You're welcome, Buttercup."

She offered him a guarded smile. "You like playing games with my name, don't you?"

His dark eyes flashed as his smile broadened. "Is it that obvious?"

She took the steaming cup from his hand. "Now, Mr. Jacob, since you are my guide on this tour, I'd like to hear about this building and the crew who stay here."

He smiled pleasantly. "It's Bane, Rose. Or, would you prefer I call you Miss Kinsey?"

"Bane—"

"Okay, Rosie—"

As they finished their tour, Bane told her, "We need to go check on Bitty," and headed for the jeep. When they arrived back at the big barn he motioned for her to wait in the jeep. In seconds, he was back again, his eyes dark as he stared blankly out the windshield at the driving snow.

She stood the silence as long as she could. "Something's wrong, I know it. What happened?"

Chapter 3

For some time, he stared through the windshield without answering. Then he yanked the gearshift into low and explained in a nearly inaudible voice, "We lost the calf."

Lost? A calf? It died? Wandered off? What? She wanted to ask, but she didn't want to appear more stupid about the ranching business than she already had. But there was no doubt about it, he was upset. Very upset.

After making the rounds of all the buildings, buildings Rose hadn't realized existed, he pulled up in front of the big barn again and turned off the ignition. She had been in the huge, stone structure hundreds of times when she was a child, and this time, she didn't wait, but hopped out and ran for the shelter and warmth of the big building. She and RuAnn used to bring their Barbies here. They'd climb up into the wonderful-smelling hayloft and dig out little rooms with their fingers for their dolls, pretending the holes were grand mansions.

Her thoughts were interrupted as Bitty came to join them in the barn, looking weary and sad. "Mornin', Rose." He glanced quickly past her toward Bane. "Can't win 'em all, I guess." With a shrug of his shoulders, he let out a deep sigh.

Bane nodded and gave the man a pat on the back. "I know, Bitty. You did all you could."

"I'll bet Charlie could have done it," the shriveled little man said as he kicked at a bale of hay with the worn toe of his boot.

"Man, you know better than that. Is it—gone?"

Bitty nodded his head and pursed his narrow lips.

Rose stared at the two men. "Is what gone?"

The old man looked to Bane for approval, then cleared his throat and answered. "The calf, Rose. I tried to save it, but the old mama delivered it breech."

Her heart ached to see old Bitty so broken up about a new calf.

"I knew you'd be comin' back here and Bane wouldn't want you to see it, so I already took it—out."

They were right. She didn't want to see it. Not a dead calf. Not a dead anything.

Bane poked at the fire and added another log. The three stood staring into the flames, watching until the sparks settled themselves and disappeared. "As soon as you're warmed up, I'll show you the rest of the barn."

She lifted her chin, glad for the change of subject. "You needn't show me the barn. I was in it many times, long before you came along. Unless some monumental renovation has taken place in the past six or eight years, I could probably show you areas of the barn you never knew existed." The thought made her smile.

Bane threw back his head with a burst of laughter. "I'll bet you could at that."

She didn't know exactly what he meant, and she had no inclination to ask him. Let him think whatever he wanted.

"It's past lunchtime, Rose." Bitty stood holding his hat in his hands as his fingers curled at the brim. "Want me to tell Nel to fix you somethin' to eat?"

Bane held up his palm toward the man. "No, Bitty," he answered for her. "We're going into town for lunch. Tell Nel she needn't bother."

Before she could rebuke Bane or answer Bitty, the door closed, and Bitty was gone.

"Look," she informed Bane as she grabbed his wrist, "it may surprise you, but I *can* speak for myself. I've been doing it for years—quite successfully, I might add. And, I'm up to your little game."

He stiffened at her touch and frowned. "Game? What game?"

She lifted her head high and glowered at him, her eyes locking with his. "What game? You and I both know what game. Even if you have the others fooled, you don't fool me. I know what you're up to. You want Sweet Water and you had something on my father. What is it? He'd never have written that stupid will otherwise. And, I'm going to find out what it is."

She placed her hands on her hips and glared at the man her father claimed as his best friend. "And, mister, for your information, I *am* staying on Sweet Water, and I'm going to be the best ranch hand you've ever seen. And you'd better plan on signing that release paper. There won't be a court in the land that will side with you if you say I haven't lived up to my father's stipulations. By this time next year, I'll be running this ranch every bit as well as my father. You can bank on it."

Bane Jacob's dark eyes rested on hers as the corners of his mouth began to curl upward beneath the black mustache. "Can we go to lunch now? I'm famished."

In the jeep they rode along in silence. Rose thought about the words she'd spoken in haste, without thinking them through first. Her words had surprised even her as they'd tumbled forth, and she was sure they had surprised him. Why hadn't he lashed out at her? He had every right. Hadn't she attacked his ethics?

She knew how she would have responded had he attacked her like that. But he hadn't lashed out. He'd not only taken her words with a smile, he'd been downright pleasant, and now they were on their way to lunch like two old friends. She had to respect him. He was more of a man than she'd realized.

And, wonder of wonders, she had told him she was staying on Sweet Water Ranch—for an entire year. Where did that come from? She hadn't been aware that her decision had been made. Whatever possessed her to make such a foolish announcement? Maybe it was Nel crying in the kitchen as she'd peeled potatoes. Or the ranch hands and their insecurity about their own futures. Or seeing Bitty feeling so bad about the loss of the calf. Or remembering the good times she'd had with RuAnn in the barn. Whatever it was, suddenly she had discovered she wanted to stay. She had to give it a royal try. A year wasn't really that long; it'd be over before she knew it. Hadn't the past twelve months passed by rapidly?

Rose sneaked a glance at her companion, who appeared to be as deep in thought as she was. Too bad he was so good-looking; she'd be able to acknowledge him as the enemy more easily if he looked like a villain. Who was this man? Was he married? Did he have a wife and kids stashed away on his ranch? No one had mentioned a family, but that didn't mean anything; why should they? She snickered under her breath. No man with eyes like that could remain unattached very long. He had to be married. Or have a girlfriend.

❧

"Like hamburgers with everything on them?"

She turned toward Bane. *What did he say? Hamburgers?* She'd been so caught up in her thoughts, and he'd been so quiet since they left the barn, she'd nearly missed his question. "Oh, sure. If I don't have any choice but to go into town with you and have lunch—hamburgers are fine."

He smiled as their eyes locked. "Promise you won't eat the lettuce and leave the hamburger?"

Not sure if his question was meant as an insult or a joke, she decided to give him the benefit of the doubt and smiled. "If I'm going to be a farmhand, I'll have to learn to eat like one."

Marilyn jostled back and forth, occasionally slipping and sliding in and out of the ruts hidden beneath the snow.

"Cold?" Bane asked without turning his head.

"A little," she replied through teeth that chattered.

He wiggled the knob on the heater. "Sorry, been having a little trouble with this heater. I figured most of the cold weather would be gone by now and I could tinker with it when I rotated the tires on Marilyn."

She pulled one end of the lap robe around her shoulders and tugged the other end over her legs. "I'm fine," she lied. "Don't worry about me. Seems I'm going to have to adjust to Kansas living."

"But doesn't it get really cold in New York City?"

"Yes, but there you jump in and out of taxis; you don't go riding around in jeeps with canvas tops."

Ten cold minutes later they pulled into town. Rock City consisted of Adams's Mercantile, Bubba's Gas-ur-up, Jim's Auto Repair, a dozen or so other businesses, and Hannah's Hamburger Haven.

"We're here." Banc grabbed Rose by the sleeve before she could move to open her door. "Let me get it. My mother always said a gentleman should open the door for a lady."

She appreciated being thought of as a lady and waited as instructed by her gentleman host as he circled the jeep and grasped the door handle. "Thank you." She shifted in the seat and dropped her booted feet to the pavement. "Your mother was a smart lady. I'm glad you listened to her."

Hannah's Hamburger Haven was a quaint place. The smell of meaty hamburgers frying on the big grill made Rose ravenous. Hefty Hannah herself stood at the grill, clad in a pinafore-type apron with ruffles over her broad shoulders. "You from around these parts, honey? Don't remember seein' ya before."

"Sure am." Rose smiled at the pleasant woman. "Probably lived here long before you arrived."

Bane spoke up proudly. "Hannah, Miss Rose is Charlie Kinsey's daughter. Charlie wanted her to take over Sweet Water, you know—now that he's gone."

Hannah stopped flattening the burgers with her big spatula and turned toward the couple. "That so, honey? You're gonna run that big spread?" She eyed the young woman with a sardonic look and frowned as she put one hand on her rounded hip and surveyed her two customers. "You two pullin' my leg? Who are you really, honey?" She shot a teasing smile toward Bane with a shrug of her hand. "One of this man's groupies?"

"I'm just who he says I am. Rose Kinsey, Charlie's daughter." She shot a stern look at the man seated next to her, then continued with determination, "And, yes! I am going to stay and run the ranch."

"Well, I'll be," Hannah muttered as she turned back to the sizzling hamburgers. "We sure miss your pop. Ya got a mighty big pair of shoes to fill, darlin'."

When they finished their burgers, Bane wiped his mouth with his napkin, wadded it up, and dropped it in the middle of his plate. "Guess I'd better get you back to Sweet Water before Nel sends Bitty out to find you."

A warm hand touched her shoulder as the jeep came to a stop in front of the picturesque farmhouse. "Did you say it because you meant it, or because you were angry with me?" He stopped and blocked her way as she started up the freshly shoveled sidewalk to the house. "You know—about staying on Sweet Water."

A gamut of emotions surged through her and ended up in the pit of her stomach. Did she really plan to stay? Or had she said it out of spite and anger?

"Well, Rose?" he asked as he stood towering over her, so close she could feel his warm breath on her cheek and catch the scent of his aftershave.

A thousand thoughts rushed through her mind and seemed to funnel into one very narrow channel. "Yes," she stated resolutely as she clenched her fists and squared her chin. "I'm staying."

When Bane dropped by the next morning, Nel handed him a message from Rose. *Gone to New York to give up my job and my apartment. I'll be back in a week. You'd better be a good teacher, 'cause this gal is gonna be one fast learner.*

He whistled on the way back to his ranch in the noisy jeep, his eyes drawn to the empty seat beside him, the one she'd occupied the day before. *So, she's made her decision. She's going to stay. Good.* That was what he'd wanted all along, because her father had wanted it. Even as Charlie Kinsey lay dying, he had asked Bane to help him get his little girl back to Sweet Water where she belonged. How could he refuse such a request? So what if he had to appear as the villain? It was a role he could live with, if necessary, to make old Charlie happy.

On his deathbed, Charlie'd revealed his plan to Bane and talked openly about his daughter. He'd known even if Rose had willingly accepted her inheritance and had taken over the ranch's operation as its manager, she'd be in way over her head within a matter of months. She needed training and experience. Bane Jacob filled his requirements for a teacher to a tee. That's when this crazy plan had hatched in his head and he'd explained it to his closest friend. He knew his daughter would have to be forced to come back; she'd never do it on her own. She needed to be there long enough to learn the ranch's operation from the bottom up as an apprentice. A full year. And, in that year, hopefully, she'd learn to love the ranch as much as Charlie had.

Bane smiled as he thought about his best friend's last wishes. *Who knows? She might even find a cowboy husband to share it with. That'd make old Charlie happy.*

"You're what?"

Rose stood before Cartee Munyo, who ran the New York division of the world-renowned *Gorgeous Woman Magazine*. "I said I'm going to stay on my family's ranch in Kansas for one year."

Cartee stood to her feet, stunned by the words of the beautiful young woman standing on the other side of her desk. "Don't kid like that, Rose. It's not funny."

"I'm not kidding, Cartee. I know I have a couple of major deadlines coming up right away, but surely you can assign them to one of the other illustrators. I need to head back to Kansas by the end of the week." She felt like a traitor, turning in her resignation like this. Cartee had taken her on when other magazines wouldn't give her work a second look. She'd been both supportive and encouraging, boosting her morale when needed, and lauding her career. She'd been her mentor, friend, and confidante.

Cartee moved around the desk and put her hand on Rose's slim shoulder. "Haven't you been happy here? Is there a problem I don't know about? Tell Cartee. We'll take care of whatever it is."

"If only it were that simple. But it's not." For the next hour, the two coworkers and friends discussed the stipulations of Charlie Kinsey's will and the options facing the young woman.

"Now, let me see if I have this right," Cartee summarized as she tapped the tip of her red, sculptured fingernail on her desktop. "If you fulfill the stipulations in your father's will, you can sell the ranch and have more money than a lifetime of illustrating will bring you? Yet, on the other hand, if you are unable to please this Bane person, you lose not only the ranch and any profits you might make from the sale, but the rest of your father's wealth as well? And you, more than likely, will have a tough time reentering the fashion world after a year of ranching. Is that about it?"

Rose leaned back in the chair, locked her hands behind her head, and crossed her slim ankles. "That's about it. Or," she added, "I could chuck it all now and turn my back on Sweet Water Ranch and all that goes with it and pretend it never existed. Stay in New York and keep on building my career."

"Whew!" Cartee dropped into her chair and tapped a pencil on the glass desktop. "I see your dilemma. But tell me more about this man your father appointed as your teacher and executor. Do you think you could work with him? Would he be reasonable with you? And, most of all—do you trust him?"

Visions of Bane Jacob paraded through Rose's mind. She shrugged. "He's highly respected by Dad's men."

"How old?"

"Maybe five years older than I am."

Cartee raised her eyebrows. "You said he was good-looking. Is he married?"

Rose shrugged again. Hannah had mentioned his groupies, but look at Garth Brooks. Having groupies didn't mean a guy wasn't married. "I don't know," she confessed.

"Rose! I'm surprised at you. You meet an apparently wealthy, gorgeous young rancher, one you're planning to give a year of your life to—and you don't even know if he's married?"

"Never gave it a thought. And," she added indignantly as she tossed her resignation onto her friend's desk, "I don't care. There's nothing about that egotistical cowpoke that interests me. The last thing I need in my life is a bow-legged, bull-headed Kansas cowboy. Now, please. Can you cover my assignments so I can head back to Sweet Water by Saturday? It seems I have to be in church as part of my daddy's little plan."

"Church?"

Rose rolled her eyes and glared at the ceiling.

Cartee walked around the desk and touched Rose's arm. "If you're sure this is what you want. You've got a good thing going, girl. I hate to see you give up the career you've worked so hard to build."

Rose nervously smoothed her dark eyebrows with her fingertips. "What choice do I have, Cartee? Dad made it nearly impossible for me to make any other decision." She slumped back in the chair, took a long breath, then exhaled slowly. "Think there's a chance I might pick up where I left off—after the year?"

Cartee grew serious and studied her friend before answering. "To be honest, I just don't know. People forget quickly. Clients forget quickly. New people come on the scene. This is a fickle industry. And," she pinched her friend playfully on her bicep, her mood brightening suddenly, "who knows what life will bring after a year of working with your cowboy?"

Rose pulled away quickly. "He's not my cowboy!"

"Whatever you say, Rose," Cartee teased with a mischievous grin. "Whatever you say."

Five days later, the men from Bingham Transfer and Storage moved the last of Rose's things out of her apartment, she surrendered her keys to the super, and headed for the airport and Kansas.

As the 747 took off for Denver, she took one final look at New York's skyline with fear and trepidation in her heart. She was leaving a lucrative and satisfying career behind. For what? A chance at inheriting her family's ranch and all her father's wealth? She wasn't a gambler. Yet here she was, taking the biggest risk of her life—and the outcome rested on a man she barely knew.

When the plane landed in Denver, Rose moved slowly along with the other passengers, tired, hungry, and dreading the long drive from Denver to Rock City in a rental car. She almost wished she'd allowed Bitty to pick her up as he'd offered, but she couldn't ask the little man to make the long round trip to and from the Denver airport.

"Hey, lady! Need a ride?"

She heard the question, but she assumed the person wasn't speaking to her.

"Hey, Lilac! Can I offer you a ride?"

This time, she spun around on her heels to face the man who stood there grinning at her. "Bane! What are you doing here in Denver?"

He grabbed the carry-on bag from her hand and slipped an arm about her waist, then ushered her toward the baggage claim area. "Picking you up, that's what." His smile was infectious; she had to admit she was glad to see a friendly face in this sea of humanity bustling through the crowded terminal.

"But, how did you know—?"

"Nel. She said you called and told her you'd be back late this afternoon. Didn't take much detective work to figure you were bound to be on one of three flights. So I decided to come and meet 'em all. And, I lucked out. You were on the second one."

She couldn't help but notice how many heads turned as her handsome escort passed. His expensive black Levi's hugged his muscular legs and his western-cut shirt tapered across his rib cage, emphasizing his broad shoulders and narrow waist. She glanced sideways at his oval, hammered-silver belt buckle and snake-skin belt, the ever-present black Stetson with the silver hatband.

"How many bags ya got?"

"Oh—er, just one, besides my carry-on. I shipped everything else."

The wait wasn't long; her bag was one of the first to hit the conveyor belt. Bane reached over the heads of the other passengers and snatched it up easily as it passed by. "Long arms come in handy."

For some reason, his smile made her suddenly warm.

"Hungry?"

Yes, she was hungry. The flight had been long, and the snack they served in coach had been hours ago. "A little," she responded.

"Then I'm going to feed you. Ever hear of Casa Benita?" He flipped the carry-on bag under his arm and shifted the suitcase into his hand, then threw his free arm about her shoulders. "Come on, little lady. That's where we're going."

Bane insisted she wait just inside the terminal while he fetched the car. He'd said *car*, but what she was looking for was a pickup or Marilyn. When a sparkling new, red convertible pulled up in front of her, she barely noticed—until Bane unfolded his long legs from the driver's seat. "Like it?" he asked as he quickly shoved the luggage into the narrow trunk. "Got it a couple of months ago."

"Sure. Yes, it's very nice," she mumbled. "Pretty. I like red."

"Tired?" he asked as he slipped behind the wheel. "We can stop at a truck stop on the way home, if you'd rather."

Is this the man I left only a week ago? He hasn't said a flippant word since I've arrived. She managed a weary smile, tired but not willing to admit it. "Casa-whatever is fine with me."

Rose decided Bane must have slipped the maître d' a good-sized bill; he seated them at a table right next to a huge waterfall on the upper level of the big restaurant, where they could feel the mist from the water as it cascaded over the rocky ledge and fell to the deep blue pool below.

"You'll like this," Bane assured her with the excitement of a little boy at his first Bulls game. "Just wait."

She had no idea what he was talking about and plunged into the Tex-Mex food they'd selected from the buffet. "Umm. Good choice. I love Tex-Mex." She twisted a long string of gooey cheese on her fork and popped it into her mouth with a grateful grin.

Bane watched curiously. "Really? You like Tex-Mex? You're not just saying that because I brought you here?"

She picked up a big taco and waved it at him. "You didn't think I would?"

Bane grabbed her wrist. "Look!"

There, on the rock ledge several stories above the pool, stood a beautiful young woman dressed in a sarong-type swimsuit, with a huge pink hibiscus tucked into her long, dark hair.

Rose leaned forward for a better look. "What's she doing out there? That's dangerous." She gasped as the woman moved to the edge of the rock and poised herself on the watery ledge amid the lush overhanging green foliage.

"Watch," Bane directed, his eyes sparkling as he gently squeezed her hand.

The woman spread her arms, stood motionless for a few seconds, then dove off the cliff into the tiny pool three stories below, barely making a splash.

"That was beautiful," Rose cried as she leaned over the railing and watched as the young diver emerged from the water to the applause of an appreciative audience. "So graceful."

Bane squeezed her hand again. "Look. He's going to dive, too." A muscular young man now perched on the ledge in a tropical print bikini, his arms spread wide like an eagle's wings, ready to dive.

"Oh, Bane. I love this. Thank you for bringing me here." Rose topped their joined hands with her free hand and held her breath as the man lifted himself high on his toes and arched into the pool.

"I thought that you would. Now, how about some hot sopapillas?"

He pulled the string on the pole in the center of their table and the little flag rose to the top, signaling their waiter they were ready for dessert. In seconds, the man returned with a basket of big, puffy, hot sopapillas and placed them on the table between them. They smelled of cinnamon and sugar.

"Honey?" Bane asked as he placed the Tex-Mex delicacy on her plate.

Chapter 4

Rose, who'd been only half-listening, her attention still drawn to the rocky ledge, gave him a startled look. "What did you say?"

He grinned sheepishly. "I asked you if you wanted honey with your sopapilla."

Her face flushed to a soft pink and a small smile danced at the corners of her mouth. "Yes, please."

They stayed long enough to watch several more dives before heading for Rock City and Sweet Water Ranch. There was little conversation on the way home; Bane loaded his CD player and they listened to music. The drone of the car's engine and the softness of the music made Rose drowsy, but she managed to stay awake all the way. If the car hadn't had bucket seats she might have been tempted to cuddle up next to the cowboy and sleep with her head on his shoulder. That would have surprised him.

When he let her out at Sweet Water Ranch, Rose stood in the doorway and watched until the little red convertible disappeared down the lane, then turned to Nel. "Do you know what time church starts at Daddy's church in the morning? Guess I'll be going every Sunday from now on."

"The morning worship service is at 10:30. Sunday school is at 9:30."

Rose tossed her head back with a laugh. "Daddy didn't say I had to go to Sunday school. The worship service is the only one I'll be attending, thank you."

"Suit yourself. Bitty and I'll be attending Sunday school, but ya got your daddy's car now, so you can come whenever you want." Nel hung her calico apron on the hook by the refrigerator.

"You and Bitty go to Mill Creek Community Church now?" Rose looked surprised. She had no idea the couple attended church anywhere.

"Sure do, honey. Started goin' there with your pa right after he met Bane. Bitty and me like it real good. You'll like it, too. The people are real nice. Pastor's good, too."

"Won't make any difference if I do or if I don't. Dad didn't leave me any choice. He specified that church and none other."

Nel just smiled. "Turn out the kitchen light when you're done here, okay? I'm headin' for bed."

Rose watched as Nel moved into the hall off the kitchen that led to the little apartment she and Bitty shared. Her father had added the addition onto the house when Rose was three. He had said she needed a woman in the house, even if it was only their housekeeper. Rose was glad he had built the addition; he worked long hours on the ranch and it was nice to have Nel and Bitty around all the time. And it was nice now that she was home again. The ranch was isolated from the main road, and she wasn't sure she'd feel safe staying here alone. Of course, some of the ranch hands stayed in the bunkhouse, but that was quite a ways from the main house. And she didn't know any of them well enough to know if she could trust them.

As she lay on her back later, staring out the window of her bedroom, the stars twinkled in the heavens and for the first time since her father's funeral, she felt at peace. Winter had changed to an early spring during the few days she'd been gone. The snow had melted and the world was beginning to take on a bright new look.

Sweet Water. . .

Home. . .

Bane. . .

She drifted off into a restful sleep.

Bane sat on the edge of his bed and tugged off his boots, wondering if Rose had fallen asleep yet. *Funny, she isn't at all like the woman I met that first day in Ben Horner's office. Actually, she has every right to be upset with her father. She's his only child and he left her inheritance with some pretty heavy ropes attached to it. Ropes that could take it all away from her. And of all things, to leave the final decision to me, a man she'd never even met.*

He padded across the room and opened the drapery. Moonlight triangled across his bed, bathing the room in its silvery glow. He slipped into his pajama pants and dropped onto his knees beside his bed, going to the One to whom he always turned when he needed answers. "Oh, Lord. Charlie placed an awesome responsibility on my shoulders. I need Your wisdom and guidance." He poured out his heart to God, then asked His blessing before climbing into bed with one last look at the moon. The day had been a good one and he was glad he'd driven to Denver. He wondered if he'd see Rose in church in the morning. He smiled. . . .

The country church's parking lot was nearly full when Rose drove in at exactly 10:30. Nel and Bitty's old pickup truck was already parked by the front door. Rose glanced at her watch as she pulled open the heavy oak door that led into the vestibule. She was two minutes late.

The pastor read the Scripture, the choir sang, and the offering plate was passed while several men strummed guitars and a woman played the violin, then the worship leader stood to his feet. "And now we're going to hear from one of our favorites. His God-given voice never ceases to bless us." He turned toward the front row of the choir. "Bane. . ."

Stunned, Rose watched as Bane moved to the pulpit and nodded to the organist. In a voice deep and rich with feeling, he began to sing.

Bane Jacob attends Mill Creek Community Church? And he sings? Rose listened intently as the congregation sat motionless; even the babies stopped their fidgeting and listened. *Is this why Daddy and Bane got so close? They attended church together? Was that why Daddy put so much faith in this man?*

At the close of the service, Rose rushed from the sanctuary, eager to avoid the questions of well-meaning people welcoming her back into the community. She hated having to explain what her father had done to her, and she didn't want the congregation to know she was in church only because her father's letter demanded it.

After one of Nel's famous Sunday dinners, Rose spent the afternoon poking around in her father's room, bagging his clothing for the mission box she'd read about in the church bulletin. She put in a separate box a few personal items she wanted to keep, labeled it, and sealed it with tape. To her delight, she had even found his wedding ring with an inscription that read, *A loves C.*

Funny, in all the years she'd lived at home she had never once realized her father and mother had loved one another. The only story she'd ever heard about their relationship was that her mother had left her father when Rose was a baby. She had no idea why, or when, or what had happened to change their love. Or whom her mother left with, or where she'd gone. Her father had refused to allow her mother's name to be spoken in the house, and no one ever mentioned her, not even Nel or Bitty. When Rose tried to ask about her, her father would banish her to her room. It was as though her mother had never existed.

Now Daddy is gone and I still don't know anything about my mother. Is she still alive? If she is, where is she living? Has she remarried? Did she have other children? These questions had plagued her since childhood. She stared at the shiny gold wedding band as she rotated it between her fingers. One question loomed larger than any of the others. *Why did my mother leave without me? Now that Daddy is gone, will Nel be willing to talk?*

At 6:00 that evening, she heard a car pull up next to the house, and then a horn honked. When she looked out the window, she saw Bane had the top down on the little convertible.

"Hi," he called out cheerfully as she opened the door. "I saw you at church this morning. Wanna go tonight?"

Rose moved down the stone steps and placed both hands on the driver's door. "Church twice in one day? Are you kidding?"

"Nope, not at all. I go twice every Sunday. Wouldn't miss it. Wednesday night, too." He pulled the black Stetson from his head and smoothed his coal black hair. "Gonna show a missionary film. From Quito, Ecuador. Wouldn't want to miss that, would you?" His smile didn't waver, even though she gave him a *forget-it-buster* look.

She gave a forced laugh, hating to be put on the spot like that. "Well, once a week is often enough for me, and I'm not sure I'd go at all if my dad hadn't forced me into it. I kinda got out of the church-going habit when I moved to New York City. Too many weird churches there, if you know what I mean. I figured it was better to not go at all."

A man driving a black pickup, which looked suspiciously like Bane's, pulled into the circle drive and came to a slow stop behind the convertible. Bane gave the man a wave of his hat. The man nodded.

"Well, then. I guess I'll be going on without you, if you're sure I can't entice you to join me. I might even treat you to a cup of coffee on the way home. Sound tempting?"

"Oh, sure. Real tempting, but I think I'll pass."

She backed away in surprise as he pushed open the door and exited the car.

"Your choice. Don't say you weren't invited." He headed toward the truck where the man sat waiting. "See you bright and early tomorrow morning," he called back over his shoulder as he slid into the passenger's seat. "Say, about 5:30? We'll start your ranching education by checking the fences. Better wear your riding clothes. We'll be going on horseback."

"Horseback?"

"Yep, horseback." He slammed the door on the pickup and rolled the window down. "Oh, yeah. Here're the keys to my new car. Thought you'd rather drive it than that tank of your father's. It's yours for as long as you stay. Even a year." The ring of keys fell with a clank at her feet.

He winked as he sped past in his truck. "And by the way, I hope you'll stay forever."

She picked up the keys and stared at the swirl of dust the truck left behind. *Why would any man in his right mind give a stranger the keys to his new car? And, whatever did he mean by that bizarre comment?*

Bane was having a cup of coffee with Nel and Bitty when Rose entered the kitchen at 5:25, dressed in her new work clothes. He saluted her with his cup. "Five minutes early, that's good. You'll have just enough time for juice and a slice of toast before we head for the west pasture."

Nel winced, and Bitty grinned.

Rose smiled and filled her cup, unsure how to take his comment.

Bane was dressed in scuffed black boots, faded jeans, and a well-worn western shirt, all of which bore evidence of many days of hard labor. He sat watching as she took each bite, then checked his watch and announced, "5:35, Iris. Let's go. Time's a-wasting."

Rose grabbed her corduroy jacket and gave him a look as he hustled her out of the kitchen and into the approaching dawn of a beautiful day. Under the yard light, tied to the post by the gate, stood Bane's stallion. Next to the stallion was a horse that could have been his twin, saddled up and ready to go.

Rose gulped as they walked toward the huge animals; she hadn't ridden a horse since she was eighteen, and she'd never been comfortable around her father's horses. Her little pinto had been horse enough for her, but now she was walking toward the big stallions with a man who apparently assumed she was at home on horseback.

"Ah—beautiful horses. They look so much alike." She was sure he could hear the quaver in her voice as she struggled to mask her fears.

He grinned proudly as he patted his horse's firm rump. "They should. This is Midnight's brother. My horse Satin was the mama and one of your daddy's horses was the papa." He untied the reins of the second horse and handed them to her. "You're a mighty lucky lady to inherit such a fine animal. His name's Ebony. Horses are one of God's greatest creations."

Slowly, she reached for the reins; once they were tightly in her grip, she carefully patted the big horse.

Ebony stood glaring at her, nostrils flared.

"Did God tell him to be kind to women?"

"Of course He did." Bane mounted Midnight with a laugh and headed down the lane. "Let's go."

Rose slid her trembling foot into the stirrup and awkwardly flung her leg over the horse's broad back. Ebony stood firm, waiting for instructions. She patted the horse's silky mane, then bent and whispered, "Look, Ebony, I've never ridden a horse like you before. You're going to have to help me. And, please, don't throw me off. I'd hate to start my year with a broken arm." Her brain struggling to remember what to do, she gently pressed her heels into the horse's side. As if he'd understood her plea, he began to amble down the lane behind Midnight. She breathed a sigh of relief and leaned back into the saddle.

Ebony followed the fences almost mechanically, as if he'd done it hundreds of times before with her father. Bane spoke into the voice-activated recorder he held in his gloved hand, and Rose smiled as she watched and listened while he barked information and locations into the little battery-operated device.

"What're you grinning about?" he asked as he swung Midnight around and trotted up alongside Rose and Ebony.

She flinched at the close proximity of the two big horses, but she lifted her head confidently, trying to mask the fear that still engulfed her. "You."

A smile played across his lips as their eyes met. "Me? What about me?"

She leaned to stroke Ebony's thick mane. "Seeing you with that recorder. I thought an old do-it-the-tried-and-true-way cowboy like you wouldn't resort to using hi-tech gadgets in your ranching."

His smile widened, revealing those perfect teeth. Her father could've bought a new pickup with all the money he'd spent on orthodontists to give her the good teeth she had. How could one human have such perfect teeth, with or without the aid of an orthodontist?

"I can hang rags on the fences where they need to be fixed, so the hands will know where there's a problem. Or I can use this thing and tell them exactly where the fences need attention and just how much I want done to them, as well as other important things. Hey, I'll use anything that helps me be a better rancher. And now the hands have gotten used to listening to this thing, they like it, too. Saves a lot of confusion. Every tenth post has a tag attached to it, with a number on it. Makes the problem spots easy to identify." He gave Midnight a slight kick and moved on ahead of her, then called back over his shoulder, "You'll have to come to the Wild Rose and see my computer setup sometime. With that baby, I can tell at a glance how my operation's doing, right to the penny."

"You leave instructions for your wife on that thing?" she asked, trying to make it sound like an innocent question that had just occurred to her.

He frowned slightly and seemed agitated, then answered in a near whisper, "I'm not married."

Embarrassed and angry with herself for her foolish question, she turned Ebony away.

By noon, Rose's thighs were groaning from straddling the big horse, so when Bane reined up and suggested they take their lunch break, she agreed readily. Other than stopping at creeks and ponds along the way to water the horses and sip hot coffee from their Thermos bottles, they'd remained astride their horses all morning.

When they reached the river, Bane tied the horses to a young sapling, while Rose pulled their lunches from Midnight's saddlebag. Every muscle in her legs ached, but she refused to admit it.

He took her hand and motioned toward a gnarled hackberry tree near the water's edge. "This looks like a good place. Sorry, I don't have a nice checkered tablecloth. Mind sitting on the ground?"

His tone wasn't unkind, but his words rankled her a bit. Of course she could sit on the ground. Did he think she was some snooty prima donna? She lowered herself onto a clump of wild grass and relaxed her saddle-sore body against the tree's trunk. "This is fine," she said.

"Shall we pray?"

Rose bowed her head awkwardly, hoping he wouldn't ask her to do the honors. "Sure. I guess."

Hat in hand, he said, "Lord, we wanna thank You for this beautiful day. And thank You for letting us share the beauty of Your creation. And lastly, thank You for this good food Nel prepared. You're just too good to us. Amen."

She lifted her eyes to the man and wondered at the simplicity of his prayer. He sounded as though he were speaking to an old friend.

They sat in silence and munched on Nel's fried chicken, the fruit salad, celery sticks, and chips.

"Bane?" she said coolly, twirling a celery stick between her fingers. "Shouldn't you be running your own ranch? What was it you called it? The Wild Rose? Surely you don't have time to be riding fences on my father's place."

"Yeah, I should be," he admitted slowly as he shielded his eyes and watched a soaring hawk. "But I promised your dad I'd teach you every phase of the ranching business if you'd be willing to learn, so—here I am."

The hawk was drifting in big lazy circles overhead. She lifted her eyes and marveled at its grace as it rode on unseen winds. She hadn't watched a hawk in years, not since she and RuAnn used to lie on their backs on the freshly mown lawn and stare up at the sky, talking about what they wanted to do when they were all grown up.

"But, why? Why would you offer to do something so demanding for my dad? Surely you knew how much of your time it would take." She shot him an inquisitive glance, still confused by his motives. "I'm sure he told you how little I know about ranching."

Bane stuck his long legs straight out in front of him and crossed his ankles as he leaned against the trunk of the hackberry beside her. "Simple. I owed your dad—big time. He saved my life."

Rose straightened up and turned to face him, amazed by his words. "Really? When? How?"

He pulled off his hat and placed it on the ground between them. "Pulled me out of the river, upstream there a ways."

Her eyes grew wide. The thought of her stocky father pulling this perfect specimen of manhood from the river was incomprehensible. Besides, her father had always feared water. "My father? Pulled *you* out of the river?"

"Yep. I'da drowned if he hadn't." He looked grim. "Guess you want to hear the whole story, right?"

She nodded and leaned toward him, her interest piqued. "Of course I do."

He pulled a small knife from the leather sheath on his belt, picked up a stick, and began to whittle idly at the bark. "Well, I hadn't lived on the Wild Rose for very long. I met your dad and he was giving me a few ideas about the new barn I was planning to build. It was a hot day. I had this wild hare notion to get into the river and cool off. It'd been raining for nearly a week straight and when that sun came out, everything was hot and muggy."

"And—?"

"And even though the river was bank full and the current was running strong, and your father had warned me against doing it, I pulled my shirt off and dove in."

"Could you swim?"

"Yes, I'm a good swimmer. I wasn't afraid of the current. That wasn't the problem."

Rose pulled her knees to her chest and wrapped her arms about them. "Then what was the problem?"

Bane lowered his head and took a few more strokes with the knife. "I slipped on the muddy bank as I dove in. I fell and cut my head on a big, old jagged rock."

Her hands flew to cover her face. "Oh, no. What did you do?"

Bane looked up with a boyish expression that tore at her heart. "Nothing. I was out cold, drifting down that river like a piece of dried-out log, bleeding like a hanging deer in hunting season. I still got the scar. See?" He parted his curly hair, exposing a long crooked scar.

"So? Did my father go for help? Or throw you a rope?"

"No time to go for help. And the water was taking me away too fast to throw a rope. Besides, I was unconscious, remember?"

Her eyes widened. It was hard to believe his story was true, knowing her father's fear of water. "So, how did you get out?"

"Like I told you, your father got me out. All by himself, without personal regard for his own safety. He raced his horse way downstream, tied his rope to a tree, and waded out in that shoulder-high water, then caught me as the current brought me by. He pulled us both up that rope and out of the river. I don't know how he did it. I'm not sure I could have done it, and I was in better shape than he was. It was quite a struggle. Not many men could have done it."

"My dad did that?"

"Sure did. I'd swallowed quite a bit of water and he had to give me mouth-to-mouth resuscitation. Like I said, I owe my life to him."

Rose looked horrified. "But—my daddy couldn't swim. He was terrified of water. He wouldn't even wade out in the shallow end of our pond."

"I know, and he put my life before his." He picked up his hat, scooted closer to her, and continued, "After he revived me, somehow he got me up on his horse in front of him and rushed me back to the house. Then he called the ambulance. They took me to the hospital and stitched up my head and checked my lungs, then kept me overnight for observation and tests. That doctor said I would have died if your dad hadn't gotten to me, if not from drowning, then from the loss of blood."

Bane closed his eyes; with a shudder, he leaned back against the tree trunk once more, as if reliving the incident all over again. "That's what made him so special to me, Rose. He risked his life, despite his fear of the water, to save mine." He grasped her arm gently. "Oh, Rose. My stupidity might have cost your father his life. That current could have easily washed both of us away, but when he saw me in trouble, he forgot all about himself and came after me. We've been blood brothers ever since." His fingers tightened. "I would've done anything for that man. That's why I said yes, without hesitation, when he asked me to do this for him."

His brow furrowed and he became serious as he reached for her hand. "After that, your dad led me to his Lord. He explained how God had given His only Son to save me from my sins and give me eternal life with Him in heaven. I gave my life to Him. And I thanked God for your dad and the kind of man he was. Guess it took that knock on the head to get me to slow down and listen, because before that I'd pretty well turned my back on God. But seeing your dad willing to give up his life for me, well, it made God's love much easier to understand."

Rose could see moisture rising in Bane's eyes; she respected him for his ability to reveal such emotions. "My dad. . .led you to a. . .a religious experience? No wonder you two were so close. It all makes sense now."

His grip on her hand tightened. "You do understand what I meant when I said he led me to the Lord, don't you?"

She lowered her head. "Kinda. At least, I think I do. I've heard the pastor ask people to come forward and have their sins forgiven at the end of the services I've attended at Mill Creek Community Church."

His hands moved to grip her shoulders as he stared into her eyes. "That was the hardest, yet the best, decision I ever made. It wasn't easy to admit I was a sinner, but in my heart I'd always known I was. I just hadn't admitted it. Your dad had tried to talk to me about God before, but like most folks, I wasn't ready to listen."

"I can't imagine you being a sinner, Bane. Not with all the wonderful things people have said about you."

He frowned. "We're all sinners. You, me, Nel, Bitty—"

She lifted a finger to his lips. "Whoa there, big fella. Speak for yourself. I don't consider myself a sinner. Sinners are those people who steal, abuse, commit murder, things like that. I've never done any of those things."

"Have you ever said no to God?"

Rose considered his question. "No, of course not."

"Have you read His Word?"

She winced. "Certainly. When I was a child I went to Sunday school every Sunday with RuAnn's family."

"When was the last time you read it?"

She turned away, irritated with the way the conversation was going.

"If you'd read much of God's Word, you'd know He says all have sinned and come short of the glory of God. You, me, all of us. Everyone." He threw back his head with a laugh. "Even Billy Graham!"

"Billy Graham, huh? Well, if he sinned, as good as he is, I surely must have sinned, too."

Bane rested his forehead against hers. "Then you need to be saved, Rose. Think about it."

"So," she said quickly, eager to change the subject, "tell me more about my dad."

"Well, the most important thing I could tell you is that your dad saved my life—twice. Once in the river."

She nodded.

"And the second and most important time was in the cabin when he explained God's plan of salvation. That second time was for eternity!"

A bevy of emotions buzzed through her as she looked at this man whose life her father had risked his to save. For a moment, she hated him for putting her father in jeopardy, but she respected him for wanting to repay her father in any way he could. She could understand his being indebted to the man who saved him from drowning. But although she didn't want to admit it to him, the spiritual part was a total mystery to her.

"And whose idea was it that the ranch and everything Daddy owns goes to you if I fail?"

He cupped her hands in his and lifted them to his chin. "Honest, Rose, as God is my witness, I didn't know about those stipulations in your father's will until just before he died. He told me in the hospital as he lay on his deathbed. I'm sure this was your father's way of forcing you to spend time at Sweet Water. He was a desperate man. He wanted you to love it the way he did. And in all honesty, would you've come back here for any length of time if he hadn't added that stipulation? I think your father was much wiser than any of us realized. It was a masterful plan."

Bane stood to his feet and gathered up all traces of their lunch leftovers and stuffed them back into a bag. "I'm glad you're staying." He extended his hand and pulled her to her feet. "It's what your father would have wanted. And, I'm going to do my part in teaching you the ranching business." He threw an arm around her waist as they walked toward where the horses were busily munching on the tender spring blades of wild grass. "I'm going to be tough, because there's no other way to learn. You'll probably hate me at times. Hopefully, sometimes you'll like me," he shot her a smile, "but my whole purpose is getting you to the point where you'll be able to take over the ranch and run it as good as Charlie."

Rose leaned into Bane as they walked toward their horses. For the first time, she thought she understood her father's *and* this man's motives. She hoped she could live up to their expectations. Bane was out to repay a debt to her father, and in some ways, she had a debt to pay, too. After all, she'd never been the daughter she should have been. Maybe this was a way to make it up to her dad, by keeping Sweet Water in the Kinsey family, at least for another year. And if she stayed a year, she could at least say she tried. Surely, her father could ask no more of her than that.

Bane pushed a lock of her hair off her face and planted a quick kiss on her forehead. "That's for being a good sport and giving this crazy thing a royal try." He mounted Midnight and circled her as she put her foot into Ebony's stirrup.

She wished he wouldn't watch her so closely; mounting the big horse was hard enough without an audience. Ebony stood his ground, as if to make it as easy as possible for her, and soon they were trotting along behind Midnight, checking fences.

Bane watched the lovely young woman as she sat tall in Ebony's saddle, her back straight, hands on the saddle horn as she held the reins tightly. He knew she was afraid of the big horse. She hadn't said anything, but he could tell. He'd wanted to offer another horse, but Ebony was her dad's. It seemed only proper that she ride him. He had to admire her guts. Those years in New York away from the ranch had made her soft, and yet her softness was one of the things that made her attractive. She was different from the other women in and around Rock City. Although she had everything going for her, she hadn't let it go to her head like he had envisioned. He'd watched her with Nel, and with Bitty, with the hired hands. At first, he'd thought she was a spoiled brat, but he had soon realized that was far from the truth. She had a kindness and a sweetness about her that amazed and intrigued him. *Those eyes. A man could get lost in them. So blue, so clear. And that skin, all silky and smooth. Now, that's a woman.*

He wanted to touch her, to rub his fingers across her cheeks. He'd wanted to rub her back and shoulders when they'd had lunch, when he knew she was hurting from riding that big horse all day along the fences and through the meadows, but he felt his touch would be out of place. *I wonder how she would have reacted. . . .*

Suddenly aware she was watching him, he was sure his eyes had betrayed his thoughts. He hadn't had feelings like this in years, feelings he'd vowed he'd never let himself feel again. He hadn't been interested in a woman since. . .

Chapter 5

I put the liniment on your dresser, Rose," Nel told her as she rapped on the bathroom door. "Are you sure you're okay? Ya didn't look so good when you came in. You looked plumb tuckered out."

Rose had been soaking in the tub for over an hour, submerged in warm water up to her neck. "Thanks, Nel," she answered with a great effort. Every bone and muscle in her body twanged with pain. She was sure her bottom was perfectly flat from sitting astride Ebony all day.

"What was that man thinkin' of? Keepin' you on that horse all day," the housekeeper snapped as she turned back the covers on Rose's bed. "You ain't no ranch hand yet! He oughta give ya a little time to get used to Ebony before keepin' ya out all day on that creature."

Rose nodded her head from the bathtub; she couldn't agree more.

"I put your plate in the oven. You have to eat supper, Rose. You can't work all day, then go without supper. You hear me?"

Rose leaned her head on the wall behind the tub and closed her eyes. "I hear you, Nel. I promise I'll eat my supper. Go on to bed and I'll put the dishes in the dishwasher before I go to sleep."

"Just see that you do, or tomorrow night I'll have to sit and watch you eat to make sure you do it! And, don't bother with them dishes."

"Yes, Nel."

The rest of the week, Bane worked mornings with Rose, then turned her over to Bitty for the afternoons while he went back to the Wild Rose, for which Rose was thankful. She missed Bane, but Bitty didn't work her nearly as hard. And with Bitty, she could quit or rest whenever she felt tired, without wondering if he was watching her.

As she crawled into bed on Saturday night, she experienced a euphoric feeling of satisfaction. She'd bonded with Ebony and was beginning to feel at home in the saddle. She had used the recorder to document fence information for the hands, and she'd learned how to saddle Ebony by herself. And much to everyone's surprise, she'd cleaned out Ebony's stall all by herself, rather than leave it to one of the hands. Maybe those things wouldn't mean much to some people, but to her, they were monumental milestones.

The little country church's parking lot was as filled as it had been the previous Sunday. She searched until she spotted the big, black pickup, and parked as close to it as she dared. Bitty and Nel were seated in their usual pew, and Rose slipped in beside them; this time she was early. Bane was sitting in the choir loft, right where she'd expected he would be, and he smiled at her over his hymnal. As they sang the hymns, her eyes met his again and again; each time she glanced his way, his dark eyes were riveted on her. Not that she minded. She found she welcomed his attention, even if from afar. If only she knew more about him. *Well, that settles it*, she decided as she gave him a demure little smile. *I'll just ask someone about him. I should have done that when I first arrived. I have every right to know about the man who controls my future. Haven't I?*

The pastor's message held her attention, despite the eye games she played with Bane. The pastor talked about things their old pastor never had—or maybe she hadn't heard when she was growing up because she hadn't been listening. She wasn't sure which was the case, but these things were new to her. The pastor said all people were sinners and needed a Savior, just like Bane had said. He talked about making a decision for God. He even mentioned her father several times during the message, praising him for all he'd done for the church during his lifetime, holding him up as a Christian example.

Example? Example of what? After all, my mother left my father, didn't she? She surely had good reason to leave. I just wish I knew why. He couldn't have been a very good husband. I wonder, did they agree to separate? Or was it all Daddy's fault? Was he impossible to live with? If only I knew what happened.

She looked for Bane after the service, but the pastor had mentioned a short deacons' meeting to be held at the conclusion. Probably Bane was a deacon.

RuAnn phoned after lunch. She'd driven over to her folks' place for a visit and hoped the two of them could get together for girl-talk, if Rose wasn't too busy.

"Me? Busy? What could I possibly do around Rock City on a Sunday afternoon? Aside from the chores, the ranch virtually shuts down on Sundays. Come on over!"

The young woman arrived at Sweet Water twenty minutes later, her naturally curly, red hair neatly woven into a long braid that nearly reached her waist. She was a good twenty pounds heavier than she'd been in high school, but Rose would have recognized her perky face anywhere. "Oh, RuAnn," she exclaimed as she opened the door and threw her arms around her old chum. "It is so good to see you."

The freckle-faced vet returned her embrace before stepping back to take a good look at her host. "You're beautiful, Rose. But you're way too thin—for Rock City."

The two girls giggled all the way to the kitchen, where Rose dipped generous scoops of vanilla ice cream into gigantic mugs, then filled them with ice-cold root beer from the fridge and inserted long iced-tea spoons and straws. "Remember these?" She handed the foamy root beer float to her old buddy. "What shall we drink to?"

The redhead lifted her mug to meet Rose's. "To old friends and new beginnings."

They clanked mugs, looped their arms, and drank, then plopped into chairs and reminisced about bygone times.

"Tell me more 'bout Bane," RuAnn coaxed as she took the last sip of the sweet, foamy concoction. "Has he been working you hard this week?"

Rose rolled her eyes and shook her head. "Nearly killed me the first few days, but I'm toughening up, I guess. He leaves by noon now, so I can slow my pace a bit the rest of the day. He's a tough teacher. But I have to say this for the guy, he knows what he's doing."

"You bet he does," RuAnn confirmed as she pushed a rust-colored spiral of hair from her forehead. "He's the greatest. You're lucky to be learning from him. There are ranchers around here that would trade half their herd for a chance to learn from Bane." She poked her friend in the ribs. "Has he made a pass at you yet?"

"Pass? Bane Jacob?" Though she'd had many thoughts of Bane taking her into his strong arms and kissing her, unfortunately it hadn't happened. "Why? Does he have a reputation for that? He's so—reserved—and businesslike. I can't imagine anything the least bit flirtatious coming from him." She twisted in her seat toward her friend. This was her chance to ask the unanswered questions that had been plaguing her.

"Which reminds me," she said, trying to sound casual. "I know very little about Bane. Can you fill me in? You know, general background stuff?"

RuAnn fingered the handle on her empty mug thoughtfully. "Some, I guess. He was already living on the Wild Rose when I came back from college. My folks really bragged him up, wanted me to meet him. Nothing would have pleased them more than to see their daughter walk down the aisle with Bane Jacob."

Rose mustered an uneasy smile. "You and Bane?"

"Well, most of the women in the county were chasing Bane by the time I came on the scene. Unsuccessfully, I might add. He's dated most of us on a purely platonic basis. More to get acquainted than anything. He very nicely made it clear he wasn't interested in a serious relationship with any of us. And goodness knows, we all tried."

"Why? Has he never married?"

"I wish I knew. Far as I know, no one knows."

Rose wrinkled her nose. "Do you think he's—you know—"

RuAnn reared back with a hearty laugh. "Bane? No way. What a thought. That's funny, Rose."

"Then, why? Why doesn't he get serious with some woman? What man would want to spend his life as a bachelor? And the right woman would be a real asset to a man with a spread like his."

"I think you said the key word. *Right* woman. Maybe Bane hasn't found her yet. I just don't know. I do know I'd jump at the chance if he'd give me a second look. He's a real gentleman and a great catch." She turned to Rose accusingly. "How about you? Maybe you're that woman."

Rose shot both hands up defensively. "No way! I'm no more interested in marriage than you say Mr. Jacob is." Her face turned somber. "One year, and I'm outta here."

"But what if you decide you like running the ranch? Wouldn't you consider staying then?"

Rose took her friend's empty mug and placed it in the sink alongside hers and absentmindedly filled them with water. "Not a chance. Oh, I may hang onto a few hundred acres, just to keep the family tradition going, maybe rent it out for pasture, but no, I'm going back. My life is my illustrating career. With the money I'll get from the sale of the ranch, I can open my own agency, do freelance work. I've had that long-range goal in the back of my mind for some time. Selling the ranch would make it possible."

RuAnn studied her high-school classmate for some time before she spoke. "But, Rose—wouldn't you like to have a family? Kids? I know I would."

Rose tapped her chin with her fingertip. "I have to admit, now that I'm older, at times I do think about having a family. I don't know, RuAnn. This thing with Daddy's will has really put my life in a quandary. I've even found myself feeling obligated to my dad, to give this ranch a fair chance like he wanted. He was so sure I'd want to stay here on Sweet Water. I try to brush the idea away, but it keeps nagging at me. *If* I found the right man, and *if* he liked ranching, and *if* I decided *I* like ranching—well, maybe I'd change my mind about this place. But," she emptied the mugs and placed them in the dishwasher, "how likely are all those *ifs* to happen? Barbara Bush pairing up with Richard Simmons would be more likely to happen."

The two laughed their way through the afternoon, and when RuAnn left, they vowed to get together again. Soon.

❧

Bane had Rose's horse saddled and waiting for her when they left the kitchen together the next morning, after a breakfast of Nel's french toast and sausage.

She gave him a smile. "More fences?"

"Nope. Thought we'd ride over to the Wild Rose and I'd show you how I keep the entries on my computer. I set your dad's up pretty much like mine, and it would be helpful if you understood the format we've used."

She nodded, but she felt suddenly stupid; she didn't want to have to admit that she was nearly computer illiterate. When her classmates had been taking computer science, she'd been taking art classes.

Bane headed Midnight down the lane. The sun was just rising over the meadow, and Rose paused to drink in its pastel beauty before mounting her big horse. Although she hated to admit it, she had missed the Kansas sunrises and sunsets.

By the time she was sitting in the saddle, Bane was already out on the country road and Midnight was galloping at a good pace. She patted her stallion's mane. "Ebony, it's up to you. I've never ridden that fast before. If you think we can handle it, let's go." She tightened her grip on the reins and gave the big horse a firm nudge with her heels. Ebony responded and took off with a rhythmic trot, his mane flying in the gentle morning breeze. Rose smiled to herself, feeling very confident sitting astride his strong back. As the horse picked up speed, she rose in the saddle, her weight on the stirrups as she leaned over Ebony's neck.

And then suddenly, she hit the dirt with a thud that knocked the wind out of her.

She rolled onto her back and gasped, struggling to refill her lungs with the clean air. The trees overhanging the lane seemed to be moving in circles overhead. Ebony seemed to be moving in circles, too, as he stood motionless beside her. She tried to sit up, but the world was spinning too fast, destroying all sense of balance. Somewhere in the distance, in the back of her brain, she could hear a man's voice, but she couldn't make out his words.

An arm slid under her neck and gently lifted her head, and she felt something soft being placed beneath her. *Think. Focus. Collect your thoughts. Get a grip.*

"Rose, honey. Are you okay? What happened? Did Ebony throw you?"

Each time she opened her eyes she could see earth, sky, trees, a horse's head, and Bane, all whirling together in a sea of visual confusion.

He tipped his water bottle to her lips. "Here, drink this. It'll help."

His voice was soothing, his body warm as he crouched on the ground beside her. She wanted to sleep. . . .

"Rose. Drink!"

She tried to sip the water, but she could feel herself slipping between reality and la-la land.

The water did help and within minutes she was able to sit up and lean into Bane's broad, firm shoulder. The world seemed to be slowing down a bit.

"I don't—" She stammered to form her words. "I was on Ebony—then—I was on the ground—" It was hard to speak, her breathing was uneven and labored, and her chest hurt.

"Ebony threw you? Maybe he's too much horse for you."

She drew in another gasp of air, ready to defend the big horse who had become her friend. "No. It wasn't Ebony," she refuted, still feeling dazed.

He pulled her close and stroked her cheeks with the back of his hand, running his fingers gently back and forth. "Well, then. If it wasn't Ebony, what? Things like that just don't happen. What did you do?"

"What did *I* do?" She fought the impulse to scream at him and pound him with her fists. Did he think she'd done something to cause this to happen? She pushed away from him and got uncertainly to her feet, grasping at Ebony's bridle for support. "Just forget it. I'm fine. Let's go."

"Rose, I didn't mean—"

Her hands flew to her hips. "Oh, didn't you? You think I did something stupid—like fall off a horse?"

As she raised her foot ready to thrust it into the stirrup, she came to a stop. The stirrup was gone! All that remained was a portion of the leather strap that had held it.

Bane saw it, too. He grabbed at the strap and held the end of it up close for a better view. A deep frown etched itself across his face and his eyes narrowed as his finger rubbed the smooth end of the leather. "From the looks of things, someone could have cut this strap on purpose."

Bane led Ebony back to the barn to replace the damaged saddle, while Rose sat trembling at the kitchen table and Nel hovered over her.

"Who could have done such a thing?" Nel asked Bitty as he opened the door and hurried into the kitchen, a worried look on his ruddy face.

Bitty pulled his hat off and knelt beside Rose. "I'm so sorry, Rose. That saddle was fine the last time ya used it. No one else touched it, until Bane saddled up Ebony for ya this morning. I said I'd do it, but he was here early and wanted to take care of it himself." He touched her skinned arm warily. "Ya okay?"

Rose rubbed the back of her neck and rotated her shoulders, feeling the inevitable stiffness already setting in. "I'm okay, Bitty. Just a little banged up from hitting the ground. Fortunately, I'd barely gotten up on Ebony's back when it happened. Thank goodness, we weren't galloping at the pace Bane was."

Nel moved behind the young woman and began to massage her shoulders as the kitchen door flew open and Bane entered.

"Calvin's finding you another saddle," he said. "Sure you don't want to go to the doc's office? I'd feel better if you'd let him check you out."

She shook her head, a little embarrassed at all the attention. "I'll be fine. Just give me a few minutes and I'll be okay."

"Few minutes? I'd say you'd better take the morning off. Tell you what, you rest this morning. At noon, if you're up to it, I'll drive you over to the Wild Rose, we'll have lunch, and I'll show you the computer setup." He took her hand and rotated her arm to check the bruises and abrasions. "Sorry, I can't imagine how that leather strap got worn like that—"

"Worn? Out there, you said it'd been cut, Bane. I heard you. Why would anyone want to do that to a perfectly good saddle? That thing was nearly new, wasn't it?" Her voice quavered as she voiced the suspicions that had been nagging at the back of her mind.

He shook his head with a deep sigh. "I don't know."

She was glad to have the morning off. A good soak in the tub helped soothe her wounds, and the extra time allowed her to scan through her father's desk. His computer loomed on his desk, as if it held secrets accessible only to those who knew how to operate it. Maybe information was in that mysterious thing about her mother. She glared at the monster and vowed to master it.

In the top drawer of the desk she found her father's address book, but there was nothing in it to indicate an address or phone number for her mother after she'd left Sweet Water.

Bane held the strap in his hand. *It's been cut all right, no doubt about it, but I sure don't want to frighten Rose. Looks like it's been slashed with a knife.* The cut was too clean to have worn that way. He thought a tiny bit, maybe a quarter inch long, had been left uncut, so the next rider would be able to mount without the thing giving away. But it would never stand any prolonged pressure.

He took the saddle and locked it in the cabinet at the back of the tack room, securing it with his own personal padlock, where no one would have access to it. Why, he wasn't sure, but until he found what evil person had done this stupid thing, the damaged saddle would remain locked up in his possession.

He mounted Midnight and rode slowly down the lane, retracing their path. Nothing looked out of the ordinary. He stopped where Rose had taken her fall and dismounted and squatted. The dirt was scuffed up, and he sifted his fingers through the fine silt, remembering how frightened he had been when he'd turned and seen Ebony standing there, riderless. Then he had caught sight of Rose, lying motionless on the ground like a rag doll. He shuddered as he relived the scene. *She could have been—*

He didn't want to think of what injuries she might have sustained. Other riders hadn't been as fortunate; he'd heard of several who had been paralyzed for life from such a fall. He bowed his head. *Lord, guide me as I track down the person who did this to Rose.*

Chapter 6

Bane returned at straight up noon in his shiny black pickup, and they made the fifteen-minute drive to the Wild Rose. Rose hadn't realized his ranch was so close to theirs; she'd known that land as the Lazy Z. The ranch had been run-down and ill-kept, with a small, battered log cabin and leaning barns and fences that sagged and dipped on rotting posts. Now, she barely recognized the place as they turned into the tree-lined lane that led past meticulously painted barns and outbuildings. The magnificent farmhouse was surrounded by a thick grove of shade trees.

"This is it. The Wild Rose," he said proudly as he rested his long arms on the curve of the steering wheel. "One of the prettiest spreads in this part of the country, if I do say so myself."

She envied the feeling of pride he felt for his ranch and wished she felt the same for Sweet Water. He sounded as though his every dream, every fantasy, had been fulfilled by the Wild Rose. "You have every reason to be proud. It's beautiful."

"Wait'll you see the house." He leapt from the truck and rushed around to open her door. "I hope you like it."

She smiled. What difference did it make if she liked it or not? *More than likely the inside is nothing but a masculine hideout, filled with animal heads hung over fireplaces with their glass eyes glaring at you, and trophies on mantels.* He probably cared nothing about endangered species or ecological imbalances.

The house turned out to be a two-story brick and cedar structure, probably no more than five or six years old, surrounded on three sides by a covered porch, with wonderful rustic, willow furniture and several porch swings. Now that the danger of frost had passed, baskets of vibrant red geraniums hung above the porch's railing, adding batches of color to the front of the house. The yard was well landscaped, with a manicured lawn. A woman in a white apron gave them a friendly wave from the doorway.

"That's Maudie, my housekeeper. Maybe you knew her—she used to work for the Grindons before she came to work here at the Wild Rose."

Rose decided the geraniums had to be Maudie's doing. A man like Bane, with all the demands on his life, wouldn't have thought of hanging baskets of flowers on the front of his house.

"Like the geraniums?" he asked as he ushered her up the stone walkway to the farmhouse. "I raise them in my little greenhouse out back. I've got plenty—I'll plant up some baskets for Sweet Water, if you like."

So, now he's a gardener, too? She scanned the line of lush, healthy flowers blooming profusely amid trailing dark green ivy in the sphagnum moss-filled wire baskets. *Is there anything this man can't do?*

A tiny garter snake slithered across the path in front of their feet. Rose bolted back with a scream.

"Now, don't tell me you're afraid of a little snake?"

Bane's chuckle brought a burst of color, both anger and embarrassment, to her cheeks.

"Yes, I'm terrified of them," she confessed as she raced up the steps onto the safety of the porch.

The woman in the white apron met her with open arms. "Now, honey. Don't you be afraid; them little snakes won't hurt you. Will they, Bane?"

"Only if you're a beautiful woman who's lost her Kansas roots," he teased.

"Bane, you stop that. This little lady's had enough excitement for one day." Maudie took Rose by the hand and led her into Bane's home, where she seated her on a massive sofa before going to fetch a glass of water.

Bane removed his hat and sat down beside her. "Sorry, Sweet Pea. Guess there are lots of ladies who are afraid of snakes. I didn't mean to make fun of you." He covered a chuckle with his hand. "But you did look mighty cute, the way you went straight up in the air when you saw that little wiggler. Ya scared him worse'n he scared you."

She saw no humor in the situation. There was nothing funny about snakes. Of any size.

Maudie returned with the glass of water and prattled on and on about what a wonderful man her boss was while Rose drank the water. "Can I get you anything else? Lemonade? Coffee? Lunch'll be ready in a few minutes."

"Nothing, thank you." She took a few more sips of the cool water, then placed the tumbler on the glass-topped coffee table next to a big well-worn family Bible; then she leaned back against the plump sofa and scanned the room. It was exceptionally large, well furnished, and quite comfortable, without animal heads and trophies. Instead, lovely lighted oil paintings hung on the walls among framed pictures of a couple she guessed to be his parents. The view from the big picture window was breathtaking. Gentle rolling hills were covered with what looked to be a bountiful crop of wheat. Off to the side stood a small greenhouse filled with flowers blooming in an array of festive colors.

Bane sat quietly beside her, saying nothing, but she knew he was watching her.

"Who's your yard man? Maybe I need to get him to spend a few hours a week at Sweet Water."

He grinned. "I'd be happy to work at Sweet Water several hours a week; the place does need a little help. Your daddy didn't feel much like worrying about the lawn this past year."

"You? You do the yard work around here?" The thought of this powerful man on his knees, weeding a flower bed, brought outrageous visions to her mind.

"Of course, me. You should see my rose garden. A number of my prize-winning roses are beginning to bloom. What can I say? I love flowers." He gave a wink. "Especially roses!"

The meaning in his voice made her heart sing.

They toured the entire home and ended up in the master bedroom, in the far upstairs corner. She wasn't sure she should be in that room, but she decided that with Maudie in the house it was okay.

"This is where I keep my computer," he explained as he lifted the tambour rolltop on the giant oak desk and exposed the computer and keyboard. "I used to keep it in the office at the end of the hall, but I like it better in here. More convenient at the end of a busy day."

She nodded, hoping he wouldn't ask her something that would force her to reveal her ignorance.

"Had a chance to look over your dad's computer files yet?" He tapped a button and the screen lit up with all kinds of colorful squiggles darting across its surface.

"No. Not yet." She tried to sound casual.

He scanned her face. "You do know how to work a computer, don't you?"

There. He'd asked her point-blank. No way around it, it was truth time. "No," she admitted softly, as if saying it softly made the *no* any less a *no*.

He frowned. "Are you kidding me? You really don't know how?" He didn't say it in a mocking, ridiculing way, just as a question, pure and simple.

"No. I honestly don't know," she repeated as she avoided his eyes. Why did it seem she'd just confessed to some awful crime? Surely she wasn't the only woman in the world who knew nothing about computers.

He seated himself before the keyboard and gave her a smile. "Then you're in luck. I happen to be just itching to teach someone how to use this thing. Your dad's is exactly like mine, so if you learn this one, you'll have no trouble with his."

This kind of knowledge would give her access to her father's files. She was sure Bane expected her to refuse his offer, but if it would let her search her father's files, the hardship would be worth it.

"Thank you, Bane. I'd like that."

For the next three hours, the two huddled over the keyboard as Bane would perform a function, then scoot over so Rose could repeat it. By the end of the afternoon, she knew how to get the machine up and running, how to access files, create new documents, add and delete, and she had set up a letter and an envelope template. Now she was glad RuAnn had talked her into taking that year of typing.

From time to time, as she was sitting at the keyboard, he'd lean over her shoulder to point something out, and the musky smell of his aftershave would cause her mind to stray; his face would be so close she could feel his breath on her cheek. She found herself enjoying their closeness and wondered if he enjoyed it, too, but she quickly put that out of her mind. She would be here for one year. That was all.

After he drove her back to her ranch, she thanked Bane for a wonderful, informative afternoon.

"I hope you're not too tired. You've had quite a day. I shouldn't have kept you out this late. You'd better go to bed early, and if you don't feel like working in the morning, I'll understand. You'll probably be plenty sore."

"And miss a day of my training? No way." She leaned nervously against the doorway like a teenager saying good night to a first date. "See you in the morning. Thanks again."

Bane tipped his hat and backed off the little porch with a smile.

Although Rose was brain-dead after working with Bane's computer all afternoon, she had one thing on her mind. Her father's files. She trembled as she sat down in front of her father's keyboard and the screen came to life with the same squiggles as Bane's. She took it slowly, step-by-step, repeating the procedures she'd learned, careful not to venture into unknown territory. She selected file after file, clicking on the little icons, scanning each document as it appeared, closing it if it held nothing of interest.

She was tired and nearly ready to click the shutdown button, when she found a file labeled *C.M. Personal*. Her heart did a flip-flop as she considered its contents. New energy flowed through her; maybe it contained information about her mother. But try as she might, she couldn't open the file; a box kept appearing, asking for the password.

By morning, some of the soreness from her fall off Ebony's back had subsided and she was ready to resume her role as ranch hand. Bane decided the time had come for her to help with the horses. Although she'd been afraid of most of the horses when she arrived, she found working with the mares and their foals gave her a joy she couldn't express. There was something about being with them that was so innocent and sweet.

He made fun of her motherly interest in them, but Nel assured her that many people who raised horses started talking to the foals and playing with them as soon as they were born, just like people did with their babies.

One little foal especially found her favor. He looked very much like Ebony, and she named him Jet. She told Bane, "This colt won't be sold like the others. He's special." Then she added with a sparkle in her eye, "And who can argue the point with me? I'm the boss."

❧

She had been working with the horses for several weeks, besides getting ready for the wheat harvest, and by the first week in July she was feeling pretty good about herself. Although she had put on ten pounds, she had more stamina and strength than she'd had as a teenager. The skin she'd once protected now glowed with a golden tan. Her blisters had turned to calluses, and she no longer had to force her weary body out of bed in the morning.

Bane seemed pleased with her progress and complimented her often on her growth as a rancher. She hadn't seen much of him during the past month, as he had his own ranch to tend to and his lead man had been laid up with a broken leg. However, he checked in every day in person or by phone. The men had come to respect her as she worked side-by-side with them, and they no longer whispered behind her back. Wheat harvest was behind them, and life on the ranch was good.

❧

Bane stopped hammering and watched Rose as she braced herself on the steep roof of the barn. She was so beautiful, even in stained, ragged jeans and a faded T-shirt. He wondered if she had any idea how many times he'd been tempted to take her in his arms and kiss her like she'd never been kissed. It was hard to believe just a few months ago all she'd been to him was a picture in a frame on her father's desk. If he was truthful, he'd admit he had dreaded meeting her; he had expected to find fake beauty or a spoiled brat. He'd realized immediately she was no fake beauty, but he had thought her spoiled that first meeting in Ben's office. Looking back, though, maybe the spoiled part was a preconceived notion on his part. He'd been so sure that her father had pampered her and given in to her every whim, so how could he have expected anything less? *I have to admit I was wrong. She's anything but what I'd expected.*

"You loafin' on the job?" she called down to him as she moved farther up the roof.

"Hey, Blue Bell, wanna cohost the end-of-harvest church picnic with me?" Bane called back. "Your daddy and I used to do it together, so I guess it's up to you to take his place. If you would."

"Sure," she agreed quickly as she pulled a handful of nails from the carpenter's apron around her waist. "Sounds like fun. Whatta we do?"

He tugged a bandanna from his back pocket and wiped the sweat from his brow. "Well, we announce the date at the church, set up the picnic area in my yard, and wait for the people to come. And you could help me decorate."

She watched as a trickle of sweat made a crooked path down his neck to the knit band of his red tank top. There was something so masculine about this man, yet so gentle. "It's that simple? Then, why do you need my help?" She anchored a piece of aluminum to the roof and pounded in six nails without bending one of them over, then threw him a victorious grin. "Not bad, huh?"

He nodded in agreement. "I didn't say *work* with me, I said cohost. All you have to do is look beautiful. Smile. Make people feel welcome." He hammered another piece of aluminum in place. "And of course you'll have to dress like a lady, instead of a ranch hand."

She shot him a grin. "Just watch me. I'll knock your socks off."

The day of the picnic arrived. They had both been so busy with the preparations all morning, they had barely had time to speak. Nel and Bitty helped them, and by noon, the Wild Rose was decorated with bales of hay, lanterns, reams of orange and gold crepe paper, and stuffed scarecrows, ready for its guests. After calling out a *be-back-later* to Bane, Rose crawled into the little red convertible to head for home, to shower and dress for the occasion.

Her bloodcurdling scream pierced the windless day and brought Bane and everyone else running to the car.

There, on the seat beside her, lay a big black snake, coiled and glaring at her with its beady eyes. She pressed tight up against the door, too terrified to move, too frightened to do anything but scream.

Bane yanked open the door and pulled her out by the arm, then grabbed the snake with a gloved hand and jerked it from its resting place. "It's okay, Rose. I've got him. He won't hurt you. He's one of the good guys."

He tried to reach out to her with his empty hand, but she only screamed louder and he turned away. "Take care of her, Nel, while I get rid of this thing."

Bitty whispered into Nel's ear. "That snake couldn't have gotten in there without a little help. I think someone put it there on purpose."

"I heard that, Bitty," Rose called out, her voice raspy and shaking. "And someone cut that stirrup strap. Someone is out to get me. I know it." She buried her head in Nel's shoulder as she fought back tears of fear and anxiety.

"Not likely," Bane countered as he joined the group surrounding the young woman. "Why would anyone be out to get you? It was just a snake looking for a ride in a convertible. That's all."

A snicker crept through the bystanders as most turned back to their tasks. Rose felt her anger rise, then she realized that to these farm people a harmless snake was nothing to get so upset about. She felt a bit foolish.

Bane wrapped her in his arms. "Don't let that old snake ruin our day, sweetie," he said softly as he nuzzled his chin in her hair. "I'm here. I won't let anything hurt you."

He nodded toward Nel. "Nel, why don't you drive Rose home, so she can take a nice bath and get ready for the picnic. A leisurely bath will calm her down."

Nel put her arm around Rose's waist and pulled her toward the car. "Sure, Bane. I'll drive her home. Bitty can come when he's finished here. We'll take your car."

He was right about one thing. The bath did help. Rose decided it must have been coincidence: the snake, the stirrup. After all, she barely knew most of the people around Rock City. Who would want to hurt her? And why?

"You're lookin' mighty purty."

Rose turned to find Nel standing in the doorway with an appreciative smile on her wrinkled face. "You think this broomstick skirt looks okay with this blouse, Nel?"

Nel nodded in approval. "Sure do. And I like your hair all swooped up on top like that. Bet Bane will fall all over himself when he sees you."

"Oh, Nel. Stop that."

"Well, he will. I've seen the way he looks at you, Rose. I think he's taken a shine to you."

The young woman took a final check in the mirror before grabbing her purse from the table. "Well, he's not any more interested in me than I am in him."

"Oh?" Nel shot back with a wink as Rose made her way past the woman.

"And how much might that be?"

"Nel!"

Bane was standing by the porch waiting for her when she pulled into the drive. His smile washed away any feelings of fear she might have had over the snake incident. She had looked forward to this picnic and she was going to enjoy herself.

He opened her door and extended his hand. "You look beautiful." His dark eyes scanned her from head to toe. "I've never seen you like this. You're so—so—feminine. What happened to that ranch hand I've been working with every day?"

She gave him a smile and accepted his hand. "Which do you prefer, sir?"

He pulled her to him and gave her a quick hug as he whispered in her ear, "Both."

She watched as Bane disappeared into his little greenhouse. He returned a minute later, carrying a gigantic pink rose in his hand, which he tucked into her hair. The sweet fragrance of the perfect flower excelled any perfume. He kissed her gently on each cheek. "There, Rose Bud. My prize rose for my prize ranch hand."

She laughed, her gaze soft and dreamy as they stood only inches apart. He could be so sweet, so gentle. Her hand sought his and their fingers entwined.

The church members began to arrive, laden with platters of fried chicken, ham, barbecued beef and other meats, big bowls of potato salad, slaw, baked beans, and all kinds of casseroles, pies, cakes, and cookies. Rose stood at Bane's side, greeting each person who came to the picnic. She blushed when RuAnn arrived and whispered in her ear as she entered the backyard, "You two make a great-looking couple. Has Bane found that perfect woman?"

Bane leaned down toward her with an accusing smile. "What did RuAnn say?"

She was sure he'd heard her friend's comment, but she answered anyway, "She said, 'What a great day for a picnic,' didn't you hear her?"

He slid his long arm about her waist with a mischievous wink and lifted a skeptical brow. "Sure she did. And I'm Elvis Presley."

Rose looked around at the smiling faces and could feel the love flowing through the sincere, gracious people of Mill Creek Community Church. She could understand her father's love for these people. No doubt they had filled the void she'd left in his life.

Bane filled his plate to overflowing and had to stuff his silverware and celery sticks into his shirt pocket. Rose laughed and nudged him as he lingered at each bowl and platter, trying to decide which one to take and where to put it.

"Ready for dessert, Delphinium?" He took her arm and pushed through the people milling toward the cakes, pies, and cookies.

"Surely, you're kidding. You have room for dessert? After two platefuls of food?" She pulled away but was glad when he wouldn't release his grip on her arm.

He selected two pieces of pie, napkins, and two plastic forks, and dropped down on one of the quilts spread on the ground, then motioned for her to join him. "I love this old quilt." He stroked it while she seated herself beside him and began to nibble on the delicious-looking pie. "Maudie made it when her kids were little. See all the triangles? Can you imagine cutting all of those?"

Rose was surprised by his appreciation for the old quilt. Most men would have called it a blanket and not even noticed the wonderful patches that made up the starlike pattern.

"I've tried to buy it from her," he continued as he forked another bite, "but she won't sell it to me. Calls it her Triangle Charm quilt. So for now, all I can do is sit on it once a year."

When the last crumb of pie was consumed, Bane joined in a volleyball game. He racked up a big score for his team before being run off by the opposing team.

Rose sat on a bale of hay and watched as he chased a ten-year-old boy around the yard and put a chunk of ice down the boy's neck, while the little girls squealed with delight. He tossed a toddler into the air as the child wiggled and giggled.

"What that man needs is a wife and family." RuAnn straddled her short legs over the bale of hay and plunked down beside her friend. "He's a natural with kids, isn't he? Or hadn't you noticed?"

Rose gave her old chum a frown as Bane joined them.

"Can I get you ladies something to drink? Or more pie?" He put his hands on his narrow hips and waited.

"How about a nice available bachelor?"

Rose flinched at RuAnn's suggestion.

"Coming right up," Bane responded with a twinkle in his eye as he moved away from the bale and disappeared into the crowd.

"RuAnn. How could you?" Rose covered a giggle with one hand and slapped RuAnn's arm playfully with the other. "What are you going to do if he brings you one?"

The young veterinarian pursed her mouth as if in deep thought. "Marry him. What else?"

Bane's familiar voice spoke up from behind them. "Ladies, meet Thorne Horner, Ben's nephew. He hired on at the Wild Rose two months ago and he's looking for a wife."

Chapter 7

RuAnn got to her feet and extended her hand. "Hi ya, Thorne. Nice to meet you." She slipped her hand into the bend of the handsome young man's elbow and led him off toward the dessert table. As they went, the last thing Rose heard her say was, "Now tell me about this wife you're looking for."

Bane dropped onto the bale beside her and they had a good laugh. "I'm sorry, Bane. I never thought she'd ask you to find her a husband. I apologize for my friend."

He grinned. "*Your* friend? I thought she was mine."

The picnic ended all too soon and people gathered chairs and dishes and kids and headed for home. Bane walked Rose to her car and kissed her on the forehead as he thanked her for being his cohost. She felt a sudden wave of longing flow through her, and she wished he'd take her into his arms and kiss her lips.

But he didn't.

Bane moved through the house, locking doors and turning out lights. It had been a good day; he loved sharing his home with friends. As he climbed the stairs, he thought of RuAnn and Thorne, and he grinned. It hadn't taken them long to get together. Then his thoughts turned to Rose and the rose he'd put into her hair. *I should have kissed her. I'll bet her lips would have been as soft and silky as that rose's petals. Yep, that's exactly what I should have done. Grabbed her and kiss her. She couldn't have done any more than slap my face, and it would have been worth it.*

Rose was up early the next morning, early enough to attend Sunday school. "But what class will I be in?" she asked Nel as she sipped orange juice and nibbled on a blueberry muffin.

"The pastor's." Nel wiped the countertop and hung the dish towel on its rack. "He teaches the singles group. Got quite a few people in it, as I recall. It'll give you a chance to get better acquainted with people your own age."

Rose tried to appear disinterested as she asked casually, "Is Bane in the singles class?"

"Mercy, no!" Nel pulled the plate from under the younger woman's muffin and shoved it into the dishwasher before spinning the dial. "He teaches the high-school class, started five or six months after he came to Rock City, I think. I hear it's the biggest class in the church. The kids love him."

Rose glanced at the clock on the kitchen wall and decided there was plenty of time for a few more questions before they had to leave for church. "Nel, what do you know about Bane? I mean, has he ever married? Does he have a girlfriend?"

Nel laughed and patted Rose's hand. "Honey, none of us knows much about Bane. He showed up one day as the new owner of the Lazy Z Ranch, worked his tail off gettin' it on its feet, built that new house, barns, and outbuildings, bought several other adjoining ranches, and put down roots in the community. Past that, we're all in the dark. He avoids talkin' about his past and we all respect his privacy." She pinched Rose on the arm and pointed to the clock. "I'd suggest you do the same thing. Leave them sleeping dogs lie, as Bitty says."

Bane smiled at her as the choir marched in and seated themselves in the choir loft. This morning she sat in the second row with new friends she'd met in class. It was nearly impossible to keep her eyes off Bane as he sat facing her. When their eyes met, they'd both smile awkwardly and turn away, embarrassed they'd been caught looking at each other. She tried to bring her errant thoughts into focus, but Bane kept creeping into her mind. The picnic had made her see him in a whole new way.

She phoned RuAnn later that afternoon. "Oh, Rose, I think I'm in love," RuAnn told her. "Thorne is all I've ever wanted in a man—and to think he's been right under my nose these past few months."

Rose stiffened. "You're serious? You just met the guy yesterday. Love-at-first-sight only happens in movies."

RuAnn's voice bubbled with joy. "Yes, I'm serious. Thorne and I talked till four this morning. We've been together all day. He's here with me right now."

Rose shuddered. "Can he hear what you're saying?"

"Sure can. Can't you, honey?"

Rose could hear him answer *yes* in the background. "This is bizarre, RuAnn. No one falls in love in twenty-four hours."

"Oh, yes they do. We did. Me and Thorne. We're even talking marriage."

"RuAnn. You can't be, you barely know each other. Slow down. Take your time. What's your hurry?" She couldn't believe what she was hearing from her old friend.

"We both want kids before we're too old to enjoy them. Aren't you happy for us, Rose?"

Rose gave a deep sigh and twisted the phone cord around her finger. "Of course, I'm happy, I just don't want to see you get hurt."

"Then give us your blessing."

"You got it," she agreed reluctantly. "You know that."

A little after six she saddled Ebony, slipped a paperback romance in the saddlebag, and rode out to the creek at the far end of the ranch. The late afternoon sun was hot, but it was cool under the shade of the trees along the creek. She tied Ebony to a big hackberry, found herself a huge clump of green grass, and spread out on her saddle blanket to read.

The warmth of the sun filtering through the trees made her drowsy, and soon the book dropped from her hands and she was fast asleep. When she awoke, the sun was beginning to slip below the horizon. She stood up and stretched, then she realized Ebony was gone.

But how could he be? I tied him to the tree with the knot Bane showed me. There's no way Ebony could get loose. She tried to get her bearings as she slipped her boots onto her feet and folded the blanket. *Let's see, if I head the opposite way the sun is setting, I'll be heading toward the house.*

Rather than take the trail, she decided to take the shortest way, diagonally across the fields. It was a long, uneven walk, but she was a big girl, and she could make it. She stumbled several times on the plowed ground, nearly falling in the freshly turned soil. Ebony was nowhere in sight.

The sun sank rapidly once it hit the treetops, and she guessed it to be at least 8 or 8:30. *Why didn't I bring my watch?*

With the sun dropping, the hot air cooled quickly. Her boots sank into the soft ground with each step, and trudging across the field took more energy than she had expected. *If Ebony goes back to the barn with his saddle on, someone will realize I've been riding and come and find me.*

But she hadn't told anyone where she was going. How would they know where to look? The sky was getting dark fast, and she wasn't totally sure she was going in the right direction. The creek wound back and forth across the pastures and she could no longer use the sun to get her bearings.

She had to face reality. She was lost.

The blanket was cumbersome to carry, but Rose held onto it anyway; she didn't want to admit she might be spending the night in the field, but she kept the blanket just in case.

She seemed to have walked for hours, and she wondered if she had been going in circles. The moon made an occasional peek from behind the gathering clouds, and the air grew cooler by the minute as clouds rapidly filled the sky. She worked her way closer to the creek and trees, in case she needed shelter from a thunderstorm. At last, she found a heavily leafed tree and curled up on a spreading clump of grass with the little blanket covering her. The night went dark and she could see lightning streaks off in the distance and hear the faint sounds of thunder. Her mind went back to nights in her childhood when she'd been alone in her bedroom, her head under the covers, scared half out of her wits for no reason at all. Now here she was, with the darkness swarming around her, more alone than she'd ever been in her life, and no one, not even her father, to care.

With each dash of lightning, she tried to make out the dark shadows around her. *What am I doing out here? Anyone with half a brain would have made sure that knot was more secure. But no. Little Miss Know-it-all took out on her own without telling anyone, and look where her stupidity got her. It'd serve me right if Bane did get the ranch. What do I know about ranching? I can't even find my way home!*

After what seemed like hours, Rose settled down and decided all she could do was wait till morning. No one was coming to find her. She was at the mercy of whatever might be around her. If a coyote or a snake or some other animal wanted her, it would have to come and get her. She was not moving until daylight. *God, if I ever needed your protection, it's now!*

The approaching storm veered in the other direction and passed on by with only a few sprinkles to indicate its presence. Many hours later, Rose fell asleep.

The morning dawned with a pinkish glow that crept across the cloudless sky. Birds flitted from tree to tree in search of breakfast. Wild rabbits hopped from clump to clump, while squirrels busily chattered as they ran up tree trunks and leapt from limb to limb. Rose stirred beneath the saddle blanket, then sat up, stretched, and drank in the cool, clear morning. She was thirsty and hungry, but those wants paled as she realized she'd made it through the night without mishap. *Thank You, Lord.*

She scanned the horizon, hoping somehow, somewhere, to see Ebony, but he wasn't there. Her mouth was dry and had a horrible taste. Food she could get by without, but oh, how she longed for a cool drink of water and a toothbrush. The sun was rising quickly as she made her way across the furrows in the freshly plowed field. At last, the outbuildings of the ranch came into view, and Rose felt like shouting hooray. Ten minutes later, she walked into the far end of the horse barn and went directly to Ebony's stall. There he was, nonchalantly munching away on his breakfast. And there was her saddle, hanging right where she normally kept it.

"Morning, Miss Rose." Calvin was the first of the group of hands who spotted her.

"Who put Ebony in his stall?"

Bobby spoke up timidly. "You did, didn't you?"

"If I'd put him away, would I be asking you who did it?" Her patience was wearing thin rapidly. The miserable night had stretched it to the breaking point. "Who took his saddle off?"

The men shook their heads with confused looks as Calvin stepped forward.

"Sorry, me and the men don't know what you're talkin' 'bout. He was in the barn when I came in this mornin' 'bout five. I saw him myself, and he weren't wearin' no saddle."

Obviously she wasn't getting anywhere with these men so she spun around on her heels and headed for the house. Nel stood at the table, rolling out pie dough. "Hi, hon. Where ya been? You look—awful."

Rose pulled the pitcher of orange juice from the big refrigerator and drank a tall glass before answering. "You'd look awful, too, if you spent the night where I did."

Nel stopped rolling and stared at her. "Ya mean ya didn't sleep here? Then where was you? I thought you'd gone to bed early."

"I wish!" Rose pulled her boots from her tired feet and dropped them onto the tile floor with a *kerplunk*, leaving a dusty residue. She explained about riding Ebony to the creek, about falling asleep while she was reading, about Ebony disappearing, her night on the ground, and finding the big horse in his stall.

Nel listened with widened eyes. "Oh, Rose, your door was closed when I locked the house up for the night. I thought ya was to bed. Then this mornin', when Bane came for you at 5:30, your door was still shut and I figured ya'd overslept. I knew ya had to be tired, with working long hours on the ranch and the picnic and all. He said he had things to do and would come back later. I shoulda knowed somethin' was wrong. You never oversleep."

Rose squared her jaw and narrowed her eyes. "Nel, someone took that saddle off Ebony and put him in his stall. And I know I tied that knot good and tight. Someone had to have untied it while I was asleep."

She picked up her boots and headed for her room. "I'm going to take a quick shower and then I'm going to get to the bottom of this. Too many things have been happening to me lately, things that can't be a coincidence. If Bane comes back, tell him to wait. Maybe he can help me find some answers."

❧

He stood as she entered the kitchen. "Nel told me about your night in the field. I'm sorry, Rose. I can imagine how frightened you must have been." He pulled her to him and held her in his arms, much like he would a frightened child. "I wish I'd known. I'd have come looking for you when I came by yesterday."

She lifted her head. "You came by? When?"

"Not sure exactly. Nel and Bitty were just getting into their pickup and told me they'd seen you heading up the trail on Ebony. So I went on without you." He rested his chin gently on her head and held her tight. The scent of his aftershave was pleasant and she enjoyed feeling the security of his arms. "None of the hands confessed to putting Ebony in his stall?"

She leaned into his chest with a deep sigh. "Bane, why would anyone do that to me?"

He cupped her chin in his hand and lifted it to his face. "Do what?"

She gave him a puzzled look. "Untie Ebony!"

"You think someone untied Ebony? Come on, Rose, you probably didn't tie the knot as well as you thought you did. I'll bet it worked loose and he wandered off."

She pressed her hands against his chest and shoved away from him with fire in her eyes. "I tied that knot just like you showed me. You said if a horse pulled on the reins, it made the knot tighter." She stomped her foot for emphasis. "Someone untied Ebony—on purpose."

A mocking smile flickered beneath his black mustache. Anyone could tell he didn't believe her, as he said, "Like they put a snake in your car?"

Her hands flew to her hips. "Yes. Exactly like that." She returned his amused grin with a fierce glare, yanked her hat from the hook, and stormed out the kitchen door, calling behind her as she went, "Forget it, cowboy. I'll find the answers without your help."

The two went on with the morning's chores, speaking only when necessary. When Bane would catch Rose's eye, she'd turn away haughtily. She had been upset with him before, but this time she was furious.

His comments about her overnight incident created a wall between the two of them. Not only had his words hurt, he hadn't believed her. She had expected sympathy and concern, and all she'd gotten was criticism. Undeserved criticism. For the next few weeks, they worked in a very businesslike manner, speaking little.

When an envelope arrived in the morning mail bearing RuAnn's return address, Rose opened it eagerly. It was an ivory lace-trimmed card, an invitation to her and Thorne's wedding at the Wild Rose Ranch, the first day of September.

RuAnn and Thorne were getting married? Rose couldn't believe it. They had known each other only a few weeks. A feeling of envy surged through her. She and RuAnn were part of the few remaining singles from their high school class, and now RuAnn was getting married. Although she thought they were rushing things, she was happy for them.

When she phoned to congratulate her friend, she found one ecstatic veterinarian on the other end of the line. "The wedding is going to be at Bane's, and you must be my maid of honor. Oh, Rose, I'm so happy. I love him so much, and to think that Bane brought us together."

Rose had mixed emotions when she finally hung up the phone. RuAnn's happiness was contagious, yet she felt sad, like life was passing her by. At this point in her own life, she had no idea what she wanted. Except to find out who released Ebony.

❧

Rose stood in front of the hay barns, now loaded with the season's freshly baled hay, with a look of pride. She'd worked hard right along with the men to fill those barns, and now they were full and overflowing. Rows and rows of big round bales stood side-by-side like Twinkies in a box around the perimeter of the pastures. Hundreds of them, plenty to take them through the hardest winter Kansas could offer.

She mounted Ebony and sat erect in the saddle, gazing at the beauty of the land. She had worked hard to learn the ranching business, and although she had much to learn yet, no one could say she wasn't giving it her best. If she could just maintain her present momentum and make it through the winter to early spring, she would have fulfilled her father's stipulations. Sweet Water would be hers.

She smiled as she thought about her father's requirement about attending church. Funny, since forcing herself to go that first Sunday, she had wanted to go. In fact, now she looked forward to attending each Sunday; it was one of the highlights of her week. She'd gotten acquainted with the singles in the church, and she'd learned to love the older ladies as well. They were so open, so honest, so willing to share of themselves and their time. And, she loved the pastor and his wife. She'd even considered singing in the choir—if it weren't for Bane. She didn't want him thinking she'd joined because of him. No, she'd watch from the second pew and sing along in her heart.

Now she had become a part of the church, she could understand her father's love for it and its people. She grinned and shook her head. If anyone had told her six months ago she'd be attending church regularly, nursing blisters, and admiring bales of hay, she'd have laughed in his face.

She brought Ebony alongside the fence rail surrounding the mares and their foals and watched Jet. He was looking more like Ebony every day. The colt had gotten used to the attention she lavished upon him and would nuzzle her pockets, seeking the treats she often brought with her.

Her thoughts turned back to Bane, and she frowned. She'd wanted to ask him to help her find the password to her father's file, but now with his pigheaded attitude toward her accidents, she wouldn't give him the satisfaction of saying she needed him. She wished she was computer savvy enough to break the code herself.

A few days later, after supper one evening, she excused herself and headed for her father's bedroom. By now, she was quite comfortable working with her father's computer, and she had been keeping a daily journal of the ranch's activities and what she'd learned about its operation.

She retrieved the file marked *C.M. Personal* and tried to open it with her father's birth date, then hers, then her name, Sweet Water, names of his horses, pets. Nothing worked. In frustration, she shoved the keyboard away, and it banged against the coprocessor case. She heard something fall, but nothing looked out of place on the big desk. Impatiently, she shut down the computer, grabbed the pad she'd scribbled potential passwords on, and jammed it into the top drawer. The drawer wouldn't close. She shoved it several times, but whatever was blocking it wouldn't give way. That must have been what she heard fall. Something behind the drawer. *Oh, no. Surely this old desk drawer didn't break. I don't have time for this right now.*

She tugged the heavy drawer to the end of its long metal slides, carefully lifted it out of the grooves that held it in place, and then reached into the opening, expecting to find one of the metal drawer guides broken and blocking the drawer. But it wasn't a broken slide. There, wedged against the back, was a small black book, and it looked like someone's journal. The name inscribed across the front was *Charlie Kinsey.*

A few minutes later, her heart pounding, Rose flipped the switch of the lamp on her nightstand and crawled onto the bed, the little book in her hand. She was sure the journal held the answers she had sought since childhood. With trembling hands, she opened it, prepared to read wonderfully detailed daily entries. But what she found instead were pages and pages of figures and notes. Until she reached page 42. There, in her father's handwriting, was her mother's name, Abigale Newly Kinsey, and her birth date.

Rose rubbed her fingers over the page's smooth surface. This was the first time she'd ever known her mother's maiden name. Newly. What an unusual name. She couldn't remember ever hearing of anyone around Rock City having that name, yet her father had lived here all his life. He'd been born right here on Sweet Water Ranch. *So where did he meet my mother?*

Abigale Newly Kinsey. What a lovely old-fashioned name. How Rose wished she could have known her mother. *Was she tall like me? Was she blond? Did she wear her hair long?* Somehow, the name conjured up images of a woman with her hair coiled in thick braids on top of her head. How she wished her father had kept a picture of her mother.

She sat up straight as an idea hit her. *Maybe he did. The attic is full of old things. Beds, chests, picture frames, old tricycles, and dozens of sealed-up boxes. Maybe they contain pictures.* When she and RuAnn used to play dress-up ladies in the attic, she would ask her father what was in those boxes, and he'd always answer the same way, "Snakes and hoot owls." She'd giggle, and he'd pick her up and whirl her in the air, making sounds like a hoot owl. She'd never touched those boxes.

Armed with this newfound information, she promised herself, *Tomorrow night, after Nel and Bitty leave for the church senior social, I'm going to search the attic.*

Early the next morning, Rose made a hurried trip to town, to the hardware store to purchase several flashlights and packages of batteries for her exploring mission. The attic had several uncovered lightbulbs hanging from the ceiling, but she'd decided it might be difficult to search boxes if she had to drag each one of them under a light. *And I'll have to watch out for snakes and hoot owls.*

"Some of us guys heard about that little snake of yours. Bane said you was mighty scared of that little wiggler," Harold, the hardware store's owner, said when she entered.

"Maybe you're here to buy some dependable rope to tie up your horsy," another man standing by the counter added with a smirk.

"Sounds like someone with a big mouth has exaggerated a minor incident to amuse some of his more gullible friends," she responded flippantly, although inwardly she felt like a fool. She could feel the eyes of several other shoppers as she passed them in search of the flashlights and batteries for her evening's quest.

"What you going to do with these flashlights, go frog-gigging?" Harold's gold front teeth glistened as he rang up her purchases on the old, ornate cash register. Several other men milling around the store paused long enough to laugh at Harold's joke.

"Not tonight. I'm getting ready for next week," Rose quipped with a smile. "I hear it's the best week in the year for frog-gigging." She winked and pushed through the door, its bell clanging.

She was glad Harold had put her purchases in a brown paper bag, for on the fender of the little red convertible sat Bane Jacob.

"Checking on me?" She folded over the top of the sack to conceal its contents.

He gave her a broad grin. "Nope, came into town for some kerosene. Why? Doing something you don't want me to know about?"

This was not the time to banter with Bane, no matter how much he irritated her. She had things to do. "I came into town to get some snake repellent and see if Harold could teach me how to tie a decent knot, one that wouldn't come magically undone and let my horse get away next time I decide to take a nap along the creek."

She left him sitting on the fender and crossed the street into Betty's Beauty and Barber Shop. She hoped Betty took drop-ins; she hadn't thought to call for an appointment.

Betty herself greeted her as she chomped on a wad of chewing gum. "Hi, honey. What can I do for ya? Want me to cut that pretty hair?"

Rose smiled pleasantly. "I'd just like a shampoo—is that possible? I don't have an appointment."

"You're in luck, sweetie pie. My next appointment cancelled. I'm free as a tick on a dog's back. Have a seat there at my shampoo bowl."

Rose sat motionless as Betty wrapped the purple plastic cover around her shoulders. "You're Charlie's girl, ain't ya? I used to cut Charlie's hair once a month. Nice man, your pa. Known him a long time. I miss him."

This was the reason she'd come to Betty's; she had hoped the beauty shop would be the gossip center of Rock City, like the one in the *Steel Magnolias* movie. "How long did you know him?"

Betty deftly ran the spray across Rose's forehead. "Honey, we went to school together. Of course, he was a few years older'n me. Guess I knew your pa all my life, had a crush on him when we was in high school. If that man'd proposed to me, I'd 'a' knocked people down draggin' him to the altar. He was quite a catch." Betty applied the shampoo and began vigorously scrubbing Rose's scalp while she chomped her gum in rhythm.

"Did you know Abigale, too?"

Betty stopped chomping and scrubbing. "Abigale? Now, why'd you ask that? Of course, I knew her."

Rose took a deep breath. She mustn't appear too interested or maybe Betty would stop talking. "Just wondered. My hair certainly isn't like my dad's. I thought maybe I looked like her."

"Yeah, you sure do. She was a pretty thing when they got married. Cryin' shame she changed like that." Betty pulled the hose from the sink and began rinsing Rose's long blond hair. "I told her she'd look like a hussy with it dyed black like that, but do ya think she'd listen to me? Not on your life. Said she was ready for a radical change and wanted it as black as night. Charlie hated it. He hollered at me fer doin' it, but like I told him, if I wouldn't a done it she'd gone somewhere else. I figured I'd do it and help Rock City's economy."

"Was that before or after I was born?" Rose shielded her eyes from the errant spray.

Betty squinted her heavily made-up eyes and looked thoughtful. "Honey, that was after. Your mama was a different woman after you was born. Restless-like. Nothin' around here seemed to suit her. Oh, Charlie tried. That man would've done anything for that woman. Given her anything she asked for, but it wasn't enough. She wanted the bright lights and the city, and Charlie couldn't give her that in Rock City and he couldn't leave Sweet Water, so they just muddled along until you was about two." Betty took a towel and began to rub Rose's hair.

"What happened when I was two?" Rose pushed the towel off her face.

Betty stopped drying and stared at her. "Honey, don't ya know? She up and left overnight, without any warning. I thought Charlie'd told you. He didn't?"

Rose blinked. "No, he never told me. He wouldn't allow anyone on Sweet Water to even mention her name. I didn't even know her maiden name."

"Newly. Abigale Newly." The voice came from behind the manicure table. "I knew her, too."

Rose turned in the direction of the voice to find a woman, probably in her late sixties, watching her. "You knew my mother?"

"Sure did. She worked down in Dodge City as a sales clerk at K-Mart for a couple of months before she and Bill Babcock took off for Colorado. I had a little cafe in Dodge and she used to come in there several times a week."

Rose's heart skipped a beat. This was the information she was after. "What was she like? I mean, did she seem happy? Sad? Did she mention me? Or my father?"

A frown crossed the woman's face. "Hate to tell you this, but your mother never mentioned the fact that she had a child. And she went by the name Newly, not Kinsey. I thought maybe she and that Babcock guy were married when she first started coming in, but she was always hanging on him. Most married folks I know don't behave that way."

Rose's heart sank. Had her mother left her father for another man? Bill Babcock?

The frown deepened. "He didn't treat her very good. Always putting her down. She paid for their meals most of the time. He'd eat and then just walk out, leaving her with the bill. I don't know why she stayed with the guy."

Betty switched on the blow-dryer and by the time she'd finished, the woman was paying her bill at the reception desk. "Sorry, honey. I wish I could have told you more pleasant things about your mom, but that's what I saw. I hope Bill Babcock treated her better after they got to Colorado. I hope she didn't lose that baby."

Baby? Her mother had been pregnant when she was in Dodge City? Had her father known? Was that why her mother left? Was it Bill Babcock's baby? Is that why her father never allowed anyone to speak about her mother?

She rushed out the door of the beauty shop, following the woman, the purple plastic still tied about her neck. "Wait, please!"

The woman leaned out her car window. "Sorry, that's all I know."

"But the baby? Do you know. . . ?"

"Whose it was? No, your mama never said, and neither did Bill. But if I had to guess, I'd say it was his." She turned the key in the ignition and drove off, leaving Rose alone in the street.

Betty was waiting in the doorway. "Sorry, honey. I assumed Charlie had told you all of this." She motioned Rose back to her chair and waited until she lowered herself into it before combing through the long, silken locks. "Honey, whatever happened between your mama and daddy, you can be sure of one thing. Your papa loved your mama like no man ever loved a woman. I know he would have forgiven most anything she'd ever done—except carryin' another man's baby."

Rose shuddered.

"Your papa was a proud man. His handshake was as good as a signed contract. Never took advantage of no one or shorted on any deal he ever made. He always went the second mile. If anyone was hungry, your dad fed 'em. I've seen him take in perfect strangers and give 'em a job, just so's they'd have a place to stay and food to eat."

Betty placed the comb on the counter and handed Rose a mirror. "Any child of Charlie Kinsey's can hold her head up high, knowin' she comes from good stock. Don't let anyone tell you any different."

Rose thanked the hairdresser and left a generous tip. She'd gotten more than she'd bargained for at Betty's Beauty and Barber Shop. As she climbed behind the convertible's steering wheel, she was eager to get home and into the attic. But when she turned the key in the ignition, nothing happened.

She tried it again.

Nothing.

At least she wasn't out on a deserted road this time. She crossed the street and walked down the block to Jim's Auto Repair Shop; Jim himself offered to check out the problem for her.

"Mighty lucky for you it happened here in town. It's probably just your battery. I'll give you a jump start and you'll be out of here in no time." He grabbed the jumper cables and the battery cart, and the two walked down the street, pulling the little cart behind them.

Jim lifted the hood and exclaimed loudly. "It's your battery all right. Someone has yanked the connectors off."

Rose peered over the man's shoulder. All the connections had been pulled from the car's nearly new battery. "Someone had to do this, didn't he? They couldn't have come loose by themselves? Right?"

Jim shook his head. "I'd say someone is pulling a mean trick on you. I'll have these put back in a jiffy."

By the time Jim dropped the hood back in place, Rose was fighting mad. Enough was enough! *Bane Jacob, did you do this to me?*

❦

Rose had already eaten her lunch by the time Bane arrived the next day. "You don't have to come every day, Mr. Jacob," she told him coolly as they drove down the lane. "I'm sure my father would allow you a day off now and then. Or are you afraid I might do something wrong if you don't keep an eye on me?" she asked with a defiant tilt of her chin.

He flashed her a wide smile. "Oh, so now I'm Mr. Jacob? You aren't carrying a grudge, are you? Just because of a few innocent comments I made?"

She twisted sideways in the seat and leaned toward him with a somber expression. "Innocent comments? I'd say any man who runs around town telling tales like you do is far from innocent."

He jammed his foot on the brakes, nearly throwing her into the dash till the seat belt grabbed hold. "What are you talking about?"

She glared at him. "Some guy at the hardware store said you told him all about how I didn't do a good job tying Ebony to the tree, and another guy repeated your cute little comment about the snake wanting to ride in a convertible. Are you saying those men were lying when they said they heard those things from you?" She crossed her arms and waited for his answer.

He reached over and rested his big, warm palm on her shoulder. "Aw, come on, Rose. Forgive me, okay? I really am sorry. I've been treating you like a helpless female, and you've proven you're much more than that." His arm drifted across her shoulders as he spoke. "Can we kiss and make up?"

She was all set to slap him for the childish kiss-and-make-up line, but before she could respond, he scooted across the seat and planted a quick kiss on her lips. Her body stiffened at his touch. Suddenly, she couldn't think of a thing to say. The desire to slap him disappeared.

Bane took her hand in his and kissed her fingertips, one by one. "We have too much to lose to fight like this."

She tried to say something—anything. She felt foolish just sitting there, the words stuck in her throat.

"I don't want any hard feelings between us, Rosie. I'm very proud of the job you're doing on the ranch. Charlie would have been proud, too. You're nearly halfway through your year, and I know you'll make it." He gathered her in his arms and traced her brows with his finger. "I promise I'll try to be more understanding. Just be patient with me. Okay?"

Her breathing came a little easier, and she relaxed a bit. He was so close she could feel each warm breath on her eyelids. She found herself wanting to give him the benefit of the doubt. "Bane, you've got to believe me. I tied that knot just like you taught me. It would never have come undone. I've had four incidents—"

He stiffened. "Four?"

She let out a deep sigh. "Yes, four. Yesterday, when I came out of the beauty shop and tried to start your car, it was dead. Zilch. So I walked down to the repair shop and got Jim. He discovered someone had yanked the battery connections loose."

"Maybe it wasn't fastened properly and worked loose."

She jerked her hand away. "Man, don't you listen? Or do you only hear what you want to hear? I said *all* of the connections were off! Not just one that might have worked loose. Ask Jim, if you don't believe me." She crossed her arms and stared straight ahead as she considered leaping from the truck and hiking back to the main house.

"So, what are you saying? You think someone is deliberately doing these things to you?"

"That's exactly what I'm saying. What other explanation could there be?" Now she was shouting.

He put his hand on her arm, but she pushed it off and moved closer to the door. "Rose, you're in Rock City territory now. Things like that don't happen around here. This is a pretty peaceful community. Who would want to harm you? You haven't had time to make enemies."

She hated to admit it, but everything he was saying was true. Who could possibly want to hurt her? Maybe it was coincidence. Most of the things could easily be explained away, except the cut stirrup strap, and it was impossible that could have happened in some freaky way. Perhaps whoever had messed with the battery thought he was playing a trick on Bane and didn't realize she was the one driving his car.

She forced a smile. She had to work with this man every day, and after all, everyone she talked to thought he was a prince. "Okay—you may be right. I'll accept the fact that all this stuff may not have been intentionally done to me, but you've got to promise you won't run around town making jokes at my expense. I mean that, Bane. No more tale-telling."

"I promise I'll try, but old habits are hard to break. I guess I tend to see the positive side of most everything that happens—it keeps life in a better perspective." He unfastened his seat belt and moved toward her. "Forgive me?" His arms wrapped around her and drew her close.

Again, she pushed away. "What do you think you're doing?"

"Making up." His arms tightened as she struggled to free herself, but he was too strong for her and his lips soon pressed against hers.

A tingle of excitement ran through her veins, and she melted into his arms. The woodsy smell of his aftershave made all her reasoning wilt, and she found herself yielding to his touch as her arms wrapped around his neck and her fingers twisted through black ringlets.

As they pulled slightly apart, his lips whispered against hers, "Truce?"

She pressed her lips against his, eager for another kiss. "Truce."

He held her there, nestled against him, his chin in her hair. "Rosebud, you're some woman."

At the sound of an approaching vehicle they separated quickly. Bitty's truck roared up beside them. "Truck trouble?" the little man asked as he leaned out the window.

Bane winked at Rose before answering. "Nope. No trouble at all. Everything's fine—now."

She wanted to wring Bitty's neck for interrupting. She loved being in Bane's arms, sharing his kisses, and Bitty's appearance had caused an all-too-sudden stop.

As Bane started the truck and it moved on down the lane, he and Rose grinned at each other, like two teenagers caught making out. He reached a hand toward her and she took it in hers. For once, they were on the same wavelength.

They spent the next day with Bitty at the cattle sale. Rose took notes as Bane explained which lots of cattle would be the best ones to purchase for Sweet Water, which would be the best for the Wild Rose, and why. He did the bidding on the first few lots, then encouraged her to do her own bidding. Her hand wavered nervously when she made her first bid, as she considered the ramifications of her actions. Thousands of dollars were at stake, but with his guidance, she soon found herself feeling confident in her own abilities.

Everyone in the county seemed to know and like Bane. She was pleased when he introduced her as the new owner and operator of Sweet Water Ranch. He'd say, "This is Rose Kinsey. She's running Sweet Water Ranch just like old Charlie did." To Rose, that was quite a compliment; her father had a good reputation as a rancher. Then Bane would put his arm around her shoulder and smile as proudly as a sixteen-year-old with his first car.

Bane dropped her off at Sweet Water a little after 3:00. She spent the rest of the afternoon checking the cattle she'd bought, making sure they had made the ride to the ranch okay; then she played with Jet and stroked his smooth, silky coat before she headed for her bath. Nel had supper ready right on time, pork chops and dressing, Rose's favorites.

Bitty chattered all through dinner, giving Nel a step-by-step description of the cattle sale. "You should have seen Rose, Nel," he said with a slap of his rough hand on his knee, "she done that biddin' like she'd been doin' it all her life. Bought some good stuff, too. Played it real cool, just like her papa used to do."

"Couldn't have done it without Bane," Rose confessed as she spooned out the last bit of tasty sage dressing from the big bowl.

"Sure you could, hon," Nel said. "He just helped ya, that's all. Ya gotta remember he's had lots of experience." She turned to her husband. "Remember,

Bitty? You said the first time Charlie took Bane to the cattle auction, he was a basket case. Charlie had to do all the biddin' for him."

"What? Did you say Dad taught Bane how to bid on the cattle?" Rose nearly dropped her fork as she looked from Bitty to Nel. "Didn't he already know about ranching when he came here, what, five years ago? I thought he'd always been a rancher."

"Nope." Bitty stabbed another pork chop and dropped it onto his plate. "Charlie taught him everything he knows."

"But he has the largest spread around here. How did he manage to do all that in five short years? That's quite an accomplishment and quite an investment. Where did he get all the money? That kind of spending would take a real bundle."

The older couple looked at each other, then at Rose. "No one knows, Rose," Nel said. "He came in, bought the Lazy Z, spent a few months building the house, barns, and other buildings, then came to your dad and asked him for help so he could build his herd. By the end of his first year in Rock City, he'd bought up enough ranches to become the largest landowner in this part of the state."

"In one year?" Rose shook her head. "And he had to ask my father how to buy cows?"

Nel stood to her feet and began clearing the table. "That's about it. Maybe he told your dad how he did it, but he sure never told nobody else."

"Do you know anything about where he came from? His family? What he did before he came here?"

Bitty and Nel shook their heads, and Rose knew she'd learned as much as she was going to from the pair.

Nel checked the clock and turned to Bitty. "Give me fifteen minutes to clean up here and I'll be ready to go."

Rose thumbed idly through a magazine as she waited for the couple to leave. Finally, their pickup pulled out of the circle drive and headed down the lane. Armed with her flashlights, she headed for the attic.

Chapter 8

After much searching, Rose zeroed in on a box marked *C.M. Personal*, the same name as the computer file. Her hands trembled and her palms were sweaty as she lifted the lid, confident the box could provide her with the answers she so desperately sought. The box was filled with pictures. Pictures of her and her father and a beautiful young woman with long, straight, blond hair and a willowy figure much like Rose's. *My mother. It has to be my mother!*

With tears flowing, she closed the lid and shoved the heavy box across the attic floor to the head of the stairs, then slid it down the steps to the landing and tugged it down the hall to her bedroom. Her heart raced with wild anticipation as she closed her bedroom door and locked it behind her.

Once the pictures were spread out on the floor, she began to sort them. The ones that contained anything that looked remotely like they might be of her family, she placed on her bed, lingering over the ones showing the young, blond woman. *This is like looking into a mirror.*

She was so like the image of the woman smiling back. Had she reminded her father of her mother each time he'd looked at her? *If only Father had told me.*

In the bottom half of the box, she found several large, framed photos of the same woman, and on the back of one of them was written in a beautiful, feminine hand: *To Charlie, with all my love for a lifetime*. It was signed, *Abigale*.

Rose wept openly. At last she had visible signs of the mother she couldn't remember. She touched the photograph lovingly with her fingertips, as tears fell across the glass. *Oh, Mother. How could you leave us? How could you leave me—your baby girl?*

Her body cringed at the word *baby*. That had to be the reason her mother had left Sweet Water so suddenly: She was carrying Bill Babcock's baby. Her father must have thrown her out when he found out. The day she was at the beauty shop, hadn't Betty said Charlie would have forgiven most anything, except Abigale carrying another man's child? Maybe she left without telling him she was pregnant. The questions plagued her long after she had scooted the heavy box into her closet and gone to bed.

As Rose lay on her back staring out the window, watching the brilliant stars as they lit up the night sky, she wondered where her mother was now. Maybe

Colorado? She'd only be in her forties, still young enough that she would be alive—somewhere.

She sat straight up in bed, wide awake. *Baby? My mother was pregnant? That means I might have a half sister or brother out there somewhere. Maybe several.* She had wanted siblings all her life and envied those who had them. A determined look crossed her face, there in the darkness, as she narrowed her eyes and clenched her fists. *I'm going to find you, Mother. You may not want me to find you, but I'm going to do it. I have to see you. I have to know.*

Rose met Bane at the door when he came at 5:30 the next morning, looking bright-eyed and ready to go, despite her lack of sleep. Just finding the pictures of her mom had invigorated her.

He tipped his old straw hat and gave her a wink as he pushed open the door. "I've missed you."

Her heart did the cha-cha as she eyed the handsome cowboy in the battered straw hat. "Good morning. I've missed you, too."

"We need to start thinking about winter," he reminded her as they rode Ebony and Midnight across the west pasture.

The young woman wiped perspiration from her brow with her bandanna. "Winter? It's nearly eighty degrees already this morning." She watched as a trickle of sweat ran down his neck and disappeared into the V of his shirt collar.

He went on to explain that each season needed special preparation. A good rancher anticipated those needs and made ready before they arrived. She mentally made a note of everything he was saying so she could discuss them with Bitty over supper.

As they dismounted by the creek to water the horses, he gave her a smile that looked almost shy. She met his smile with one of her own. "Come here," he said softly, his eyes as warm as the morning sun.

"Why?" She pushed a length of long hair behind her shoulder.

"Because I want to hold you in my arms and kiss you, that's why."

She watched as he moved slowly toward her. She longed to be held and kissed by this man of mystery. Halfway toward her, he held out both arms and she ran into them, abandoning any questions she had about his past.

His lips eagerly sought hers, and then his kisses trailed to her chin, went slowly down her neck, and stopped at the little indentation at her collarbone. She lifted her head, loving each tender kiss and wanting more. She'd dated a few men, been kissed by a few men, but no one ever kissed her like Bane.

He drew back slowly and gazed into her eyes. "Every time I see those lovely, pink lips I go crazy. Even at the cattle auction I wanted to grab you and kiss you." He gave a laugh. "Now that would have surprised a few of those old codgers."

She looped her arms about his neck and drew his face to hers till their foreheads touched. "And I've longed for those kisses, Bane. Even when you've made me so mad I wanted to slap you."

"Who, me?"

"Yes, you. You know, the last thing I wanted when I came to Sweet Water was to be domineered by some grumpy know-it-all guy my father had assigned to teach me to be a rancher. But because of my dad and his stupid ideas, I met you." She kissed his chin, then brushed her lips across his mouth, avoiding it as his lips hungrily sought hers. "I've been fighting my emotions, Bane. Since that first day out on the road. Remember? When you offered me a ride on Midnight?"

Bane snickered, then gave her a peck on the end of her nose. "Do I!"

They walked arm in arm to the water's edge. Bane bent and scooped up some of the cool water with his straw hat, and they splashed themselves. The cool water trickled down their necks and arms.

Rose jerked the hat away from his hand, threw back her head, and splashed herself again. He grabbed it back, filled it, and poured the cool liquid slowly over his shoulders and let it run down his shirt, over his jeans, and onto the ground as she watched.

They laughed and hugged each other. Rose giggled when Bane lifted a hat full of the cool water and placed it on his head, letting it flood down his face, through his eyebrows, over his mustache, and drip off his chin. He was such fun when he relaxed. She hated to see their time come to an end, but they both needed to get back to work.

He pulled her to him one last time and smothered her with sweaty, damp kisses, which she returned with the same fervor, as Midnight and Ebony stood by waiting patiently.

On the way to church Sunday morning, Bane stopped the car by a hedgerow and turned to the woman who had penetrated his self-imposed shield, finding her way into his heart. "I haven't been able to get you off my mind." His mouth covered hers as he kissed her tenderly.

"You know we're going to be late, don't you?" she whispered as she leaned against him, begging for more.

After a long, lingering kiss, he backed away and headed the little red convertible toward the church. "You sure I can't convince you to skip RuAnn's shower and spend the afternoon with me instead?"

Her finger tapped the tip of his nose playfully. "RuAnn would never forgive me—but I have to admit, spending the afternoon with you does sound tempting."

It was fun seeing old friends again and watching RuAnn open the wonderful array of wedding gifts. Rose found herself envious of her old friend, as she wondered what it would be like to be married to Bane. Her thoughts skipped ahead to Bane's children. Funny, she'd never given motherhood a thought before meeting him and spending time with him.

Once back from the shower, she headed for her room to sort through the rest of the things in the box she had hidden in her closet. Beneath the framed pictures, she found several other treasures. Her mother and father's wedding pictures, their marriage license, and in a little velvet box were her mother's engagement and wedding rings. Her heart ached to see the photograph of the happy couple and hold the rings in her hand. Where had it all gone wrong?

With tear-filled eyes, she slipped the rings onto her finger. *If only we could have been a family. Surely you loved Daddy once. Yet something caused you to leave your wedding ring behind.*

It was hard to imagine her crusty old dad as a handsome young lover, but he must have been to have caught such a beautiful bride. *Mother. Mother. Where are you?*

After carefully arranging things back in the box, she shoved it back into her closet and climbed into bed. She had so much to think about.

Sleep eluded her, as her mind whizzed back and forth. Eventually, she crawled out of bed and stepped outside her bedroom door onto the patio. She breathed in the brisk night air.

Is that smoke? Has Bitty been burning trash outside in the big barrel?

She gave a big stretch, then leaned against the patio railing as she scanned the sky for shooting stars. She sniffed the air again. The smell was stronger. She couldn't see the barns or the outbuildings from her side of the house, but that was the direction the scent seemed to be coming from. After pulling on her robe and slippers, she moved quickly down the hall and out the kitchen door. It *was* smoke, she realized. The horse barn was on fire!

She screamed for Bitty and Nel and they both came running in their nightclothes. "Call 911, Rose. Quick!" Bitty barked as he stuffed his feet into his boots and rushed out the door.

Her hands trembled as she tried to hit the right numbers on the phone. By the time she'd made the call and reached the barn, the crew had gathered and were attaching hoses to the big pump, dragging them toward the barn.

"Ebony!" she cried out. "Get Ebony and Jet!"

The men were running in every direction as the flames rose higher and higher, fueled by the hay inside and the big timber trusses that held up the roof.

When Bitty tried to open the barn's big door, thick smoke, heat, and flames leapt out at him. He rushed back to Rose with a troubled face. "I can't get in there. It's too hot. I'm sorry, Rose."

She tried to push past him; she had to get her horses out of there. Nel pulled her back and held tightly onto her arm. "Now, honey. There's nothin' you can do for Ebony and Jet. Just hope they can save the barn."

The volunteer fire department's trucks roared in with their sirens blaring and their red lights flashing. They had arrived in record time, but it appeared to be too late for the horses. If the fire didn't get them, the smoke would.

Rose cried uncontrollably as she stood with the neighbors and friends who had arrived to lend help and encouragement. Ebony had been the first real friend she had made since coming home. She had never feared the big horse, although Bitty'd told her most of the ranch hands refused to ride him. It must have been because Ebony had been her father's horse that he had accepted her so readily. And Jet. How she loved that colt. She'd been with him from his birth and had spent many wonderful hours playing with him, stroking his smooth back.

"Hey, look!" one of the firemen shouted over the roar of the trucks and pump as he aimed a hose on the burning barn. There, coming around from the backside of the barn, was Bane. He was leading Ebony and Jet.

Rose ran to him and threw her arms about his neck. "Oh, Bane. Thank you, thank you, thank you!" He smiled and handed her the reins of the two horses. She stroked first Ebony's nose, then Jet's. It was then she noticed Bane's head was bleeding. "Oh, Bane, you're hurt. What happened?"

He seemed dazed and unsure of his footing as he crossed the barnyard and dropped onto the fender of Bitty's truck. "I'm not sure. I decided to come over to see if you'd want to drive into town with me, for ice cream. I knew you were home because the convertible was here, so I knocked on the kitchen door. But when you didn't answer, I decided to check the horse barn. I thought you might be out there with Jet."

"But what happened to your head?"

"Yeah. What happened to your head?" The sheriff approached and shone his flashlight on Bane's wound. "Ya got quite a goose egg there. Looks like ya could use a few stitches."

Rose wrapped her arm around Bane's shoulder and blotted his wound with the sleeve of her robe. "Bane, you'd better let me take you in to Dr. Kane."

He pushed her hand away and tried to stand to his feet, then dropped back onto the fender, shaking his head as if disoriented. "Sheriff, someone hit me on the head when I went into that barn. I don't know what they hit me with. I don't even remember hitting the floor. I haven't any idea how long I was out, but when I came to, the entire loft was on fire and it was so smoky I could barely see. The horses were going crazy and I figured I couldn't do much about the fire, but I could get the horses out."

He turned toward Rose and added, "I turned the whole lot of them loose. You know how spooked horses get around a fire. No telling where we'll find them all. Better get the men rounding them up first thing in the morning."

She nodded, grateful all the horses had been spared, thanks to Bane.

The sheriff squinted his eyes and frowned. "Are you telling me someone may have set this fire intentionally? After he knocked you out?"

Bane's jaw tightened and vertical lines creased his forehead. "That's exactly what I'm saying."

"You need medical attention for that cut. You might have a concussion from the blow you took." The sheriff gestured toward Rose. "Take him on in to the doc. I can talk with him more tomorrow. I'll know where to find him if I need him."

Bane started to protest, but he gave up and went along peacefully to the car. She knew he was hurting when he closed his eyes and leaned his head against the seat back.

"Bane, thanks for saving my horses," she told him as soon as he was settled. "They would have died if it hadn't been for you. And for that, you got that nasty cut and a knock on the head. I feel responsible."

He groaned with pain. "Rose, I couldn't let anything happen to Ebony and Jet. I know how much you love those horses. I don't know who hit me, but believe me, I'm going to find out." He sat up straight in the seat. "And when I do. . ." He slammed his fist into his other hand.

"Well, not tonight you're not. I'm taking you in to doc."

She smiled grimly. *At least now maybe he'll believe me. That my incidents weren't coincidences after all.*

The first thing in the morning, Rose phoned Maudie and checked on Bane. The housekeeper assured her he'd had a fairly restful night and wasn't going to do anything but rest.

"Tell him I'll be by later today and he'd better be sitting in that recliner with his feet propped up."

She drove into town with a broken tractor part that needed to be welded. She had wanted to go to town anyway, and the part had given her the needed excuse. After she dropped the part off at the welder's shed, she made her way back to Betty's Beauty and Barber Shop. Some beauty shops closed on Monday, but not Betty's.

The shop was nearly empty, except for one woman sitting under the hood of a dryer, reading a magazine. "Just a shampoo, kiddo?" Betty asked.

Rose nodded and sat motionless as Betty wrapped the plastic around her neck. She hoped Betty's tongue would be as free as it had been the last time she'd been there. "Betty, how well do you know Bane?" she asked, trying not to sound too interested.

" 'Bout as well as anyone, I guess. Met him the first week he showed up in Rock City." She quit scrubbing and turned on the spray. "Kind of a private guy, yet friendly. Know what I mean?"

Rose decided to push for more. "Where'd he live before he came here?"

"Kansas City, I think." Betty shifted the spray to her other hand. "Yes, Kansas City, I'm sure of it."

Rose held her breath as Betty began to run a comb through her long hair. "Did he ever mention his family?"

Betty quit combing and scratched her chin. "No, don't think so. Except his father-in-law. He said Charlie reminded him of his father-in-law. Never mentioned a wife, but I guess if he had a father-in-law he must've had a wife. I think his father-in-law had some kind of manufacturing business. I know Bane worked for him. That's about all I know." She resumed combing.

"Did he ever mention children?" Rose asked carefully.

Betty quirked up her face. "Not that I heard. But I know the guy loves kids. I wish some woman'd sweep him off his feet and give him some. He'd make a great daddy."

"I wonder how he got started in the ranching business," Rose prodded as she watched Betty's face in the mirror.

"I'll bet that father-in-law had something to do with it. Maybe he was the moneyman. Bane got all that money somewhere. I hear he paid cash for everything."

Rose placed enough money on the counter to pay for her shampoo and blow-dry, then added an extra five dollars. Betty pocketed the five and put the rest in the cash drawer.

Rose filtered the new information through her mind as she drove back to Sweet Water. So Bane was from Kansas City and he'd worked for his father-in-law in manufacturing. It wasn't much to go on, but it was a start. She had to know more about this man. Dare she ask him?

After supper, Nel handed Rose a bag of cookies. "These'll make him feel better. Tell him Nel sent 'em."

Bane was waiting on the big front porch, swinging idly in one of the porch swings, his open Bible in his lap. "Thought you'd never get here. It's been a long day."

Maudie came out the screen door with a pitcher of iced lemonade. "He's a terrible patient, Rose. I've had to ride herd on him all day. That man needs to be tied down. He don't know the meaning of the word *rest*. It'd take an entire posse to keep him in line."

Bane pulled a frown as he gestured toward his housekeeper. "That woman's a tyrant, Lilac. She's been hoverin' over me all day. Had to lock myself in the bathroom to get a few minutes' privacy."

Maudie picked up the scattered newspaper from the porch floor, rolled it up, and swatted her employer on his arm. "And I plan to do the same thing tomorrow. Doctor's orders," she cautioned as she moved back into the house, leaving the two alone on the porch.

Rose kissed Bane's forehead near the bandage, then sat down on the swing beside him and slid her arm around his broad shoulders. "I wanted to get by earlier."

"I've missed you," he whispered as he nestled his face in her hair, the scent of her rose shampoo still lingering.

The early evening was warm, but the sun's last rays were filtered by the autumn clematis that climbed the porch's trellis. The white clematis was in full bloom, its sweet fragrance filling the air.

He leaned against the cushion and cradled against her arm, his feet gently pushing off against the floor as the swing moved back and forth rhythmically. She felt strength emanating from this man with whom she'd become so comfortable, a strength that seemed to engulf her whenever he was around, a feeling he could handle anything set before him.

They sipped lemonade as they sat swinging, thinking private thoughts about each other as the sun slowly found its way to the waiting horizon and butterflies savored the nectar of the lacy clematis. Bane's hound dog lay sleeping on the welcome mat and his calico cat perched on the railing, its head drooping lazily in the heat of the Indian summer. Life was good.

Their attention was suddenly drawn to a car as it barreled up the lane toward them. It came to a stop and Sheriff Johnson crawled out and tipped his hat. "Evening, Bane. Miss Kinsey. How's that bump? Doc Kane said it was a pretty nasty cut. Took quite a few stitches, I hear."

Bane's free hand moved to his head. "Sore."

"I'll bet." The sheriff pulled a notepad from his pocket. "Been talkin' to a few people. No one seems to know anything or have seen anyone around the barn, but I'll tell you one thing—that fire was set a'purpose and so was that bump on your head. We found what they used on you, a crowbar. Found it tossed into one of the stalls all covered with your blood. We sent it off for tests, but it'll likely not show much. They probably had gloves on when they hit ya."

Rose shook her head sadly. "Why would anyone want to do such things? Bane hasn't an enemy in the world."

Sheriff Johnson poured himself a glass of lemonade and shielded his eyes from the sun's rays that were now streaming low across the porch. "You got any enemies, Miss Kinsey?"

She turned to look at him. That was something she'd never seriously considered. "I don't know the people around here well enough to have made enemies." Yet someone had deliberately burned out her barn.

The sheriff removed his hat and scratched his head. "Just asking. Procedure, you know."

"Well," Bane declared with an iron set of his jaw, "I'll tell you one thing, Orin, you'd better find out who did it, 'cause if you don't—I will."

Rose stayed later at the Wild Rose than she'd intended, but she made sure Bane rested in the recliner most of the evening, and he promised he'd go directly to bed when she left. She had hoped for a good-night kiss, but somehow it didn't seem appropriate with Maudie standing there looking at them, so she settled for his wink.

Bane lay awake in the darkness for hours after Maudie quit fussing over him and turned out the light. So much had happened. *Has Rose been on the right track all along? Was someone deliberately trying to hurt her? Or was it me they were after?* He'd have to be more on guard in the future, but what about her? He couldn't be with her all the time, to protect her and watch over her. *I wonder if Rose got home okay, and if she's in bed yet? I wish I'd asked her to call.* He flipped the bedcover off his feet and rearranged the pillow beneath his head. *What if she decides to go back to New York at the end of the year? Or if she decides to stay in Kansas, what then?*

Could they continue this courtship indefinitely? It had to go somewhere; it couldn't stand still forever. She was bound to get tired of a relationship in constant limbo.

Am I ready to move forward? Can I make that kind of commitment again? After all that's happened to me? Lord, I need Your guidance. You know how I want nothing but Your will in my life. I'm Yours, Lord. Show me what's best. For all of us.

He desperately wanted to have a permanent relationship with Rose, but could he? Could he take a chance at repeating a hurt like that a second time? She was a lovely young woman; how long would she wait for him to make up his mind? He knew he'd have to decide something, and soon. Things with Rose were heating up rapidly. They might already be past the point of no return.

He reported a good night's sleep when she phoned the next morning. He was itching to get back to work.

By Friday, Bane was driving Maudie crazy, and Rose as well. He was ready to get those stitches taken out and take up where he'd left off before the fire.

"You're fine, Bane, good as new. 'Course that cut's going to take a little while to heal completely, but it's lookin' good," Dr. Kane advised him as he removed the last stitch from Bane's head.

"You're sure, Doctor Kane? He doesn't have to take it easy because of the concussion?" Rose asked with open concern.

"No, he's fine, believe me. That crack on the head just slowed him down a bit."

The two drove from the doctor's office directly to Sweet Water. Bane was anxious to check the progress on the rebuilding of the horse barn.

Rose went on to the house to alert Nel they had a guest coming for supper. As she stood at the window in front of the sink and poured herself a glass of water, she watched as Bitty handed Bane a large brown sack. The two men looked around as they spoke to each other, as if in confidence. Then Bane made his way to his pickup, put the sack in the cab, and locked the door. Something he never did. What was in that sack that needed to be locked up?

After supper, while Bane, Bitty, and Nel discussed cattle prices and current world happenings, Rose excused herself by saying she had to call RuAnn. With a set of keys in her hand, she slipped out the side door of the big farmhouse and made her way to the shiny black pickup. She hoped Bane wouldn't remember he'd given her a spare key to the truck one time when she had run into town to pick up supplies.

Stealthily, she opened the door and cautiously reached inside the brown sack. It held none of the things that had crossed her mind. Instead, there was a small gas can, maybe a gallon-size, and on the side in big red letters was painted *The Wild Rose.*

Why did Bitty have the can? And why did they put it in a brown paper sack? Was he covering up for Bane? And why were they so secretive about it?

She unscrewed the lid and took a small whiff. *Whew, gasoline!* Just like the can said in raised letters on the outside.

With the door locked once more, she moved quietly back into the house and joined the group at the kitchen table as unsettling thoughts filled her mind. *What would a Wild Rose gas can be doing at Sweet Water? And in a sack?*

When it came time to say good night to Bane, Rose found herself pulling away from him. Her trust was once again broken.

Bane was so far behind in his own work, he decided to spend the next few days at his ranch. The Wild Rose crew did a good job, but they did a better job under his leadership. With Rose at the helm, Sweet Water was functioning much like it had when Charlie was alive, and they both agreed he could be spared.

She tried to keep her mind off the gas can, but it kept confiscating her thoughts and twisting them in convoluted ways. *Could someone from the Wild Rose have set the fire? If so, who? And why?* The unexplained incidents she'd experienced kept reappearing in her thoughts, mingling with visions of devouring flames.

She knew she'd have to watch her backside at all times, but she couldn't deny the love for Bane that was building up inside her. Against her better judgment, she found herself giving him the benefit of the doubt.

Sunday after church, she and Bane planned to spend the day together. She wished either she sang in the choir or he didn't. She would much prefer to sit by him during the service, feel his arm around her, his body next to hers, and enjoy the woodsy scent of his aftershave.

After Nel's tasty lunch of baked roast smothered in its own gravy, Bane pulled her to one side. "Go put your jeans on. I want to show you something."

In no time they were in his truck heading down the lane. "Where are we going?" Rose watched his face as he gunned onto the gravel road; she slid over close and poked him in the ribs with her finger.

"Eeeoww! Don't do that, I'm ticklish!" The truck veered to the left, then to the right, as he grasped the wheel with one hand while covering his ribs with the other.

"Oh? That's something I didn't know about you." Her eyes sparkled as she continued to jab at him.

He brought the truck to a screeching halt as he hit the brake pedal and turned to his giddy tormentor. "Hey, you. Two can play that game. Let's see if you're ticklish." He leaned over and quickly pulled off her boot and began to tickle the arch of her foot.

"Bane! Oh, Bane! Stop that!" she begged as she giggled and wiggled and tried to tug her foot away from his grasp. "Please, stop. You'll make me st–st–stutter!"

They wrestled on the seat and finally fell exhausted into each other's arms, gasping for air. He pushed the blond hair behind her shoulders and gazed into her eyes. "You're beautiful when you laugh," he whispered as his lips brushed her cheeks, then lingered on her receptive mouth. The inside of the cab grew warm in the afternoon sun, but neither seemed to notice as they enjoyed their playful time together.

He was so thoughtful, so tender, always the gentleman. Rose loved to gaze into his dark eyes and try to imagine what was going on inside that head of his. Was he really interested in her? Or was this truly some game he was playing?

Bane wiped a bead of perspiration from his brow and pulled away from Rose with one final kiss. "Better get goin', Pansy. Or we may not make it to our destination."

She smiled at his play on her name, no longer irritated by his teasing. "Where are we going?"

"Around two more curves and we'll be nearly there."

She smiled to herself. "You're impossible."

Soon the truck stopped in front of an iron gate with a No Trespassing sign. Bane jumped out, pulled a key from his billfold, and opened the padlock. He motioned to Rose, and she scrambled over into the driver's seat. With Bane guiding her, she steered the truck through the narrow opening. His eyes twinkled as he slipped back into the driver's seat beside her. "Hang on, Larkspur, this ride could get a little rough."

They took off across an open field, following two nearly invisible tire tracks. Rose covered her eyes with her hands and held her breath, fearing the truck would turn over on its side at any moment. With a cloud of dust, they came to a sudden stop. "You can look now." He pinched her arm playfully.

Her eyes scanned the area. It was beautiful and so wild and isolated. "This is it?" she asked with a bewildered expression. "Your surprise?"

"Almost." Bane moved around to her side of the truck and opened her door. As she planted her feet on the ground, he whipped her up in his arms as though she were a child and began to carry her.

She tried to escape his hold, but he held her all the tighter as she looped her arms about his neck and smiled into his suntanned face. "If you're kidnapping me, Mr. Jacob, there's no one to pay my ransom. Have you thought of that?"

He kissed her lips and pretended he was going to drop her as he jumped over the narrow branch of the stream. "Close your eyes, no peeking." For several minutes more, he carried her, then announced, "You can look now."

There before them, nestled in the trees as if it had always been there, a part of the forest itself, was a small log cabin that looked to have been hewn out of the very trees that surrounded it.

"Oh, Bane. I love it. Whose is it?"

He lowered her feet to the ground and hugged her close to him. "Yours."

Chapter 9

Mine? You mean this is on Sweet Water land?"

He nodded and took her hand as they walked up the newly cleared trail to the cabin. It seemed to beckon to the young couple with its geranium-filled planter and heavy, crosshatched front door.

"Geraniums don't grow wild in containers. Know who planted them there? Maybe someone with a greenhouse?"

Bane shot her a quick sideways smile as he pulled another key from his wallet and handed it to her. "Open it."

Her heart pounded as she pushed the key into the big padlock and they moved inside. It was like going back in time, like an old movie of the untamed West. Red and white checkered curtains hung over the windows, and a kerosene lantern hung from its hook on the ceiling. A bed made from willow and slats and roping stood in the corner by a chest. But along the wall by the door hung an assortment of very modern fishing rods and gear. She laughed at the contrast between the old cabin and the new ultra-modern fishing gear. "Who did all this?" she asked as she examined the dishes and other items lining the shelves.

Bane lowered himself onto a chair and wiped his brow with his bandanna. "Your dad and I. This was our hideout. Our escape."

She turned to him in amusement. "You and my dad? Why? There are many places much closer to fish than here. Like that big pond out behind the barn. I've seen Dad pull some pretty big fish out of there."

"Ahh. But none so private. This was where we came to escape. Just the two of us." He took her hand and led her out of the cabin, down a path through the trees; there, sparkling in the sunshine, was a gently flowing river winding through the rocks like a ribbon set with jewels.

She clung to his hand as they stood on a big overhanging rock. "It's magnificent. I didn't even know any of this was here on Sweet Water property."

Bane pointed to the low bank downstream. "See that area way down there, where it gets flat? That's where your daddy pulled me out when I nearly drowned. Only the river wasn't nice and peaceful then, it was at flood stage, like I told you, and flowing like crazy." He stepped behind her and wrapped his arms around her waist as they stood gazing at the tranquil river. "It was the first time your dad ever brought me up here." He let out a chuckle. "After those shenanigans, I'm surprised he ever brought me back. I owe him a lot."

Rose decided now was as good a time as any to get her questions answered, while he was in a mood to talk. "Bitty mentioned my dad took you to your first cattle auction," she said casually as she seated herself on the rock and dangled her feet over the edge.

Bane looked wistfully out over the rippling water. "He did. I was as green as a field of winter wheat. Didn't know anything about cattle and ranching, except I wanted to do it."

She tugged at his pant leg and he squatted down beside her. "Then why did you buy a ranch?"

He lifted his eyes to watch two geese gliding through the sky above them. "Wanted one. Had to start somewhere."

"But," she asked, trying not to press her luck too far, "why Rock City? Did you have relatives here?"

He stroked his mustache and continued eyeing the geese. "Nope. Just read about the Lazy Z in a real estate catalogue, thought it sounded like the kind of place I was looking for. And," he said as he seated himself beside her on the rock and stretched out his long legs, "I bought it sight unseen."

"You didn't."

"Oh, but I did. And fortunately for me, the advertisement didn't do it justice. It was even more than I dared hope for." He leaned back on the rock and crossed his arms behind his head. "Your dad was one of the first people I met when I came out here to stake my claim."

"But," she asked with hesitation, "wasn't that expensive? To buy a ranch, I mean. They're not cheap, even when they're run-down. I remember Dad saying if he hadn't inherited Sweet Water, he could never have afforded a ranch like this." She turned to look up at him and discovered his eyes were closed against the bright sunshine. "Where did you get that kind of money?"

There. She'd blurted it out. She'd finally asked the question that had been plaguing her.

He opened his eyes and peered at her with a strange intensity. "I'm sure there are a lot of people in Rock City who've asked that same question. Did they put you up to asking me?"

"No!" she replied nervously, wondering if she'd put their relationship in jeopardy. "I wanted to know."

He sat up straight on the rock and cracked his knuckles as he stared off in space. "Do you want the whole story? Or the condensed version?"

"Whatever you want to tell me," she answered softly.

He stiffened slightly. "I've never told anyone my story, except Charlie. And as much as I think of you, Rose, I'd prefer to keep it to myself, at least for now.

Let me just say I came by my money honestly. And another thing: I don't know what you've heard about me, but I haven't been interested in a serious relationship with a woman, and I've had my reasons. Sure, I've been friendly with some, even dated some, but I assure you, nothing serious with any of them." He grabbed her hand and kissed her fingertips. "Until now."

There was so much more she wanted to ask, so many things she didn't understand. "But, Bane, why did—"

"In time, Buttercup. In time." He pulled her to him and wrapped her in the security of his arms.

They huddled there on the rock as the afternoon sun swirled around them and the bees sipped nectar from the late blooming wildflowers in the field. Two people, who had been strangers before Charlie's death, mused Rose. Two people from different worlds, who had found each other on the plains of northwestern Kansas. This place was now their place, a place known only to them, a place where they could be together. Their sanctuary.

As the sun began to sink behind the trees, and the river grew orange and pink, the two made their way, arm-in-arm, to the pickup and back to civilization.

The day of RuAnn's wedding arrived. Rose drove to the Wild Rose early in the morning, laden down with the punch bowl Nel had sent and the long red dress she would wear as RuAnn's maid of honor. An hour before the wedding, she moved into Bane's room to take her bath and dress for the occasion.

She felt strange to be in Bane's room alone. His scent was everywhere. As she sat soaking in his tub, she could imagine him standing before the mirror, rubbing thick, white foamy lather between his palms and spreading it on his face and neck. Then she imagined him shaving with an old-fashioned razor, shaping the area around his mustache, moving his jaw from side to side to get a clean, smooth shave. As she stepped out of the tub and wrapped herself in a thick, plush towel from the shelf, she visualized Bane standing before the sink, combing his wet, wavy locks, wrapped in that very towel. *Get your thoughts back to the wedding where they belong.*

He was waiting in the hall when she stepped out wearing the red satin dress with its fitted waist and sweetheart neckline. Bane let out a long, low whistle, and she blushed and curtsied as she accepted his hand. "Your beauty never ceases to amaze me," he said with a sincerity that touched her heart.

"You're pretty handsome yourself." She eyed his black tuxedo and white pleated shirt.

When the wedding march began, Bane offered his arm and the two walked slowly down the hallway and stood on either side of the arch, followed by four bridesmaids in pink satin.

As the electronic keyboard rose in volume and the pianist began to play "Here Comes the Bride," RuAnn in her gown of white lace, with its long train of white satin, moved slowly toward the man with whom she intended to spend her life. Thorne beamed. Rose couldn't resist a peek at Bane and found his eyes fastened on her. As they smiled at each other, he mouthed something she didn't understand.

She lifted one eyebrow, and he repeated the words: *I—love—you.*

Her heart danced, and her cheeks turned as pink as the roses that twined the ivy-covered arch. She tried to listen to the words of the ceremony, but her eyes were constantly drawn back to Bane's, and his to hers. She kept imagining what it would be like to be in RuAnn's place, with Bane as the groom. To be pledging to love, honor, and cherish him, this man of her dreams. In sickness and in health. In good times and bad. For richer, for poorer. That type of commitment overwhelmed her. It was so—forever. Yet as she listened and watched the joy and eagerness on the faces of the bride and groom, she knew in her heart that was what she wanted out of life. To spend it with someone she loved more than herself, to share her life, her love, and even her body with a man who deserved her commitment. And, if God willed, to bear his children. All else in life paled in comparison.

Bane's fingers closed over hers as they followed the happy couple down the aisle to the sound of the "Wedding March." She almost felt like the bride instead of the maid of honor. Bane grabbed her into his arms and kissed her passionately the second they hit the entry foyer, a kiss she'd remember the rest of her life.

After the reception, Rose changed back into her jeans and helped Maudie, Bane, and several other guests who had stayed to help with the cleanup. In no time things were back in order at the Wild Rose.

"Guess I'd better be going," she said wistfully as she and Bane shared the porch swing and sipped one more glass of wedding punch. "Big day tomorrow, remember? You promised to go over the winter schedule with me."

He put his arm around her and pulled her body close to his. "Stay a little longer." She could feel the slight roughness of his face and the scrape of the familiar five-o'clock shadow as his cheek touched hers. How could she refuse?

Life seemed so simple, sitting there on his porch, lazily swinging, his strong arm wrapped around her. Rose no longer thought of herself as independent and self-sufficient, but as a woman who wanted to walk side by side on an equal basis with a man, sharing their strengths and weaknesses, becoming one. . . .

She returned to her room after a quick supper, eager to get back to the box.

Beneath the cardboard divider she found her mother's wedding gown wrapped in layers of tissue paper, the same dress she had worn in the photograph.

She clutched the dress to her bosom. If only it could talk, could tell her about her mother, tell her what she was really like. If she had loved her father, really loved him. Was there another side to the story Betty hadn't told her? Her mother's side?

Pinned to the dress was a folded piece of paper, and on it in a strong, masculine hand was written: *Thank you for our beautiful daughter. I'll love you and take care of you both forever. Love, Charles.*

Rose bowed her head and let the tears fall. At last she knew—her father *had* loved her mother.

After the box had finally been shoved back into the closet, sleep evaded her. She gazed at the glowing red numbers on the clock next to her bed.

Then, she heard it. A soft, scraping noise. It seemed to be coming from the direction of the window that earlier had allowed moonlight to splash across the wedding gown and veil she'd spread out on the lounge. Her body stiffened as she peered through the darkness and stared at the blackness outside.

What was it?

Her heart thumped against her chest so wildly she could almost hear it. She pulled the quilt up about her neck and snatched the phone from its cradle and dialed the number for Nel and Bitty's room. A sleepy Bitty answered immediately.

Rose grasped the phone tightly, as if it were her only link to safety. "Bitty, hurry. Someone is trying to get in my window!"

Within seconds, Bitty was pounding on Rose's door. She vaulted from the bed and turned the knob.

"You okay?"

"Fine. But, I know someone was there." She pointed an accusing finger. "At that window."

Nel arrived, wide-eyed, her long, unbraided hair tumbling down her back. "Stay with her, Nel," Bitty ordered. "I'm going outside and have a look."

The two women stood huddled together as they watched the long streaks from Bitty's powerful flashlight move across the window and wall of the big ranch house.

"Better call the sheriff," Bitty directed. "Someone cut a sizable hole in this screen and there's footprints below the window in the dirt."

Sheriff Johnson arrived in short order. He and Bitty searched the surrounding area, although they were both sure whoever cut the window screen was long gone. Orin Johnson shook his head as he sat in the living room and wrote in his report book. "I'll be back in the morning and check out the area in the daylight. Can't see much tonight with that cloud cover. Sure looks like rain."

Nel spoke up. "Me and Bitty'll check all the windows before we go back to bed. And the doors."

So much for sleeping with fresh air in my room, Rose thought as she pulled down the shade and climbed back into her bed to finish out the remainder of the short night. *Who would want to frighten me like this? And why?*

The sheriff arrived just as Bane came riding up the lane on Midnight. Nel invited them both to come in and have breakfast, but as soon as Bane heard about the would-be intruder, he offered to help Sheriff Johnson with his search. Rose joined them, and the three of them moved around the house to the area where her room was located.

Bane touched the jagged hole in the screen. "If you hadn't heard him and turned on that light, whoever was there was within seconds of gaining entry. Oh, Rose. . ." He grabbed her by the shoulder and spun her around into his arms. "If anything had happened to you. . ."

Sheriff Johnson ruffled the dirt with the side of his boot, then leaned down and pulled something from behind a yellow chrysanthemum plant. "Well, would you look what I found." He held up a small, ivory pocketknife and twisted it in his fingers.

Bane blinked in disbelief. "That's my knife!"

Two sets of eyes drilled Bane's, the sheriff's and Rose's. The sheriff stared intently, his eyes narrowing suspiciously. "How did your knife get here? Under this young woman's window?"

Bane brushed dirt from the knife with a puzzled look. "I don't know. The last time I saw it was when I used it to cut the tape off the roll of table covering for the wedding reception. I'm sure I put it back in my pocket. Or at least I thought I did. How'd it get here?"

Sheriff Johnson's look switched from Bane to Rose. "I'm sure she'd like to know that." He tilted his head toward Rose.

There had to be an explanation. Bane would never do her harm. Rose mulled over the episode as Bane walked the sheriff to his car. Yet who had been there when she'd fallen off Ebony? Who'd been there when she'd found the snake? Who had she seen the day she'd gone into town and someone had jerked the connections from her battery? Who had taken the horses from the fire after it had been set? And whose gas can was in the sack Bitty had given Bane the day after the fire? Now this. She didn't want to believe there was any connection to Bane Jacob. *He can't be involved in any of these incidents. Can he?*

Despite her feelings for this man, she had to be cautious. Her life might depend on it. Until she had answers, she could trust no one.

For the next few weeks, Rose discreetly sidestepped Bane's advances and avoided being alone with him as much as possible. The horrible mistrust she felt wrenched her heart. There seemed to be only one explanation if Bane was involved: to scare her off before the year was up. She'd been doing so well at the ranch, learning the business and enjoying the hard work it required. Had that frightened him into doing something so desperate as to frighten her like this? Did he want Sweet Water that badly? Weren't the Wild Rose and his other ranches enough for him?

She constantly watched her back, wary of trusting anyone who might put her in a vulnerable position.

Especially Bane.

❦

A month passed and she saw very little of Bane. At first, he phoned several times a day to make sure things were going okay on the ranch.

Then, once a day.

Now, he was only calling every three or four days.

She longed to talk to him, to laugh with him, to hear him call her Buttercup or Petunia or some other ridiculous flower name, but the feeling of insecurity and doubt in the pit of her stomach made her draw back from him, even on the telephone.

❦

Nel invited Bane for Thanksgiving dinner without asking Rose's permission. It was a miserable day; the two almost-lovers had nothing to say to each other. The conversation was strained with small talk, weather talk, how're-things-going talk.

After a wonderful dinner, Bane suggested the two of them take a ride on Ebony and Midnight; he wanted to talk to her. The weather was crisp and cool, but the sun was bright and inviting, a typical Kansas Thanksgiving Day, with the heat of summer over and the invigorating cold of winter peeking over the horizon.

Rose hesitated; she was sure the cabin was his intended destination, and she couldn't bear to be in such an intimate setting with this man she no longer trusted. "Sorry, I can't go. I want to watch a Thanksgiving special on TV."

Bane seemed hurt when she rejected his offer with such a flimsy excuse. His look made her heart constrict, and she longed to run to him and beg him to take her in his arms. But she couldn't. Her old fear welled up and seized her tight.

"Sorry. I really wanted us to have some time together. It's been awhile." When she didn't respond, he moved toward the housekeeper. "Thanks for inviting me, Nel." His arms encircled the housekeeper's waist and he gave her a bear hug. "You're the best cook in the county. Nobody makes mincemeat pies like you, Nelly-girl. They're even better than Maudie's. Just don't tell her I said so."

He added a quick, "Thank you, Rose, for your hospitality," shook Bitty's hand, and was gone.

Rose went to the front hall and watched through the leaded beveled-glass window as he rode down the lane. Together, the man and horse looked like an ad from a magazine as the dust puffed up behind Midnight's hooves and Bane sat straight and tall in the saddle, his black Stetson perched low on his brow. *Oh, Lord. Am I doing the right thing? Or am I ruining my chances with the finest man I've ever known? If only I knew the truth.*

❧

The first snowstorm of the season hit western Kansas with all its fury the second week in December, four inches the first day, with six more falling overnight. Winds whipped it in every direction, banking high drifts.

Rose stood in the bunkhouse surrounded by the hired hands. "I arrived in the spring in time for the last snow of the season, but I wasn't in charge then. You guys have to help me. I have no idea what kind of problems this presents to us as ranchers." She stood confidently, yet open to those who would offer their expertise.

Bobby stroked his handlebar mustache. "Why don't ya ask Bane? We thought he was helpin' you, but we ain't see'd much of him lately. He always knows what to do."

She narrowed her gaze and shifted from one foot to the other. "Even so, we can't expect Bane to keep running over here to tell us what to do. He has the Wild Rose to worry about. Surely you men have been here long enough to know the routine. Didn't you learn anything from my dad?"

"I'll get with the men and work up a schedule of the things we need to get done," Bitty offered as he surveyed the rag-tag crew of men. "If that's okay with you."

She wished there was someone besides Bitty to turn to. Try as she might to dismiss her fears, she felt uneasy about his part with the gas can. But there was no one else. "Thanks, Bitty," she said as confidently as she could. "I'd appreciate it."

By Sunday, most of the snow had melted; only the drifts around the buildings, barns, and fences remained. After church and a quick lunch, Rose took the keys to her dad's old jeep. In no time she was opening the gate with the key Bane had given her and following the tire tracks through the field to the grove of trees at the far end of the ranch. Something about that cabin magically drew her to it. Maybe it was the pleasant memory of being held in Bane's arms, of his kissing her and of her returning his kisses. She only knew she had wanted to return since the day she'd been there with him.

It was freezing cold inside, but she was dressed for it, and she went about checking inside the cupboards and drawers for anything that might give her information about her mother or her father. Or Bane.

"I thought I'd find you here."

She gasped and spun around to see Bane's body silhouetted in the sunny, open doorway. She placed her hand over her heart and breathed deeply. "You scared me."

He strode up beside her, his dark eyes searching hers. "How could you ever be afraid of me, Rose? I'd never hurt you. I thought you knew that."

She pulled away slightly.

"You are afraid of me, aren't you? Why?"

She didn't know how to answer. Her eyes skidded around him and back again, trying to avoid his penetrating gaze.

He shook his head sadly as his shoulders slumped. "I don't understand, Rose. You've avoided me ever since that day Orin found my pocketknife by your window. Surely, you don't think I tried to break in, do you?" He stood firm, his hands on his hips, his eyes pleading for answers.

"I don't know. What would you think if you were me?"

He dropped onto one of the chairs at the little table and rested his chin in his hands. "Probably the same as you." He sighed. "But honest," he lifted his eyes to hers, eyes that said they could be trusted, "I wouldn't do that—or anything—to hurt you. Please believe me."

He was hurt; she could see it in his eyes. It took all her strength to keep from running to him and kissing the pain away. Maybe he was simply putting on a good act.

"Why would you ever think I could be capable of such things?" He folded his arms across his chest and leaned against the chair's back with another deep sigh.

She stepped toward him, hands on her hips. "Then who, Bane? Who? You're the only one who would profit if I left Sweet Water. Too many things have happened, and you were there for all of them."

Now she was glaring at him, afraid she was already in danger by being there alone with him, so far from the main house. No one would know to come looking for her there if she failed to return. A sudden wave of fear shot its way through her body and she knew he saw it.

He got to his feet, then turned on his heels and headed for the door.

She watched him go and wanted to cry out, *Bane. I was wrong to doubt you. I love you. Please convince me it wasn't you.*

He stopped at the threshold. "I love you, Rose. Remember that when you're looking over your shoulder, afraid I'm going to hurt you. I'd give the Wild Rose and everything I own to be able to have you love me in return. And to have you trust me." Then he was gone.

The roar of his jeep and the spin of his tires made her cringe. Had she made the mistake of a lifetime with her foolish suspicions?

Bane Jacob sat in Marilyn, his head resting on the steering wheel, his hands lying idly in his lap. He'd done it again. Fallen in love with a woman and now he was about to lose her, just as he'd lost the other one. Hadn't he promised himself he'd never let that happen to him again? Until now, he'd never allowed himself to love a woman like he'd loved Carol. It'd nearly killed him when he lost her; how could he have let himself fall so crazy in love again?

"Bane find ya?" Nel asked as her employer entered the cozy kitchen. The room smelled of freshly brewed coffee. "He came by and I told him ya didn't say where ya was goin'. He seemed to think he could find ya." She poured a cup of the rich, brown liquid and handed it to Rose.

"I think he misses ya, Rose. Bitty says he asks about ya all the time. Ya been avoidin' him?" She placed two cookies on Rose's napkin. "I know. It's none of my business. It's just that you two seemed so happy, like two robins in springtime. Then, all of a sudden, you was like banny roosters."

Rose didn't answer. She just forced a weak smile and drank her coffee.

One week before Christmas, the UPS man arrived with a long box addressed to Rose Kinsey. No return address.

"Probably from one of them New York friends of yours," Nel suggested as the two of them scanned the package. "Why don't ya go ahead and open it? It don't say ya have to wait till the twenty-fifth." They giggled like naughty children as Nel handed her a pair of kitchen shears.

Rose let out a scream as the box fell to the floor with a thud. There, on a bed of black tissue paper, lay a dozen roses, dried and shriveled, topped with a tarantula spider, all fuzzy and menacing—and dead. Her eyes widened with horror.

Things had been quiet, too quiet, since the cut-screen episode. Rose had hoped the weird incidents had come to an end. But apparently not. The roses and the spider had to be a part of them, the newest addition.

Who knew she was terrified of spiders?

Bane.

Sweet Water Ranch took on a festive look for the Christmas holiday season. Bitty helped Rose bring the decorations down from the attic and Calvin helped her cut an old-fashioned tree from the pasture. She and Nel spent most of the day decorating the house and trimming the tree while they talked about Rose's growing-up years on the ranch.

"Your papa was always sad at Christmas. That's when your mama left, Christmas Day." Nel looked nostalgic as she lifted the tree-topper angel from its box.

Rose frowned. "I didn't know that, Nel. How awful for him. No wonder he was so grumpy at Christmas. I remember the wonderful presents he bought, but he seemed to take no joy in giving them to me. Did I remind him of her?" Her expression was melancholy as she exchanged a red lightbulb for a blue one in the string of lights she was draping over the staircase greenery.

Nel stood still, the angel in her hand. "Yep, ya sure did. He never said nothin' 'bout it, but you was the image of yer ma. Still are." She pulled the stepladder to the tree and climbed up on it. "She was beautiful, too."

Once the angel was resting on its place on top of the tree, Nel climbed back down to admire it. "Your mama made that angel, did you know that?"

Rose looked up at the treetop in surprise. "I didn't know that. Are you sure? Why didn't anyone tell me?" She pulled the ladder back to the tree and hustled up the steps, gently lifting the delicate angel from its place. "I needed to know and no one told me," she said with misty eyes as she fingered the embroidered features on the angelic cloth face.

Nel lowered her eyes and rolled up the hem of her apron nervously. "Yer daddy wouldn't allow it. He said we was to say nothin' about it, it was just an ornament. But each Christmas, he put that angel on the tree, and then he'd sit on the couch and stare at it for hours. I wanted to tell you, but I worked for yer dad. He was my boss."

Rose touched her fingertip to the little angel's face lovingly, then climbed the ladder slowly and placed the exquisite doll on top of the tree where she belonged. She felt as if touching the little angel brought her one step closer to the mother she'd yearned for all her life.

Bane appeared at the door Christmas morning with presents for all three of them, Rose, Bitty, and Nel. He placed them under the tree, wished them a Merry Christmas, and left. Rose felt bad she hadn't bought him a present; he'd been such a help to her since she had arrived in Kansas. That was the least she could have done.

She took her present to her room to open it. What could Bane have given her? The box was wrapped in a lovely embossed paper of pink and red, tied with velvet ribbons. A sprig of fresh mistletoe was tucked beneath the knot. It was almost too pretty to open. The card read:

> *To Rose, who has taught me the meaning of true love and how to love again. I miss you and the time we used to spend together. I love you.*
>
> *Bane*

She lifted the card to her lips and held it there, her heart fluttering as she thought about the words. If he did love her as he claimed, he couldn't have done those awful things. She carefully removed the ribbons and paper and folded them neatly, then opened the box. Inside was a scarlet leather Bible. On its cover in gold letters was printed *Rose Jacob.*

Chapter 10

She did a double take when she read the name. *Rose Jacob?* A piece of parchment paper was tucked inside the cover and on it was written in Bane's masculine handwriting:

> *When the clerk asked what name I wanted on the cover, I said Rose Kinsey. Then I thought, if Rose consents to be my wife her name will not be Kinsey, but Jacob. I decided to throw all wisdom to the wind and go for it. Will you marry me, Rose? You'd make me the happiest man on earth if you'd say yes. I won't rush you, darling. I don't want to crowd you. But know that I love you and am willing to do whatever it takes to win your love and make you trust me again. I'll be waiting.*
>
> *Bane*

Rose brushed her eyes with the back of her hand. She loved Bane. She'd known it almost from that first day. Now he was asking her to be his wife. How many times had she dreamed about hearing those words? She opened the Bible to 1 Corinthians where the red satin ribbon marker rested, and read the verse he'd marked with a yellow highlighter: "If you love someone you will be loyal to him no matter what the cost. You will always believe in him, always expect the best of him, and always stand your ground in defending him."

A tear fell onto the page and she quickly blotted it with her sleeve. *Oh, how I want to trust you, Bane. But all evidence seems to point to you.*

Even as her fingers stroked the smooth leather of the Bible, another thought niggled at the back of her mind. One she didn't want to acknowledge, but knew she must. Perhaps this proposal was the cheapest and easiest way Bane could get his hands on Sweet Water—by becoming her husband. She had such little time left to fulfill her year, and he certainly couldn't say she hadn't completed her part of the bargain. She had learned her lessons well, and the ranch was running smoothly and showing a good profit. Marrying her was the only way left he could add Sweet Water Ranch to his other land conquests.

No, she decided, she had a ranch to run. Nothing and no one could take her attention from her goal. If Bane loved her as he said he did, surely he'd be willing to wait until the time was up and the ranch was hers.

She wrote a very formal note, thanking him for the beautiful Bible, reminding him she had three months to make her decision about the ranch. She would take his marriage proposal into consideration at that time.

A heavy snow fell the week after Christmas, followed by a freezing rain that hit on New Year's Day and covered the snow with an icy glaze. After that, the temperature dropped to below zero for fourteen days straight. The ponds and creeks were nearly a solid mass. Bane phoned to warn Rose about the danger to the cattle if they didn't get enough food and water, and offered to come over and help. As much as she hated to be obligated to him, she gladly accepted his offer.

He arrived right at five in the blackness of the cold morning and began barking out orders. Although he protested and warned against it, she stood her ground and convinced him she was going with them.

The winds were biting cold as they climbed into the back of the pickup and headed for the big barn. Rose had no idea why they loaded the rectangular bales onto the truck when there were hundreds of big round ones lined up in the field, but she did as she was told and loaded the bales right along with the men.

Bane tossed in two pitchforks, two axes, two sledgehammers, and a pair of wire cutters, then instructed her to climb into the truck's seat between him and Calvin. The truck jostled and jiggled across the fields to where the first herd of cattle stood huddled together. Bane stopped the truck and motioned for Calvin to slide behind the steering wheel while he and Rose moved out and climbed into the truck's bed with the bales. He dropped to his knees and began clipping the wires that held the bales together.

"Grab a pitchfork," he ordered as he stood to his feet, "and do what I do." He banged on the cab with his fist and Calvin began to drive slowly alongside the black cattle as their eyes reflected in the headlights.

Bane jabbed a pitchfork into the loosened bales and thrust big chunks over the side of the truck onto the frozen ground. The cattle moved up to the piles and began to eat. "Do it," he snapped with authority. "We've got a full day's work ahead of us."

She jabbed her pitchfork into the broken bale and emptied it over the truck's side. Her fingers were so cold she couldn't get them to unbend from around the fork's handle, but she wouldn't admit it. Instead she worked alongside him, matching him forkful to forkful.

About one o'clock, they stopped for the sack lunches Nel had prepared for them. Rose wanted to say *I give up* and go back to the warmth of the main house, but she couldn't; she was too stubborn. After all, Sweet Water was her responsibility.

After lunch, Bane drove the truck to the largest of the ponds and stopped.

Calvin hopped out and pulled axes and sledgehammers from the back.

"Now what?" Rose tugged the wool scarf over her face. Bane's mustache was tinged with ice, and any other time it would have made her laugh, but not today. Today, she was too cold for anything to be funny.

Bane winked at Calvin, then grinned at her. "Hey, this'll warm you up. Grab a sledgehammer and follow me." He headed for the pond, his long legs taking great strides.

Rose tried to pick up the sledgehammer, but she found it was much heavier than she had anticipated.

"Here, you take the axes. I'll get the sledge," Calvin offered.

"No. I can do it." With a mighty grunt, she hoisted the sledge as best she could and carried it across the frozen ground to the pond.

Calvin shook his head and picked up the axes and followed his boss.

Bane began swinging the sledge in large, open circles over his head, crashing it to the ice, sending chunks flying across the glassy surface. After several more powerful hits, the hole became bigger and the water splashed through. "Gotta break this up so the cattle can get water." He motioned to Rose. "Have at it."

She tried to swing the sledge like he had. At first it was impossible, but as she expended energy and her blood began to flow again, she found she could do it. Not as well as Bane, but she could break up the ice and that was her target. He seemed surprised at her determination and smiled at her.

Rose's hands ached inside her gloves. She was sure there were blisters swelling and bursting with each swing, but when Bane tried to get her to climb into the truck and let Calvin take over the sledge, she refused.

By five o'clock, the daylight had come and gone, and they were far from through. But at least the cattle had food and water. Tomorrow would be another day, and they'd repeat their performance until they were sure there was adequate feed and water.

In the ranch house kitchen, Rose smiled through masked pain as she struggled to pull her gloves from cramped fingers that burned with broken blisters.

"You should've seen Marigold, Nel," Bane bragged. "She surprised me. I never expected she'd last an hour."

Rose turned to him with a forced smile. "I told you I was going to fulfill my part and I will." An involuntary frown wrinkled her forehead, and she flinched as she removed the second glove from her blistered palm. She quickly put her hand behind her back, but it was too late.

"Give me your hands," he demanded.

She shook her head and backed away. "They're fine."

"I said give me your hands." He grasped her arm and reached behind her, pulling her hand into his. "Rose, you should have told me. Those blisters have popped open and they're bleeding." He lifted her wounded hand to his lips and kissed it tenderly. "You stubborn woman. You should never have been out there today. I don't care what your dad said. I shouldn't have allowed it. What was the matter with me? Letting you do the work of a man like that? Tomorrow, you're staying home."

She pulled her hands away. "No, I'm not. I'm going out again. There's still work to be done and Sweet Water is my responsibility." She nearly added that he could go back to the Wild Rose, but she knew they'd never finish without him. "Who's taking care of the Wild Rose herds?" She had almost forgotten he had cattle of his own to feed and water.

"Don't worry your pretty little head." He gave an affectionate jab to her chin. "I've got my bases covered. I promised your dad and I'm not about to let him down. My word can be trusted, Rose. Honest."

She knew his words had a double meaning, and she was grateful to him for his loyalty to her father.

"Get some supper in you and go to bed early, Rosebud. You deserve a rest." He winked at Nel as he shoved his Stetson onto his head and reached for the door. "And forget about coming out tomorrow."

She lifted her chin and squared her shoulders. "I'll be ready at five. Stop by for me."

He took a step forward and faced her squarely. "Only if you'll drive the truck and stay in the cab. Deal?"

She took a deep breath and felt the pain in her palms. "Okay, but only till these heal a little."

He smiled broadly. "You got it. Five it is."

For three days they hauled feed and broke up ice. It was hard, tiresome work. Rose had a renewed appreciation for her crew. Bane worked with the men, side by side, the entire three days. At last, the cold spell broke and the blazing sun broke through. They'd made it with no losses, just a few close calls.

After a proper thank you from Rose and her crew, Bane went back to the Wild Rose to see how his own cattle had weathered the cold.

❧

"He's a fine Christian man, Rose. Not many of those around these days, especially with the standards Bane sets for himself," Nel told her as she stood before the sink washing vegetables for a stew. "Bitty and me was hopin' you two'd get together."

Rose slowly sipped her hot coffee and gazed out the kitchen window at a pair of flame-red cardinals perched on the cedar bird-feeder Bitty kept filled with sunflower seeds. "Yes, he is. At least I think he is—a fine man."

Nel turned off the water and wiped her hands on her apron. "Think he is?

What does that mean?"

Rose bared her soul to Nel. She reminded her of all the incidents that had happened to her and how Bane was either there at the time, or had been.

Nel listened with wide, doubting eyes. "Oh, honey. Yer wrong. Bane would never do any of those things, for any reason. He ain't no greedy man." She placed her wrinkled, blotchy hand over the young woman's. "Bitty helps the church treasurer when he gets overloaded. He's told me how much money Bane gives to the church and to the families and neighbors who was ahavin' trouble financially. Bitty says he does it through the church so those people don't even know he's the one who gives it to 'em. Bitty shouldn't have told me, but he did. It's not that *Bane* wants Sweet Water, honey. He wants *you* to have Sweet Water—like yer pa wanted." She patted Rose's hand and went back to the sink. "You're abarkin' up the wrong tree if ya think Bane would do any of those things. I know the man. He ain't got a selfish bone in his body. Just ask the pastor, he can tell you."

That was a new thought, one that bore consideration. She trusted Pastor Nelson. She'd talk to him.

The frame parsonage sat next door to Mill Creek Community Church at the end of a long sidewalk. Pastor Nelson greeted Rose at the door and invited her inside. His wife smiled, offered coffee, and then left them alone.

"Well, it's certainly good to see you. It seems you've been avoiding us lately." He lifted the palm of his hand toward her and continued. "I know you've been regular in your attendance, but for a while now, you've come in late and left the second the service was over. As if you didn't want to be bothered. I've considered calling on you, but hoped you'd come to see me if there was a problem. I hope none of us have offended you."

She hadn't realized her quick comings and goings on Sunday mornings had been so obvious. "Oh, Pastor Nelson, it has nothing to do with you or the church. I love Mill Creek Community Church, more than I ever thought I could. And its people. It's. . ." She couldn't find the words to explain what was troubling her mind and heart. "Bane."

"Bane?" He leaned forward in his chair with a puzzled look. "I don't understand. I thought he'd been helping you at Sweet Water. Just this week, Eddy Murdock told me he'd been by the Wild Rose and the hands told him Bane was spending all his time helping you feed and water cattle."

She took a deep breath and let it out slowly, feeling very foolish, then spread the entire history of their relationship before Pastor Nelson.

He sat silently, holding his coffee mug in his hands, listening to every word until she was finished. "Umm. I can see why you're in such emotional turmoil about this. Things don't look so good on the surface, do they?"

She lowered her head and clasped her hands in her lap. "That's what I thought."

He put his mug on the table and stood to his feet, then moved to the window and fully opened the blinds, letting the bright sunlight fill the room. "The Scripture says even a child is known by his doings, Rose. Certainly a man is known by his doings." He moved back to his chair with a warm smile. "I remember the day your father brought Bane into this very room. He and Bane had been out fishing somewhere and Charlie—bless him—had led Bane to the Lord. Bane sat in that very chair where you're sitting, as I recall, and told me he'd confessed he needed a Savior. That he'd done things in his life he wasn't proud of, and he'd asked God's forgiveness. I've no doubt the man was sincere."

The pastor paused as if giving her time to think over the things he had said before continuing on.

"What happened after that? Let me tell you. Bane became active in our church immediately, and he began to memorize Scripture. Sometimes he'd call me several times a week to ask me what certain passages meant. That man had a hunger for the Word. Still does." His eyes went from the young woman to the window, as if he was reflecting on his admiration for the man they were discussing.

"Right after Bane began attending church, he began a vigorous program of giving. At times I wondered if he could afford it, but he assured me the Lord had been good to him and he wanted to return all he could to Him, by giving to His work. I could tell you stories about his giving, but that information is confidential. Bane never wants people to know what he's done. He says it is between him and the Lord. But that man is always ready to help anyone in need. Does that sound like a man who is out to get you?"

Rose twisted the ring on her finger as she listened. Could she have been wrong? "But, Pastor. It seems no one knows anything about Bane's life before he came to Rock City. Why, if he's such a great guy?"

"When your father brought Bane to meet me, I asked him that very question. People were asking about that young man."

She shifted in her chair. "What did he say?"

He smiled and rubbed his chin. "I can't tell you. Pastor-client thing, you know. But I can tell you he had his reasons, and I respect him for them.

"Your father and Bane had a real kinship, Rose. That's what happens when one man leads another to Christ. An unbreakable bond, even by death. Bane was like the son Charlie never had. Charlie was like a father to Bane. Bane trusted and respected him, and your father felt the same way about him. Bane seemed to fill a void in your father's life when he arrived in Rock City. You were gone. Charlie was alone, then Bane came along. I wish you could have heard those two. They'd tell stories on each other, tease each other, like two old ladies. And Charlie loved it. Bane brought him out of the depression he'd been in since your mother left him. I saw it happen."

She lifted watery eyes and pursed her lips. "Did you know about my daddy's will?"

He nodded his head and leaned back in his chair, locking his fingers behind his head. "Yes. He brought it to me after Ben had drawn it up. I asked him why he wanted to do it that way, rather than just leave you everything outright. You know what he said?"

She shook her head and breathed deeply.

"Two reasons." He paused thoughtfully. "I guess now Charlie's gone, I can tell you. First, because he wanted you to have one last chance to fall in love with Sweet Water Ranch, before you sold it. And, second—and most important—he wanted to make sure you and Bane spent as much time together as possible, getting to know each other. He felt if he could get the two of you together, there was a good chance you'd hit it off. It was his way of bringing the two most important people in his life together. That old dreamer was sure you'd end up getting married and the ranch would remain in the family."

"Did he tell this to Bane?"

"No, he didn't want him to know."

Although Rose was shocked by what she was hearing, she had to smile. That old rascal. Her father had planned this. He was trying to play Cupid; that's why he'd written that ridiculous will!

Pastor Nelson continued. "Now, considering all the trouble and planning, do you think your father would have given all that power to Bane, if he didn't think he could trust him?"

The words echoed through her mind and ricocheted off her good sense. *Trust him—trust him—trust him.*

"Have you ever read that passage in the Living Bible in the seventh verse of the thirteenth chapter of First Corinthians? It says, 'If you love someone you will be loyal to him no matter what the cost. You will always believe in him, always expect the best of him, and always stand your ground in defending him.'"

Rose nodded. "Yes, I read those very words in the Bible Bane gave me for Christmas."

"From my vantage point, young lady, I'd say you're in love with Bane, and I know he loves you."

The young woman let out a sigh. "I do love him, Pastor. Is it that obvious?"

"To those who know you both, it is. I've watched the love grow between the two of you these months since you've come back to Rock City. A number of people in our congregation have, too."

Rose grinned as she felt a tinge of pink rise to her cheeks.

"Your father could've set it up so you would have to have sold Sweet Water to Bane. He certainly could afford to buy it. But that way, you two would have met briefly, and you'd have been off to New York. Bane would never have seen you again. I'd say your father had a brilliant plan. He only delayed your inheritance for one year and forced the opportunity for you to spend time with his friend. I think he knew you'd take the challenge. He wasn't a gambling man, but he knew the odds were in his favor."

"Then, you think Bane had nothing to do with those awful things that happened?" Somehow she knew what his answer was going to be. The man was in Bane's corner.

Pastor Nelson rose and placed both hands on the arms of Rose's chair, looking directly into her questioning eyes. "Me? Think he did it?" He shook his head. "No. I don't. But," he added without breaking eye contact, "you are the one who has to decide if he's trustworthy. You alone will have to live with the consequences of your decision. But I'd think long and hard before condemning him without knowing for sure. A man like Bane Jacob may only come around once in a lifetime."

She thanked Pastor Nelson for his time and wise counsel. Apparently everyone who knew Bane thought he was a saint.

But was he?

Valentine's Day came and went, and other than a lacy, sweet, sentimental card reminding her of his love, Bane left Rose pretty much to herself. He came by two or three times a week to see if his services or expertise were needed at the ranch, and he checked over the book work and visited with the hands. But other than that, he stayed at the Wild Rose.

A few days later, RuAnn called and invited her friend to join her for a shopping trip to Kansas City to buy baby furniture. She and Thorne had decided not to wait to have children and were happily expecting their first baby in late fall. Rose consented eagerly. She could use a break.

On a whim, while RuAnn was ahhing and oohing over a very expensive round canopy baby bed, Rose crossed the street to a secondhand bookstore. The clerk barely looked up over his half-glasses when she entered.

"You wouldn't happen to have any old Kansas City phone books, would you? Say, five to ten years old?" It was a long shot, she was probably wasting her time, but it wouldn't hurt to check.

"Maybe," the man returned with a weary sigh as he dragged himself off the stool and moved to a back shelf. "Got two." He plunked them both on the counter.

She smiled and began thumbing through the yellow pages, looking for the manufacturing section. If Bane had been working for his father-in-law, the business wouldn't be in his name. She had no idea what she was looking for, but ran her fingers up and down the columns anyway. Nothing rang any bells. She handed the heavy books back to the little man with a disgruntled, disappointed look. "I was looking for an old friend who used to live here."

"What's their name? Maybe I knowed 'em."

She adjusted the strap on her shoulder bag and gave him an appreciative grin as she turned toward the door. "I doubt that you would have known Bane."

He frowned, pulled off his thick glasses, and rubbed at his eyes. "Only one man I ever know'd named Bane. That was Bane Jacob. Me and his father-in-law used to belong to the same VFW post. We was good friends."

She stopped in her tracks. Had she heard him right? "You know a Bane Jacob? Was he tall, with black hair and a mustache? Maybe six-foot-two?"

The man rubbed his bald head thoughtfully. "Sounds like him. Let's see—he'd probably be twenty-nine, maybe thirty by now. I think he went out West somewhere. Started raising cattle."

Rose's heart thumped wildly and her hands felt sticky from perspiration. "Tell me about him. Anything you can think of."

He pulled a hanky from his pocket and wiped his forehead before propping himself back up on the stool. "Well, he was a good-lookin' kid. I went to his and Carol's wedding. His pa invited me."

Rose's jaw dropped. "Wedding?"

"Yep, wedding. You know, Bane went to work for old Bud Cantrell right after he got outta school. Worked all the way to the top and took over after Bud retired. That company made the finest metal buildings you'd ever want. Made old Bud rich. Not to mention that special truss those two invented and patented. Brought 'em more money than a guy could spend in a lifetime when they sold the patent."

"Why did Bane leave the company? And where is his wife now?" Rose prodded carefully, not wishing to push.

He shot her a questioning glance. "You know Bane and you don't know that?"

She hated to lie. "It's been a long time since I've seen him, but I'm very interested in finding him and hearing what he's been doing since I saw him last."

The store owner gave her a once-over and a frown, but he must have believed her story. He continued, "Old Bud was still chairman of the board even though Bane was president and general manager of the company. With such a big company, Bud insisted one of them be in town at all times. So when Bane decided he wanted to fly Carol and little Carrie to Disney World in the company plane—"

Rose edged toward the man. "Carrie?"

"Yeah, Carrie, their little girl. Must've been about two at the time. As I was sayin', when he wanted to take Carol and Carrie to Disney World, Bud offered to stay behind and run things. But at the last minute, one of their big clients insisted on meetin' with Bane to sign a big contract, so's he sent Bud in his place and stayed in Kansas City. Real sad about what happened."

She leaned both elbows on the counter and cradled her chin in her hands. "What did happen?"

"They crashed! Lost all three of them. Gone, just like that." He snapped his fingers for emphasis. "And Bud was a good pilot, flew during the war. They said it was wind shear or somethin' like that. I never really understood that kind of stuff. I was an infantry man myself."

Her eyes widened. "They died? Bane's wife and baby and father-in-law?" Her heart ached for him.

"Yep. Bane took it real hard. He loved Carol, but, oh, how he loved that baby girl. I'd say he near worshipped her from what old Bud used to tell me. She was a purty little thing, looked more like Bane than her ma. Bud showed me lots of pictures of that family." He fingered a mole on his chin and squinted his eyes again.

"Bane tried to run the business for a while, but he couldn't. Too many memories. He and Bud was mighty close, thick as pudding. Last I heard, Bane'd sold the business, sold the house, and took off for Montana, Colorado, or some such place. I lost track after Bud died and couldn't come to the VFW no more."

Rose gulped and tried to keep her composure. How awful to lose them all at once like that. Poor Bane.

The old man stared off in space. "Ya know, that man blamed himself for them dying like that, thought if he'd been flying them instead of Bud, they might not've crashed. Changed his life in a matter of seconds. He got real withdrawn, wouldn't talk to nobody, about became a hermit."

"Er—thanks. You have no idea how helpful you've been." She got to her feet, eager to be gone. Her emotional rubber band was about to snap.

She walked out into the sunlight with mixed emotions: a heavy heart for all Bane had gone through and a new confidence in him as a man.

"Where in the world have you been?" RuAnn asked as Rose slipped into the chair at the ice-cream parlor where they'd agreed to meet. "I was about to give you up and walk back to the Ritz-Carlton."

Rose only smiled. "You wouldn't believe it if I told you." She'd decided to keep her information to herself. If Bane hadn't told anyone, she felt she had no right to either. She could hardly wait to see him again and try to make amends for ever doubting him.

As soon as she got back to Sweet Water, Rose determined to call Bane. She needed to hear his voice, to talk to him, and to feel his touch—if he'd let her, after the way she'd mistrusted him. But she decided to wait till morning; the trip had been tiring and she needed a good night's sleep—and time to think before doing something she might regret later. She still needed answers.

Bane phoned early the next morning and invited Rose to have lunch with him. He didn't say where, but since their choices were somewhat limited, she decided jeans and a plaid shirt were in order. And, of course, boots. She was a little surprised when he arrived in the canvas-topped jeep, but she said nothing and climbed in. The March winds were cool, but the day was bright and sunny.

He grinned as he removed his black Stetson and dropped it onto the backseat. She watched, wondering how she could have ever been afraid of this man. She had so many things to tell him, but she decided after lunch would be a better time; she wasn't sure how he'd react to her prying into his life. For now, she'd just enjoy his company. She knew in an instant where they were going, and even though she hadn't turned to check out the backseat, she was sure there'd be a picnic basket waiting there.

They rode along, making small talk about Sweet Water, the Wild Rose, their horses. Make-do kind of talk, the kind of talk people make when they're not sure what to say.

The jeep came to a stop in front of the cabin, just beyond the nearly dried-up stream. Bane whipped Rose's door open and scooped her up in his arms before she could set her feet on the ground. "Let's do it right, like we did the first time we came here, okay?"

She looped her arms about his neck and allowed him to carry her to the porch before he went back after the picnic basket. Maudie had not only prepared a delicious picnic, she'd even added a freshly pressed red and white checkered tablecloth, which Bane spread out on the porch in the warmth of the sunshine.

They were like two old friends, and much to her disappointment, he made no move to kiss her or even hold her hand. Once the picnic leftovers were placed back in the hamper, Bane pulled a large manila envelope from the back of the jeep and placed it on her lap as she sat cross-legged on the porch.

She frowned. "What's this?"

As he sat down beside her, his face took on a serious look she'd rarely seen. "I wanted you to have this before you announced any decisions you might make. About staying on the ranch or selling it. Open it." It was almost a command.

She scanned his face but his expression didn't change. She lifted the flap and slid out the contents. It was some kind of legal document.

"Read it."

She unfolded the papers and began to read. It was a deed, made out to her. She gave him a puzzled look and he pointed back to the document. She read a little further, then backtracked and read it again. Surely she'd misread it the first time. "The Wild Rose? I don't understand."

Without a trace of a smile, he answered, "I've deeded the Wild Rose and all my other ranches over to you, Rose. It's that simple."

She shook her head and leaned against the cabin's wall. "I don't get it. Why would you ever do that?"

He took her hand in his and looked intently into her quizzical eyes. "I've deeded it all to you, to show you I never had any intention of taking Sweet Water from you, and to convince you I never had anything to do with those things that happened to you, no matter how it looked."

She gazed at the deed through misty eyes. "You'd sign over everything you own, just to prove that to me?"

He squared his jaw and nodded. "I not only would—I did. This document is legal. Ask Ben Horner. He drew it up and it's been filed. You own it all."

She pushed back a tear and swallowed hard. "But, why? Why would you do such a thing?"

"Because I love you," he declared, his words solid and unwavering.

"How could you? After all I've accused you of?"

He touched her hand with the tips of his fingers. "In two weeks, I'll sign the release paper Ben is holding on Sweet Water and you'll own that, too. I want you to stay, to become my wife. I now have nothing to offer you but myself and my love. Everything is yours. Now, after turning all my wealth over to you, you should know my love is true, I have no ulterior motives. I come to you empty-handed, Rose. The rest is up to you." He stood to his feet and headed for the jeep. "I'm ready to go back when you are."

"Bane. Oh, please, Bane. Wait. I had so much I wanted to tell you."

He stopped and turned. "It isn't necessary. I just wanted you to have the document before your year was up. You've more than met the stipulations in your father's will. Charlie would be proud of you." With that he moved on down the trail toward the waiting jeep.

"But, Bane—I haven't fulfilled the one thing that was most important to my father." She was weeping openly now. His great unselfish gesture had been far too much for her.

He swung around and faced her with a frown. "One thing? What is that?"

She ran from the porch straight to him and threw her arms about his neck. "I haven't married you!"

Chapter 11

Their eyes met as he tilted her chin upward with his palm. "What? What do you mean? I don't get it."

She blurted it out. "My father did it all to bring us together. The will, asking you to mentor me, everything. He wanted us together."

Bane raised his eyes heavenward. "That is so like Charlie. He sang your praises from the first day I met him. I never suspected. That ornery old geezer. Why didn't I see it?"

"I wanted to tell you I was sorry. Sorry for ever suspecting you of foul play. Sorry for being afraid of you. I owe you an apology, Bane. I should've known better. Everyone thinks so highly of you. Even the man at the bookstore in Kansas City—"

He grasped her by the shoulders. "Bookstore? In Kansas City? What are you talking about?"

It was time to come clean; it was only fair he knew everything she'd learned. She told him about her meeting with the bookstore owner and how he'd told her about Carol and Bud and little Carrie. All of it.

He lowered his head and touched his fingertips to his temples. "I guess I should have told you myself. I—I just couldn't. I wasn't sure you'd understand. That anyone would understand. No one will ever know the pain I went through when I lost my wife and my baby girl. I didn't want to live. If it hadn't been for my decision to stay behind and let them go with Bud, they might still be alive. It was all my fault."

"No! It wasn't your fault. It was part of God's plan. You should know that, Bane. Someday you'll understand it all, but for now, God must want your life to go on. I think He wants us to be together." She put a hand on his shoulder; she knew she was resurrecting old memories he'd worked hard to bury. "I'm sorry for asking questions about you. But when you love a man you want to know all about him."

"Why didn't you just ask me outright?" he rebuked softly. He blinked through misty eyes, as if his emotions were tearing his insides apart.

She raised her face to his. "I did. Remember? You didn't want to tell me. Bane, no one seemed to know anything about you or your background. You appeared in Rock City out of nowhere, a man with enough money to buy the

Lazy Z, purchase all the equipment you'd need, build a fine house—"

He dabbed at his eyes with his sleeve, then put his warm hands on her shoulders, warming her heart as well.

"You could have been a member of the Mafia, for all we knew," she added with a wide smile.

He reared back his head and gave a laugh, a sound she welcomed. "Mafia? Me? I wish Charlie could have heard that one." He bent and kissed the top of her head. "Really, Rose. I guess I never realized how mysterious I must have seemed to the people around here. I can see why they all wondered about me." His lips slowly grazed her forehead. "I guess if you know about Bud's company and his death, you know where I got my money to do all this. He not only owned the business, half of which he'd given me when he took me in as a full business partner, he was heavily insured. So was Carol. It all came to me. With that, and the money we'd gotten selling off the patents, I was set for life." His arms circled her shoulders and she could feel him tremble as he went on with his story.

"But without my family, life was meaningless. I loved Carol. And Carrie. I didn't know what to do. I should have died with them." He paused. "They were everything to me. I'd always wanted to be a rancher, and I thought the physical exercise might help keep my mind off losing them. So after a year, I sold everything and moved out here and started the Wild Rose operation. Shortly after, I met Charlie and we became friends. He was a lot like Bud. But I had made a vow. I'd never put myself in the position of loving another woman like I had Carol. I didn't want to ever lose another child. I couldn't take a chance on being hurt like that ever again. I pledged myself to a life of celibacy." He took both her hands in his.

"Then Charlie died and you marched into my life." He gave a slight chuckle. "And I haven't been the same since. That first day, when we met in Ben Horner's office, I knew if I didn't fight as hard as I could, I'd fall for you. And I did, in nothing flat, but I couldn't let myself believe it."

Rose could stand it no longer. She stood on her tiptoes and wrapped her arms about his neck. "Quit talking and kiss me, Bane Jacob."

Somehow that kiss was different from the other kisses they'd shared. There was a surrender, a pledge, a commitment to each other that hadn't been there before. It was a coming-home kiss. An I-love-you kiss. A passionate kiss. An I-want-to-be-with-you-forever kiss. And they both knew it.

Rose tried to give the deed back to Bane, but he wouldn't take it. "The only way I'll ever take it back will be as your husband. It's yours. No strings. You have two weeks to finish out your time. I'll abide by whatever decisions you make. In the meantime, I plan to court you like you've never been courted."

She loved his humor. It was one of the things that drew her to him in the first place. She touched his smooth-shaven face with her fingertips and smiled into his eyes. "Oh, Bane. I want you to court me, but I want something else, too."

He bent and trailed kisses down her face all the way to her mouth. "What? Anything."

"Help me ask God to forgive me for my sins. I want everything in my life to be right with Him. I want to know your Lord like you do." She lowered her eyes. "I've been reading the Bible you gave me."

Once again tears filled the big man's eyes, only this time he made no attempt to brush them away. "Oh, Rose. Of course, I'll help you. This is the happiest day of my life." He took her hand and led her back to the porch steps where they knelt together. Bane pulled a little New Testament from his pocket and together they read John 5:24 aloud. "Verily, verily, I say unto you, He that heareth my word, and believeth on him that sent me, hath everlasting life, and shall not come into condemnation: but is passed from death unto life." Then Bane carefully explained the simple plan of salvation to the woman he loved. Together, they bowed their heads and prayed.

A feeling of euphoria rose between them, a newness of life, and a love that was overwhelming as they walked hand in hand back to Marilyn. He kissed Rose again before closing the jeep's door and getting in on his side. "I love you, Rose Kinsey, and so does God."

"I know that now and I praise Him for the love of both of you." She leaned her head onto his broad shoulder as the little vehicle dipped and dropped across the furrows, then made its way down the gravel road toward the ranch. All was finally right with her soul.

Sheriff Johnson's car was parked in the circle drive and Nel and Bitty were standing in the yard when the two lovers reached the farmhouse. Bane pulled up alongside and bailed out. "What's up, Orin?" he asked as he bolted around the jeep.

"I need to talk to both you and Rose, Bane. I think you'll be interested in what I've got to say."

"Come on in the house, Sheriff," Nel offered. "I just made a fresh pot of coffee."

Orin Johnson tipped his hat. "I'll take some of that coffee, Nel. But this isn't a social visit."

Bane frowned as his arm circled Rose's waist. The party made their way to the kitchen door. Once everyone was seated and Nel had filled tall mugs, Sheriff Johnson began. "You know, when Rose first told me about the stirrup strap, I said to myself, that wasn't much. That strap could've been accidentally cut in the barn by a tool or something. Then she comes to me with that tale about the snake. I laughed and figured someone was playin' a joke on Bane, bein's it was his car they put it in. Next, old Jimmy at the garage tells me about those battery connections, and again, I wrote it off, since I figured it was some kid's sick joke. But when that fire hit the barn, I knew somethin' was up. Especially when that gas can turned up with the Wild Rose painted on it. It had to be someone who had easy access and who knew you both well."

Rose placed her mug on the table with a thud. "You knew about the gas can?"

Bitty spoke up. " 'Course he did, he's the one who found it."

"But—I saw you give it to Bane, in a brown bag."

"I suggested that," Orin volunteered. "I didn't want whoever left it to know we'd found it. It was obvious it'd been planted to throw us off the trail. Then, there was the problem of the shoe print under your window. Bane always left a pair of his boots in Rose's barn, ever since he started helpin' her with the work. Then, there were the flowers and the spider. Anyone could send those."

Rose smiled sheepishly at Bane.

The sheriff continued. "As things progressed, and each thing happened, a definite pattern began to form. All evidence led to Bane. But those of us who know Bane knew he'd never do those things. For any reason. So—that meant someone else was out to see he took the fall. But who?"

The group's eyes were glued on Sheriff Johnson as he continued. "It had to be someone who'd gain from either Rose leavin' early, before her year was up. Or—someone who'd gain by Bane taking the rap. I'll tell ya, I felt I'd reached a blank wall. There didn't seem to be anyone to blame. Until. . ."

"Until?" four people around the table asked in unison.

The sheriff narrowed his eyes. "Until I heard a big conglomerate was lookin' to buy property round here, thousands of acres for a feed lot. I couldn't get much information about it, but one day when I was havin' a burger at Hannah's, I saw Calvin sittin' in a corner booth, havin' what looked like a confidential conversation with this big, beer-bellied fella. The guy was dressed in a fine suit and wearin' one of those big, diamond horseshoe rings on his fat finger, like ya see in the movies. I asked Hannah who he was; he didn't look like he'd be a friend of Calvin's. She said when she filled their cups, she heard him tell Calvin if he'd do his part, they'd soon have what they needed and he'd be rich."

"Calvin?" Rose screamed as her hands flew to her face. "Not Calvin!"

The sheriff nodded his head. "Yes, Rose, Calvin."

Nel gasped and clamped her hands over her mouth. "You mean they was after Sweet Water?" she asked.

"That's the conclusion I came to, so I thought about the things happenin' to Rose, and the coincidence that Calvin worked here at the ranch, and I decided to do some checkin' on old Calvin. Guess what I found out?"

Bane spoke up as his fingers tightened around Rose's. "I'm almost afraid to hear. I'd never have believed it was Calvin. He was such a good worker. Did everything the way he was told. More than carried his share of the load. I thought I was a better judge of character than that. Guess I was wrong."

"We all make mistakes in judgment it seems." Rose shot him a look of remorse.

"He's been in prison three times, for fraud," Orin told them with a flare of his hands. "And he's needin' money real bad. Got gamblin' debts ya wouldn't believe."

Rose closed her eyes and felt sick to her stomach. "Poor Daddy. Do you think he knew about Calvin's record?"

Bane squeezed her hand again. "Probably. Knowing your dad, he'd give the guy the benefit of the doubt in a heartbeat. He believed in second chances."

Bitty chimed in. "Even third and fourth chances."

Orin took charge of the conversation again. "Well, Rose, you're going to have to find yourself another ranch hand. I picked Calvin up in town this morning and arrested him. He had an outstanding warrant in Indiana for guess what—arson. When I hit him with the facts, he confessed to setting the fire and all the other things. Seems he figured if he could scare Rose by making her think Bane had done all those things, she'd sell out cheap, rather than let Bane buy Sweet Water. And he figured if she was considering stayin' on the ranch and running it herself, maybe she'd be frightened enough to sell out anyway. Either way, he was making sure the conglomerate would get Sweet Water—and he'd get his money."

Bane pulled Rose into his arms. "Sorry, Rosebud. I should have listened to you and realized those things were serious, instead of making jokes about them."

She kissed his cheek. "I'm the one who should apologize. You did nothing wrong, but I blamed you for all of it. I should have known better. You'd never be a party to anything so cruel."

"Well," Orin interjected, "we all should've done things differently. But we didn't. I'm just glad it's over. And," he said, turning to Rose, "I don't know what your plans are, but I for one hope you'll decide to stay in Rock City and run your daddy's ranch. Permanently. You're a real asset to our little community."

Bane gave the sheriff a wink. "I think so, too, Orin."

The next two weeks were busy ones, with much work to do on the ranch. Bane tried to give Rose some space, but he couldn't leave her alone. If he wasn't on the phone with her, he was on her doorstep delivering cut flowers from his green-house or e-mailing her love notes, but he never pressed for her decision. He'd promised he wouldn't.

On the final day of her year, they met in Ben Horner's office and Bane signed the release paper. Sweet Water and all her father's holdings belonged to Rose Kinsey at last.

As they left the office, Rose stopped on the narrow sidewalk, just outside the building where she'd met Bane Jacob exactly one year ago. With a deadly serious face, she took him by the hand and looked directly into his dark eyes.

"I'm sure you're wondering about my decision, Bane. I've weighed things from every direction. With what I could get from the sale of Sweet Water to the conglomerate, and with what I could get from the sale of the Wild Rose and the other property you deeded over to me, I could live quite comfortably the rest of my life."

He moved to speak, but she silenced him with a motion of her free hand.

"You were a fool to deed that all to me, Bane Jacob. Now you have nothing and I have everything!" She dropped his hand, took one step back, and glared at him as he stood gaping at her, startled by her words. "I have one last thing to ask you."

He shuffled his feet, then planted them firmly as if to brace himself for what was to come.

"Where is the nearest place a couple in love can get a marriage license?" She grinned with an impish grin that spread into a broad victorious smile as she ran to the man she loved and flung herself toward him. "Hey, cowboy. Will you marry me?"

Bane caught her midair and whirled her about as he covered her face with kisses. "Rose, my wonderful Rose. I love you. Of course, I'll marry you. Just say when. How about now?"

The fifteenth of April, their wedding day, Rose stopped packing her suitcase for their honeymoon and listened. It sounded like Bane's truck. But why would he be coming to Sweet Water now? Didn't he remember it was supposed to be bad luck to see the bride on their wedding day?

"Rose, come down here," his voice echoed up from the kitchen.

She clutched the negligee she was folding to her bosom, her face shining with love for the man whose voice sent shivers up her back. "No. You're not supposed to see me today!"

"Rose, please. It's important," he begged. "Come down here, I have your wedding present."

Muffling a snicker, she pulled a chiffon scarf from her dresser drawer and draped it over her face, then made her way to the kitchen. She laughed aloud as she entered, until through the chiffon she saw a strange woman standing next to

Bane. He was smiling as happily as he did when a new colt was born.

Embarrassed, she jerked the scarf off quickly. "Sorry, I didn't know there was someone with you." She went to stand beside her fiancé and snuggled into the crook of his arm.

He reached for the stranger's hand. "Rose, this is your wedding present from me."

"I—ah—don't understand, Bane," she whispered as she searched his eyes for a clue.

"Meet Abigale. Your mother!"

Rose gasped and threw both hands to her mouth. "Mother?"

Abigale lunged forward and pulled her daughter into her arms. "Yes, Rose. It's Mother. I'm here. Bane found me and brought me here for your wedding, if you'll let me stay."

Rose hugged her mother close. "Of course, I'll let you stay. This is the best day of my life." Her body trembled with excitement as she turned to Bane. "Oh, Bane, I love you so. I'm not worthy of you."

Bane stood watching as mother and daughter embraced, pleased to have been the one who brought them together after all these years. "For you, Rose, I'd do anything."

He slipped his long arms about both women.

Rose's laughter faded as she turned to her mother and took her hand in hers. "Why, Mother? Why?"

Bane backed off a bit. "Why don't I leave you two alone? I know you have things to talk over—"

Rose grabbed his sleeve. "No, Bane. Stay. You're my family now, I want you here."

Abigale tugged her daughter onto the window seat beside her. "I owe you an explanation. Where do I begin?" She took a deep breath as she unfolded her story.

"Rose—I was so stupid. I met your father at the bus station in Hays when I was sixteen. I'd run away from home, from an abusive stepfather. I was hungry and your father bought me a meal, then brought me to Rock City and got the little cafe in town to hire me as a waitress. He even paid my first month's rent for the little room in an old boardinghouse. He was so kind to me, and although he was eight years older than I was, we enjoyed being together. When he asked me to marry him, I jumped at the chance to have a real home with a man who wanted to take care of me—"

"But—" Rose tried to ask a question, but her mother shook her head.

"Let me finish, then I'll answer your questions, okay?" She blinked hard and continued. "I loved Charlie, Rose. Honest I did. And I tried to fit in, to be the kind of wife he deserved. But I was so bored in Rock City. Then you were born and Charlie was the perfect father. Every minute he could steal away from the work on the ranch, he spent with you. After a while, I found myself jealous of my own daughter. When I'd complain, he'd say we'd have time to be together later, when you were grown. I can't believe I was so selfish. I thought maybe if I could change myself, my hair color, my makeup, wear fancier clothes, he'd notice me more. But even after I tried all those things, he barely noticed."

Bane pulled out his hanky and handed it to Abigale.

"I decided if your father wouldn't pay attention to me, I'd go places where someone would, and I left you with Nel and started hanging out with some of the not-so-nice women at the local bar. That's where I met Bill Babcock. He was a trucker from Boston. He was exciting and hung on me like I was the most beautiful woman he'd ever seen."

"But did you love him? Like Daddy?"

Abigale lowered her head and twisted the hanky in her hand. "Umm, I thought so at the time. Well, I'm sure you figured out what happened. I discovered I was pregnant again, only this time, Charlie wasn't the father. I didn't know what to do. I knew Charlie'd never let me take you from him, but I had another baby to consider. Before I made a decision, someone told your father about the affair. He shoved me down in a chair and asked me about it. I tried to deny it, but his source had seen us together a number of times, so eventually, I confessed. The next morning I threw up for three hours straight and he knew I was pregnant. He told me I could stay on as his legal wife and we'd live in separate rooms. We'd raise you together, he said, so you'd have both parents, but the baby I was carrying would have to go as soon as it was born. Either Bill could take it, or it could be adopted. Charlie said he still loved me, and could have forgiven almost anything, except his wife carrying another man's child. Bill wanted to take me with him, so I asked your father for a divorce. The only way he would give it to me was if I'd leave you behind with him. Either way, I would lose one of my children."

Bane sat down beside Rose and snuggled her close to his side. She grabbed his hand and held it fast in her quivering grip. "Then he didn't throw you out?"

Abigale laughed through her tears. "No, he'd never do that. He let me stay until Bill and I got things worked out. He was kind to me up to the day I left. I'll never forget him standing in the doorway waving good-bye, with tears running down his cheeks, as I drove away with Bill. I made a terrible mistake, Rose. Bill didn't want a wife and baby. He was a selfish man, and he was mean. Greedy and mean. It was like living with my stepfather all over again."

Abigale took a deep breath. "Our little boy was born with Down syndrome. Bill had a hard time accepting him, and he has spent all the years since Billy's birth on the road. He only gets home six or eight times a year, and then I count the days till he's gone again. We're both miserable when he's home."

"And Billy?" Bane asked.

"He's doing okay. He goes to a day care while I work. It's a lonely life, Rose. I've wanted to contact you so many times. But what could I have said to you? That I left you for a man who beats me? To give birth to a child who wasn't wanted? No, I knew you had a good life with Charlie. To contact you would only ruin it, and I knew Nel was here for you."

Abigale reached for her daughter's hand. "And look at you now. You're all grown up and getting married to a fine man who loves you dearly. Bane went to a lot of trouble to find me and he wouldn't take no for an answer when he wanted to bring me to you. You two have a wonderful future ahead of you. I am so proud of you, Rose, and I pray that one day you'll find room in your heart to forgive me."

Rose cupped her hand under her mother's chin and gazed into eyes as clear and blue as her own. "Mother, I've made mistakes in my life, too. We all have. Of course I forgive you. Just as God has forgiven me. I've been desperately trying to find you, ever since I discovered the box in the attic. There'll always be room for you and Billy here at Sweet Water. Come anytime you can, and for as long as you want. I want you to be part of my life." She reached a hand toward her soon-to-be husband, her soul mate. "Our life."

Bane took her hand and rubbed his fingers over the gold engagement ring he'd placed on her hand so recently. "And Abigale, you'll never have to worry about your daughter. I would lay down my life before I'd let anything happen to Rose. She's my family now."

At exactly seven o'clock, wearing her mother's wedding gown, Rose stood at the back of the church, waiting for the organist to begin playing "Here Comes the Bride." As perfect as the day was, she felt a sadness that her father wasn't there to give her away. Her fingers rose to the tiara, and as she touched it she thought about Abigale wearing it so long ago; wondered if Abigale had been as happy on her wedding day. The music started, and Rose moved down the aisle on Bitty's arm toward Bane Jacob, the man she loved. As she slipped her hand into his, she felt his fingers tighten over hers. At last, she was to become his wife.

Pastor Nelson smiled at the couple and began the ceremony, then asked, "Who gives this woman to be married to this man?"

"I do!" Abigale answered proudly, her head held high.

Pastor Nelson smiled first at Bane, then at Rose, then at the woman. "And how are you related to the bride?"

The slightly graying blond woman stepped from her place and kissed her daughter's cheek. "I'm Abigale. Her mother."

Bane bent and whispered into Rose's ear, "How do you like my wedding present, Petunia?"

"Which one?" Rose whispered back with a silly grin as she hiked up the hem of the delicate satin gown. There on her feet were the flame-red boots Bane had given her that first morning at Sweet Water. "I told you I'd save them for my wedding, and I did!"

Bane let out a chuckle loud enough for all the wedding guests to hear. "You're wearing the boots I gave you!"

It was a good thing they were videotaping the wedding, because the bride was afraid she wouldn't remember a thing that was said. Except when Pastor Nelson proclaimed, "I now pronounce you husband and wife, united together by the love you have for each other and for God. You may kiss the bride."

And he did.

Bane Jacob kissed Rose Jacob with a passion that had been smoldering for one full year.

THE GROOM WORE SPURS

Chapter 1

Unpleasant thoughts plagued Dina Spark as the endless, barren miles of Nebraska's West I-80 ticked by on her car's odometer. Every ranch, every herd of cattle, every fence post brought back memories of the way her rancher father had been before a wheelchair had become his prison and his only lifeline to mobility. He had known the risks and been more than willing to take them, regardless of the costs to him and those around him. "What price we humans pay for glory," she proclaimed aloud with a shake of her head.

She glanced at a road sign as it whizzed past her window, then at her watch, before leaning back in the seat to enjoy the remainder of her ride. This extended weekend at her friend's house was exactly what she needed. Thirty miles later, when she came to the familiar little town of Chitwood, she signaled her turn and headed south, eventually making a left onto the road she thought was the one to take her to Burgandi's house. After driving nearly another fifteen miles, and the country road morphing into nothing more than two dusty tire tracks, she realized she was hopelessly lost. In near panic, she scanned the road ahead of her, looking for a safe place to turn around when, suddenly, the engine died and her car came to an abrupt stop. *Oh, no. This can't be happening! I have no idea where I am!*

Instinctively she did what she always did when faced with a problem, closed her eyes and prayed. But, even then, the car refused to start. Frustrated, she pulled her cell phone from her purse and dialed Burgandi's number, hoping she and her father would come and help her. But that idea, too, proved futile, as the message on her phone's screen read NO SIGNAL.

The heat from the afternoon sun bore down on her, turning her perspiration into outright beads of sweat. They trickled down her forehead as she exited her car, lifted the hood, and peered at the many belts and gadgets. Other than checking the battery terminals, she had no idea what else to do. Maybe she could walk to a farmhouse and they could call Burgandi. But after sheltering her eyes from the blinding brilliance of the sun, she realized there wasn't a farmhouse in sight. Hot, annoyed, and very much alone, she climbed back inside to contemplate her options. Walk or stay in the car until someone happened down the road, which might be hours.

Walking won.

Yanking her keys from the ignition, she placed them in her purse and was about to sling its strap over her shoulder and roll up the window when she heard the faintest sound of an engine. Glancing over her shoulder she saw a truck of some sort wending its way toward her, leaving a curly trail of dust in its wake. As it came closer, she could plainly see its worn paint job and cracked windshield, as well as numerous dings and dents. The old truck looked like a junkyard reject. Why hadn't she brought the can of pepper spray her mother had suggested?

She sat, half grateful, half in fear, as the truck came to a stop a few feet behind her rear bumper and the driver emerged, his face nearly hidden by a voluminous scruffy beard, and wearing worn clothing that didn't look much better than the truck. She was about to reach for the lock button and raise the window when the man walked toward her.

"Got car trouble?" he asked simply.

She nodded. "Yes. It quit on me. It won't start."

He tugged at his stained ball cap, pulling it lower on his forehead. "Don't you know this road doesn't go anywhere? It dead-ends down there a mile or so, where the old bridge finally washed out. Didn't you see the sign?"

What sign? Had she missed it? "No, I guess I didn't. I was looking for the Leyva place."

He frowned, or so she thought. It was hard to tell with that full beard and his ball cap pulled low. "No Leyvas on this road. You must have made a wrong turn."

"Maybe. It did seem like I drove more miles after I turned off at Chitwood than the other times when I've been in this area."

"Don't feel bad. The roads around here can be pretty confusing." He gestured toward her hood. "Did you check your battery terminals?"

She nodded. "Yes."

"You didn't run out of gas?"

"No, my gauge is still showing a quarter of a tank."

He moved to the front. "Pop your hood. Let me take a look."

She pressed the hood release then climbed out and stood watching over his shoulder as his hands moved capably from one area to another. If he didn't know what he was doing, he had her fooled. After a few minutes he lowered the hood, letting the latch engage with a snap. "It kinda looked like the connection on one of your battery terminals was a bit loose, so I tightened it. Jump in and see if she'll start."

She crawled in and gave the key a turn. Nothing. If he hadn't been standing there she would have cried. "How far is it to the nearest repair shop?"

"One that could fix a car like yours? Maybe twenty miles."

Dina leaned against the headrest with a sigh of defeat. "Is there a farmhouse nearby where I could call someone? My cell phone isn't getting a signal."

"Yeah, I know. Mine isn't, either," he said slowly, as if contemplating the nearest place. "The Coulter ranch is about three miles from here. I could take you there."

While his offer was generous and she appreciated it, she was still afraid of him.

What if he was telling her that her car was unfixable so he could lure her into his truck and take her to some even more isolated spot? No one would ever know he was the one who had picked her up. "But if you want me to take you, you'd better hurry. I gotta get back and do my chores."

Frazzled thoughts ran through her head. Normally, she would never crawl into a truck with a stranger, but it appeared she had no other choice. "Thank you," she struggled to say, still not sure what she was about to do was wise. "I'd appreciate a ride to the Coulter place."

She grabbed her purse from the seat and, as an afterthought, the small case containing her makeup and a few other things she hated to leave behind, locked her car, then followed him to his truck.

After opening the passenger door he went to work brushing the seat off with the palm of his hand. "Sorry about the mess," he told her as bits of straw, paper, broken Styrofoam cups, empty pop cans, and a few things she didn't recognize fell out onto the dirt road. "It's usually not this bad."

Without a word of response, she climbed inside, cradling her bag and her purse in her lap.

He rounded the truck and climbed into the driver's seat, slamming the door three times before it finally caught hold. She grabbed the armrest as his truck backed over the ruts and headed in the direction they'd come. They rode in awkward silence for quite some time, which was just fine with her.

Finally, he said, "I take it you're not from around here."

"No. I'm from Omaha."

His gaze left the road long enough to give her a half smile. "Omaha, huh? Big-city gal?"

"I guess you could say that. I used to live in Farrell, a small town northwest of there, but I moved to Omaha after. . ." She paused. He didn't need to know her family history. "When I went to college. I'm a nurse."

"Good profession. I guess a nurse could live about anywhere and find a good-paying job."

She nodded and then, despite the heat, quickly rolled up her window, the dust from the road nearly gagging her. "Yes, I guess I could."

"Me, I'm a rancher."

"You enjoy it?"

"Oh, yeah. It's a hard life, and some years the pay is lousy, but I couldn't live in the big city like you. I have to have the wide-open spaces. It's not much farther to the Coulter place."

That was good news. Despite the kindness he'd displayed so far, she was anxious to get out of that truck and call her friend.

"Too bad you couldn't have broken down closer to civilization. Hardly anyone uses that old road. I haven't been on it in months myself, but I wanted to check out a piece of property down by the creek I heard might be for sale."

"I'm glad you came along." And she was glad. Now that they were near the Coulter place, most of her fear had subsided and she'd begun to think of him more as an angel sent from God than the villain she'd been afraid of when he'd first come along.

The Coulter ranch turned out to be a lovely place. A woman came out onto the porch and waved as his old truck rolled to a stop in her driveway.

"Brought you a damsel in distress," he explained good-naturedly as he helped Dina exit the truck. "Her car broke down out on the old Bennington road. I did all I could to get it started but nothing worked. Our cell phones couldn't get a signal. We hoped she could use your phone."

"Of course she can." The woman motioned to Dina. "Come on inside where it's cool. You two look like you're about to melt."

He lifted his hand. "Thanks, Mrs. Coulter, but not me. I gotta scoot. Got chores to do."

Before Dina realized it, the man had climbed back in his truck and started the engine. With a wave, he was gone, and she hadn't properly thanked him or even asked his name.

"You're mighty lucky Will happened down that road," Mrs. Coulter said, smiling as she closed the door behind the two.

Dina nodded. "Yes, I am. I'm sure he was sent by God."

Mrs. Coulter spun around, her brows raised. "By God? Does that mean you believe in Him?"

Dina smiled proudly. "Yes, ma'am, I do."

The woman smiled back. "I'm mighty proud to hear that. That makes us kinfolk. The phone is right there on the table."

Will checked his watch. He'd have to hustle to get everything done before he headed out for his long weekend. But he was glad he'd taken time to help that woman. He was just sorry he hadn't been able to get her car running. Too bad such a rotten thing had to happen to her. She seemed like such a nice person. Pretty, too. He wished they had exchanged names. Not that it made any difference. They'd probably never see each other again. But it would have been nice to think of her by name and not just as the nice woman he'd tried to help.

He pressed the accelerator closer to the floor. He had to put all thoughts aside and concentrate on his own weekend. Because being distracted in his line of work could cause things to happen that never should. His mind needed to be clear, with his thoughts totally focused on what he was doing. Anything else could bring injury, or maybe even worse.

Chapter 2

Burgandi grinned at Dina as the two friends floated on the creek on their air mattresses the next morning. "I'm glad you came. I've missed you."

"I'm glad, too. Getting to spend time with you was well worth the long drive. But I have to admit I was terrified of that man when he stepped out of that truck, looking like he did."

"Other than his scruffy appearance and your description of his dilapidated old truck, you haven't told me much about the man himself. How old was he?"

Dina giggled. "I have no idea. With that heavy beard, I couldn't see much of him. I can't believe I missed my turn."

"Some of the road signs out here are so faded they're hard to see."

Burgandi took a cautious step onto the rickety dock at the creek's edge then tossed Dina a towel. She caught it and wrapped it, turban-style, around her wet hair.

"That's what Will said."

"I thought you said he didn't tell you his name."

"He didn't. That's what Mrs. Coulter called him. I wish I would have asked his full name, his address, too, so I could have sent him a thank-you card."

"Do you realize it's only three weeks until our committee meeting in Cheyenne?"

Dina nodded. "I know and I'm excited about it. I've never been there before."

"Me, either." Burgandi picked up their bottles of suntan lotion and her own towel. "Come on. We'd better hurry. Mom's probably got lunch ready."

By the time they got back to the house, Dina's car was sitting in the driveway. Burgandi's mother smiled as she greeted them. "Guess what the mechanic found? Your gas gauge had stopped working. You only *thought* you had gas. Of course our little repair shop didn't have a one in stock. You'll have to have a new one installed when you get back to Omaha. But they filled your tank and set your trip meter at zero, so you'll know when it needs filled again."

"No wonder it quit on me! Where is Mr. Leyva? I want to thank him."

"He's out in the barn. He said to go on without him. By the way, Dina, how is your father doing?" Mrs. Leyva asked as the girls sat down at the table.

Dina fingered her napkin. "He's about the same, and I guess always will be."

"Is he bitter about his accident? So many people who suffer injuries that incapacitate them like that tend to get bitter."

"He's not only bitter, he's vindictive, arrogant, hateful, and, worst of all, he takes out his anger on my mom. I hate him for it. If it wasn't for wanting to be with her, I'd never go to that house."

"Dina, don't talk that way. He *is* your father!"

"But, Mom," Burgandi pled on Dina's behalf, "he brought it on himself. Dina and her mother begged him to give up bull riding after that first brush he'd had with death and he wouldn't. If he didn't care about himself, he should have cared about his family. He's in a wheelchair for life. He can't even go into the bathroom without someone's help."

Dina hesitated, unsure she wanted to admit what she was about to say but forged ahead anyway. "I took it as long as I could before I moved out and got my own apartment. I tried to assume some of Mom's responsibilities, but he wouldn't let me. He said it was her *duty* because she'd vowed to take care of him for better or for worse when she married him. Get that? It was her duty, as if he owned her."

Mrs. Leyva's hand went to her chest. "I—I had no idea."

"As a Christian, I know I shouldn't harbor such bad feelings toward him. He wears his disability like an award for bravery, but I see it as punishment for not listening to his family and quitting while he was ahead. That's why I've made myself a vow that I will never, ever, date a man who has anything to do with rodeos. I refuse to end up like my mother."

"But, Dina, you used to be a barrel racer."

She lowered her gaze. "Yes, I did. In fact I had hoped I'd get to be good enough to someday win the regional finals. But that all ended the day my father got hurt. Although injuries in barrel racing are pretty rare, it does happen. I decided then, the risk of being injured wasn't worth the thrill and the excitement of winning. I just wish my father had realized it before he ended up in that chair."

"But, dear, very few are injured as seriously as your father," Mrs. Leyva countered. "Rodeo is a sport. A lot of people here in western Nebraska take part in rodeos."

"That's true. Some rodeo events are fairly harmless and participants rarely injured, but those events don't attract as many dedicated fans and spectators as bull riding. Why? Because people like to see someone put their life on the line. If they took the bull-riding event out of rodeos, the attendance would drop considerably."

"Mom, if you'd seen how Dina's dad has changed since his last encounter with a bull, you'd understand why she feels the way she does. That man is nothing like he used to be."

Mrs. Leyva took Dina's hand. "From what you say, I assume he isn't a Christian. It sounds as if that man desperately needs the Lord. Considering the way he's confined to his home, you and your mom may be the only ones who will be able to reach him for Christ." Dina felt a slight squeeze on her hand. "Think about it, honey. Keep the door open, if only a crack. He may be all you've said, but he is your father."

As if eager to change the subject, Burgandi tugged on Dina's free hand. "Speaking of fathers, Mom has Dad's lunch in the oven. Why don't we take it out to him?"

Dina sent a gentle smile toward Mrs. Leyva. "Thanks for the great lunch, Mrs. Leyva. I especially loved the salad."

It was nearly ten thirty the following Monday morning before Dina was able to take a break at the hospital where she served as a nurse in the trauma unit. Two shootings, a drug overdose victim, and a man whose arm had been badly mangled in an industrial accident had taken up most of her time since she'd reported to work a little before seven. She twisted the lid off the juice bottle she'd selected from the vending machine and took a long, cool, refreshing drink. It tasted good. On impulse, she stepped outside and pulled her cell phone from her purse, turned it on, and dialed Burgandi's number. "Hi, sweetie, I just wanted to thank you again for our wonderful weekend. I had a great time." She could almost see her friend's smiling face on the other end.

"Hi, yourself. I loved having you here. How's it feel to be back to work?"

"Good. This has really been a morning. How's it going for you?"

"Busy. I was about to call you. I just heard from Celeste about the committee meeting we'll be having in Cheyenne. She had a request for us."

"What kind of request?"

"She explained that each year during the planning session for our convention the chairperson arranges for those on her committee to perform a number of public service hours in whatever city we're meeting. She said the media is always eager to cover things like that, and it's a great way to let people know what's happening in the field of nursing. Since you and I are both on the planning committee, and both nurses in emergency-type areas, she asked if the two of us would mind volunteering."

"To do what exactly? I hadn't realized we'd be doing anything except working on next year's convention plans."

"She gave me a few examples from last year, when the committee met in Atlanta. Two nurses helped with the administering of flu shots to senior citizens; a couple spent several evenings helping a new industrial plant set up their first-aid facility. I think she said one or two others assisted by passing out brochures in a kiosk set up in one of the local shopping malls."

Dina shrugged. "If it means you and I will be working together, tell Celeste to count me in. Sounds like fun."

"Great! I was sure you'd say yes."

"Dina! Come quick!"

She turned at the sound of her name to find one of her coworkers hurrying toward her, and from the expression on his face she knew it was anything but good news.

"Bad accident out on 680! The ambulances will be arriving any minute."

"On my way, Jim!" Dina tossed her juice bottle into the trash can near the doorway then hurriedly said into her phone, "Sorry, sweetie. My break's over. Incoming emergency. Gotta go. See you in Wyoming."

Awestruck was the only word Dina could think of to describe the way she felt as she sat in Cheyenne's Nagle Warren Mansion's parlor, waiting for Burgandi to arrive. The entire place was far more grandiose than she'd expected, from its ceiling-high mirror above the magnificent cherrywood fireplace to its lovely Aubusson rug. The brochure she'd found on the table said the mansion had been built in 1888 by Erasmus Nagle and later purchased by Jim Osterfoss, who had turned it into the present bed-and-breakfast establishment.

"Hi, girlfriend. Can you believe this place?"

Dina spun around to face her friend. "Hey, hi. I was beginning to wonder when you'd get here. When you told me Celeste had been lucky enough to get us into one of Cheyenne's nicest B and Bs, I never expected it to be this nice. I can hardly wait to see our rooms." Her eyes narrowed as she suddenly sobered. "But—nice rooms or not—if I'd had any idea the Cheyenne rodeo would be going on at the same time as our meeting—I might not have come."

Burgandi reached out and gave her a hug. "That's why I didn't mention it. But, buck up, kiddo. One more day, and this year's rodeo will be history. Besides, you and I aren't here to be entertained. We're going to be stuck in meetings for the next four days."

"Whew, I had no idea the Saturday morning traffic would be this bad. I didn't think I'd ever get here."

The two turned in unison as a pretty redhead with a soft-sided briefcase tucked under each arm hurried toward them.

"The others are already upstairs in our suite." Celeste nodded toward the elegant cherrywood stairwell. "I haven't had a chance to tell you why we're staying in such a luxurious place. Mr. Bellows, a wealthy man who lives in Casper, ended up in the hospital with back surgery and couldn't make it to the rodeo. And of course his family didn't want to come without him. So, since I had taken such good care of Mr. Bellows' mother, who lives here in Cheyenne, when she was in the hospital, and I'd mentioned to him that I was looking for a place to house our committee, he phoned and offered me his suite. And, get this, since he'd paid for it in advance, he's not charging us a dime!"

Dina's jaw dropped. "You're kidding! This place is magnificent. The cost per night must be astronomical!"

"I'm sure he's writing it off on his taxes as a public service donation."

"Even so, that was really nice of him," Burgandi inserted.

Motioning for them to follow, Celeste began climbing the stairs. "He said we should enjoy ourselves, that he considered it his privilege to help us out."

The suite Mr. Bellows had reserved took their breath away as they entered it. It was comprised of two completely autonomous rooms, joined by a common door.

"This is the Francis E. Warren Room," Celeste explained, lowering her briefcases onto the desk. "That other door leads to the Clara Warren Room. You two will be staying there. Since this is the larger room, there is plenty of space for four of us in here."

Dina couldn't help but gasp as the three of them stepped into the Clara Warren Room. With its ceiling-high windows, authentic rose-encrusted Victorian wallpaper, and its king-sized wicker and leather sleigh bed, it was truly one of the most richly decorated and feminine rooms she had ever seen.

Celeste scurried about the room, lowering the blinds, plumping bed pillows, and checking the thermostat. "We're due at the Synergy Café in an hour. Maybe you'd like to freshen up and then rest until the others are ready." She moved quickly to the door leading into the adjoining suite. "I hope you don't mind but, since we hadn't planned to officially start our meetings until tomorrow, I've scheduled several of our volunteer public service assignments for this evening."

"That's fine with me. What will Burgandi and I be doing?"

Celeste frowned. "The list is in one of my cases, but don't worry about it," she added with a smile. "Trust me, whichever task I've assigned you will be fun. I'll be delivering you to your location and picking you up after you're finished."

Since all of the members of the planning committee already knew one another, they had a great time visiting over lunch as they renewed old friendships and caught up on the four months since they'd last seen one another. Knowing most of the restaurants would be overflowing with rodeo patrons during the dinner hour, the six had opted to have pizza delivered to their room. By five thirty they had eaten, freshened up, changed clothes, and were on their way to their first assignment.

Barbara and Tracy were the first two to be dropped off. Their assignment was handing out brochures at the kiosk in the Frontier Mall.

"You still haven't said where the two of us are going," Dina reminded Celeste as the minivan exited the mall parking lot.

Celeste grinned at Dina's image in the rearview mirror. "I'm keeping it a surprise until we get there."

Kitty was the next one to exit the van. Her assignment was at the Aspenwind Assisted Living Community on College Drive. "The head nurse is expecting you. I'll come back and help you as soon as I deliver Dina and Burgandi," Celeste told her, handing her a fancy pink tote with the words NURSING IS MY BAG embroidered on its side. "Take this with you. I told them we'd be showing a video on the importance of geriatric exercise."

Though Kitty seemed a little apprehensive about working alone until Celeste returned, she waved and offered a faint smile.

"You're next. We'll be there in less than ten minutes."

Dina and Burgandi exchanged glances then settled back in their seats and relaxed. It was obvious Celeste wasn't about to tell them where they were going. But wherever it was, from the line of traffic in which they were tangled, Dina concluded it must be somewhere near the rodeo grounds.

Minutes later as the van turned onto Carey and Celeste flipped on her turn signal, Dina thought she was going to be sick.

Chapter 3

The sign straight ahead read Frontier Park—Home of the Cheyenne Rodeo.

Seeming to sense Dina's fear, Burgandi grabbed her arm. "It's okay, honey. Maybe—"

But before she could finish her sentence Celeste blurted out, with all the pride of a newly proclaimed Miss America, "We're here! You two are going to have the privilege of working in one of the famous Justin Sportsmedicine Team mobile centers. Aren't you excited?"

Excited was definitely not the word to explain how Dina felt at that moment.

Celeste beamed. "Normally, the only persons allowed to work on the Justin team are those who have been prequalified and officially authorized. But when I explained the kind of work you two do, and the world of experience you've had in your trauma units, they were eager to have you serve." She showed the man at the gate some sort of pass, then pulled on through and came to a stop near a big, shiny red gooseneck-trailer that had to be thirty-five or forty feet long. "I'll try to be back by ten o'clock. Dr. Pratt, the doctor in charge, is expecting you."

Just the thought of seeing a cowboy risk his life by participating in something so dangerous, then expecting others to volunteer to help put him back together again, made Dina want to turn and flee on foot. However, rather than make a scene, she forced herself to calm down. It was apparent Celeste thought she was doing them a favor when she had assigned her and Burgandi to work as part of the Justin team. After all the trouble the woman had gone to, she certainly didn't want to appear ungrateful. Celeste had been nothing but kind to her.

Burgandi grabbed the handle and pulled open the door. "I'll stay, but Dina's not much of a rodeo person. Maybe it would be best if she went back and spent the evening working with you and Kitty."

Dina hurriedly slipped out of her seat to join her. "No, it's fine, Burgandi, honest. I'll stay with you." Then forcing a smile, she turned to Celeste. "We'll see you about ten."

As Celeste drove off, Burgandi lodged her hands on her hips. "Why'd you tell her you'd stay?"

Dina rolled her eyes. "Because I didn't want to look like a baby. I'm a professional. It's about time I decided to act like one. But don't expect me to set foot outside of this trailer. The only cowboys I plan to see are the ones who need medical assistance, and I'm not too crazy about seeing them."

Burgandi followed Dina as she made her way up the steps of the trailer. "Yes, ma'am, whatever you say."

"You must be Dina and Burgandi," the man who greeted them at the door said as they entered the trailer. "Sure glad you're scheduled to be here tonight. Somehow we ended up shorthanded. In addition to one of our doctor's wives going into labor, there was a twelve-car pileup out on I-80. Two of our nurses are stuck out there. I understand you're trauma nurses and you've both had some training in physical therapy."

"Yes, that's true, but Dina is far more qualified than I am." After a quick glance in Dina's direction, Burgandi gave the man a smile. "I live in a small town in southwestern Nebraska, but she works in a large hospital in Omaha and treats many more injuries than I do. We're both glad to be here. Just tell us what to do."

To Dina's surprise, meeting and working with the medical staff on board the mobile unit turned out to be a real treat. She had assumed the doctors were local doctors who volunteered each time the rodeo came to their city. But, instead, these were people who, many times a year, traveled from one rodeo to another, giving as much of their time and professional expertise as they could, because of their love of the sport.

Fortunately, other than a couple of possible concussions and a broken wrist, most of the injuries they treated during the evening were minor, with most only requiring some taping up. With her father being involved in rodeo as long as he had, Dina, much to the surprise of the doctors, was well versed in the proper taping technique and wrapping of rodeo injuries.

"Hey, that rookie bull rider Wayne Warner is up next," Dr. Pratt told them as he finished up on their latest patient. "You girls ought to go watch him."

Dina shook her head. "Let someone else go. I'll stay here."

The man shrugged. "Suit yourself, but right after Wayne rides, Billy Bob is the next one up. You sure don't want to miss him. He's the main reason some of these fans come. He's had a terrific week. I wouldn't be one bit surprised if he didn't break his own record tonight."

"He's a bull rider?" Burgandi asked, as if considering his offer.

Dr. Pratt reared back with a laugh. "You haven't heard of Billy Bob? Oh, yeah, he rides bulls, the meaner the better for that man. I hear he's drawn a mean one tonight. Between him and that bull they may score as high as ninety. Maybe even higher."

Though the evening was warm, Dina wrapped her arms about herself and felt a sudden chill as vivid pictures of her father flying off that bull's back and onto the dirt beneath the huge animal's hooves filled her mind.

"Do you care if I go, Dina?" she vaguely heard Burgandi ask.

"No—go, if you want. It's fine. I–I'll stay."

Later, as she applied tape to a sprained wrist for one of the bareback contestants, Dina could hear the announcer's voice and the roar of the crowd. *Billy Bob*, she thought to herself. *Stupid man. He might be a hero today, but tomorrow he may be wishing he'd never even heard of rodeo. One fall, one misplaced step, one moment of hesitation and his career could be over.*

After she'd finished taping the man's wrist she busied herself by checking out the many nooks and crannies of the well-equipped mobile unit. It surprised her to find they had not only an intermittent compression unit, but a number of TENS units—nerve stimulation devices used to relieve pain—as well as any kind of first-aid supply they would ever need. Once the two men Dr. Pratt had mentioned had finished their rides, Burgandi returned, all excited about the way the one called Billy Bob had stayed on his bull for the full eight seconds.

"You should have seen him, Dina. He was amazing! I've never seen anyone like him. He—"

Dina lifted her hand to silence her. "No more, please. I don't even want to hear about it, okay?"

Burgandi raised her shoulders in a shrug. "Okay, if you say so. Now, tell me what you've been doing while I was gone."

Since only a couple minor injuries happened after Billy Bob's ride, and the other members of the team were taking care of those contestants, Dina and Burgandi decided to wait outside the trailer, enjoying the night's breeze until Celeste arrived.

"How'd it go?" Celeste asked as Burgandi slid open the back door and the two climbed in. "Did Billy Bob have a good ride?"

Dina flinched at the sound of his name. *Billy Bob! Is that all people around here think about?*

"He was wonderful!" Burgandi responded immediately, sounding awestruck. Then glancing at Dina, she added less exuberantly, "Strange, but wonderful."

Celeste shifted slightly in her seat. "Now that we all know what we're supposed to do, I thought we would each take on the same assignment tomorrow night."

Dina couldn't believe what she was hearing.

"I'm hoping both Channel 5 and KLWY Fox will show up, someone from the newspaper, as well. I figured, if we got one evening under our belts, we'd be better prepared in case they wanted to interview us." She twisted in her seat to glance back at Dina and Burgandi. "Your assignment probably has the best opportunity for coverage. Around here, rodeo is always top news. You don't mind doing it again, do you?"

Dina and Burgandi raised their brows at each other. "No, I guess not," Dina said slowly, her response lacking proper enthusiasm. But, knowing it was for a good cause, she added a smile. "They really seemed to appreciate our help."

Celeste grinned at her in the rearview mirror. "Good. I knew I could count on you. Our meeting in the morning will start at eight. It looks like tomorrow is going to be a very long day. I hated for our first meeting to be on a Sunday, but I was trying to schedule things so you wouldn't have to be away from your jobs any longer than necessary. I know several of you normally attend church. Maybe, while you're getting ready in the morning, you can find a good preacher on TV."

It was nearly three thirty the next afternoon before the nurses got away from their meeting at the bed-and-breakfast, and a few minutes past five before they returned from having a nice dinner at Celeste's favorite Mexican restaurant.

"I know I'm pushing you, but let's plan to leave here in no more than thirty minutes," she told the group as they entered their rooms. "Since this is the last night of the rodeo, the traffic is going to be heavier than usual. Oh, and you might want to wear something with a Western flair if you have it, in case you're interviewed."

"I guess you could call my blue jeans 'Western,'" Dina said in a hushed voice as she and Burgandi stepped through the adjoining door and into their room. "I'm fresh out of Western-cut, plaid, gripper-fastener shirts with saddle-stitching."

Burgandi gave her head a shake. "Aw, come on, Dina. Give Celeste a break. She's doing her best. You have to admit we did get a lot accomplished at our meeting today. Celeste is a good organizer."

Dina kicked off her shoes and stretched out full-length across the bed, clasping her hands behind her head. "I know and, even though I don't sound like it, I appreciate her efforts. It was really rude of me to make that comment, and I apologize, but this rodeo thing is getting to me. The whole town is rodeo crazy. I've never seen anything like it."

"They don't call the Cheyenne rodeo the daddy of all rodeos for nothing. I'm sure it deserves that name," Burgandi countered with a glance at the clock on the nightstand. "I hate to rush you but. . ."

Dina pulled herself into a sitting position. "I know. I'm moving."

"Wish I would have known how to reach you," Dr. Pratt told the two as they entered the Justin trailer. "You wouldn't have had to come. More volunteers showed up tonight than we could possibly use. Probably because this is the night the big winners are announced."

Burgandi wrinkled up her face at the news. "Our driver just let us off at the gate, and she won't be back after us for several hours."

He gave her a wink. "Well, lucky you. I guess that means you two can go out into the arena and watch the show."

She brightened. "Really?"

"Sure, go out there and introduce yourselves to any of the men wearing a Justin shirt. He'll find you a good place to sit. Should be a great night. I heard Billy Bob drew Gray Ghost again. That bull is one of the meanest around. Other than Billy Bob, no one has been able to stay on that monster for more than a few seconds. Who knows? He may be the man to do it again!"

Dina turned to face the doctor. "If you don't mind, I'd rather stay here. I–I'm not interested in rodeo. Let someone else go in my place."

"Suit yourself. I can always use the company. Unless things go crazy out there and someone needs our services, it gets pretty boring in here just sitting around waiting for something to happen." He flashed a toothy grin before hastening to add, "Which is good, of course. The fewer people injured, the better."

With her expression displaying disappointment, Burgandi took hold of Dina's hand. "You might enjoy watching. You don't even want to give it a try?"

Dina gave her an emphatic, "No, I'm sorry, but I'm not going out there. You know how I feel about rodeos, especially bull riding!"

"Yes, sweetie, I do know, and I know how you feel about your dad. But not all cowboys are like him. Come and watch a couple of the events, then you can come back to the trailer when it's time for the bull riding, okay? I sure hate having to sit by myself again."

Dina never liked disappointing anyone, especially Burgandi, but what her friend was asking was too much. There was no way she was going into that arena and watch grown men, most who had families who loved them, pay their hard-earned dollars as entry fees then put their lives on the line, all because of the possibility of winning a little extra money and basking in a few minutes of glory. Maybe not every rodeo cowboy ended up like her dad, but some did. "I'm sorry, Burgandi. I can't. I just can't."

Burgandi gave her shoulder an affectionate squeeze. "Oh, honey, I understand. Forgive me. It was cruel of me to even ask."

Swallowing at her emotions, Dina forced a smile. "No harm done, but I don't want my hang-ups to keep you from enjoying yourself. Go on. You won't be alone. You'll be sitting with some of the other Justin volunteers."

Burgandi stood gazing at her for a long moment. "You sure? You don't mind?"

"Absolutely sure. Besides, we don't want Dr. Pratt getting lonely, and one of us has to stay in case any of the media show up and want an interview. After all the trouble she's gone to, Celeste would have a fit if we missed out on that." She reached out and gave Burgandi a little shove toward the door. "Have fun, but don't flirt with too many of those cute cowboys, you hear?"

Burgandi giggled. "I'll try to control myself, but some of those guys look pretty tempting in their worn jeans and cowboy hats." She headed for the door. "I promise I'll come back right after Billy Bob rides."

"No hurry. Don't worry about it." Dina followed her to the door, then stood watching until she disappeared into the crowd.

"Sure you don't want to go?" Dr. Pratt asked as he walked toward her, holding a box of Ace bandages.

"Thank you, but no. I–I'd rather stay here." She took the box from his hands and placed it in the cabinet where, she'd learned the night before, the bandages were stored.

Other than some minor injuries to a few calf ropers, a dislocated shoulder, and a badly twisted knee, very few came into the trailer for help. Dina felt good when Dr. Pratt asked her to assist instead of a couple of the regular volunteers who had also decided to remain in the trailer. He was a nice man who loved rodeo and, she found out as they conversed between patients, had been volunteering his expertise as part of the Justin medical team for the past ten years, often traveling great distances at his own personal expense to assist at his favorite rodeos.

Burgandi came back to check on her before the second-round bull-riding event started, all excited about the way Billy Bob's first ride of the evening had gone, though Dina had little interest in what she was saying.

"Heads up!" Dr. Ryan called out as he rushed through the door and hurried to one of the open beds in the trailer. "Wayne hit the dust big-time—probably got a monster of a concussion. The team is bringing him in now."

Dina pressed herself against the wall as they entered and carried the man on a gurney past her. "Too bad, folks," she heard the announcer's voice boom through the open door. "Hopefully, Wayne was only stunned and will be back soon. Up next is the man you've all been waiting for. One of your favorites! Bil—ly Bo—b!" he drawled dramatically as the crowd went wild with applause and shouting. "And he'll be riding one of the roughest, toughest, meanest bulls around. The bull that, three times, has deprived Billy Bob of his highest wins! Grraa—ay Ghoo—st! Who'll be the winner tonight? Our mysterious Bil—ly Bo—b? Or Grraa—ay Ghoo—st? Give Billy Bob a big Cheyenne Rodeo cheer, folks!"

Dr. Pratt let out a, "Yee haw! I gotta go watch that boy ride this time." Then turning to Dina he asked, "Sure you don't want to go?"

She shook her head. "Thanks for asking, but no."

"I'll be back as quick as his ride is over."

As soon as he was out the door, Dina moved toward Dr. Ryan to see if she could be of any assistance.

Billy Bob positioned himself along the top of the chute and watched as the big bull snorted and pawed his way along the narrow-railed wall toward the gate. He'd faced hundreds of bulls since he had started bull riding, but none as fierce as this one. In his opinion, Gray Ghost was the meanest, most cantankerous bull on the circuit. You never knew what he was going to do. Sometimes he came out of the chute, his head held low, his nostrils flaring, his eyes filled with fire, and headed straight toward the center of the arena before he began to kick and leap in the wild, unbridled dance for which he had become famous. No bull could kick as hard and leap as high as Gray Ghost. Other times, he'd start his leap-and-pivot routine the moment the gate opened, as if trying to crush his rider's shoulder or legs against the steel posts, dislodging him and causing great pain before the seconds had even begun to tick away.

But the thing that sent fear into the hearts of most of those who had been unfortunate enough to draw his name was the way Gray Ghost was able to defeat most riders with what his dedicated fans had begun to call his Tornado Twist. But Billy Bob had not only experienced that tornado twist and been defeated by it, he'd studied it by watching countless hours of videotape taken by other cowboys, of Gray Ghost in action, and he was ready for him. Though that bull had a mind of his own, and you never knew how he'd come out of the chute, he did have definite patterns, and if a rider could anticipate those patterns and work them to his advantage he'd have a far better chance for a winning ride.

Take your time, Billy Bob told himself, striving to be oblivious to the yelling of the crowd as he straddled the top rail and looked down at the beast he'd come to know so well. *Forget about the noise. There's no reason to hurry. This is our time together. It's Gray Ghost and me, just the two of us. Put everything else out of your mind. Concentrate on the bull. What is this beast thinking? Can he smell me? Does he know who I am? Does he remember me as the man who, several times, has stayed on his back for a full eight seconds and vowed to keep riding him until he scores over ninety?*

Almost as if the bull had read his mind, Gray Ghost reared back his head and for one brief second their eyes met. And in those eyes, Billy Bob could see a fierce determination, a doggedness, a resolve he had never before seen in a bull's eyes. It was as if Gray Ghost did remember and that his goal was to put an end to this man who dared to attempt to again ride on his back for eight seconds. And, for just the tiniest of moments, sweat poured from Billy Bob's forehead and dripped from his chin as he felt a trace of fear. He wiped at the sweat with his sleeve, leaving smudges of white and red face paint.

The fear he felt was not the fear any normal person would feel at being so close to such a powerful animal, but downright palpable fear—fear that he could taste and the feeling scared him. But, not about to let that bull rob him of the win and score he hungered for, he shook the feeling off and glared back, narrowing his eyes menacingly as he leaned closer to that massive head and the long horns that could tear a man apart. He had to let that bull know who was in charge. With the pang of fear behind him, now nothing more than an insignificant blip in his memory, he reached out, grabbed hold of a single horn, and gave it a yank, releasing it quickly, as the giant creature lunged upward in anger. Billy Bob gave Gray Ghost a grin of satisfaction. He'd shown him who was boss. All he felt now was the rush of adrenalin flowing through his veins as he sensed a win was in the making. After lifting his hat high above his head and waving it while smiling at the crowd, with the help of the chute workers, he lowered himself onto Gray Ghost's broad back, quickly slipping his hand, palm-up, into the braided leather loop of his favorite bull rope to stabilize himself.

"Watch him, Billy Bob!" one of the chute workers shouted above the roar of the crowd. "This one's dangerous!"

How well he knew. Though the bull was bucking and thrashing to the right and to the left within the confines of what little space the chute allowed him, Billy Bob took his time, making sure his leather glove was tied securely around his wrist before wrapping the rope around his hand. One error and it could be all over. When satisfied everything was as he wanted, he lifted his hand high over his head and yelled out, "Let 'er go!"

As keyed up as Gray Ghost had been while in the chute, Billy Bob fully expected him to plow out at full speed, kick and spin a few times, then go into his tornado twist. The bull had other ideas and thrust his body against one of the steel posts as he exited the chute, momentarily crushing Billy Bob's leg between the unyielding post and the bull's two-thousand-pound body, but Billy Bob barely noticed the pain. Pain went with bull riding. He'd learned long ago to ignore even the worst of pain and not allow it to rob him of his goal.

Gray Ghost zigzagged his way to the center of the arena, leaping what seemed to be straight up into the air, his hind legs flying upward and outward like an unsecured sail in a massive ocean storm. He lunged his body close to the ground, as if renewing his strength from some unseen power source. Then, using his strong legs to propel himself even higher, he thrust, kicked, and twisted, his horns seeming to be in every direction at once.

Despite Gray Ghost's sudden release of fury, Billy Bob held on, his mind concentrating on the points he intended to make as he mentally checked the position of his legs and feet, the placement of his body on the bull's back, the reach of his hand above his head. Gray Ghost was doing his part to score as many of his allotted fifty points as possible. Billy Bob had to do his part to score his fifty. Bull and man, though enemies, were a team. They had to make it into the nineties. Nothing less would be acceptable.

Finally, after what seemed like an interminable amount of time, the buzzer sounded.

❧

"Well, there goes the buzzer," Dina told the team with an indifferent shrug as they continued to work on Wayne. "I guess that means old Billy Bob stayed on the bull's back the full eight seconds. Good for him." Her tone was mocking. "I hope he's happy."

Dr. Ryan nodded toward the door. "Leave it open so we can hear how many points he scored."

She nodded then hurried to the scrub area to wash and sanitize her hands again before returning to the table.

"What a ride," a voice boomed over the loudspeaker. "That had to be one of Billy Bob's best rides. Folks, that boy is taking the rodeo world by storm. I fully expect we'll be seeing him in Las Vegas."

"That's where the finalists from all the rodeos go. The top rodeo in the country," Dr. Ryan explained. "Dr. Pratt and I always try to make it to that one."

Billy Bob smiled victoriously as he waved at the crowd. He and Gray Ghost had made it to the eight seconds, but apparently the big, angry bull didn't care. As two rodeo clowns came running toward them to make sure Billy Bob made a safe dismount, the bull changed directions, throwing him off balance. He leaned toward the opposite side, hoping to compensate, but Gray Ghost changed his plans again and immediately twisted in an unexpected direction. Rather than be thrown, Billy Bob leaped off the bull's back, hoping to land on his feet and make a quick exit, but his plans went awry and he found himself dangling at the enormous bull's side, his hand helplessly caught in the rope.

Everyone in the Justin trailer snapped to attention when suddenly the announcer screamed into the microphone, "No! Trouble! Trouble! Trouble! His hand is caught in the bull rope! Clowns, help him! Get him out of there! Help that man before he's dragged to death!"

Then silence.

No applause.

No yelling.

No whistling.

Absolute silence.

Dina's heart pounded wildly as she and the others listened, waiting for news of what was happening out on the field.

"Oh, folks," the announcer continued, his voice high and shrill from excitement. "I can't believe it. It looks like Gray Ghost is out to put an end to our Billy Bob. If those clowns don't get in there soon and cut that rope. . ."

Dr. Ryan pounded his hands on a nearby table. "Come on, clowns! Get in there! Hurry!"

Billy Bob couldn't believe what was happening. One moment his feet were hitting the ground. The next, he felt as if he were flying as his body was powerfully thrust into the air by Gray Ghost's erratic kicking and bucking movements.

And the pain, oh the pain, as his arm and shoulder bore the full brunt of his weight as his body hurled into the air then crashed to the ground. With his head bouncing and rebounding off of the bull's side, he was only vaguely aware of the clowns reaching and grabbing at the rope as Gray Ghost continued to move and grind, blocking their way to his prey. He tried in vain to reach out for the rope, but his strength was nearly gone and he was getting dizzy, light-headed, and—

"Whew, they've done it!" the emcee announced with great relief. "He's loose—and he's on the ground, but he doesn't look good!" A hush remained over the audience, until from somewhere in the stands, a slight applause erupted, then more followed. Soon everyone present was applauding. "That's the Justin Sportsmedicine Team putting Billy Bob onto that stretcher," the man boomed.

"Good work, boys!" The announcer heaved a heavy sigh and sounded greatly relieved. "What would we do without our bull-fighting clowns? These men risk their lives night after night to save others. What an unselfish group of men." He paused, as if so caught up in the scene playing out before him, he found it hard to express himself. "Billy Bob is young," he finally managed to say, "and he's strong. We'll have to pray that Gray Ghost didn't put an end to Billy Bob's bull-riding days."

Dr. Ryan gave his head a sad shake before turning to Dina and nodding toward the open bed next to Wayne. "Stand by, Dina. I'm sure Dr. Pratt is going to need all the help he can get. Too many things are happening too fast. First Wayne, now Billy Bob."

When Dr. Pratt rushed into the trailer, shouting out instructions to the men who carried the second gurney, Dina let out a shriek of surprise. She had expected to see a cowboy, a typical bull rider dressed in denim and leather chaps, but the injured man looked like one of the clowns. His red shirt was dotted with big yellow polka dots and he was wearing clown makeup! Surely this wasn't the famous Billy Bob. Had a clown been injured, too, while trying to save the man? If so, why hadn't the announcer mentioned it?

Dr. Pratt nodded toward the Justin team carrying the gurney. "Good job. Thanks, men." Then, turning toward Dina and the others who were ready to assist, he added as he leaned over the man, "You wouldn't believe how that bull threw him around. He took a lot of punishment. It looked like old Gray Ghost was determined to do him in. I'm concerned about his leg, but it's his arm and shoulder I'm worried about most," he said in a hushed tone, lifting his face toward Dina.

"He's fortunate his injuries weren't any worse."

"Come on, man," the doctor said, lifting first one of the man's eyelids and then the other as he shone a light in his face. "Come on, Billy Bob. You can't let Gray Ghost win."

Dina's jaw dropped. "That's Billy Bob?"

He nodded. "Yeah, what's left of him."

"He's a clown?"

"No, even though he looks like one. Nobody knows why he wears these silly shirts and that makeup. We've never seen him without it. He had a beautiful ride but as he tried to dismount, somehow his hand got tangled in the bull rope and that beast dragged him around the arena, kicking and throwing him like he was a rag doll. Then, when they finally got him loose, Gray Ghost turned and tried to trample him. For a second there, I thought it was the end of Billy Bob."

Dina reached for a tissue, intending, for cleanliness' sake, to remove the man's makeup, but Dr. Pratt hurriedly stuck out his hand to stop her. "No, don't! He left emphatic orders with all of us, if he were ever to be unconscious or impaired in any way we were not to remove his makeup. Why, we don't know. He never told us. But we all respect him and his wishes. Leave it on."

"But it would be—"

The man shook his head. "Leave it, Dina. If Billy Bob wants it left on, that's the way it's going to be." Then in a whisper, he added, "I'm sure they'll take it off at the hospital but for now we'll abide by his wishes."

She withdrew her hand then stood staring at the bull rider's face. Even though his forehead was painted a chalky white, his eyelids and the area around his eyes, a brilliant blue, his shaggy eyebrows, outlined in red, something about him looked familiar. She shrugged. Maybe she'd seen him on the news. "I've never seen a shirt with that many colorful polka dots," she said, her gaze still fixed on him. "Why would a guy go to all the trouble to wear makeup and a silly-looking shirt just to ride a bull?"

The doctor shrugged. "Who knows? Some guys carry a rabbit's foot, some throw salt over their shoulder before a ride, some do even more ridiculous things to bring them luck."

She huffed. "Luck? The luckiest thing that could happen would be if they decided to give up bull riding and take up a less life-threatening form of recreation. Riding a bull does nothing but invite disaster."

"You're right about that, but I have to admit I enjoy watching them do it."

"Have you ever seen Billy Bob ride?" one of the team members asked her.

"No, and I wouldn't want to. Billy Bob, or any other bull rider."

Dr. Pratt let out a sigh of relief as a long, low groan sounded from his patient. "I knew Billy Bob was too tough to give up that easily. It may be a long time before he's able to compete again, but I have a feeling old Gray Ghost and Billy

Bob will be meeting again someday."

Dina gasped as her hand went to her chest. "You honestly think he'll want to ride again? After that bull nearly killed him?"

Dr. Pratt snorted. "Sure he will. Bull riders are a whole other breed of men. Once a bull rider, always a bull rider. They never quit. It's in their blood."

Though she knew the doctor couldn't see her, Dina rolled her eyes. Then, rather than have a verbal sparring match with Dr. Pratt, who obviously loved the sport of bull riding, she said to herself, *They never quit—unless a bull takes that option away from them and they end up in a wheelchair like my dad. Then it's too late.*

He removed an instrument from the tray on the table and began to cut away at the injured man's sleeve. After one of the other team members removed Billy Bob's chaps, Dr. Pratt carefully cut away his left pant leg.

"Augghh. What happened?" the man on the table asked in a distorted whisper as his eyes opened in a narrow slit. Then, forcing them wider, he squinted and blinked at the doctor, as if trying to focus in on him. "Did any of the clowns get hurt?"

Dina was surprised the man's first words were of concern for the clowns. He didn't even ask about his own injuries.

"Other than a few scratches and scrapes, the clowns are fine." Dr. Pratt nodded toward Dina. "Alert the ambulance crew. We need to get this man to the Cheyenne Regional Medical Center."

Dina did as she was told then watched the ambulance crew as they quickly entered and snapped into action.

"I'd go with him but. . ." Dr. Pratt motioned toward Dr. Ryan who was still working with the other bull rider. "I'd better stay here, in case anyone else is injured. Would you mind going with him, Dina? I'm sure one of the officers at the hospital will see that you get back to where you're staying when you're ready. I'd feel better if, considering your experience with your trauma unit, you rode along."

She really didn't want to go with him. He'd brought his injuries on himself. But her caring side, the side that had made her want to be a nurse in the first place, kicked in and forced her to say yes.

"I got here as soon as I could!" a breathless voice said. Dina turned as wide-eyed Burgandi rushed into the trailer. "They made everyone stay in their places until the EMTs got Billy Bob off the field. How is he?"

"Not good, but he's conscious. They're taking him to the hospital. Dr. Pratt wants me to ride along with him."

Burgandi's expression showed concern. "Are you up to it? I could go."

"Thanks, but I'll go. I'll meet you back at the bed-and-breakfast. Dr. Pratt said one of the officers would bring me." Dina took her purse from the cabinet where she'd placed it then followed the EMTs to the ambulance. Once she'd settled herself inside and had a chance to lean closer to her patient, she had to clamp her hand over her mouth to keep from shouting out that the man looked so much like Will, the man who had rescued her when she ran out of gas. The resemblance was uncanny. Of course with the makeup on, she couldn't be sure about his face, but that beard? She'd recognize it anywhere. But what would Will be doing riding bulls at a rodeo? And if it were Will, why would everyone be calling him Billy Bob? The whole idea was ludicrous.

Ludicrous or not, she had to ask. "I know this sounds strange, and I hate to ask since you're in so much pain, but—isn't your real name Will?"

A sudden look of panic came over his face. "Don't tell, please don't tell."

"That you're Will?"

"Yes. Don't want anyone to know. Important to me."

Though her curiosity was trying to get the better of her, she wasn't about to ask why. She was nothing more to him than the nurse who was accompanying him to the hospital. What he said or did was of his own choosing. "Then I won't say a word. It's none of my business anyway."

"Was Dr. Pratt—telling me—the truth?" he asked as Dina turned her full attention to checking his vitals.

She frowned. "About your injuries?" She never liked discussing a patient's injuries with them, not even a famous bull rider's. That was the doctor's area.

He opened his eyes a slit. "No. The clowns."

"You mean about none of them being hurt?"

His only response was a slight nod.

"None, as far as I know. I'm sure if any of them had sustained serious injuries, we would have been told about it."

After a nearly undetectable sigh, he closed his eyes. "Good. I was worried about them."

His concern about their well-being touched her heart, especially in light of his own injuries. Though she rarely touched a patient except in the line of duty, she felt compelled to give his good shoulder a comforting pat. "And I'm sure they're worried about you."

They arrived at the hospital much sooner than she'd expected. "The hospital is going to expect some means of identification, you know," she told him with concern.

"Insurance card." With his good hand, he gestured toward his left side. "Back pocket."

Dina waited until they had rolled him inside and were ready to transfer him to an examination table then asked one of the technicians to take it out of his pocket.

Knowing from experience how important it was for the trauma crew to have as much information about a patient's injuries as possible, she quickly gave them a rundown of how the bull had tried to crush his leg as they came out of the chute, and how his hand had gotten entangled in the rope, being sure to add Dr. Pratt's findings as well as Will's vitals since his accident had happened.

The doctor on duty thanked her then motioned to the nurse. "Get that stuff off his face. I'm surprised the Justin team didn't take it off."

Knowing he'd be none too pleased about losing his makeup, she cast a glance in Will's direction before moving to an inconspicuous place along the wall where she stood watching as the doctor resumed his examination. There really wasn't any real purpose in her staying. Her job was finished. But for some unknown reason, especially now that she knew he was really Will, she felt an obligation to be there.

"Hey, you're a pretty good-lookin' guy," the doctor told him, pulling off his latex gloves with a chuckle once he'd finished his examination and Will's makeup had been removed.

Dina was in total agreement.

"Now, cowboy, we have to get you up to Radiology. I don't like the looks of your arm or that shoulder—or your leg. Doesn't look like you'll be riding bulls for quite a while."

"But—"

The doctor held up his hand to silence him. "No buts about it, young man. I hate to say it, because I know you don't want to hear it, but you're going to need months of healing time and a lot of physical therapy to get you back to where you can tangle with bulls again." He added a snicker. "Of course my best advice would be that you forget about rodeo, except maybe as a spectator."

He turned to Dina. "Thanks for coming in with him, but you can go now."

"No, I'll stay awhile." Dina's words surprised even her. "He needs someone here with him. I'll call whoever he wants called and let them know what's happened."

"I'm sure he'd appreciate it." Lowering his voice, he continued. "I'm bringing in an orthopedic specialist. If the X-rays show what I think they will, Mr. Martin will probably end up in surgery early tomorrow." He motioned toward the bed. "Someone will be here shortly to take him to Radiology."

"Is there anyone you'd like me to call?" Dina asked, bending over him as soon as the doctor had gone. "A relative or friend maybe?"

Will opened his eyes wide then answered with a weak, "No."

She stared at him for a moment, taking careful note of his shaggy beard, his heavy eyebrows, and his wild, thick hair, but mostly his eyes. She'd thought of those eyes, those beautiful sky-blue eyes, countless times since she'd visited her friend's home in southwestern Nebraska. "I still can't believe you're the man who was nice enough to try to start my car and then drove me to the Coulters' ranch."

He stared at her, his eyes almost pleading. "Promise you won't tell anyone. Please."

Dina lifted her hands in a surrender fashion. "Don't worry about it. I won't say a word. Whatever name you want to call yourself is really none of my business."

"Don't mention Nebraska."

Now she was really confused. "You don't want anyone to know you're from Nebraska?"

He moved his head in a slight bobbing motion. "Yes. Don't tell."

"Okay, I won't mention it, though I can't imagine what difference it would make. Are you sure there isn't someone you'd like me to call?"

"No!" His answer was so quick and firm it caught her off guard.

"There *has* to be someone," she told him, unable to imagine him going through this ordeal alone.

"No. No one."

Dina glanced at her watch. Her roommates had probably already gotten back to the hotel and were soaking in the hot tub. "I'd planned to stay, at least until you went to Radiology, but I guess I could stay longer, if you want me to."

"Don't want to take your time."

She sent him a gentle smile. "Don't worry about it. I'm a nurse, remember? I'm used to hospitals and working the late-night shift."

He fixed his gaze on her and almost looked as if he wanted to tell her something but wasn't sure if he should.

"What? What is it?" she asked, curious but not wanting to pry.

He hesitated then answered in a whisper so soft she couldn't be sure she'd heard him right. "You're scared? Is that what you said?"

He nodded.

"There's nothing wrong with being scared," she told him, wanting so much to console him. "You wouldn't be human if you weren't. But usually things don't turn out half as bad as we imagine they will. You have to believe you'll be fine."

What else could she say? What could she do to comfort him? Even though he was a bull rider and had no one to blame for his injuries other than himself, what she wanted to do was wrap him in her arms and tell him he would soon be back to his old self. But that would be a lie. Until the results of the X-rays were read and the severity of his injuries known, there was no way of knowing much of anything. He might recover fairly quickly, or he might end up like. . . She shuddered at the thought. *No, not like my father!* Just thinking about that possibility made her stomach quiver. Grasping his hand in hers and holding it tight, she decided to do what she should have done in the ambulance. Pray.

Chapter 4

Will felt like Gray Ghost had not only mashed his leg against the chute post and dragged him about the arena by his arm, but had plopped all of his two thousand pounds right down on top of him. Every bone, muscle, and nerve ached.

Now what? Though he'd done well at the Cheyenne rodeo, his winnings wouldn't begin to cover his doctor and hospital costs. What little insurance he carried might help, and he knew he could count on the Rodeo Contestant Crisis Fund to give him some financial assistance, but those things wouldn't come close to taking care of his medical bills if his injuries were half as bad as he suspected. If he hadn't felt so rotten, he would have given his head a sad shake. He not only couldn't afford the costs his bout with Gray Ghost had caused him, he couldn't afford the time it would take to recover, not with the amount of responsibility he carried on his shoulders. His family needed him.

He glanced up when someone took hold of his hand. It was Dina. That woman had the face of an angel. He'd thought of her day and night since he'd found her stranded on that abandoned road. What was it about this beautiful person that made his head swim, his knees shake, and his heart beat like it was in a race for first place? She was beautiful, that was for sure, but she was far more than that. She was a wonderful, caring person whose smile lit up the room and made his dire situation almost hopeful.

"Do you mind if I pray for you?" she asked, breaking into his thoughts. "I quite often pray for my friends and patients when they ask me to. God is the Great Physician, you know." She smiled as she gave his hand a slight squeeze. "During my time as a nurse I've seen many miracles happen when people pray."

"Sure. Thanks. I'd appreciate it." Her words excited him. He'd seen miracles, too, and was trusting God to perform a much-needed miracle for him.

He listened with rapt attention as she spoke aloud to God, asking Him to touch him, comfort him, calm his fears, lessen his pain, and be with him as he went into Radiology. He'd never had a near-stranger pray for him, and certainly never anyone as pretty, or as capable of understanding his injuries, as the woman who had come into his life in such unexpected ways. She was like an angel sent from God to not only pray for him and bring hope into the most frightening time of his life, but to encourage his faith in the God he had known since he was a child. The God in whom, at times, he'd nearly lost confidence because of the circumstances his family had found themselves in the day he turned twelve, a birthday he'd never forget.

When she finally said, "Amen," Will had to fight back tears. After all, grown men like him didn't cry.

"Do you know the Lord, Will?" she asked as he opened his eyes.

But before he could answer, two men in blue scrubs appeared with a gurney. Dina quickly tucked her long blond hair behind one ear then leaned close to his face and whispered, "You shouldn't be alone at a time like this. I'm going to stay until they're finished with you, and I'll be praying for you," before stepping back out of the way.

Within minutes, they had transferred him from the table to the gurney and, though it pained him to do so, as they rolled him out into the hallway, he turned his head for one final glimpse of Dina. He wanted to remember her beautiful face forever. Would she really stay until they'd finished with him? With all the injuries he had, it could be hours.

As he relaxed his neck, in his heart he cried out to God. *God, I've faced some scary things before, but I've never been this afraid. I know I don't deserve to ask, but please bring me through this, not for my sake but for the sake of my family. I know a person isn't supposed to try to bargain with You, God, the Ruler and Creator of the universe, but, I promise, if You bring me through this, I'll do the best I can to live for You.*

Dina followed the gurney into the hallway then smiled at Will as he turned his head and their eyes met. She waited in the hallway until the gurney disappeared into an elevator before going down to the main floor, stepping outside, and dialing Burgandi's number.

"Where are you? Do you have any idea what time it is?" her friend nearly shouted into the phone. "I thought one of the officers was going to bring you back."

"I'm still at the hospital. They've just taken Wi—ah, Billy Bob up to Radiology. I'm. . ." She paused, knowing her roommate was going to think she had gone bonkers. "I'm going to stay until they finish with him." Dina wanted to tell her who he was—the man who'd helped her when she'd had car trouble—but she didn't. He'd asked that she tell no one, so she wouldn't. Not even Burgandi.

"You have got to be kidding! What's wrong with you, Dina? Aren't you the woman who refused to have anything to do with a man who rode bulls? You wouldn't even go watch him ride."

She searched her heart. Why *was* she staying? Why was she helping a near-stranger? She didn't know the answers. All she knew was that she had to do it.

"I was shocked," Burgandi went on, not even stopping long enough for a breath, "when you consented to ride along in the ambulance. I never thought you'd *stay* with him!"

"I have to stay. He—he needs me." She'd no sooner said it than she realized how stupid her answer must sound to Burgandi, after all the raving and ranting she'd done about bull riders.

"He *needs* you? You don't even know the man. How could he need you?"

"I can't explain it. I just know he does, and I promised I'd stay."

"Are you forgetting about our meeting? It starts at eight. Celeste is going to sizzle if you don't make it. Your report is the first one of the morning."

"No, I haven't forgotten, but. . ." She didn't want to let Celeste down, but right now, Will and what he would be facing in the weeks, probably even months, to come, were uppermost on her mind. "I'm planning on making it back in plenty of time." Again she paused. "But if, for any reason, I don't, you will explain my absence for me, won't you?"

"How can I explain something I don't understand myself? But I'm your friend. I'll do the best I can."

"Thanks, Burgandi. I knew I could count on you. Will you do me another favor? Pray for Billy Bob. He needs it."

"You got it. I love you, sweetie. Wake me up when you get back. *If* you get back."

Dina thanked her again, said good night, then hung up the phone.

"Are you the woman who came in with the man from the rodeo?" a nurse asked as she approached Dina. "He wanted me to give you this and tell you thanks for staying."

Dina took the plastic bag then said a grateful, "Thank you. Do you have any idea how long it will be before he's finished in Radiology?"

"We're pretty busy up there tonight, so I'm guessing it could be as much as a couple of hours. But you can come up and wait in the Radiology waiting room, if you like."

Dina thanked the woman then followed her. She found a comfortable-looking chair in the corner of the room and then, not sure it was any of her business, sat down to open the bag she'd received. It didn't contain much, probably because, when they ride, bull riders wanted as little as possible in their pockets. There was a single dime, an old key, and a small crumpled snapshot of a man and a young boy. That was it. Why would a grown man, especially a strong, tough one like Will, carry such insignificant items with him while riding bulls? To bring him luck maybe? And why did he feel they were important enough to make sure someone would hold on to them for him?

She picked up a magazine and then, after flipping through the pages, placed it back on the coffee table. It seemed nothing could take her mind off him. She adjusted her position several times, trying to find a comfortable way to curl up and maybe catch a little sleep, but it didn't work. No matter how tightly she closed her eyes, her thoughts kept going back to the man in Radiology.

"Oh, Dina, there you are." It was Dr. Pratt. "I don't know if the rest of the bull riders were spooked because of Wayne's and Billy Bob's injuries or what, but after you two left, it seemed every contestant ended up with injuries of one kind or another." He quickly seated himself next to her. "How is he?"

She sighed. "No news yet. He tried to put on a brave front and act like he wasn't in pain, but he was. I could see it in his eyes."

"I was surprised you were still here. I felt bad after you left, that I had asked you to ride in the ambulance, knowing how you felt about bull riding."

She gave him a sheepish grin. "I'd planned on going to our hotel as soon as they got him checked in, but I couldn't leave him. He looked so sad, and he was alone."

"I'm glad you stayed. I know you haven't been around Billy Bob long enough to get to know him but, in my opinion, he's one of the finest men I've ever met. I'm sure they took off that makeup."

She nodded. "Yes, they did. Do you have any idea why he wears it?"

"Only reason most of us could come up with was that he wanted to remain anonymous and that was his way of doing it." He freed a small chuckle. "If I didn't hold him in such high regard, I might think he's running from the law."

"It's a shame he wears it. I liked him so much better without it."

"Liked? Past tense? Does that mean you knew him before?"

Dina had been guarding her words so carefully she couldn't believe she'd goofed. "I'd met him once, briefly, under entirely different circumstances and in a different place. I hadn't realized the man I'd met and Billy Bob were one and the same. Until tonight," she hastened to add. "But his eyes were a dead giveaway. I could never forget those beautiful blue eyes." She felt herself blushing. She'd said far more than she should have.

Dr. Pratt scooted his chair closer then leaned toward her. "I don't want you to betray any confidences, but is there anything you can tell me about him? I promise anything you say will be between the two of us. I'd never do anything to hurt Billy Bob." His eyes narrowed. "Or is that his real name? I have a feeling you know."

This time Dina was extremely careful with her words before uttering them. "Actually, other than seeing his face and having a general idea of where he lives, I doubt I know any more than you do."

"Where did you meet him? You haven't said."

"I'm sorry, Dr. Pratt, but I'm afraid anything else you'd like to know will have to come from Billy Bob himself."

He gave her arm a pat then moved his chair back to its original place. "I'm sorry to have put you on the spot, but all of us who love rodeo are in awe of Billy Bob. If you just recently met him, you may not know this, but a couple of years ago he showed up on the rodeo circuit, registering himself as simply Billy Bob, no last name. No address. And where the form said state, he wrote in USA. And the craziest part? He was wearing that same makeup he was wearing tonight. Everyone loves a mystery. The fans immediately went crazy for him, partly because of the mystique that surrounded him, but mainly because he proved to be one of the best bull riders around. After a decent night, he'd collect his purse, disappear, and no one would see him 'til rodeo time the next night. Then, once that rodeo was over, we didn't see or hear from him until time for the next one. Some folks even began to call him the Rodeo Phantom, but it didn't stick. I guess they liked the name Billy Bob better. It was obvious that boy had been riding bulls for a long time, probably in competition under another name, without the clown face. He won that first big event as Billy Bob and has been winning ever since."

"I can see why the fans like him. You're right. Everyone loves a good mystery."

"Yeah, and it couldn't happen to a nicer guy. It's sure been fun watching him rise to the top. I had fully expected to see him make Las Vegas next year." His shoulders rose in a sad shrug. "But—now—after what happened tonight—who knows? His bull-riding days may be over."

As far as Dina was concerned, nothing would please her more than to hear Will say he was through with rodeo. The man had no business even entertaining the thought of ever climbing onto a bull's back again. Hopefully, the injuries he had sustained would be a wake-up call before some bull caused his death.

Dr. Pratt stood to his feet and, with a yawn, stretched his long arms first one way then the other. "Well, since you're staying, I guess I'll go. It's been a long day." After fishing around in his pocket, he handed her his card. "Call me when you find out about his surgery."

She thanked him for coming then said good-bye. She'd barely settled down in her chair again when he hurried back into the room. "Oh, yeah. I forgot something. If you get to talk to him and you want to cheer him up, tell him he and old Gray Ghost scored a 94, and he won first place in bull riding. That, and the money it'll bring him, should make him feel better."

Even though she hated bull riding, she couldn't help but be pleased. She knew enough from her father's rodeo days to know a 94 was nearly unachievable. If his ride on Gray Ghost had to be his last ride ever, it would be of some comfort to know he'd gone out at the peak of his career. She could hardly wait to tell him.

Nearly an hour later, the nurse who had brought her up to the waiting room appeared. "We're finished. They'll be taking him to his room in a few minutes. Dr. Grimes will be in shortly to discuss their findings with you. After you've met with him, I'll take you to Mr. Martin's room."

It seemed an eternity before Dr. Grimes joined her. She couldn't believe how fidgety she had become waiting for him.

"I'm Dr. Grimes, and you're. . ."

"Dina. Dina Spark."

"I wish I had better news, Miss Spark, but Mr. Martin took quite a beating by that bull." He pulled a chair up in front of her and sat down. "I've discussed our findings on the phone with Dr. Farha, an excellent Denver orthopedic surgeon who is part of the Justin team of volunteer doctors. He's flying into Cheyenne in the morning. We've scheduled Mr. Martin's surgery for two o'clock tomorrow afternoon."

"Dr. Farha is coming all the way from Denver?"

"Yes. As a matter of fact, he called us. Being a part of the Justin team, he was already well aware of what had happened and was eager to come. The good news is your friend's leg isn't as bad as we'd first feared. Our main concern is the shoulder, and the way his arm was twisted while bearing Mr. Martin's weight as that bull dragged him around the field. I'd try to better explain the extent of his injuries, but it's usually hard for a layperson to understand."

"I'm a trauma nurse, Dr. Grimes. I'd appreciate anything you can tell me."

"Oh? In that case, there are a few things you should know." He went on to explain the various arthroscopic surgery procedures Dr. Farha had recommended with hopes that their use would help shorten Will's recovery time. "But don't worry. Dr. Farha is one of the best arthroscopic surgeons around. He'll put Mr. Martin back together. That young man should be able to walk on his leg by the end of the week, but his shoulder and arm are going to take time to heal, and he'll have to go through weeks of physical therapy. But who knows? He may be back riding bulls before we know it."

Dr. Grimes might have thought his last words would cheer her up, but they didn't. Be back riding bulls? She hoped Will wouldn't be that stupid.

"Maybe you'd better go on home and come back in the morning."

"I have to go to him," she told him adamantly. "I promised."

He stood then reached out and shook her hand. "Then, by all means, Miss Spark, go. But you'd better hurry. We'll soon be giving him something to make him sleep. We want him to be well rested for tomorrow."

Will was asleep when she entered his room, or at least that was the way it appeared. Though he was a big man, with muscles any bodybuilder would be proud to claim, he looked as helpless as a premature newborn as he lay there. Dina approached his bed cautiously and stood gazing at him. *Why would any man go to all the trouble to put on makeup to ride a bull? Unless he had something to hide.*

She startled when he opened his eyes and gazed up at her.

"I—I didn't think you'd stay." He groaned as he attempted to shift his arm. "Thanks."

"You're welcome." She held up the little bag. "The nurse said you told her to give this to me. I'll keep it for you until after you've had surgery if you like."

He fingered his beard with his good hand. "I wish they would have left my makeup on."

She smiled at his words. "Only women are allowed to wear makeup in hospitals. But don't worry about it. I doubt anyone will recognize you without it, especially since you're registered here as William Martin. But if any of your fans were determined to find you they might recognize your hair and that beard. Yours is very—unique."

"You're probably right."

"You won't be riding bulls again for quite a while. I'm certainly not a barber but when I was in high school I cut my friends' hair all the time, and I used to trim my dad's hair between haircuts. They all said I had a knack for it. I could borrow a pair of scissors from one of the nurses and trim your hair quite a bit shorter if you like. You could have a barber touch it up later."

He fingered his beard with his good hand. "What about this? I don't want it shaved but I wouldn't mind a close trim."

"I've never trimmed a man's beard before. I'll bet a male nurse would do it for you. I could ask."

He appeared to be thinking it over then nodded. "Yeah, sure. That's a good idea. Thanks." A smile quirked up the corners of his lips. "That way, for sure, no one will recognize me. I'm not even sure I'll recognize myself without this mass of hair and my beard trimmed short."

"I'll bet you'll be quite handsome." Her expression softened. She sure didn't want to talk him into anything he didn't feel like doing. "I know you're hurting, Will, but would you like me to cut it now? I might even be able to talk someone into trimming your beard right away, too. Before they give you something to make you sleep?"

"Sure, why not? Let's get it over with while I'm in the mood."

Though she wanted to ask him more about why he wore his hair and beard that way, she didn't. He was entitled to his privacy. Instead, she excused herself and hurried out of the room in search of a pair of scissors and a willing male nurse.

Within less than an hour a weary, near-stranger smiled up at her from his bed. "How do I look?" Will asked with a happy smile and more of his face showing than she'd ever seen.

"I can't get over the way cutting off your hair and trimming that shaggy beard changes you."

"For the better, I hope."

"Much better, but I have to admit I was beginning to like it the way it was."

"Maybe I should have left it."

She gave his good shoulder a pat. "Oh, no. You're—gorgeous this way."

He scrunched up his face. "Gorgeous?"

"Well, maybe not gorgeous, but I can safely say you're extremely handsome. I'm. . ." She stepped back, twisting her head first one way and then the other. "I'm having a hard time realizing it's actually you."

"It's me alright. But I can tell you I'd much rather be riding on a bull's back than be in this hospital bed."

She snapped her fingers. "By the way, Dr. Pratt was here earlier. He said to tell you that you and Gray Ghost scored a 94 on your last ride."

His eyes widened. "A 94? Really? I'll have to thank Gray Ghost when I see him."

"You want to thank that bull? After what he did to you?"

"He only did what came naturally to him. He meant me no harm."

She let out a sardonic laugh. "No harm? That bull nearly killed you!"

"He didn't set out to kill me. He only did what bulls do. I agitated him by climbing on his back and spurring him. If a stranger climbed onto my back and tried to ride me like that, I'd buck them off just like he did me."

"But he dragged you around the arena!"

"Not by choice. It wasn't his fault my hand got tangled in the rope. It was mine. If I'd done things the way I was supposed to, I would have slipped off his back after the buzzer sounded, gotten out of his way, and I'd be back at the hotel in bed instead of lying here in the hospital."

"That isn't all Dr. Pratt said. He wanted you to know you were named this year's Bull Riding Champion. The big number one."

He brightened. "That's great! Wow! Being named Bull Riding Champion of the Year has been my goal ever since I started rodeoing. Too bad I wasn't there to enjoy it, but there's always next year."

She gave her head a sad shake. "What's with all you cowboys? You get hurt and then go back again and again. It's like you're challenging fate. Do you think you're invincible?"

"No, ma'am. I know I'm not invincible but I have to keep riding. Bull riding gets in your blood. It's like you're not complete unless—"

"Unless you're challenging fate, with hopes of staying on a bull's back for eight seconds and making the highest score."

"I guess you could say that, but—ah—the money is nice, too. Where else can a guy win that much?"

"But is the money worth it?" She gestured toward his battered body as it lay covered with a pristine white blanket. "Look at you! You told me you were a rancher. Who is going to do the chores and take care of your herd while you're recovering from surgery and going through the many months of healing and physical therapy you're facing?"

He let out a slow breath of air. "That's the question I've been asking myself. I don't know. My mom is pretty good at it but she can't handle it on her own. I have two brothers but one of them, Ben, lives in West Virginia. Jason is still in college in Kentucky. He's working on his Masters in biology. Teresa, my little sister, is great help around the ranch during her summer breaks from college, but there's only so much two women can do. Maybe my neighbor will help me out."

She felt like a heel for pushing him. The poor guy was facing surgery, with no idea of how he was going to come out. "You shouldn't be worrying about things like that now. It may not be as bad as it seems." Her gaze went toward the open door. "I'd better be going. The nurse will be here soon with something to make you sleep."

"My surgery is tomorrow."

"I know. I spoke with your doctor." His sad expression was almost more than she could bear. Wanting him to know she really was concerned about him and his uncertain future, she moved closer and gently placed her hand on his good arm. "I'm sure Dr. Farha will do everything he can to get you back to normal as soon as possible."

They both turned as a nurse breezed into his room. Her smile alone would have put anyone at ease. "Sorry to break into your conversation, but I've got something that will make this man sleep like a baby."

Will puckered up his face. "It won't make me sick, will it?"

She laughed. "No, only sleepy. You'll be out before you know it."

After giving him his medication, she refilled his water glass, asked if there was anything else she could do, then disappeared as fast as she'd appeared.

"Thanks for staying. It means a lot to have you here."

"You're quite welcome. Are you sure you don't want me to call someone to come and stay with you when you come out of recovery?"

"No. No one."

"But you need someone here with you." His pitiful expression broke her heart. "If you want me to, I guess *I* could come back." The words slipped out of her mouth before she had time to think them over.

"Would you?" His eyes were pleading, almost begging.

"I have a report to give in the morning, but I'm sure I can slip away after that. I'll try to be here before they take you to Prep."

"Thanks. I'll feel better knowing you're here. You've been so kind to me. I hate to ask, but there is something else you could do for me, if you would."

"Oh, what?"

"You've seen my pickup. It's parked out behind the Super 8 on West Lincolnway. Is there any way you could get my wallet from under the seat and bring it to me?"

She couldn't keep a frown from creasing her forehead. "You left your wallet in your truck?"

"Yeah, I always keep my insurance card in my back pocket when I ride bulls—just in case—but I put a bag with everything else in it under the front seat and locked it. The truck key is in that bag the nurse gave you."

"No problem. I'll be glad to get it for you." She straightened his covers and pulled them up about his neck, not sure if she was doing it because she was a nurse and that was what she did for her patients, or if she was doing it because she felt sorry for him. Maybe both. By the time she finished, his eyes were already closed, the medication the nurse had given him already taking effect. "Sleep tight," she said in a faint whisper, leaning even closer to his ear. And then on impulse she lightly kissed his cheek.

As she backed out of the room, she took one final glance at the man in the bed. It almost looked as if he was smiling. Surely he hadn't realized she'd kissed him!

Once outside the hospital she hailed a cab. "Super 8 Motel, please."

Chapter 5

Burgandi's clenched hand anchored on her hip as the two sat in their hotel room the next morning. "You have got to be kidding!"

Dina put her favorite tube of lipstick back into her purse then zipped it shut. "I promised. I can't go back on my promise. He's counting on me."

"But you barely know the man! And he's a cowboy. A bull-riding cowboy! Have you forgotten what you told me?"

"No, I haven't forgotten, but I didn't say I'd never talk to a cowboy or treat one like a human being if he needed it. I just said I'd never have anything to do with one—on a serious basis," she hastened to add. "He's merely a man facing surgery alone. Being there to encourage him is the least I can do."

"Do you have any idea how upset Celeste is going to be when she finds out you're missing this afternoon's meeting?"

"You can take notes for me."

"And you think that will appease her?"

"I guess it'll have to, because I'm going." Dina picked up her jacket and tugged it on.

"You, my friend, are a stubborn, unpredictable woman."

She reached out and gave the strap of Burgandi's shoulder bag a tug. "I know, but you love me anyway, right?"

"Yeah, I love you. What choice do I have? You're my closest friend."

They decided not to tell Celeste she was leaving until after she had given her report and, like they had expected, the woman didn't like the idea one bit. "You're a vital part of this committee, Dina," she nearly shrieked at her. "It's nice of you to offer to stay with the man, but he is not your responsibility."

"You are absolutely right," she told the woman in a soft, controlled voice. "But everyone deserves to have someone there with them when they come out of recovery. Knowing how thoughtful you are," she decided to add honestly, "I'm sure you would do exactly the same thing if you were in my place."

Celeste, apparently dazzled by Dina's compliment, gazed at her for a moment, then smiled. "Yes, I'm sure I would. Go on and go to him. We'll bring you up to speed later."

She left the hotel by noon, hoping she would make it to the hospital in time. Fortunately, Will was still in his room when she arrived, his bed propped up slightly. He smiled at her as she entered. "Thanks. I—I was afraid you wouldn't come."

"Didn't I tell you I'd be here?"

"Yes, ma'am, but even people I thought I could trust have let me down."

"Well, *I* didn't let you down." She held up his blue canvas bag. "I got it for you last night, just like I said I would." The smile that formed on his face made her late-night trip to the motel worth the effort.

"I appreciate you going to all that trouble. I'll find some way to repay you."

"No payment necessary. I was glad to do it. Did you sleep well?"

He nodded. "Yes, ma'am, but I had the strangest dream."

"About the bull?"

"No, ma'am." He gave her a sheepish grin. "I dreamed someone kissed me."

She felt a flush rise to her cheeks. "Oh?"

"I've never had a dream like that. It was—sorta nice."

Dina pulled off her jacket and draped it over a chair. "Sometimes medication causes dreams."

His grin broadened. "Maybe. I sure appreciate your being here. I'm never keen on having surgery."

"I guess that means you've had surgery before." *Probably from other rodeo injuries.*

"Yeah, simple stuff, like having my tonsils out. Nothing major like Dr. Farha is going to do."

"I thought maybe you were talking about rodeo injuries."

"Oh, I've had lots of those, but none serious enough to require surgery. I never ride without my protective vest. That helps. Mostly all I needed during those times I got hurt was a bit of taping up or a few stitches."

Again, she thought of her father. "If that's all you've had, and you're a bull rider, you're a mighty lucky man."

"I know. I thank the Lord for it every day."

"You do?"

His brows narrowed. "What? Thank the Lord?"

"Yes. I mean—do you really thank Him, or was that just a figure of speech?"

"Are you asking me if I'm a Christian?"

"I tried to ask you before, but the men with the gurney came for you and you didn't have a chance to answer me."

"Yes, ma'am, I—"

"You have got to stop calling me *ma'am*. We're friends, Will. Call me Dina."

"I like your name. It's pretty. Just like you."

She felt as if she were blushing. "So—are you a Christian?"

"Yes, ma'am—Dina—I am. I'd be afraid to ride bulls if I wasn't. I ask God to protect me before every ride and I give Him the full credit when He does."

"Does that mean, just because you know God, you think He approves of your taking ridiculously dangerous chances with the life He gave you?" She had to ask, because what he did just didn't make sense to her.

"I know riding bulls must seem stupid to you, but other than the fact that I enjoy it, I do have my reasons."

Smiling, a slightly rotund nurse came in and circled his bed. "They'll be here to take you to the surgical floor any minute now. Are we ready?"

Dina laughed to herself at the woman's use of the word *we*. As a nurse herself, she avoided asking patients, *Are we ready*? as if she were going to go into surgery and be operated on right along with them. "Could we just have a moment? I'd like to pray for him."

The nurse's smile broadened. "Of course you may. A person can never have too much prayer. I'll be right outside."

He reached out his good hand. "I was hoping you'd pray for me, 'cause I admit it. I'm scared, Dina, really scared."

She moved closer to the bed and entwined her fingers with his. It was hard to imagine big, tough Will afraid of anything. But, in his eyes, she saw fear. Fear of what, she wasn't sure. Fear of coming under the surgeon's knife? Of never being able to ride bulls again? Or losing the full use of his arm? The man before her was a man of mystery, not only to her but to everyone else. Yet, mystery or not, for some reason she couldn't understand, God had brought them together. And that was reason enough for her to be there, praying for him and holding his hand. Though she didn't feel very strong at that moment, whatever strength she had, she wanted to share with Will.

"I know you are. We're all scared when we face the unknown but God is with you, Will. You're far from alone." She tightened her grip on his hand. "I'm here, too, and I'll be here waiting when you come back from surgery."

"You'll do that for me? It'd sure mean a lot to me to have you here, but didn't you say you're in town for meetings?"

The look of gratitude on his face brought tears to her eyes. "Of course I'll do it. Being here is far more important than any meeting."

"You mean it?"

"Absolutely. There's no place I'd rather be today than here with you."

He closed his eyes and swallowed hard. "Somehow—I'll find a way to repay you for all your kindnesses toward me. Not many women would give up their time to stand by someone they barely know."

"We're even. You were kind to me when you found me stranded on that road."

"I didn't begin to do for you what you've done for me." He gazed into her face. "Other than my mom, you're the most wonderful woman I've ever met." His fingers tightened around hers. "You're an angel sent from God."

She smiled down at him. "I don't know about the angel part, but I'm glad God brought us together."

"Me, too."

Bowing her head, she began to pray aloud.

She stayed by his side until they'd loaded him onto the gurney, then lingered in the doorway, watching until he disappeared out of sight. When the phone on his night table rang she hurried to answer it, hoping it would be Burgandi since she had given her the direct-dial number.

"Wow, you answered quick." It was Burgandi. "Has your cowboy gone to surgery yet?"

Dina rolled her eyes, ready to chastise her friend for her comment, then decided not to. "Yeah, they just took him."

"We caught the noon news while we were having lunch. From what the TV anchor said, I guess everyone is concerned about your Billy Bob, even those not interested in rodeo. But no one seems to know anything, other than that he's facing surgery and probably many months of recovery."

"I know, and I feel bad about it. From what I've heard, he has thousands of loyal fans, but I'm sure Dr. Farha will do a news briefing later on today to bring everyone up to speed on his condition. Right now, there's not much to tell. And, by the way, he is not *my* Billy Bob."

Burgandi responded with a teasing huff. "You could have fooled me. He still hasn't told you why he wears that makeup?"

"No, but whatever the reason, I'm sure it's important to him."

"You don't think it's simply a gimmick?" Burgandi asked. "You know, something different and unusual to make him stand out from all the other bull riders and to keep people talking about him."

Dina considered her friend's words. "He's not like that. He's actually quite shy. You'd like him."

"He's sure got you wrapped around his little finger."

"Me? How can you say that? I feel sorry for him, that's all."

"Hey, this is your best friend you're talking to. I know you, Dina. I've seen you get interested in other guys, date them a few months, and then drop them for one reason or another. But I've never seen one sweep you off your feet like this man. And you haven't even seen his face!"

But I have seen his face! Dina wanted to scream out, but the loyalty she felt for him kept her from it.

Burgandi uttered a slight giggle. "What's he got that the others didn't have? Is there some secret magnetism you're not telling me about?"

"Of course not. He's just a very nice man. I like him."

Her friend huffed again. "A very nice cowboy/bull-riding man, and he's sure got you mesmerized."

"I am not mesmerized!" Dina replied indignantly. "As a nurse, I'm merely concerned about him, as I would be about any of my patients."

"You're forgetting one very important point. That man is *not* one of your patients. Plain and simple—you're there with him because you want to be."

"That's foolishness! Dr. Pratt asked me to accompany him to the hospital. Otherwise, I wouldn't have come."

"But once you were there, Dina, your responsibility was over. You had no more obligation to stay there than the EMTs or the man who drove the ambulance. Your job was finished."

Dina wanted to reply, to refute her words, but she couldn't. Ethically, Burgandi was right.

"Look, Dina, what you do with your life is your business but, as your best friend, I don't want to see you get hurt. I'm sure Billy Bob is as nice as you say he is, but I'm worried about what all this unusual allegiance you feel toward him will do to you. What if you fall for the guy?"

Dina gasped. "Fall for him? Are you crazy? He's everything I *don't* want in a man! I'd never fall for someone like him!"

"I hope you mean that."

"Just the idea of me falling for a *cowboy* is ridiculous, especially a bull-riding cowboy."

"What was it Shakespeare wrote in *Hamlet*? 'The lady doth protest too much, me thinks'? From my vantage point, it seems you're protesting way too much for someone whose sudden friendship with a near-stranger, who is a total opposite of the man she'd like to marry, becomes the primary focus of every breath she takes."

"Well, you're wrong," Dina told her adamantly. "Like I've already said, I feel sorry for him, that's all! End of discussion! Now, unless you have something else to chat about, this conversation is over."

"Other than to check on Billy Bob's condition and try to talk some sense into your head, I called to tell you that our committee is planning on finishing its work by late this afternoon, and we'll all be leaving for home in the morning. I was wondering if you'd be staying at the hospital or in our room tonight, because if you were staying at the hospital, I was going to offer to pack up your things."

"The committee is finishing today? I didn't think we'd be through until tomorrow afternoon."

"I didn't either, but things came together more easily than any of us had anticipated. By finishing today, that means everyone will have time to check out after breakfast, then head for home and arrive before dark." She paused. "You *are* planning on heading back to Omaha tomorrow, aren't you?"

Chapter 6

Dina froze at her question. "I–I'm just surprised we're finishing so soon."

"Dina, be sensible. Forget about that man and go home like the rest of us. Surely you're not thinking of staying on."

"I— I don't know. I haven't decided."

"Look, sweetie, you're my friend. We've been best friends since our nurse's training days. And, knowing you and loving you like I do, I'll give you a bit of advice. After Billy Bob comes out of recovery and he is rational enough to know what you're saying, tell that cowboy good-bye, get in your car, head for Omaha, and never look back."

Dina knew her friend meant well, but Burgandi hadn't been around Will. He was more than just a cowboy. She hadn't been there when he'd shown more concern for the clowns who had tried to help him than he had for himself. She hadn't seen the respectful way he treated her, as well as the nurses and doctors who cared for him. No, the Will she'd come to know and respect in the few short hours she'd been around him was nothing like the man Burgandi thought he was. This man was kind and gentle and had a certain charm about him that was—

"Earth to Dina. Did you hear me? Are you heading back to Omaha or not?"

"Oh, Burgandi, I don't know," she said honestly. "It depends on what Dr. Farha says after he comes out of surgery, but I am staying with Billy Bob tonight. If his prognosis is good and he doesn't need me, I'll leave tomorrow."

"And if it isn't?"

"If it isn't—then I'll stay, at least through tomorrow afternoon. I can't leave him alone. You're a nurse. You know how difficult it is for our patients who have no one to be with them when they come out of surgery."

"Yes, I know, and I always feel bad for them, but that doesn't mean I'm obligated to stay by their side when my shift is over. I've said my piece, but it sounds like your mind is already made up."

"I'll slip away long enough in the morning to come back to the hotel. That way I can tell you and the others good-bye and pick up my things. Don't worry about packing for me. I really don't have that much."

"Promise you'll think about what I've said, Dina. I can't stand the idea of your being hurt. And considering how little you know about this man, and the fact that he *is* a bull rider, I'm afraid if you get involved with him, you'll have nothing but heartache."

"I'm not getting *involved* as you call it. I'm only helping someone who needs my help. Don't worry about me. I'll be fine." Dina hung up the phone then stood staring at the empty bed where a short time ago Will lay smiling at her. *I'll stay tonight and maybe tomorrow night if he needs me, then I'm gone.* But as she reached out and touched his pillow, she knew she was involved. To what extent, she couldn't be sure. All she knew was that leaving him and heading back to her busy life in Omaha was going to be one of the hardest things she had ever done.

Several others were already there when Dina made her way up to the surgical floor waiting room, apparently waiting for loved ones or friends who were also having surgery. She took a chair in a far corner then picked up a magazine and opened it.

A pretty, middle-aged woman leaned toward her. "You have someone in surgery?"

Dina nodded. "Yes, a close friend. How about you?"

"My husband. My sons and I were finally able to talk him into having his torn rotator cuff repaired. That thing has been paining him like you wouldn't believe."

"Have you heard the rumor?" the woman seated on her other side asked in a hushed voice. "Someone told us that Billy Bob—you know, the cowboy who got hurt at the rodeo the other night—is in this hospital."

Dina purposely raised her brows and tried to appear nonchalant. "Oh?"

"I've heard he's one of the nicest cowboys around but, for the life of me, I can't figure out why he'd wear that awful clown makeup. Do you suppose he's got some terrible scars on his face he doesn't want anyone to see?"

"Maybe he's just plain ugly!" the first woman said with a snort.

"Well, I know one thing," the second one replied. "I'm gonna keep my eyes open as I walk around the hospital halls. I've heard they're not giving out his room number, but I might just happen to get a peek at him."

"What makes you think you'd recognize him if you did see him? They probably took that stuff off his face when they brought him in here."

"Hey, not many men have as bushy a head of hair or a heavy beard like that cowboy does, and who wouldn't recognize those biceps of his? Believe me, I'll know him if I see him."

Good thing he let us cut his hair and trim up that beard, Dina thought.

"And if I do see him," the woman continued, waving her arm in an animated fashion, "I'm gonna run into his room and get his autograph. In fact, I might buy myself one of those disposable cameras and keep it in my purse. Wouldn't that be something if I could get a picture of that man without his makeup? I'll bet I could sell it to one of those rodeo magazines for big bucks."

"Yeah, but if he decided to sue you for invading his privacy, it might cost you a whole lot more than what you'd make."

Dina was glad when the doctor who'd performed the surgery on the first woman's husband came into the waiting room for his briefing. But hearing the women's discussion had made her begin to understand why Will had felt it necessary to keep his makeup on at all times. The thing she didn't understand was why he was so determined to keep his true identity a secret. What difference did it make?

Soon, both the doctor and the man's family left the room and she was alone again, her erratic thoughts her only companion.

As she had predicted, it was nearly two hours before Dr. Farha appeared. "We had quite a job putting Mr. Martin"—he paused and gave her a knowing wink—"back together." He glanced around and lowered his voice. "I was kind of surprised when I arrived at the hospital and learned Will Martin, the person I was going to be performing surgery on, was really Billy Bob. I didn't recognize him without that wild head of hair and that beard."

"We thought a trim was a good idea since we had to give the hospital his real name when we checked him in. You won't tell anyone who he is, will you?"

He shrugged. "Not unless it became absolutely necessary, which is highly unlikely. What he wants to be called elsewhere is his business."

"Thank you. I know Will would appreciate it."

Dr. Farha pulled a chair up in front of her and seated himself. "His shoulder was a mess and his arm wasn't much better. But with a few months of physical therapy, not to mention a lot of patience and hard work, he should regain full use of that arm."

"What about his leg?"

"I understand that bull pinned him against one of the steel posts as they came out of the chute. I haven't met a cowboy yet whose leg could take that kind of pressure without sustaining some type of injury. Not even rough-and-tumble cowboys like our Billy Bob. But it'll be okay. He's young and used to pain. He'll have to stay off of it for two or three days to give it time to heal. Sad thing is, with that shoulder, he won't be able to use crutches or a walker to support his weight. Which means he's going to be pretty much either bedfast or in a wheelchair until he can stand to walk on it." His face took on a smile. "He won't want to hop around on one leg, either."

"But he won't be able to ride bulls again, right?" she asked hopefully.

"He could, if he works hard at getting himself back in shape. That boy loves riding bulls!"

Her blood ran cold at the thought.

"But I'll be honest with you. He is going to have a lot of soreness. Most cowboys rebel when I tell them they are going to have to work with a physical therapist. They think they can do it on their own, but they can't. You're a nurse. You know what I'm talking about. If they don't do it right, they can cause even more damage." His expression brightened. "Dr. Grimes tells me you're a trauma nurse. I'm sure that means you've had some physical therapy training. Maybe you can help him."

"I'd like to, but he lives clear across the state from me."

He shrugged. "Too bad. Do you know of any physical therapists in his area you could recommend to him?"

She shook her head. None of what he was saying was good news. "No, and finding a good one may be difficult. The area where he lives is pretty isolated. The nearest hospital is probably a number of miles away."

Again he shrugged. "That definitely presents a problem. He needs to get that therapy started as soon as he gets home."

"Do you have any idea when he might be released?"

He paused as if giving his answer some thought. "Barring any complications, I'd say in two days at the most."

"I know you're a busy man, Dr. Farha. I can't thank you enough for coming all the way from Denver."

"Like Dr. Grimes probably told you, I'm a big fan of rodeo and a part of the Justin Sportsmedicine Team. I'm like an old firehouse dog; that's why I bought my own plane. Tell me there's a rodeo anywhere nearby, or a cowboy who is hurt and needs my services, and I'm off and flying—literally." He rose and extended his hand. "Well, I've got to get back to Denver. Dr. Ken Flaming, the doctor who assisted me during surgery, is taking over for me now. Don't worry about your cowboy. This hospital has some fine doctors. While he's here, I'm sure he'll get the best of care. It's been nice meeting you, Miss Spark."

She started to tell him Will was *not* her cowboy, that they had only known each other a few days, but what difference did it make? She'd probably never see Dr. Farha again so she simply shook his hand, thanked him again, and said good-bye.

It seemed like forever before someone came to take her to Will's cubical in SICU. "He's still pretty groggy," the woman told her as Dina hovered over him. "Dr. Farha told us you were a trauma nurse. He left orders that we were to let you stay with him as long as you like. If he gets nauseated, just push the button and one of us will be here right away."

The nurse went about checking his vital signs, his IV, then the machines to which he was attached before nodding to Dina and leaving the two alone. Dina moved as close to the bed as she dared, then stood gazing at his nearly clean-shaven face. It wasn't that she hadn't liked his wild look; she had, though not at first. But that look had grown on her. Somehow, it suited him, at least in his role as a bull rider. Maybe that wild hair had helped cushion his head when Gray Ghost had finally thrown him off his back and he had hit the ground. She straightened as a second nurse appeared in the doorway.

"Has he responded to you yet?"

She shook her head, then answered in a mere whisper, "No, but I've only been here a few minutes."

The nurse leaned over him and gave his good shoulder a slight shake. "Will, it's time to wake up. Your surgery is over and you have company."

He stirred slightly and seemed to be struggling to open his eyes.

She nodded toward Dina. "Go ahead. Talk to him."

After looping her hair over her ear, she again leaned close. "Will, it's me. Dina. Wake up, sleepyhead."

He responded with a slight moan.

"Dr. Farha said your surgery went just fine. With some physical therapy and a lot of work, you should be. . ." She paused. She wasn't about to say he should be riding bulls again. "You should be—like your old self."

"It might help if you'd take his hand and give it a good squeeze every once in a while. As I'm sure you know from experience, a personal touch does wonders for our patients."

She smiled as the woman headed for the door. "I will." Though his hand was rough and dry, she loved the feel of it as she cradled it in hers. It felt strong, earthy. He'd said he was a rancher. She could almost visualize him going about his daily chores—feeding cattle, mending fences, shoveling hay, cleaning stables. . . . Ranching was hard work. She knew, having grown up on a ranch herself. But, thanks to her father's injuries, her family's ranching days were a thing of the past. She had loved living on that ranch, helping care for the animals, riding her horse, watching the calves being born—but that was all behind her, never to be experienced again. She was a city gal now, living in one of Omaha's beautiful apartment complexes. She'd sold her horse and moved away the week her father had leased their Madison County ranch out to someone else. He and her mother had stayed in the house, but the ranching duties now fell upon other shoulders.

She startled as his fingers tightened around hers then relaxed. "Will, please wake up. I want to see those beautiful blue eyes."

He opened one eye, just the faintest crack, and stared at her, as if trying to focus on her image. "Dina?"

She bent nearer his face. "Yes, it's me. I'm here, just like I told you I would be."

"It's over?"

"Yes." With the tip of her finger, she pushed a wisp of hair away from his forehead. "All over. I'm right here."

"You're so bootiful. . . ."

She had to laugh. If people had any idea of the things that came out of their mouths when they were still under the effects of anesthetics, they would probably refuse to have surgery. One man she had attended in recovery had even confessed to stealing money from his employer.

When he began to gag, she burst into action and punched the button for the nurse. But rather than wait for her, she hurriedly began going through the cupboards in search of the nausea pan and, when she found it, lifted his head a bit and placed it beneath his chin. Although nausea was a perfectly normal reaction from someone just out of surgery, she felt sorry for him anyway and wished he didn't have to go through it. She could only imagine how uncomfortable being sick to his stomach was on top of everything else he was going through.

She stepped out of the way when the nurse entered and took over. Within minutes, his episode had run its course, the woman had cleaned his face with a wet cloth, and he was quiet again. Dina thanked her then moved back to his side and, once again, took his hand.

Though his eyes didn't open, the corners of his mouth lifted ever so slightly. "Glad you're here."

"I'm glad, too. I like being with you."

"Staying?"

"Yes, I'll be staying at the hospital all night. If they won't let me sleep here in the chair, I'll be in the waiting room just down the hall."

"Good." He sighed then took several shallow breaths. "Sleepy."

"You go ahead and rest. I'll be close by if you need me."

"Pray?"

She smiled. "Yes, I'll keep praying for you."

"There's a phone call for you at the desk," the nurse said in a whisper later that evening as her face appeared in the open doorway.

After a quick glance at Will, Dina hurried after her, then went in the direction the woman pointed and picked up the phone. "This is Dina Spark."

"Good, Dina, I was hoping you'd be there. I spoke with Dr. Farha. He gave me Billy Bob's floor number and said you were staying with him for a while." It was Dr. Pratt. "How's he doing? Did he come through the surgery okay?"

"Yes, he's getting along fine. The surgery went well. Dr. Farha said he should regain full use of his shoulder and arm if he works with a physical therapist like he should. He didn't seem overly concerned about his leg, just that it would take time to heal." Apparently, since Dr. Pratt had referred to Will as Billy Bob, Dr. Farha had kept Will's secret.

"That's good news. I'll pass the word around. I wanted to let you know they've gathered up Billy Bob's things, but the problem is no one is sure what to do with them. I removed his boots and spurs when they brought him into the Justin unit. If he's like most cowboys, he'll want to make sure he gets them back."

Dina searched her brain for an answer. She would like to tell them she had the key to Will's truck and would meet them there, so she could lock his belongings inside. But she wasn't sure, considering how far away Will had parked from the arena, that he wanted them to know which truck was his. All a resourceful person would have to do to learn his identity was get his truck's Nebraska license number and do a little detective work. "If someone is willing, they could deliver his things to the Nagle Warren Mansion. I'll be going back there early tomorrow morning to pick up my suitcase. I'll be glad to see that he gets them."

"Good. I'm sure that will work out fine. I'd bring them myself but I have a plane to catch. I'll put your name on the box and make sure someone takes it by. Other than his spurs and his boots, gloves, extra bull rope, that sort of thing, there wasn't much else, so everything should fit in one large box. Thanks, Dina. I know Billy Bob will appreciate your efforts. Be sure to tell him hello for me and wish him a speedy recovery. It was nice meeting you."

"I enjoyed meeting you, too, Dr. Pratt. I'll give him your message and I'll make sure he gets the box."

After she hung up, she stood gazing at the phone. *Exactly how am I going to do that? I'd planned to head out of town myself tomorrow. I can't just lug that heavy box into his hospital room and leave it. Most of the cowboys and others who are associated with rodeo will be gone by tomorrow, so none of them would be around—even if he trusted one of them to help him out. And how is he going to get back to Nebraska? He won't be able to negotiate crutches, and he certainly won't be in any condition to drive his old truck for weeks, maybe even months.*

A sudden realization hit her. *I'm the only one he has! There is no one else!*

Dina stayed by his side until about midnight then went to the hallway vending machine for a sandwich and something cold to drink. He was stirring when she reentered his room. "Hi, sleepyhead. I'm glad to see you're awake." She pulled the chair closer to his bed and smiled at him.

After blinking several times, he opened his eyes wide. "Is it over?"

"Yes, it's over. Dr. Farha said everything went well."

"Thanks for. . ."

"For being here? I told you I would." Inwardly she laughed. His question made her realize, since he hadn't been fully conscious when they'd had their last conversation, he wouldn't remember the part about telling her she was *bootiful*. Maybe this time, now that he was more fully awake, he'd remember things. "How do you feel? Are you in a lot of pain?"

"Not much."

"Are you sure there isn't someone you'd like me to call for you? An aunt or maybe a cousin who should know where you are?"

He shook his head. "No."

"Come on. Everyone has someone."

He merely shrugged his good shoulder. "Don't need someone. Just you."

"But my meetings here in Cheyenne are nearly over. I might be able to stay until noon tomorrow, but I have to get back to my job in Omaha."

His eyes widened. "Want you here."

"I have to go. My boss is expecting me to come back to work." She could tell her words upset him, but what else could she do? Like Burgandi had said, her obligation to him was over.

"You're my angel."

She bit at her emotions. "I'm no angel, Will. Just a nurse who happened to be on duty when you had your accident."

"No. *My* angel," he insisted.

Dina grinned. "You only think that because the anesthetics are still affecting you."

Smiling, the nurse flitted back into his room. "Well, I see our patient is finally awake and responding better now." She checked his vitals before taking hold of his foot through the sheet and giving it a squeeze. "By morning, we should be able to transfer you to a room on the post-op floor. If your wife's up to it, she can spend the rest of the night right there in that chair."

She kept her peace until the nurse left the room. "Great. She thinks I'm your wife."

He reached for her hand as he gave her a sheepish grin. "Would that be so bad?"

She took it then entwined her fingers through his. "Of course not, but I should have told her."

"What difference does it make?"

She wanted to argue with him but what he'd said was true. Wife, sister, cousin? It really didn't make any difference what anyone thought. No one really cared who she was to him.

Though at times as they visited he still seemed a bit confused and unable to quickly sort out a few of his thoughts, they shared a fairly intelligent conversation before the other night nurse came in at about two o'clock to give him his pain medication and something to make him sleep.

She went about the task of straightening his covers and filling his water glass then left them alone again. A few minutes later she returned, handing Dina a blanket and pillow. "You'll be needing these. Those recliners aren't nearly as comfortable to sleep in as they appear."

Dina took the items and thanked her. "I'm sure I'll be fine." She placed the things in the chair as soon as the woman left then gave her full attention to Will.

"I wanted to let you know I'll be leaving for an hour or so in the morning. I have to go back to the hotel, pack up my things, and say good-bye to my friends, but I'll come back as soon as I can."

"I really like having you here. You promise you'll come back?"

"Yes, I promise. I like being here with you." She bent and lightly kissed his forehead. "It's after two. You'd better get to sleep. I'll be right there in that chair the rest of the night. If you need anything just tell me."

Other than Will moaning in his sleep a number of times, the rest of the night went fairly well. He stirred about five thirty when the night nurse came for her routine check, which gave Dina the opportunity to once again remind him she'd be going to the hotel, but she'd be back as soon as possible.

At seven thirty, she slipped quietly out of his room.

Will slowly opened his eyes and gazed about the room, hoping to catch a glimpse of Dina, but she wasn't there. Ugghh, his mouth tasted like rotten eggs smelled, and his shoulder felt as if an elephant were sitting on it. He could shift his good leg but his injured leg refused to move. His entire body felt like he'd tangled with a bull and lost the fight—which he had. *Well, I didn't exactly lose*, he told himself with a trace of a smile. *Gray Ghost might have dragged me around the field, but I stayed on that awesome beast for the full eight seconds. Surely, that was a victory.*

But where was Dina? She'd promised she'd stay. He needed her, not because of his helplessness, but because he couldn't get her off his mind.

"Well, good morning!"

He blinked then focused his eyes on the pleasant-looking woman coming through the door, carrying a tray. "What time is it?"

"A little past eight thirty. Are you hungry? I've brought breakfast." She placed the tray on the over-bed tray table then smiled at him. "Um, looks like your right arm isn't going to be of much help. I hope you're left-handed."

He shook his head. "No, I'm not."

"Well, don't worry about it. I can help you."

He didn't want *her* to help him; he wanted Dina.

He gazed at the tray. Not one thing on it looked good. As far as he was concerned they could take it away. "Yuk! That looks like the stuff my mom fed me when I was a baby. Can't I have some scrambled eggs, or at least a hard-boiled one?"

"Don't like what we've given you, huh? Well, I don't blame you. Our post-op menu is pretty boring, but it's what your body needs. You do want to get well, don't you?"

He nodded. "Yes, ma'am, but I'd sure rather have something else. I'm a meat-and-potatoes kind of guy."

"You men! You're all alike." She pushed the uninviting bowl of what looked to him like unbuttered, seasoned grits to one side then took the spoon and filled it with an equally disgusting-looking goldish-colored liquid from the other bowl. "Open up."

He did as told then sputtered as a weird flavor hit his tongue.

She gave him a sympathetic frown. "I know. It tastes awful, doesn't it?"

Again he nodded.

"But you have to eat. Come on, open up again. I may not be as pretty as that wife of yours, but—"

"You've seen her?"

"Yes, not more than an hour ago. She said she had some errands to run and would be back as soon as she could. I imagine she'll be back in plenty of time to feed you your lunch but, in the meantime, you're going to have to put up with me."

He smiled at the congenial woman then opened his mouth. Dina hadn't left him. She was coming back. Though it was torture, he finished the bowl of chicken broth, or whatever it was, drank a full cup of coffee, and even consumed a small glass of juice. Once the helpful woman had adjusted his pillow and removed the tray, he settled back to await Dina's return.

Just the thought of seeing her lovely face made him smile. He'd never known anyone like her. He felt bad that she'd missed some of her meetings because of him, but how thankful he was that she had been on duty in the Justin trailer when they'd brought him in and then gracious enough to ride along with him in the ambulance. It had to be a *God thing*, he concluded, the way he was beginning to feel about her, that the two of them had been brought together.

He had to get that notion out of his head. Dina had simply been the one on duty when they'd carried him in on the gurney. She hadn't asked to ride to the hospital with him. That had been Dr. Pratt's idea. And what had he done? Gone all googly-eyed and begged her to stay with him, put the heavies on her by making her feel sorry for him, which probably did nothing but make her think of him as a wimp. Well, he wouldn't do that again. The best thing he could do for her was thank her for being there and send her back to Omaha. Though the last thing she would probably want was a relationship with cowboy who lived clear across the state, personally, he liked the idea. He had come to care for her in ways he never expected to care for a woman but he had to forget about her. Send her on her way, no matter how reluctant he was to see her go.

By the time Dina reached the Nagle Warren Mansion, the rest of the committee members had already assembled around one of the tables and were enjoying their breakfast. She selected several items from the attractively displayed assortment on the cherrywood credenza then slid into the empty chair next to Burgandi, with a nod to everyone else. "Sorry I had to miss most of yesterday's meeting."

Celeste cocked her head to one side and eyed her. "So? How is your cowboy?"

Though Celeste's words, and the way she'd said them, agitated her, Dina responded with a friendly smile. "If you're asking about Billy Bob, he's doing as well as can be expected, considering the severity of his injuries."

Barbara leaned toward her. "It's nice that you've been staying with him, but you are going home today, aren't you?"

"She's not sure," Burgandi answered for her. "There's no one else to stay with him."

"Surely he has a relative, or at least a friend, who could stay with him."

Dina gave her head a shake. "No, there's no one, and he won't be able to drive himself home when they release him. I have no idea how he is going to get there."

Celeste appeared thoughtful. "Where does he live? Has he told you?"

"No, I only know it's a small town, miles away from a hospital."

Tracy did a *tsk-tsk*. "Too bad. From what the sports announcer on TV said about his injuries, he's going to need weeks, maybe months, of physical therapy. How's he going to do it if he lives that far from a hospital? If he doesn't have family to come and stay with him here, there probably isn't going to be anyone to take him to a physical therapist either."

Burgandi poked Dina's leg under the table then whispered, "Unless one would come to him."

Kitty's eyes widened. "I hope he has good insurance coverage. Working with a physical therapist every day, or even just several days a week, can get pretty expensive."

Dina took a final sip of juice then rose to her feet. "I'd like to stay but I have to—"

Burgandi rolled her eyes. "I know—get back to the hospital."

"No, I was about to say I have to pack up my things and put them in my car."

"By the way, someone from the hotel desk called our room last night. They're holding a box for you in the lobby."

Dina could tell by the look on her face that Burgandi was dying of curiosity, but she wasn't about to explain the box's contents or why it was delivered to her, so she feigned surprise. "Oh? I'll have to ask about it when I check out." She folded her napkin and placed it on the table. "I'm sorry to leave such good company but I really do have to get moving. It's been a delight seeing all of you again, and I'm looking forward to getting together with you at our convention." She placed a hand on Celeste's slim shoulder. "You've done a magnificent job on this, Celeste. Because of your close attention to detail, it seems everything came off without a hitch. I couldn't believe it when Burgandi told me the committee was finishing a day early. Even though I didn't do nearly as much work as the rest of you, I'm proud to have been a part of it." Before anyone had time to respond, she gave them a little wave and headed for the stairs.

She packed as quickly as she could, in hopes of getting out of the room before Burgandi finished her breakfast and came upstairs to confront her, but she didn't make it.

"You *are* staying, aren't you?" Burgandi asked, waving her arms as she flew into their room. "I knew it. I just knew it. You're in love with that guy. Dina, I thought you were smarter than that. I suppose next you're going to tell me it was love at first sight and you couldn't help yourself."

"I'm not in love with anyone, least of all a cowboy," Dina assured her indignantly.

"Yes, you are; it's written all over your face. How could you do it, Dina? A bull rider of all people? I've seen you turn down handsome, well-mannered, educated men with good jobs and brilliant futures ahead of them, guys who were crazy about you. Now you've gone gaga over some broken-down cowboy who wears silly polka-dot shirts and clown makeup! Sure he's popular, and probably making some pretty decent money at rodeos, but how long can that last? Especially considering his latest injuries? For all you know, the guy may have a wife and kids stashed away somewhere. He might even have a criminal record. Did you ever think that may be why he wants his face covered?"

"He's none of those things. He's a fine, decent man."

"You know that? After only two days, when much of that time he was still under the affects of drugs?"

"It's just something I know." She closed her suitcase lid with an impatient snap.

"Do you even know his real name?"

"Most of it."

"Where he lives?"

"Almost."

Burgandi threw her hands up in frustration. "Dina, how could you be in love with that man? Think! Don't be dazzled by his charm and the mystique that surrounds him. Go home. Go back to Omaha and forget him. Can't you see? He's using you! He knew when he came here he might get hurt. He's a big boy. Let him find someone else to take care of him. He is not—and I emphasize *not*—your responsibility. I'm sorry to be so emotional about this, but I'm your friend. I can't stand idly by and watch you get hurt."

Dina wrapped her arms about her friend. "I told him I would stay today but I was going home tomorrow, and that's what I intend to do. Does that make you feel any better?"

"Yes, if you actually mean it and are not just saying it to get me off your case."

"I do mean it."

Burgandi sighed. "I should have known you were too smart to do something that foolish. Can you forgive me for my raving and ranting?"

Dina tightened her grip. "I already have."

Since she wasn't quite sure what to do with the box when she got to the hospital, she temporarily left it locked in her trunk. Will was waiting for her with the head of his bed raised, cradled in clean sheets, fresh from a sponge bath, his hair still damp. "Well, don't you look nice?" she asked as she breezed into his room.

"Thanks." His warm smile made her smile. "I was hoping you'd come back."

She pulled her purse strap from her shoulder then placed her purse in the chair before moving up close to his bed. "If you knew me better, you'd know I always keep my promises."

His smile broadened. "I'd like to know you better."

"And I'd like to know you better. You know I'm Dina Spark, a trauma nurse who lives in Omaha. All I know about you is that your real name is William Martin, and you're a rancher/bull rider who lives somewhere in southwestern Nebraska. That's about it."

"I'd tell you more, if I could."

"When I visited with my friend at the hotel this morning, she said the best thing I could do would be to head back to Omaha and forget about you, that I didn't know the real you—only what you wanted me to believe, which may not be the truth. Truth is very important to me."

He winced at her words. "She's probably right, but you're not going to take her advice, are you?"

"I told you I'd stay until tomorrow, and I will, but I'll need to leave no later than noon. I need to get back to my own life. I like you, Will, I really do, and I've enjoyed every minute of being with you, but your recovery is not my responsibility. Surely when you got into bull riding you knew something like this was bound to happen eventually. Didn't you have a plan in mind? Someone you could call in case of an emergency like this?"

He shook his head as he lowered his gaze. "Not really. I never expected something like this to happen. I'm very grateful for all you've done. I realize that, like the others who brought me here in that ambulance, you could have walked off, left me, gone back to whatever you were doing, and thought of me as nothing more than another patient among the many you see every day. But you didn't. You stayed."

"But—"

"Let me finish. I wish there was some way I *could* repay you for staying but"—he gestured his good hand toward his injured shoulder then his leg—"until these things heal and I'm back on my feet, there is no way I can do it. Maybe I can send you a present. Just know you are the best thing that has ever happened to me."

"No presents, please. I'd do more if I could, but I can't. I have to get home."

He gazed at her, his blue eyes seeming to penetrate her very soul. "You're a pretty little thing. Did anyone ever tell you how beautiful you are?"

She sent him a shy smile. "Yes, you. You did."

His brows rose. "I did? When? I've wanted to tell you but I don't remember actually doing it."

"The afternoon you came out of surgery." Her smile turned to an embarrassed grin. "You probably don't remember it because you were still a bit loopy at the time."

"Good for my subconscious mind. It did what I'd wanted to do a number of times, because you are beautiful."

Though Dina often received compliments from her friends and coworkers, she never knew how to respond. "Thank you. It's nice of you to say so."

"I only said it because you are. You're a real knockout, Dina. I envy the guy who marries you."

She felt a flush rise to her cheeks. "I–I'm not sure that marriage thing will happen too soon. Not unless Mr. Right comes along. My standards are pretty high."

"Yeah, I hear that. You sure wouldn't want to make a mistake. As Christians, I'm sure we both think marriage should be forever."

"Oh, yes, for sure. Being married to the wrong person could be miserable."

The silence in the room was palpable.

Finally, lifting his head, Will motioned toward the door. "I've been thinking, as much as I hate to see you go, if you leave now you can still get to Omaha before dark. Go on, Dina. Don't worry about me. Dr. Flaming and the nurses are giving me great care. I'm sure you need to get back to your life."

"But I promised I'd stay until tomorrow."

"I know you did but, believe me, other than the fact that I enjoy your company and your smiling words of encouragement, there really isn't any reason for you to stay. Go on home. The doctor said they'd be releasing me in a day or two, so I'll be going home, too." With that, he turned his head to one side and closed his eyes. "I'm getting kind of sleepy. If you don't mind, I'd like to take a nap."

"Are you sure? I could stay."

With his eyes still closed, he took a deep breath and let it out slowly. "No. Go on back to Omaha. Like I said, I'll be fine."

"But I have your boots and spurs."

He opened his eyes and stared at her. "How did *you* get them? I figured they were long gone and I'd never see them again."

"Dr. Pratt had someone deliver them to my hotel, along with a few other items you'd left behind. I have them locked in the trunk of my car."

He continued to stare at her, as if trying to come up with a place she could leave them.

"The box isn't heavy; it's bulky, but I think it will fit in your closet. Do you want me to bring it up here?"

"I hate to ask you to, but I sure don't want to lose my boots, and especially not my spurs. They're kind of special to me."

"You didn't ask. I volunteered. I'll do it now." She glanced down at the sheet covering his leg. "By the way, how are you going to get home when they release you? Even though you have one hand to steer, with your injured leg being your right one, you won't be able to drive yourself."

He shrugged. "I can probably find someone to drive me."

"But all the rodeo people you know have gone home."

"Then I'll hire someone."

"They had to cut your shirt and pant leg to get to your wounds. You don't even have clothes to wear."

"I can call one of the local stores and have jeans, a shirt, underwear, and socks delivered. That's all I need."

He seemed to have an answer for everything.

"Then I'll be back in a little while." With an assortment of confused feelings, she turned and walked out into the hall.

Will stared at the ceiling. When he had promised himself he would send Dina on her way, he'd had no idea it would be so hard. The idea of never seeing her again made him ache. He wished there could be something between them but she was on her way up in her profession. He might still have a few good years in him, if he were ever able to ride bulls again but, after that, he'd be on his way down. A man's body could only take so much abuse. He'd already had his share. When his bull-riding days were over, he would go back to being nothing more than a plain old cowboy.

He closed his eyes and listened to the slight sound of her heels clicking across the marble floor as she crossed the room and opened the closet, then the sound of the box as she scooted it into the closet. He held his breath as her footsteps came closer to the bed and she opened and closed the drawer of his nightstand. When all sound ceased, he visualized her blue eyes gazing down at him. Every bone in his body cried out for him to take her in his good arm, kiss her, and tell her how much he cared for her. But what right did he have to do such a foolish thing? Besides, she would probably be furious with him for being so brash and they would end up parting on bad terms.

What is she doing? Simply standing there looking down at me? He tried to keep his breathing even, but with the emotions raging inside him at the thought of letting her walk out of his life it was impossible.

How much longer could he lie there without giving himself away? She'd brought his boots and spurs. Why didn't she leave? He was about to open his eyes when he felt her warm breath on his face, then the sweet touch of her lips as they grazed his cheek. He lay as still as stone, his heart hammering against the wall of his chest. When he felt her lips touch his cheek, he thought he would die from gladness. He'd never felt anything so delicious. It was all he could do to keep from kissing her back. How he wished he hadn't faked sleep. But if he hadn't, maybe she would have put the box in the closet, said a simple good-bye, and left without kissing him.

"Wake up, Will," she murmured softly, her lips feathering against his.

He opened his eyes slowly. She was so close he could see the soft green flecks in her blue eyes. "You're back," he said, trying to sound as though he had just awakened from a sound sleep.

She moved a fraction away from him. "The box containing your boots, spurs, and those other things is in the closet. I hope you didn't mind my waking you but I couldn't leave without saying a proper good-bye."

"Thanks for bringing the box. A cowboy isn't a cowboy without his spurs." Oh, how he wanted to reach up and kiss her.

"Well, I guess I'd better be going. I really want to make it to Omaha before dark."

He nodded. "Yeah, good idea. Have a safe trip."

"You will look me up if you ever get to Omaha, won't you?"

"I've only been there once. It's not likely I'll get there again, but you never know." He sucked in a deep breath and held it when her finger touched his cheek.

"Then I guess this is good-bye. It's been nice knowing you, Will."

"It's been nice knowing you, too, Dina. And thanks again."

Before he knew what was happening, she bent and kissed him on the lips again, this time, long and lingering. Then, before he could respond or say another word, without even a backward glance in his direction, she was gone.

His hand slowly rose and touched his lips.

Dina may be walking out of his life, but he'd remember her beautiful face and that kiss forever.

Chapter 7

"Whoa, Miss Spark, wait up!"

Dina turned at the sound of her name. "Oh, hi, Dr. Flaming."

"I thought you would like to know, since Mr. Martin is doing so well, I plan to release him tomorrow."

"Tomorrow? I hadn't realized it would be that soon."

"Well, there's really nothing more we can do for him here. The rest of his recovery is up to him."

She asked a few questions about the type of therapy he thought would be best and then, once again, thanked him for his part in Will's recovery.

"No thanks needed." He glanced at his watch. "Oops, I'm late. I have to be going, too. Have a safe drive back to Omaha."

Dina sat in her car a full ten minutes before inserting the key in the ignition and giving it a turn. The news that they were going to release Will that soon had come as a real shock. "I don't care if he is leaving early and has nothing to wear and no one to drive him, it's not my problem," she told herself aloud, thumping her hands on the steering wheel in frustration. "Let him find his own way home. He's nothing but an arrogant—self-centered—independent—broken-down—bull rider! How dare Burgandi accuse me of being in love with someone like him! A man who wears makeup and silly shirts—and—and rides bulls?"

She yanked the gearshift into reverse, hurriedly looked both ways, backed, then fell in line with the other cars waiting to exit the hospital's parking lot. *Okay, I admit I felt sorry for him. And was maybe a little dazzled by the mystique that surrounds him, but I could never love him.*

As the cars ahead of her began to move, she inched cautiously forward. *If I were interested in finding a man, which I'm not at this stage of my life, a rodeo would be the last place I'd look for him.*

When she came to the intersection of Warren and 24th, though she was tempted to turn right and circle back to the hospital and Will, she made a left at 24th, then turned south onto Central and headed toward I-80 and home. *That man is on his own now. There is nothing else I can do for him. But pray,* she reminded herself as the miles ticked by on her odometer. *In a few days he'll be nothing but a memory.* But in her heart she knew forgetting him wasn't going to be that easy, not after the once-in-a-lifetime experience the two had shared together.

Nearly an hour later, when she reached I-80's exit 21 near Kimball, Nebraska, she changed her mind, pulled off the road, and dialed a familiar number on her phone.

Her boss answered on the first ring.

Next, she called her mother. "Hi, Mom. I know you're going to think I'm crazy but I won't be back to Omaha for another week or two. A friend of mine has been injured and needs a ride home and someone to stay a few days to help with physical therapy."

"Oh, sweetheart, I'm sorry to hear about your friend's injuries. Is it anyone I know?"

Dina hesitated, not wanting to upset her mother by letting her know the person was not only a man but one she barely knew. "No, it's someone I met in Cheyenne. I've already called my boss. She okayed my using my vacation time."

"Was this another nurse?"

Not wanting to lie to her mother, she decided to give her the whole truth. "No, a bull rider. It's a long story. I met him at the rodeo—"

"What were you doing at a rodeo? You hate bull riding!"

"Yeah, I know. I wasn't there to attend the rodeo. I was helping out in the Justin Sportsmedicine trailer and ended up riding to the hospital in the ambulance with him. He lives not far from Burgandi, and since I was driving home in his direction, I offered to drive him."

"And you're staying there? At the man's house? That's not like you, Dina."

"He and his mom live on the family ranch in Belmar, a little town in southwest Nebraska. Don't worry, he's not much of a threat. He isn't able to get around on his own. I'm only staying until he can find a physical therapist to take my place." She went on to explain both his injuries and his prognosis. "He needs my help, Mom. It's the right thing to do."

"Call me every day. I want to know you're getting along okay. Don't take any chances. If he gets—well, you know—get out of there fast."

Dina laughed. "He's not that kind of man, Mom, and even if he was, with his injuries he'd have a hard time catching me." They visited a few more minutes then she hung up, still smiling as she thought of Will chasing her with his bad leg and an unusable arm.

Will did everything he could to keep his mind off Dina, but nothing worked. Her lovely vision was always with him. He couldn't even nap without dreaming about her.

"Good morning. How's my star patient?"

He turned his head at the sound of his doctor's voice. "Good morning, Dr. Flaming. I'm doin' okay."

Dr. Flaming glanced at his chart then moved to the side of the bed. "Actually, you're doing better than okay. Fortunately, much of what Dr. Farha and I had to do to your knee we were able to do using arthroscopic surgery, which is helping shorten your recovery time. In fact, by tomorrow, you'll be ready to go home. I'm sure that's good news."

He gave his good shoulder a slight shrug. "Yeah, I guess it is."

The doctor frowned. "Is there a problem?"

"No, not really. Since I won't be able to drive myself, I'm just not sure how I'll get there."

"I would think, as popular as you are, there would plenty of people who would be willing to drive you."

"Yeah, probably. I'll think of something."

"Then I'll see you in the morning." He headed for the door. "I'll sign your release and you can go home."

"Thanks, Dr. Flaming. I appreciate all you've done for me." As the doctor left his room, Will leaned his head against the pillow and closed his eyes. He knew he had no right to ask God why this catastrophe had happened to him. He had put himself in harm's way. No one had twisted his arm and made him do it. He'd known from the moment he'd straddled himself over that bull's back he was inviting injury. He'd made the decision; now it was up to him to suffer the calculable consequences. What did they call it? Paying the piper? He'd danced to Gray Ghost's tune; now it was his turn to pay the piper, whatever the costs. *Lord, You know the mess I've gotten myself into. I really need Your help. Getting this battered body back to Belmar is going to take nothing short of a miracle.*

Dina couldn't keep from smiling as she strode across the hospital lot nearly four hours later, a shopping bag in her hand. Her unexpected decision had been the right one. She could feel it in her bones. James 4:17, one of the scriptures she had learned as a child, kept ringing through her mind. *"Therefore to him that knoweth to do good, and doeth it not, to him it is sin."* What she was about to do was good, the right thing to do. Surely God would be pleased.

She smiled a friendly hello to several nurses as she exited the elevator and swung left. The beat of her heart seemed to quicken as she turned and entered a very familiar room.

"Dina? What are you doing here? I thought you went back to Omaha."

Grinning with anticipation and excited to see how Will would react when she explained, she moved close to the bed and placed her hand on his good shoulder. "I've come to drive you home!"

"You can't. You're supposed to get back to your job."

"I had some vacation time coming so I called my boss, explained your circumstances, and asked if it would be okay if I used it. She said yes, she could find someone to take my place, and here I am!" Out of habit, she began tugging at the covers on his bed, straightening them for him as she had done since he'd been admitted.

"But—"

She put her finger to his lips to silence him. "I know what you're going to say. That I shouldn't use my vacation time that way, and if I drive you home in my car your pickup will be left in Cheyenne with no way for you to get it." She paused long enough to grab a breath. "My friend Burgandi and her parents live less than fifty miles from where we met. They'll drive to Cheyenne this weekend, get your pickup, and drive it back to their house—if that's okay with you. They would never tell anyone who you are, Will. Then, when you feel like it, you can have someone drive you those few miles to their place to pick it up, and no one will know where you live and you can remain as mysterious as ever, whatever your reason for wanting to do so. See, it's all taken care of. You don't have to worry about a thing. From what you've said, I assume you live with your mother. If it's all right with her, I'll stay at your place for a few days, help you with your physical therapy until we can get someone else lined up, then I'll go back to my life in Omaha. You came to my rescue, now it's my time to come to yours."

"My mom would be happy to have you there, but—"

"Okay then, don't try to argue with me. I'm driving you."

"But—"

"I know. You don't have any clothes to wear home." Spinning around, she took the shopping bag from the chair where she'd left it and dumped its contents onto the bed in front of him. "See? All taken care of. New shirt, jeans, underwear, and socks. I even got you a new pair of sports shoes. I checked the size on your boots, so I know they'll fit."

"But you've already done. . ."

She reached out and took hold of the hand that had become so familiar to her. Despite its roughness, she adored the feel of his skin against hers. "Quit making such a big deal out of it. It wasn't as if I really did anything. Mostly, I just stayed here with you."

His smile broadened into a grin. "Having you here is what has kept me going."

"Then it's settled. I'm driving you home."

The physical therapist came in about two o'clock and spoke with them, explaining the type of exercises that would be necessary to bring his body back to where it had been before his accident and how often he should do them.

"I'm really glad you'll be helping him," she told Dina after handing her some written information she thought would be helpful. "Hopefully by the time you have to leave him, he will have found a good therapist to take your place."

They both thanked her then spent the rest of the afternoon and most of the evening either visiting or watching television. When the ten o'clock news program ended, she switched off the TV, pulled the blanket up over him, then curled up in the recliner.

By the time Dr. Flaming came in early the next morning, Will had not only finished his breakfast, he was dressed, ready, and eager to leave.

Dina settled herself in the driver's seat then turned to gaze at the tired face of the man sitting next to her. Even with the assistance of the two men from the hospital, it had taken some doing to get him out of the wheelchair and into the front seat of her small car. But, with the help of the pillows she'd bought—one to prop behind his shoulder and one to put under his leg—Will finally found a position that was comfortable and began to relax.

She shoved the key into the ignition and smiled at her passenger. "Ready?"

He nodded. "Yeah, but now I'm really worried."

"About what?"

"I'm wondering how I'm going to get from your car into the house when I get home. Those two big, strong orderlies aren't going to be there to help me, and I'm way too big for you and my mom to carry."

As she pulled out of the parking lot, she sent him a playful grin. "We could rent a forklift."

"That's funny, but this isn't a joke. It's serious. With my bad leg, I can't even crawl."

She felt sorry for making light of his situation. "What would you say if I told you I rented a wheelchair? It's in the trunk."

His expression brightened. "Did you, really?"

"Hey, I'm a nurse. I think about those things. It'll probably still be a struggle to get you into it, but we'll make it. Don't worry about it. You're dealing with a professional."

"I should have known. You think of everything."

"Not everything, but I try. It's about two and a half hours to Ogallala. I thought we'd stop there for lunch." She gave him an impish smile. "Are you ready to tell me your full name or am I going to have to read it off your mailbox when we get to your ranch?"

He grinned back. "I guess, after you've been so patient with me, it's only right that I tell you. It's William *Robert* Martin."

She threw her head back with a laugh. "Oh, I get it! William Robert Martin—Billy Bob!"

"Yep, that's me. Now you know."

"Now I feel like I'm privy to some big national secret."

"Hardly, but the name has served me well."

"But why use it? Why not just go by your real name? And why the makeup? Was it, like some people say, all just some big promotional idea? To get you noticed by the fans?"

He huffed. "I wish I could say that's why I did it but, no, promotion had nothing to do with it."

She frowned. "Then why? I don't understand."

He gazed at her for a moment, as if considering his answer before voicing it. "I'm going to tell you, Dina, but not here. About fifty miles after we leave I-80, we'll be driving past the little town of Hayes Center. Turn off there, find a nice shady tree, and park, and I'll tell you my whole sordid story."

"Why there? That's a long way from here. Why not tell me now?"

"Number one. Because I'm sleepy." He stifled a yawn then leaned his head against the headrest and closed his eyes.

"And number two?"

He opened one eye and peered at her. "Because I don't want to tell you while we're driving down the road at seventy miles an hour. I want to tell you face-to-face. It's better that we wait until we get to Hayes Center."

She wanted to argue with him but decided not to. He'd agreed to tell her: that was something. She'd just have to wait. By the time they reached I-80, he was sound asleep.

After a pleasant lunch at Ogallala, she continued on to Highway 83, turning south toward Wallace where it intersected with Highway 25. "You'll have to guide me from here," she told him, after glancing in her rearview mirror. "I've never been this way before."

"We've got another fifty miles to go on this road before we hit Hayes Center. It's sure nice to be back in Nebraska again. I love this state." He shifted his weight then let out a slight groan.

"I wish my car was bigger. I hate it that you're so cramped up. Too bad you can't get out and stretch your legs."

"That would be nice, but we both know that won't work. I'm fine. Don't worry about me."

Her anticipation rose with each mile as they headed toward Hayes Center. It seemed to take forever before the city's road sign appeared in the distance.

"The town is to your left, a mile or so off this road," he told her, pointing east.

She made the turn then drove through the tiny town until they came to a tall tree, its branches fanning out over the dirt street, its thick green leaves filtering out the hot afternoon sun. "This okay?"

When he nodded she parked and turned off the engine then rolled down her window and twisted in the seat to face him. "I'm listening."

Chapter 8

Instead of responding, Will just sat there, staring straight ahead, wondering where he should begin. How much he should tell her. . .

"Are you okay?"

"Yeah, I'm okay."

She reached to help him adjust the pillows when he tried to angle his body more toward hers. "You have to be tired. We can go on if you want—you can tell me your story later."

He was tired, and he'd like nothing more than to head on to Belmar, lie down in his own bed, and stretch out his limbs. Sitting cramped up in her small car had been much harder on him than he'd let on. "No. I'd rather tell you now."

She gazed at him for a moment, her eyes betraying her concern for him. "You sure you feel up to it?"

No, I hurt like crazy but, right now, that isn't important. What is important is being honest with you. "Just let me talk, okay? You have to know everything before we get to the ranch."

A frown creased her brow. "Why before then?"

"Because, Dina, you'll be the first one to hear my story. No one else knows it. Not even my mom."

Her eyes rounded. "Your own mother doesn't know?"

"No, but I hope after you hear me out you'll understand why I haven't told her. Just sit back and listen, okay?"

She nodded.

"Several years after my parents married, my mother's father died and she inherited our ranch. Unfortunately, she also inherited the huge mortgage he'd put on it, as well as a number of bills he'd left unpaid. Mom loved the ranch. My dad hated it, which meant my mom ended up being the one who ran it and did most of the chores. Until us four kids came along." He paused with a half smile. "Actually, about the only thing he was good at was giving my mom babies."

When he turned to look at Dina, she was smiling, too.

"Anyway, he was always after my mom to sell the ranch, which she refused to do, knowing that by the time the mortgage and the bills were paid off they'd be walking away with nothing. To her, that ranch meant security. As long as she could scrape up enough to keep the bank happy, we had a roof over our heads, meat on the table from the cattle we could raise, and vegetables from our garden."

Dina gave her head a sad shake. "Poor woman. Sounds like she had it pretty rough."

"She did, but she rarely complained and never thought of us as poor. Lacking in some of the nicer things of life, yes, but never poor."

"I didn't mean—"

Will lifted his hand. "I know. We might not have had as much as our neighbors, but we were rich in other ways. No one ever had a better mother. She raised us kids to be strong in body and mind, and strong in the Lord. For that, I'll always be thankful. Our faith is what got us through when everything else failed. By the time I was ten years old, I had taken over a good part of my mom's responsibilities and I was literally running the ranch, under her watchful eye, of course, and I did a good job. Summers, I even helped some of the other ranchers in order to earn extra pay to put in the sugar bowl where my mom kept the next month's mortgage payment. My dad? We didn't see much of him. He never did anything around the ranch, but he did work an odd job now and then, digging ditches, whatever he could find, but most of his time was spent at the pool halls or playing horseshoes for money. He turned into quite a gambler. Well, to make this very long story short, he came to me the morning of my twelfth birthday and told me—because my mom was pregnant and about ready to go into labor—he was going to drive into McCook to buy me a present and, when he came back, we'd all have cake and ice cream and celebrate."

"I'll bet that made you happy."

Will smiled. "Yeah, it did. He'd never bought me a present before. I waited for him all day. . . ." He felt the smile fade as he took on a frown. "But he didn't come back."

Dina flinched at his words. "Ouch, that must have hurt. Did he apologize?"

"No. In fact, we never saw him again."

"Ever? He just up and left?"

"That's exactly what he did. To make matters worse, the next morning my mom discovered he'd taken every penny out of the sugar bowl. Then, when she went to the bank to tell them she'd be late with her payment, she found out he had also taken the few dollars in savings she'd accumulated toward buying another calf to raise for our herd. Plus, he owed others in town, and soon they were constantly at our door, trying to collect those debts from my mom."

"How could he do such a thing? To his own family? Especially when his wife was about to go into labor?"

"Beats me. He walked off and left the woman he had vowed to care for and protect, after giving her four kids and leaving her buried in debt, and never looked back. And I've hated him for it ever since. What he did was unforgivable."

"I know."

He drew back in surprise. "What? No lectures on how a Christian should be willing to forgive? No comments on how my dad is as much a child of God as you and me?"

"No, I can't point a finger at you without pointing one at myself."

"Dina, what do you mean? Point one at yourself?"

"I'll tell you later, I promise. Right now, I want to hear about you."

"Okay, but I'm going to hold you to it." He uttered a slight moan as he shifted his leg. "Well, like I said, I was running the ranch by then. My two younger brothers helped as much as they could—my sister, too—but I was the one who ran things, with my mom overseeing everything, of course. I knew from going over the books with her that if we didn't do something, we weren't going to be able to keep that mortgage paid. I'd had a love of bull riding ever since I was old enough to straddle the old barrel another kid and I suspended between the trunks of four trees. Every spare moment I could get, I'd ride that old barrel and got pretty good at it. So, when one of our neighbors offered to let me try to ride his bull, I took him up on it. I was sixteen by then. Next thing I knew, I was ready for our local rodeo."

"So that's how you got into bull riding!"

"Yeah, at first my mom didn't mind, but then one of the guys, who shouldn't have been riding bulls in the first place, got a little cocky and stayed on the field too long after he'd been thrown off, shaking his fist in the bull's face, challenging him to come after him. Then when the bull did, he tripped over his own feet and fell."

Dina's hand flew to cover her mouth as she gasped. "Oh, no! What happened?"

"The bull trampled him to death, right there in front of our eyes. My mom was so scared she went crazy. She told me right then and there—absolutely no more bull riding for me. It scared me bad, too, but it also taught me a lesson. To never take my eye off a bull and to get off that field as quick as possible and let the clowns handle him. But, even though I knew I was riding without my mom's knowledge, I couldn't stop. I was twenty by that time and, as a grown man I felt it was up to me to make my own decisions and I told her so. I had just begun to make a little money—money we badly needed. So, since she was used to me spending time away from home by hiring myself out to other ranchers, she didn't suspect a thing when I kept taking off on weekends to do rodeo. I'd just tell her I had work to do out of town."

"That's when you started wearing the mask?"

He shook his head. "No, I just made sure any rodeos I entered were far enough from home my mother wouldn't hear about it. Anyway, when I was twenty-four, and riding even better, and word about the high scores I was making began to get around, I decided I'd better either quit or figure out a way to ride so my mom wouldn't accidentally find out. I couldn't quit. Those winnings were beginning to mount up, enabling me to pay the mortgage payment each month and actually put a little money in the bank. About that same time, while watching some of the cowboy clown bull fighters on TV, I came up with the idea of wearing a painted-on half-mask and the funny shirts, letting my hair and beard grow longer, adding a few extra pounds, and changing my name. So over that winter, I took about four months off to let it grow and add the pounds. I sure didn't want to register under my own name so, overnight, I became Billy Bob, the bull rider who came out of the blue, one that no one knew or recognized."

Dina let out a sigh and gave her head a shake. "And your mom never knew. That's why you didn't want me to call her and let her know about your injuries."

"Yes."

"But you said you'd had other injuries. Didn't she wonder about those?"

"Naw, I'd tell her they were all in a day's work, which was true."

She leaned back in the seat and stared straight ahead. "And you did all of this to save your family's ranch."

"Yes, and take care of a lot of other family expenses. Remember, I had three siblings to help care for. My two brothers, who never cared about staying on the ranch, are out on their own now. Ben is working in West Virginia and Jason is in college, studying for his Masters. My little sister Teresa, the one Mom was carrying when my dad left, is in college, too."

Dina took hold of his good hand and smiled up at him sympathetically. "And now you're on your way home and you're going to have to tell her."

He hung his head. "Yep, and I'm not looking forward to it. It's going to be one of the hardest things I've ever done."

"That's why you wanted to tell me before we got there."

He nodded. "Yes. Telling you was almost as hard as it's going to be to tell her, but I had to do it. Does it make any sense to you, when I say I'm both ashamed of what I've done, yet proud that I did it? Because I am proud. Rodeoing made it possible for me to nearly pay off the mortgage on our ranch. Since I've been handling the books and writing the checks, although my mom doesn't even know it yet, my plans are to have it paid off in one year, by her fifty-ninth birthday, and throw a big burning-of-the-mortgage party for her. That way, my sweet mama, who was born on that place, the place where she bore and raised her children, will also be able to die there."

Dina dabbed at her eyes with her free hand, so touched by his words she could barely speak. "I had no idea."

"Don't you see, Dina? What I've done, I didn't do for me. I did it for my mom and for our family. While I admit I love the thrill of riding bulls and the roar of the crowd when I've had a good ride, participating in rodeos was my means to an end. A job that paid me far better than any other job I could find in our area, one I could do while also taking care of the ranch. Why do you think I drive that old truck? Because every penny I've made has gone into that ranch, its improvement, or our savings, so my mom wouldn't lose it."

"And that's why you're going to *keep* riding bulls."

"Yeah. With the herds and the bulls we have now, in a little over a year, with the ranch paid off, our cattle operation should be self sustaining and provide a fairly decent living."

"*Then* you'll quit the rodeo business?" Oh, how she hoped his answer would be yes.

A shy grin formed beneath his mustache. "Someday maybe, but not that soon. I plan to ride for as long as I'm able and then go into business for myself. I'll still be around rodeos. I just won't be riding the bulls myself. I'm hoping to eventually raise several mean, cantankerous bulls as rodeo stock for others to ride." He chuckled. "Billy Bob's Bulls. Don't you think that has a nice ring? Hopefully, my reputation as a winning bull rider will open a few doors for me."

He's going to keep riding bulls? His words really upset her. Why hadn't the man learned his lesson? Well, it was his life, not hers. What he wanted to do with it was his business.

"Well, that's pretty much it. Do you hate me for it?"

"Hate you? I could never hate you—especially not after what you just told me about riding because of your family's ranch. Your motives were pure. If I would have been in your shoes—I probably would have done the same thing." She gave him a half smile. "Well, maybe not ride bulls, though at one time I had aspirations to rise to the top in barrel racing. But I would have done whatever was necessary to care for my mom." Her heart skipped a beat when he allowed his thumb to rove over the back of her hand.

His brows rose. "Barrel racing! You never told me."

"I know. I should have told you but after all the fuss I've made about you and bull riding, I guess I hated to admit that I, too, had been caught up in the thrill of participating in rodeo."

"When did—"

"We'll talk about my barrel racing days later, but right now we need to get you home." Reluctantly, she pulled her hand free from his and reached for the key in the ignition, giving it a turn.

They rode the rest of the way in silence as Dina ran his story over and over in her mind. She could only imagine how hard it was for him to tell her all those things. No wonder he had worked so hard at keeping his identity a secret. It was all for his mother.

Chapter 9

"Turn left at that next road," he told her just before they reached the little town of Belmar. Two miles later, when they came to a mailbox marked MARTIN, she swung a right and headed down the dusty road toward the old farmhouse that loomed in the distance, pulling up in front of the porch when they reached it.

"It's beautiful!" she said, meaning it. She gazed appreciatively at the two-story frame house, with its brown shutters, flower-filled window boxes, and fretwork-trimmed porch. "No wonder you and your mother wanted to keep this place in the family."

Before he could comment, the front door opened and a feisty little woman donned in an apron came flying out and rushed down the stairs toward them. "Her friend has a car similar to yours," he explained, dipping his head low. "She thinks it's her. She's really gonna be upset when she finds out it's me."

The woman's smile disappeared when she reached Dina's side of the car. "Oh, sorry. I thought you were someone else. What can I do for you?"

Dina gestured in Will's direction. "Someone here wants to see you."

The woman bent, giving her a full view of the front seat, let out a cry of joy when she realized it was her son, then raced around to the other side and flung open the door.

Will held his breath as she moved toward him, knowing no matter how glad she was to see him he was in for the worst verbal thrashing he'd ever had. As she flung his door open, despite the pain vibrating through his shoulder and arm, he swiveled in the seat to face her. "Hi, Mom."

Instead of ranting at him, like he'd expected, she threw her arms around his neck and began to cry, calling out between sobs, "You're home! I've been so worried. You're home. Praise the Lord for answered prayer." Then backing off a bit, she surveyed the shirt he was wearing, noting how only his left arm was in a sleeve with the other sleeve merely draped over his shoulder. "What happened to you, son? Did you have a wreck in that old truck of yours?"

He grabbed on to her with his free hand and smiled up at her. "No, Mama, I'll tell you about it later. Right now, I'd like to get in the house, but I have a problem." He gestured toward his right pant leg, the one Dina had slit to above his knee. "My leg's hurt, too. I can't walk."

He was glad when Dina hopped out of the car and hurried around to join them. "Mama, this is Dina. She's a nurse. She was nice enough to drive me here. She's gonna stay with us for a while and help me get started on my physical therapy."

"If that's okay with you," Dina hastened to add. "I don't want to be a bother."

His mother gave her hand a shake. "Of course it's okay with me. Welcome, girl. We always have room for visitors."

"I have a wheelchair in the trunk, but we may need someone else to help lift him into it."

"Stay right here. I'll call my neighbor. As if he doesn't have enough to do on his own place, Brian's been helping with the chores since Will's been gone, but his boys have been helping him, so he hasn't minded. Will's covered for him quite a few times."

The two watched as his mother hurried back into the house. In a matter of minutes, Brian Canter, who lived on the adjoining ranch, was there to assist. A big, strong man, he literally scooped Will into his arms and into the chair, then pulled it up the porch steps as it if weighed not much more than a feather. Brian even went into the bathroom to assist Will before lifting him onto his bed.

As soon as he was gone, Mrs. Martin seated herself beside Will and began stroking his hand. "Tell me, son, what happened to you, and where have you been so long? Why didn't you call me?"

Dina placed a reassuring hand on Will's shoulder. "You and your mom need some private time together. I'll get our things out of the car and bring them inside."

The last thing she heard before she stepped out onto the porch was Will's mother yelling out, "You've been riding bulls? After I told you that you had to stop?"

After everything had been unloaded, Dina wandered into the kitchen, poured herself a glass of iced tea, then moved out onto the porch. She settled herself in one of the rocking chairs and sat gazing out over the pasture, watching brilliant orange and red streaks from the sun decorate the cloudless blue sky above the trees, listening to the twittering of birds somewhere off in the distance, and worrying about the conversation going on inside the house.

Thirty minutes later, Mrs. Martin joined her, her eyes red and rimmed with dark circles. "William told me all the things you've done for him and how you stayed by his side in the hospital. Thank you for being so good to my boy, Dina. He's the best thing that ever happened to me. I just feel bad that I forbade him to ride those bulls like he was some little kid. He's a grown man, old enough, and certainly capable enough of making his own decisions. As his mother, I could give him my opinions, but I had no business *telling* him what he could and couldn't do, much less forbidding him."

"He's a great guy. Your son loves you very much. He never meant to hurt you. You know that, don't you?"

She nodded. "Yeah, I do. I would have lost this ranch without him. Oh, I was upset with him, and wanted to wring his neck for what he'd done, but I'm just glad to have him home. Do you think he'll ever have full use of his arm again? And be able to walk?"

Dina nodded. "With a lot of work, yes, I'm sure he will. And I'm going to do all I can to help him. Within a few days he should be able to get around by himself. His arm and shoulder sustained the worst damage. They'll take a little longer to heal but, hopefully, he'll regain full use of those, too."

Mrs. Martin slid into a rocking chair next to her, her face suddenly taking on a look of pure joy. "I'm so glad you were there for my William. He's sure God sent you to be with him."

"It is kind of uncanny the way we met out on the road that day and then again in Cheyenne. When things like that happen, it's hard to believe God wasn't in it."

"You got anyone waiting for you back in Omaha?"

Dina wrinkled up her forehead. "You mean like. . .a boyfriend?"

The woman nodded.

"Occasionally I date one or two guys I work with at the hospital, but none seriously. Why?"

His mother gave her a mischievous smile. "Just curious."

"I don't know if Will told you but I was raised on a ranch. I'll be happy to assist around here in any way I can. And I'm not much of a cook but I'd like to help with meals, laundry, cleaning, and anything else I can do while I'm here. Is there any chance one of your other sons can come and help with the ranch work until Will can take over again?"

She shook her head. "They might be able to come a few weekends and help out, but you know how it is when you have job and school commitments. It's tough to get away, but they help when they can. All my children enjoy being here but none of them loves this old ranch the way my William does."

"Hey!" a male voice rang out from inside the house. "What are you two talking about out there? Come in here where I can hear you!"

The two women laughed then exchanged glances and headed for his room.

"I like your mom," she told him later as she carried his supper tray in to him.

"And she likes having you here. She told me so." He sniffed the air. "Umm, ham. No one fixes it like my mama."

She placed the tray on his lap then hurried back into the kitchen to get her own tray before seating herself in the chair his mother had placed beside the bed.

"I really like being here. This place is magical."

He gave her a sideways grin as he unfolded his napkin and placed it beneath his chin. "I love this place but I never thought of it as magical."

"It's like stepping back in time with all the wonderful antique furniture, the heavily starched crocheted doilies, old dishes, that marvelous grandfather clock chiming every hour, the magnificent stairway, the fretwork—all of it. I feel like I've walked into a storybook." She gestured toward his food. "Let's go ahead and pray. We don't want it to get cold."

She remained quiet while he bowed his head and prayed a simple prayer. When he finished, he picked up his fork and speared a piece of the sugar-cured ham his mother had cut into small pieces for him. "Most of what you see around here belonged to my grandparents. Other than adding a few of her own touches, Mom has kept everything pretty much as they left it."

"That's wonderful. So many people get rid of old things, preferring to have the latest and the newest. Not me. I'd love to have a house just like this one and filled with furniture this lovely." She ran her fingers over the heavily carved rose pattern on the front of his nightstand, taking time to feel each indentation. "They don't make things like this anymore."

He glanced around the room. "I know. I've refinished a few things for Mom. Unlike what you find on the market today, this furniture was built to last."

She sighed. "It breaks my heart when I go to a yard sale or a flea market and see the way people get rid of things they should value."

He speared another piece of ham then gazed at her. "Did Mom have you put your things in that pink room?"

She nodded. "Yes, it's beautiful, and that quilt on the bed—well, I've never seen anything like it. I can hardly wait to crawl under it tonight. Everything about this house is amazing."

"You're not just saying that to be polite?"

"No! It is amazing. I just wish I'd brought my camera so I could get some pictures to take home with me."

"You will stay the whole two weeks, won't you?"

"If necessary, but we need to find you a physical therapist before I go. I'm going to check with the hospital in McCook and see if they know of one who lives nearby." She offered a hearty laugh. "You may be wishing for someone other than me. I'm a pretty tough taskmaster."

"I'm going to do everything you say, Dina. I really appreciate your doing this for me."

She gave his hand a pat. "I'm impressed by how brave you've been through all of this. The pain you've gone through has had to be nearly unbearable yet you've never complained."

"Nothing I can't take. Injuries come with the territory when a guy rides bulls. But God answered prayer. And He not only kept me alive, He sent you to me. What more could I ask?"

She snapped her fingers with a loud snap. "I nearly forgot. Your mom told me Brian Canter was coming over as soon as he finished his chores. He thought you might like to sit in the wheelchair for a while, to change your position."

Will stretched out his good leg. "He's right about that. Though I've only been in this bed for a few hours, it feels like I've been here for days." He popped a cherry tomato into his mouth then smiled at her. "Can I talk you into going out on the porch with me? There's nothing prettier than seeing a Nebraska sunset."

She treated him to her best demure smile. "Why, sir, I'd be honored to sit a spell on the porch with you."

They had no more than finished their supper when Brian appeared at the door. "Ready?" he asked as he pushed the wheelchair close to the bed.

Will nodded. "Oh, yeah. I got a date with this pretty little gal to watch the sunset."

Dina grinned as she picked up their trays and headed for the kitchen. "I'm going to do the dishes for your mom then I'll meet you on the porch."

❧

Will watched her go. He still couldn't believe she had not only driven him home, she was actually going to stay with him for the next two weeks.

"How'd an ugly guy like you snag a beautiful woman like that?" Brian asked as he lifted Will and lowered him into the chair. "What'd you do? Lie to her and tell her there's oil in *them thar* hills?"

Will groaned as he lowered his injured leg onto the footrest. "She is beautiful, isn't she?"

"And nice," Brian added. "If I was you I'd hog-tie that little gal and never let her go."

"I'd like to do that very thing, but she's got a great job in Omaha with a brilliant future ahead of her. What have I got to offer her?"

"A nice home and the love of a good man. Isn't that what most women want?"

He shrugged. "Dina was raised on a ranch, but she's a city gal now. I doubt she'd be interested in living out here where it's so isolated."

Brian pushed the wheelchair toward the bathroom. "Take it from me. I'd say from the way she looks at you, she just might be more interested in you than you think."

Will rolled his eyes. "I wish!"

❧

Dina was already sitting in one of the rocking chairs and staring at the sky when he rolled up beside her. "Look!" she said turning and pointing toward the horizon.

"Did you ever see anything so magnificent? It's like God took a paintbrush and generously spread stroke after stroke of red, purple, and orange across His blue sky canvas."

"It's magnificent all right."

"What a beautiful picture that would make. We have some extraordinary sunsets in Omaha, but none the equal of that one."

"Our western Nebraska rainbows are great, too."

"I love rainbows!"

"Maybe you'll get to see one while you're here. Brian said we're supposed to have rain. We could sure use it. Things are really dry."

She turned her attention to him. "You really love this place, don't you?"

"Sure do. Wouldn't want to live any other place. How about you? You really like living in Omaha?"

"Yes, I guess so. It's a nice, friendly city. I like my job and my church. And I like my apartment."

"But if you could live wherever you wanted, would it be Omaha?"

"There are dozens of places I'd like to visit but. . ." She paused and stared off in the distance. "But Nebraska is home to me, and there's no place like home."

"I guess a big city like Omaha has its advantages."

She nodded. "Oh, yes. Omaha is large enough to have everything you want, yet small enough that all of those things are easily accessible. But don't get me wrong. I like living in a big city but I also miss the life I had growing up on our ranch."

"Really?"

"Oh, yes. I hadn't realized how much I'd missed it until I came here with you. Being out in the country again, smelling the fresh, clean air, listening to the mooing of the cattle, hearing the neighing of your horses, even seeing your chickens run free, brings back memories of the wonderful years I spent on my parents' ranch."

"That's good news. I was afraid you'd get bored, living isolated out here for two weeks."

Her eyes widened. "Bored? No way! I'm going to enjoy every minute of it."

"You said you were a barrel racer. I wish I could take you horseback riding."

"I'd like that. Maybe I can stop by the next time I come to visit Burgandi."

They visited, laughing and talking like old friends until Brian appeared. "Your mom and I got most of her chores done. I told her I'd be back early in the morning to help you get out of bed. You ready to call it a night?"

Although he'd rather stay on the porch with Dina, he nodded.

"It's such a beautiful evening, I think I'll stay out here a bit longer. I'll look in on you later," she told him as Brian rolled him toward the door.

Oh, how he wished he could stay out there with her, but he was grateful for Brian's willingness to help him do what he couldn't do for himself.

"You'd better get a good night's sleep," she told him when she stopped by his room as promised. "I'll be putting you through your physical therapy paces in the morning and I'm not going to be easy on you."

"How soon do you think I can start using this leg? I hate being helpless."

"As soon as you can put your weight on it."

Her words were music to his ears. Though he'd had other injuries before, he'd never been immobile and he hated it.

Bracing her hands on the edge of his bed, she leaned over him. "This has been a long, hard day for you. I'm amazed at how well you've done."

"Only because you were with me. I can't thank you enough for driving me here and giving up your vacation time to help me."

"I wouldn't be here if I didn't want to be." She bent and gently kissed his cheek. "Now get to sleep. I'll see you in the morning."

He watched her until the door closed behind her then sighed. She truly was an angel sent from God.

Chapter 10

After nearly three intense hours of physical therapy the next morning, Dina gave her head a shake. "Will, you can't expect to get back on your feet after only one session of physical therapy."

He turned his face away with a groan. "But I feel so helpless." He slammed his good fist on the table in frustration. "You're giving up your vacation to be here, I'm causing extra work for my mom, and Brian is taking time away from his own chores to help with mine."

Dina slipped her arm about his shoulders. "Your situation is only temporary. Before long, you'll be back to where you were before this happened. You have to have faith, Will. God is able to heal you."

Blinking, he locked his gaze on the ceiling. "He could also have protected me."

"Do you love the Lord?"

"Of course I do. You know that."

"Then you have to have faith. He had a purpose in it or He wouldn't have allowed it to happen."

He snorted then lifted his bad arm. "What good could come out of it?"

"You won the prize money."

"Which probably won't even pay my doctor and hospital bills."

She playfully tapped his nose with the tip of her finger. "You and I met. I think that's good."

He reached up and grabbed hold of her hand. "Is it? Do you really think it's good? I've caused you nothing but trouble."

Smiling, she tightened her fingers about his hand. "A little inconvenience maybe, but certainly not trouble. Like I said, I like being here with you, and I like being here on your ranch."

He pulled her hand to his lips and kissed it. "I'm sorry for being such a dork, but most of my life I have been the one taking care of others. I'm not used to having someone take care of me. Have patience with me, Dina. You're the last person on earth I want to upset with my ravings and carrying on."

"I'm not upset *with* you, Will. I'm upset *for* you. I know how hard this has to be but you will get back to normal. Things like this take time and effort. There are no shortcuts but it will happen." Then cuffing his chin with her free hand, she smiled at him. "Trust me. I'm a professional."

"You two ready for lunch?" his mother's voice sounded from the kitchen. "William's favorite. Fried chicken and corn on the cob."

He grinned at Dina. "Yeah, Mom. We'll be right there."

Dina smacked her lips. "Yummy. I love fried chicken." Turning loose of his hand and grabbing on to the handles on his wheelchair, she pushed him into the kitchen. "I hadn't realized you were going to have lunch this early. I should have helped you with it," she told his mother.

Mrs. Martin motioned her toward a chair. "Cooking's my job. Your job is getting that boy of mine back to where he was before—"

Will lifted his hand to silence her. "Now, Mom, no more of that. I did what you didn't want me to do and I'm paying the price. Can we just forget about it?"

His mother leaned over him and gave him a hug. "Yes, my precious son, we'll forget about it. But if you ever do that—"

"Mom!"

She lifted her hands in surrender fashion and backed away. "Okay, 'nough said. I'll keep quiet. I'm just thankful you're home. Let's enjoy our lunch."

Dina ate until she could eat no more then leaned back in her chair with a groan. "I'm stuffed. I can't remember the last time I had home-raised, free-range fried chicken and homegrown corn on the cob. You are a wonderful cook, Mrs. Martin."

The woman laughed. "Not much you can do to fried chicken and corn on the cob to ruin them, but I'm glad you enjoyed it."

"Wait'll you taste her rhubarb pie," Will inserted while reaching for another chicken leg. "It's the best I've ever tasted."

"Don't listen to him. He's biased." Mrs. Martin smiled at her son then passed him the gravy bowl. "Do you like to cook, Dina?"

"I like to, and I used to help my mom, but I don't do it often. It's no fun to cook for one."

"You plan on rising to the top of your profession or do you want to get married and have a family someday?"

Dina sent a nervous glance toward Will. "I guess that depends on when and if I find my Mr. Right. I love my job but I really do want to have a family. I've always felt being a wife and mother is one of God's highest callings."

"And, take it from me, it is." Mrs. Martin lowered her eyes and smoothed at her apron. "But I didn't do too well in the wife department. Will may have told you my husband ran out on us when he was twelve, but I like to think I've done a pretty good job at being a mother."

He reached across the table and took his mother's hand. "Good job? You've been the best mom in the world."

Mrs. Martin dabbed at her eyes with the tip of her apron hem. "And, despite the fact that you go against your mother's wishes sometimes, you're the best son a mother could ask for."

Watching that loving scene play out between Will and his mother touched Dina's heart so deeply she wanted to cry. From the time she'd been a little girl, her grandmother had told her if she wanted to see how a man would treat his wife all she had to do was watch how he treated his mother.

The three startled when the doorbell rang. It was Brian. "I've come to see if you need any help getting in or out of your chair before I go to town for some tractor parts."

Will sent him a grateful smile. "Yeah, I do. Thanks."

An hour later, after Dina had convinced Mrs. Martin to let her run the sweeper and dust, she and Will began their second therapy session.

"Higher. Take it slowly but lift that arm higher," she told him, holding his elbow and adding a bit more pressure.

"Ouch, that hurts."

"Come on, macho man. No pain, no gain—remember?" She watched as he swallowed hard, making his Adam's apple rise and fall. "I know it hurts but it has to be done."

He closed his eyes and gritted his teeth. "If I don't want you to think I'm a sissy, I guess I'd better keep my mouth shut and just do it."

"No, you tell me when if it hurts too much. I need to know when we get to that point so we can stop. Then the next time we do it, it will be a little easier. We don't want to push it too far at a time."

"When can I try to stand on my leg?"

She glanced down at his footrest. "We could try it now but it might be a good idea if we wait until after supper when Brian comes back from helping your mom with the chores. I don't want you falling."

"How soon do you think I can get rid of this chair?"

"Maybe in a couple of days. Thankfully, your leg didn't suffer nearly as much damage as your shoulder and arm." She jabbed at his good shoulder playfully. "Now, enough of this idle chitchat. Lift that arm again."

After a nice supper of homemade vegetable soup made with mostly vegetables from their garden, Dina and Will moved out onto the porch to once again watch the sunset. "You did great today," she told him, reaching over to pat his hand. "I'm proud of you."

He grinned the sideways grin she was beginning to love. "I'm proud of me, too. Boy, you are one tough therapist."

"Oh, that reminds me. While you were resting this afternoon, one of the administrators at the hospital in McCook returned my call with the name of a physical therapist that would be interested in working with you. I called her. She said she already has one client in this area, so it would be no problem for her to work with you, too."

His face took on a look of dismay. "Does that mean you're leaving early?"

"I told her I planned to be here for two weeks, which was fine with her. She's ready to take over when I leave. We're lucky to have found someone."

He huffed. "Yeah, lucky."

"You don't sound very enthused. You do want to get well, don't you?"

"Yeah, sure I do, I just—well—I don't want you to leave."

"I can't stay indefinitely. I have a life to get back to."

He nodded. "I know, but I like having you here."

"And I like being here, but we both knew when I came this was to be a temporary thing."

"Yeah, but I was hoping. . ."

"Hoping what?"

"I don't know. I guess that you'd—never mind. It was a stupid thought."

"Come on. Tell me."

"Naw. Forget it."

"Okay, I'm finished with the chores," Brian's deep voice boomed out as he climbed up the stairs to the porch. "You ready to try to get out of that chair?"

Will sent a quick glance Dina's way. "I am if she is."

Both upset and disappointed that she and Will hadn't had a chance to finish their conversation, Dina hurried to his side. "Brian, I'll hold his good arm to stabilize him while you lift him from behind."

Brian moved into position. "Okay, I'm ready. Go ahead, William. See if you can stand but take it easy. We don't want you hurting yourself."

"Brian's right. Don't rush it. Let us do the work until you're in a standing position. Then slowly put a little weight onto your right leg. If it hurts too bad, quit, and we can try it again tomorrow."

Will nodded then sucked in a deep breath and held it while they helped him out of the chair and onto his good leg. "Here goes."

Dina tightened her grip. "Slowly. Go slowly."

He cautiously leaned slightly to the right, allowing some of his big body weight to shift to that leg then grimaced. "Whoa, I think that's about it."

Dina let out a yelp. "That was great! Before you know it, you'll be walking all over the place."

He looked at her as if she were crazy. "Great? I barely put any weight on it!"

"But it's your first time," she countered, still smiling. "We'll try it again tomorrow, and the next day and the next day, until you're able to stand alone."

He huffed. "If I'm ever able to stand alone."

Brian frowned as he helped Dina lower him back into the chair. "If? Where's your faith, man?"

Will watched as Dina placed the footrest beneath his foot then leaned back with a heavy sigh. "Sorry, guys. Don't pay any attention to me. I know God is able. I just have to trust Him more."

Dina waited in the living room until after Brian had helped Will with his bathroom tasks and assisted him to bed.

"He's all yours," Brian told her when he joined her. "Sure tough to see him like that. I'm really glad you're here to help him."

"So am I, but he's the one who has to do the work. All I can do is assist him, make sure he does it right, and encourage him."

"He's a very special person. The whole community has been asking about him, wanting to know when they could come and visit him. I've told them to give him a day or two to adjust, and then they can come. I don't think there is a person in or around Belmar that Will hasn't helped in one way or another. I remember when his daddy left. It nearly killed that boy. What kind of father would leave his family like that? Especially on his son's birthday?"

"Did you know his father?"

He shook his head. "Not well. No one around here really knew him except the guys at the pool hall. That's where he spent most of his time. To be honest about it, his family is better off without him. He wasn't much good to them and he was mean to Will's mother, and he sure didn't contribute anything to the family finances or the work around here. If it weren't for Will, the Martin family would have lost this ranch. I've never seen a boy work so hard in my life. I guess that's why I wasn't too surprised when his mother told me he'd been off making money bull riding instead of working for other ranchers like she'd thought he was." He tugged his ball cap lower on his brow. "Well, I'd better get going. I wanna help my boys with a few more chores of my own before I go to bed."

Dina walked him to the door then thanked him for helping with both the chores and Will.

"No thanks necessary. He would have done the same thing for me and probably more. That's what good neighbors are for. By the way, tell Will that my brother and I are going to drive over to near where your friend lives tomorrow, to take a look at some cattle, so you'll need to draw me a map. We'll plan on driving Will's truck back so he can use it when he's ready."

"Oh, Brian, that is so nice of you. I know he will appreciate it. He loves that old truck."

"I'll park it out by the barn and bring the keys by in the morning if it's very late when we get back."

She thanked him again then filled a glass with water, wandered into the hallway, and rapped on Will's door. "Can I come in? I've brought you some water."

"Sure, come on in."

After placing the glass on his nightstand, she stood gazing at him.

"What? Why are you looking at me that way?"

"I had quite a talk with Brian about you."

He rolled his eyes. "Oh, no. I suppose he told you about the time I shattered a window in his barn with my BB gun."

She let out a giggle. "You did that?"

"Yeah, though I'm not very proud of it. I had no idea that thing would shoot that far."

"Well, you can relax. That's not what he said. He told me how you'd helped practically everyone in the community with one job or another. How did you find time to do all of that when you were taking care of this ranch?"

"A guy always has time to help his friends."

"You"—she paused to point her finger in his direction—"are amazing. Little did I know when I met you out on that deserted road and was almost afraid of you, that you were such a kind, caring, helpful man, with a boundless love for his family and friends. It's an honor to know you."

"Pshaw. Any guy worth his salt would do the same thing."

"Your father didn't."

"My father wasn't like most men I know, and he sure wasn't worth his salt."

She glanced at the clock on his nightstand then gave his arm a slight pinch. "Brian will be here bright and early and I have a grueling day of therapy planned for you."

He grinned at her. "Don't remind me. You about killed me today."

"If you think that was bad. . ."

He grabbed on to her arm and pulled her close. "No problem. I'm determined to take whatever you can dish out."

Dina felt her pulse quicken as she stared into his blue, blue eyes. "I was hoping you'd say that. Trust me, Will. You'll be back on your feet in no time." She hesitated for a moment then bent and kissed his cheek. "Sleep well. I'll see you in the morning."

He tugged on her hand, drawing her so close it made her feel giddy, and for a brief second she thought he was going to kiss her.

But he didn't.

"Good night, Dina. You're the prettiest thing that has ever happened to me."

Dina lay in her bed staring out the window at the moon for a long time before falling asleep. Being surrounded by the amazing antique furniture and pictures that had belonged to Mrs. Martin's grandparents *was* like taking a step back in time. There was something magical about being at the Martin ranch and she liked the feeling. Though she needed to get back to work, she almost hated the idea of returning to the city and its rush and hubbub. No wonder Burgandi and her family liked living where they did.

She flipped onto her side and pulled the quilt up about her, a quilt Will's grandmother had made. Though it was old and slightly tattered, it smelled nice, like fabric softener. The last thing she remembered before drifting off was the sound of a turtledove cooing in the tree next to her window.

Friday went pretty much the same as Dina worked with Will on his therapy and assisted his mother in the kitchen. Several neighbors and friends dropped by, bringing him flowers from their gardens, some brought casseroles, while others even stayed to help Brian with the chores.

"I'm going to run into town and pick up a few items I need and do a little grocery shopping for your mom," she told him Saturday morning after they'd finished their therapy session. "Anything you need?"

"Nothing. Just make sure you come back."

She gave him a coy smile. "Wild horses couldn't drag me away."

Though the little town of Belmar didn't offer much in the way of shopping other than groceries, she found almost everything she needed at the local mercantile store, buying a new pair of jeans and a couple of T-shirts for herself, a darling pink apron for Mrs. Martin, and a nice leather wallet for Will to replace the worn one she'd gotten out of his truck for him when they had been in Cheyenne.

Once she got back to the ranch and walked into the house, her arms loaded with groceries, and took one glance at Will, a shiver of delight ran through her.

Chapter 11

She hastily dropped her sacks into a chair as she hurried toward him. "I adore Vandykes. Surely you didn't trim your beard that way by yourself."

"Mom helped. It was pretty tough to do with one hand."

"Well, you both did a terrific job."

She leaned back and sized him up. "You're positively handsome. Now all you need is a little gel to make your hair stand on end like all the guys are wearing it."

"So you like the way my boy looks?" Mrs. Martin said, nodding toward her son as she came in from the kitchen, drying her hands on her apron.

"Absolutely."

Will rolled his eyes. "She told me in the hospital I was gorgeous."

Her eyes shining, Mrs. Martin chuckled. "You are!" Then turning to Dina she added, "He wanted to trim his beard into that Vandyke before he goes to church tomorrow. You will go with us, won't you?"

Dina slipped her arm about the woman. "I'm looking forward to it."

"What a nice bunch of friends and neighbors you have here," she told Will as they sat on the porch later that evening, gazing at the moon. "Everyone in town was so friendly."

He reached over, took her hand, and enfolded it in his. "You could stay, you know."

"Live here in Belmar? How would I make a living?"

"I couldn't pay much but I could hire you on as a ranch hand."

She threw back her head with a laugh. "Me, a ranch hand? At any price you wouldn't be getting your money's worth. In fact, I'd probably be a detriment."

"Detriment or not, my offer still stands. You can hire on anytime you're ready."

She playfully chucked him under the chin. "Don't tempt me. I might take you up on it. I love it here on your ranch."

"Or if you'd rather not be a ranch hand, you could marry me and be my wife."

Though she was sure he was only teasing, his words stunned her. "Don't kid about something like that. Marriage is a serious thing."

"What if I was serious?"

She grinned then swatted at his arm. "If I married you, you'd have to move to Omaha. That's where my job and family are."

"I could never leave this ranch."

"And I could never leave Omaha, so you're off the hook. Besides, I could never be married to a man who fights bulls. Of course you could always give it up. Quit the rodeo."

"I can't. You know that."

"Well then I guess that means I'll spend the rest of my life in Omaha." She rose and stretched her arms. "I hate to end this evening so early but I have to take a shower and shampoo my hair if I'm going to look presentable for church tomorrow morning. Brian said for you to call when you're ready to go to bed and he'd come right over. Want me to call him for you on the way to my room?"

He nodded. "Yeah, sure, I'll see you in the morning."

After a leisurely shower, Dina blow-dried her hair then crawled into bed, taking time to read her Bible and pray before settling down for a good night's sleep.

But at four in the morning, she was awakened by a loud crash from somewhere in the house.

Chapter 12

Without even taking time to pull her robe on over her pajamas she leaped out of bed and rushed into the living room, fully expecting to find an intruder had broken down the front door, or at least the wind had knocked off a table lamp and shattered it into many pieces. But nothing looked amiss. Everything in the living room appeared to be the same as when she had gone to bed.

"What's going on? What was that awful noise?"

Dina spun around to face Mrs. Martin. "I don't know. I thought someone was trying to break in—"

The two women turned as a low groan sounded from the hallway.

"William?"

Instantly, they rushed down the long hall to Will's room where they found him lying on his back, the bed on one side of him, the upset wheelchair on the other.

Dina dropped to her knees and, looping her hair over her ear, bent close to him. "What happened? Are you all right?"

He closed his eyes and let out another groan. "Yeah, I'm as all right as a one-legged man can be, I guess."

She wrapped her arms around him and held him tight. "I'm so, so sorry."

"How did you get down there on the floor like that, son?"

"I needed to go to the bathroom but I didn't want the two of you trying to lift me, so I tried to get out of bed by myself." He gave a disgusted grunt. "I was managing fairly well until that chair scooted out from under me." He gestured toward the pile of broken glass and the water on the floor. "Sorry, Mom, my arm must have hit the water pitcher you'd brought me when I fell."

Dina freed one hand and stroked his forehead. "You poor thing. You should have called us. Your mom and I would have been happy to help you."

He inflated his cheeks then slowly let out a breath of air. "I'm too big for you two to handle."

"We might not have been able to lift you but we could have kept you from falling." She bent and began picking up the glass and depositing it in the small wicker wastebasket they'd set beside his bed.

"Dina's right, son. You should never have tried to get out of bed alone. Are you sure you didn't hurt yourself?"

He lifted his good arm and gave her a half smile. "Other than what will probably be a pretty nifty bruise on my elbow where I banged it on the chair on my way down, the only other injured thing is my pride."

Dina carefully examined his elbow. "You're lucky that's all that was hurt. The way it sounded when you and that chair hit the floor, I thought someone had kicked in the front door."

He glanced down at the water spots on his pajama legs. "I must look like a real doofus."

"You don't look like a doofus to me." Dina tossed the last bit of glass into the wastebasket then stooped down and wrapped her arms around Will. "I have patients who do far more bizarre things than trying to get out of bed by themselves. If I would have been stuck in a bed like you have and needed to get up during the night, I would have done the same thing." She glanced about the room. "Where'd your mom go?"

He shrugged. "I don't know. She was here a second ago."

"Maybe she went to get you another pitcher of water."

"Water is the last thing I need right now."

A shy grin tilted at her lips. "Oh, yeah. I guess it is."

His mother came into the room, carrying a pair of his freshly laundered pajamas. "Brian will be right here."

Will wrinkled up his face and groaned again. "Aw, Mama, why'd you go and do that? It's the middle of the night."

She bustled about the room, straightening his bed and making neat little piles out of his things on the nightstand. "Brian told me to call him anytime you needed help. He didn't care what time it was. I only did as I was told."

"She's right, Will. I heard him tell her that very thing," she said in Mrs. Martin's defense.

"Thanks for leaving the front door open for me." Three sets of eyes turned as Brian came into the room, unshaven and his hair all askew. "I'm glad you called me."

Will huffed. "Mama shouldn't have called you. You need your sleep."

Brian bent and gently cuffed Will's bicep with his fist. "You tryin' to tell me you wouldn't do the same for me?"

He shrugged. "You know I would."

Brian gave him a wink. "Case closed. You call me anytime you need help, William. I mean that." Then turning to the women, he motioned toward the door. "Why don't you gals give us men a little privacy?"

"Ah, sure." Dina grabbed on to Mrs. Martin's hand as the two walked out of the room. Once they were out of earshot she said, "It really scared me when I heard that crash but I never dreamed it was your son."

"Me neither, but knowing how stubborn he can be, I shouldn't have been surprised. I just praise God all he got out of it was a bruised elbow."

Dina led her to her room. "You need your rest. Go back to bed. I'll stay up until Brian leaves and make sure the door is locked." She was relieved when Mrs. Martin didn't protest and went right to bed. She sat on the sofa, leafing through a magazine until Brian appeared.

"We got him changed into dry pajamas and he's back in bed now. I'm goin' home. I'll be back in the morning, probably about seven."

Dina thanked him and locked the door then headed for her room, but on impulse she paused at Will's door.

"I'm awake. Come on in."

She stepped inside then flipped on his bedside lamp before seating herself in his righted wheelchair. "Are you sure you didn't get hurt? From the sound of it, you had quite a fall."

"No, I'm okay. You know, I think I could have made it if that chair hadn't rolled out from under me. I thought I could get in it without setting the brake but I know better now."

"We can work on it after we get home from church. You're getting stronger every day. Since you can stand on one leg, with a little practice I'll bet you can get yourself in and out of that wheelchair."

His face took on a slight smile and he almost looked happy. "You really think so? That would sure make me feel more like a man instead of—what I am now."

"I not only think so—with your determination—I know so." When he reached out his hand she took it and cradled it in hers. Then grinning, she added, "Take it from me, even in that wheelchair, you're very much a man."

"Thanks, Dina. After my falling fiasco, I needed the encouragement. I can't tell you how embarrassed I was to have you and my mom find me splattered all over the floor like a helpless baby."

She rose and kissed his cheek. "You, my big, strong man, are anything but a helpless baby. Now get some sleep. I'll see you in the morning."

To Dina's surprise, the little country church was filled to near capacity when they entered its sanctuary the next morning. And as expected, everyone flooded around Will, warmly greeting him and asking how he was doing. She smiled and nodded as he introduced her to each one, honestly saying how nice it was to meet them and how glad she was to be in Belmar. "It must be rewarding to have so many friends," she told him as the organ sounded and everyone moved toward their places. Grinning, she grasped the handles of his chair. "You'll have to fill me in on the protocol. Do we sit just anywhere or do you have a special pew?"

He gestured toward the second row on the right. "That one right there but it might be a good idea if we sat in the back. I don't want to be in anyone's way and

I sure don't want to block their view."

The music was far more than she had expected. A young couple did a marvelous job, singing a duet; and an older woman's solo, which Dina could tell came right from the heart, was one of the best she'd ever heard. Even the congregational singing was superb. "You've got a great voice," she whispered to Will as the pastor moved to the pulpit to deliver his message.

He grabbed her hand and gave it a squeeze. "Funny you should mention that. I was going to tell you the same thing."

Though she wondered what people would think when the two of them held hands during the entire message, she made no effort to pull away. She liked holding hands with him. It made her feel secure, safe, and yes—warm and fuzzy.

"So what did you think of our little church?" he asked as the two sat in the living room after a delicious dinner of barbecued brisket and baked potatoes.

"I liked it. Everyone made me feel right at home. Your mom told me four generations of your family have attended Belmar Community Church. Did your dad ever go to church with you?"

He responded with a disgusted grunt. "My dad go to church? Not on your life. He even tried to keep Mom and us kids from going."

"That's too bad."

"Speaking of dads, you promised you'd tell me your story but you never did. How about now?"

She blanched. "You sure you want to hear it?"

"Dina, I want to know everything about you, both the good and the bad."

After propping her foot up on the footstool, she leaned toward him. "Like you, my father was a bull rider."

His eyes widened. "He was? Why didn't you tell me?"

"And like you," she went on, preferring to leave his questions unanswered until he'd heard her story, "despite sustaining a number of injuries, he kept riding, totally ignoring the pleading by those of us who loved him and begged him to quit while he was ahead. Eventually, he was gored by a bull, Will, badly gored—bad enough that he spends all his days and evenings in his wheelchair. The only way he can get out is by using a sling-type apparatus, and even then my mom has to operate it for him. With his back problems, he can't do it by himself. The man will never walk again. He's turned into a vindictive, demanding old man, expecting my mom to come at his beck and call and wait on him like she's his servant."

Will shook his head. "No wonder you're so against bull riding."

"He's the reason I quit barrel racing. Even though I enjoyed it and got pretty good at it, even barrel racing has its injuries. I couldn't stand the idea of someone having to take care of me like that. That's why it is so hard for me to believe you'd go back to it."

"I have to, Dina. It's the only way I can make that kind of money."

"But you said you'd have this place paid off in a year."

"And I will, but I don't want to live with my mom all my life. I'd like to build a house down by the creek and have a family. Families cost money."

"Are you and your dad on good terms?" he asked as if wanting to move the conversation back to her father instead of trying to explain himself.

"Not really. When I go visit my mother, he and I don't even speak to each other. I hate him for the way he treats her. He wears his injuries like a badge of honor for bravery."

"I guess we have more in common than we'd realized. We both hate our fathers."

"Yeah, I guess we do." On impulse, she jumped to her feet. "Let's forget about our dads. We have work to do. You need to start trying to put more weight on your leg. Other than being badly bruised and painful from your run-in with that bull, there's really nothing wrong with it. You've already been able to put some weight on it. Remember Dr. Flaming said you should start trying to take steps and walk on it as soon as you felt like trying it."

"Sounds good to me."

"Then let's give it a try. Back your chair up against the wall so it can't roll out from under you." After he did as instructed she bent and locked the wheels then reached out to him. "Grab my hand with your good hand and try to pull yourself up like we've been practicing but keep the weight on your good leg until you're on your feet."

"I weigh too much. Maybe we should wait for Brian. You'll never be able to hold me."

"If I can't, we'll wait for Brian."

He locked his good hand with hers and slowly pulled himself to a standing position, groaning with each inch as he moved. "I did it!"

"See, I told you I could hold you."

"I wish I could use a crutch."

"Impossible, with that shoulder. Don't even think about it. Wrap your arm around my shoulders and lean on me. You doing okay?"

"With you holding me up I am."

She looped her arm around his waist. "Now shift some of your weight over to your injured leg and then try to take a step."

He winced then sucked in an exaggerated breath. "Wow, the muscles in my calf feel like they're about to explode."

"And they will for a while but it'll get better. Let's try another step but keep it small."

"Yes, boss."

Her arm still looped around his waist, they moved in sync as he took one, then two more small hobbling steps, his face contorting each time he shifted his weight from one foot to the other.

"Good job. Would you like to sit on the sofa for a while?"

He bobbed his head. "Yes, but let me walk there."

"It's too far."

"Let me try."

"Okay, but keep leaning on me. I don't want you to fall."

"Hey, I like this. I've been wanting an excuse to hold you in my arms." He grinned. "Correction—arm—singular."

"I like it, too, but you'd better quit joking and concentrate on staying on your feet."

Although it was a bit of a struggle for him to make it and get seated, he finally did. "Maybe Brian won't have to come over and help me anymore."

She sat down beside him. "You're doing great but let's not rush things. By the time I have to leave. . ."

He quickly held up his hand to silence her. "Don't even mention it. I can't imagine my life without you."

"Your new therapist will probably do a better job with you than I'm doing!"

"I'm not talking about my therapy, Dina, I'm talking about you. You've become part of my life."

"And you've become part of mine, a very pleasant part, but life goes on."

He shrugged. "Yeah, I guess you're right, but you won't forget me? You will keep in touch?"

"You know I will. And when I come to western Nebraska to visit Burgandi, I'll plan on leaving early enough to stop here on my way to say hello, that is unless you're off somewhere riding bulls."

They sat on the sofa for another hour or so, laughing and talking, enjoying each other's company, and sharing stories of their high school times. When his mother came home from visiting one of the neighbors, she and Dina helped him back into the bedroom so he could stretch out awhile before supper.

"You have a wonderful son," she told Mrs. Martin later as they stood side by side doing the supper dishes.

"He thinks you're pretty wonderful, too."

She finished drying a bowl then placed it on the shelf. "Only because I offered to drive him home and help with his therapy."

"I'd say it's much more than that. He's sure gonna miss you when you're gone. So am I. You've been a real blessing to this family."

"I hope so. That's the reason I came."

"Dina!"

She turned at the sound of Will's voice. "I'm in the kitchen!"

"Can you come and help me? I'd like to go out on the porch for a while."

Mrs. Martin took the towel from her hands. "Go on. I'll finish here."

By the time she reached his room, he had already slipped his feet into his loafers and was ready to stand.

"Put your arm around me."

A mischievous smile curled at his lips. "Be glad to."

She gave him a playful nudge. "You're pretty frisky tonight."

"Probably because I can finally get out of that bed without Brian's help. I'm not used to depending on other people. Usually I'm the one who does the helping."

"So I've heard."

"From Mom and Brian, right?"

"Uh-huh, and your pastor, and some of the ladies I met at your church. Shall I go on?"

"They're all exaggerating."

"What about me? You helped me. Remember?"

He tightened his arm about her shoulders. "Only because you were so cute. If you'd been ugly I would have turned my truck around and gotten out of there fast."

"You know that's not true. You'd help anyone in distress."

He groaned as he lowered himself into the old metal porch glider. "Yeah, I guess I would. Like the Bible says, it sure is better to give than to receive. I'd much rather help than be helped."

When she sat down and scooted up close beside him, he slipped his good arm around her. "Thanks, Dina."

"For what?"

"Everything. Staying by my side in the hospital, encouraging me, driving me here, giving up your vacation to help with me—but mostly—for just being here. As big a mess as I'd gotten myself into, I'm not sure I could have made it without you."

"Sure you could. You're a fighter."

"I always thought I was, but I'd never been injured this badly."

"You're going to come through this as good as new. You know that, don't you?"

"I'm hoping so but. . ." He paused.

A chill of excitement ran through her when he smiled down at her.

"Dina, what would you do if I tried to kiss you?"

With the beat of her heart quickening, she gave him a blank stare. "I—I don't know."

"Would you shove me away?"

"I—don't think so." She held her breath as he drew closer and closer.

"Would you slap me?" His voice was a mere whisper.

"Ah—probably not." Her toes curled up as his lips feathered against hers.

"Would you be upset with me?"

"No."

Dina felt light-headed, dizzy, as his lips claimed hers in a slow, almost child-like kiss.

"Wow, that was nice!" he murmured as their lips parted.

Not sure what to do or say, she simply gazed into his beautiful eyes and nodded.

Then, without asking permission, he kissed her again. And this time, instead of sitting like a concrete statue, she participated. A feeling of giddiness came over her as she cupped his cheek with her hand and pressed her lips to his. She had kissed a few of the guys she had seriously dated but none of those kisses had made her heart flutter and her head reel like Will's kisses. He kissed her a third time, a fourth, then a fifth before loosening his grip on her.

Reluctantly, she pulled away and gave him a shy smile. "I think it's time we call it a day. You need your rest. I'm planning on taking you through at least four therapy sessions tomorrow."

"Can we make it three?"

"Three? Did I tire you out too much today?"

"No, but now that I can get around some, I want to have plenty of time to show you the rest of the ranch. I thought we could go horseback riding. That is, if you think you can handle saddling up the horses."

Her jaw dropped. "Sure, I can do that but how—"

"How am I going to get on my horse? Brian offered to help in the morning when he comes over to do the chores. I figured if you could maneuver Goldie up next to the porch, Brian could hang on to me as I throw my bad leg over the saddle and help me get centered."

"Won't it hurt to lift your leg that way?"

"Yeah, I'm sure it will, but I really want to show you around. Is it a date?"

Dina let a big smile burst forth. "It's a date!"

Will grinned over his shoulder at Dina the next morning as they rode through a grove of trees near the creek. "Getting up on Goldie's back was easier than I thought it'd be—thanks to Brian."

She gave her horse's neck a gentle pat. "I've missed having a horse. I'd like to take Silver home with me."

"You think there'd be room for him in your apartment?"

"Maybe, if I took the furniture out, but I doubt he'd be as happy there as he is here in this beautiful place."

He slowed Goldie's pace, giving her time to ride up next to them. "You really like it here?"

"Are you kidding? A person would have to be crazy not to like it."

"The barn and the outbuildings are old, the fences need replacing, the windmill's about to fall down. . . ."

"That's what gives this place charm. I'm amazed you've been able to keep things up as much as you have. Those buildings may be old but they are in such good shape and so well painted. And the windmill? I wish I had a picture of it just the way it is."

He chuckled. "Charm, eh? I never thought of it that way." Tugging on the reins, he brought Goldie to a halt. "Look over there. See those stakes I've driven into the ground? That's where I'd like to build a house. Do all the work myself. Make it really special."

"Oh, Will, what a lovely place for a home. The trees are gorgeous and there's such a great view of the creek."

He gave the reins a gentle flip and Goldie moved forward. "Gotta find me a wife first."

Dina took one last look at the area he'd pointed out. It *was* a beautiful place. The perfect spot for a house, and she found herself envious of the woman who would someday become Will's wife, live there with him, and bear his children.

"You coming?" he called back to her.

"Right behind you."

Chapter 13

The next week flew by as Dina and Will spent nearly every waking moment together, enjoying each other's company and working to get his arm and shoulder in the best shape possible before she left and his new therapist took over. In addition to their therapy sessions, they'd driven into town, attended a concert in the little city park, visited with friends and neighbors, and even witnessed the wedding of one of Will's high school buddies. She was extremely pleased with his progress, but in some ways she felt like she was running out on a job half done.

"I can't believe this is our last day together," he told her as they rode Goldie and Silver on the winding trail that ran along the creek's edge.

She sighed. "Me, either."

"You've done nothing but work since you've been here. I guess you're looking forward to getting back to your big-city job."

"Yeah, sorta."

"You don't sound very enthused."

"Only because I hate to leave this place—and you."

"You could stay."

Dina huffed. "And do what? I'm a single gal, remember? I have to make a living." She allowed a teasing grin to quirk up her mouth. "And don't tell me again you'd hire me. I'd make a lousy ranch hand."

"You could get a job at Community Hospital over at McCook. It's not that far away. They just built a 3.8-million-dollar rehab center."

"Why would I want to live in McCook? I don't know a soul over there."

"You could live here on the ranch and drive back and forth. We could fix up the old ranch hand's cabin."

"Um, as much as I like it here, I don't think that would be a good idea." She turned to him with an impish grin. "Race you back to the house!" Then before he could take her up on her challenge, she gave Silver's sides a kick and they were off.

"Hey! Not fair!" Will shouted as he and Goldie followed in hot pursuit.

With the wind whipping through her hair, she gave him a wave then called back over her shoulder. "Whoever said life was fair?"

When they got back to the barn Dina applauded as Will dismounted by himself, without her or Brian there to help ease him down. "Good job. I'm so proud of you. You've worked really hard. You're able to walk, ride your horse, and help with some of the chores. Do you realize how far you've come in two weeks?"

He lifted his bad shoulder with a wince. "Yeah, but I still can't use my arm much."

"But you've admitted it's getting better every day. If you continue to work with the therapist and do your exercises regularly like we've been doing, you'll be back to normal before you know it." She reached out for his hand. "Speaking of working with your therapist, we'd better get back to the house and get started on this morning's session."

Mrs. Martin was all smiles two hours later when she greeted them as they entered the kitchen. "Since this is the last time the three of us will have lunch together before you go back to Omaha, I've fixed all your favorites, Dina. Fried chicken, mashed potatoes, pepper gravy, and my sour cream coleslaw."

Dina lifted the lid on the skillet. "Oh, yummy, that smells wonderful! But you shouldn't have gone to so much trouble."

"After what you've done for my boy, there is nothing I could do to repay you." She gestured toward Will. "Look at him. He'll soon be back to his usual ornery self and we have you to thank for it."

"You give me way too much credit."

"Just remember, Dina. You'll always be welcome in this home. Come as often as you can and stay as long as you like."

She bent and kissed Mrs. Martin. The two had become close friends. It was going to be hard to leave her, too.

"Dina worked me pretty hard this morning," Will told his mom as the two women washed the dishes and cleaned up the kitchen after their sumptuous lunch. "I think I'll go stretch out until she's ready for our afternoon session."

Dina flipped at him with her dish towel. "If you think I worked you hard this morning, wait until you see what I have planned for this afternoon."

He grabbed hold of the towel, yanking it out of her hand, and flipped it back at her. "Bring it on, babe. You don't scare me."

His mother stepped in between them. "You two sound like a couple of kids."

Dina set the last dish on the shelf then closed the cabinet door. "Well, this kid has got to stop her playing and do some packing. I have a long drive ahead of me tomorrow and I want to stop and spend some time with my mom on the way back."

Will let out a grunt. "You that anxious to get away from me?"

She tapped the tip of his nose playfully. "You know better than that, but my time here has come to an end. I have to get back to my job."

Though Dina gathered most of her things from the closet and drawers and placed them in her suitcase, she did it with little enthusiasm. *Come on, girl,* she told herself, trying to sound convincing. *You've done all you can for that man. It's time to get back to Omaha, to your job, your friends, your church, to the life you had there before you came to this ranch. You were happy there, remember?*

She turned and stared at her image in the dresser mirror. "If I was happy living there and had such a great life, why am I so sad about leaving?"

Though she had posed the question, in her heart she already knew the answer.

Will.

Their afternoon session was every bit as vigorous and demanding as she'd promised it would be. Although Will complained about it, she could tell his complaining was nothing more than good-natured kidding and was pleased with how hard he worked.

After a light supper, he disappeared for an hour or so to write some checks and take a quick shower. Dressed in the white peasant-type blouse and the full-tiered denim skirt she'd bought in town on one of their shopping trips, Dina was waiting for him on the porch when he returned. To make her outfit even more festive and memorable for their last night together, she had pulled up one side of her long blond hair and anchored it with a red silk rose. She'd even touched a hint of her favorite perfume behind each ear.

"Um, you smell nice," Will told her as he bent to kiss her cheek before seating himself close beside her in the metal glider. "And you look—beautiful. That's the stuff you bought in town, isn't it?"

"You like it?"

"Yeah, I like it. All I can say is wow!" He slipped his good arm about her shoulders and drew her close. "So you're really going to leave me."

"Yes, I have to."

"I—I don't want you to go."

"I don't want to go but. . ." She held her breath as he lifted her face to his.

"You know I'm crazy about you, don't you?"

"You never told me."

"Only because I didn't think you'd want to hear it. I–I've never felt this way about a woman. You're in my every thought all day and I dream about you at night. Being with you each day and having you so close has been driving me crazy."

Dina found herself nearly speechless. She had felt a real connection between them, but she'd had no idea he cared for her that deeply.

"I've wanted so much to hold you in my arms, smother your sweet face with kisses, and ask you to stay."

"I can't. As much as I'd like to stay here and live in the old cabin, I hate the idea of having to drive back and forth to work every day at the McCook hospital."

"Sweetheart, you don't understand. When I said I wanted to ask you to *stay* with me, I didn't mean as a tenant in our cabin, I meant as my *wife*. I want you to marry me!"

His unexpected words nearly knocked the wind out of her. "Me—marry you?"

"Look, don't get mad at me. I didn't mean to offend you. I know I have nothing to offer. That's why I didn't tell you." He backed away, leaving her sitting with her mouth hanging open. "I should have kept my big mouth shut. Now you *are* mad at me! I love you, Dina, but I know you could never love me."

"But I do love you!" The words slipped out before she could stop them.

He stared at her. "You do?"

"Yes. I've never believed in love at first sight but I think I've loved you ever since the night I rode with you in the ambulance."

He gave his hands a despairing lift. "The only things I can give you are myself—a broken-down cowboy—and my love. And, someday, this ranch. I can't offer you the glamour and excitement of living in the city and the wealth some other man or maybe one of the doctors you work with can give you. You deserve so much more. I guess I shouldn't be surprised that you'd turn me down."

She grasped the biceps of his good arm with both hands. "But I haven't turned you down."

He shifted around to face her. "You mean you might say yes?"

"I'm thinking about it. The last thing I expected when I came out here on the porch this evening was a proposal." She gave him her most demure smile. "That was a proposal, wasn't it? Or did I only assume it was? You said you *wanted* me to marry you, you didn't exactly *ask* me to marry you."

Using his good hand to brace himself, he struggled to drop to one knee in front of her. "Well, I'm asking you now. Dina Spark, I love you more than my humble words can ever express. Would you marry me? Do me the honor of becoming my wife?"

Chapter 14

Will's words were the ones she'd longed for but never expected to hear. The kindest, sweetest, most caring, self-sacrificing man she'd ever known was asking her to marry him and spend the rest of her life with him. And best of all, he loved her and he loved her Lord. She was about to say yes and throw her arms about his neck when the sudden image of her father, imprisoned in his wheelchair for life, day after dreary day, with nothing to look forward to but more misery and pain, swept across her mind.

"I want to, Will. Oh, how I want to, but first I need to ask you something. Do you, or do you not, intend to return to bull riding? It's important that I know and I want an honest answer."

When he gazed at her for a moment without answering, something in his eyes told her she already knew what he was going to say.

"I have to, honey. It's the only way I can pay this ranch off," he said, holding tightly to her hand. "One more good season, two at the most, and I'll quit."

She tugged her hand away and swallowed at the lump in her throat. "No! That's not acceptable! What if you were injured again, maybe even gored by a bull like my father was? I can't take that chance, Will. I've seen what his accident has done to my mother, and I've seen what it has done to him. If you don't love me enough to. . ."

He reached out for her but she backed away.

"I do love you and I'd do anything for you—except what you're asking. Dina, I've worked since I was a kid to make sure this old ranch stayed in our family. I'm within a year or so of seeing all my work pay off. I can't quit now. It's not fair that you even ask."

Her hands went to her hips. "You're a man of God. Where's your faith? Why can't you trust God to meet your financial needs?"

"Trust Him?" he shot back. "Who do you think gave me this talent in the first place? Dina, when life looked the bleakest for my mom and us kids, and like there was no way we could hang on to this place, I won a hundred dollars at a local rodeo, riding bulls. That was enough to keep the banker happy for a while. From that time on, every penny I made at rodeos went to help make those mortgage payments. God gave me the talent for riding bulls. Not only did He give me the talent, He gave me the courage. Facing an angry bull takes courage.

Not many men can do it."

"And I can't face being married to a man who does. If you won't give up bull riding, I can't marry you! I'm sorry. That's just the way it is."

"Even if I promise I'll be careful?"

"I'm sure you were being careful the night you rode Gray Ghost. Being careful is not enough."

"Dina, please. See it from my side."

"No! You see it from my side. I refuse to be married to a bull rider! I can't stand the idea that you might end up like my father—or maybe even dead! No! I love you, but I won't marry you, Will, not unless you quit the rodeo now! That's my final word!" With that, she whirled around and ran into the house, into the privacy of her bedroom where she could cry her eyes out.

A few minutes later, she heard his labored footsteps in the hall as he headed toward his room. *Lord*, she cried out from within her heart, *why? Why would You allow me to fall in love with this man, a professional bull rider, when You knew how I always kept my distance from every guy who had anything to do with rodeos? Now here I am, head over heels in love and going home with nothing but wonderful memories and a broken heart.*

When morning came, Dina dragged herself out of bed, tidied up her room, then took a quick shower before dressing and going into the kitchen for breakfast.

"I didn't mean to eavesdrop last night," Mrs. Martin said, standing in front of the range, shifting the sizzling bacon around in the pan, "but you two got pretty loud out there on the porch."

Dina sat down at the table and poured herself a glass of orange juice. "Sorry about that but we had some pretty heavy things to discuss."

"From the way you stormed down the hall when you passed my bedroom, I guess things didn't end well between the two of you."

She sighed. "No, not well at all."

"Morning."

Dina stared into her glass and didn't bother to turn around at the sound of his voice. "Morning."

"Beautiful morning out," his mother inserted cheerfully, as if trying to break the gloom that suddenly engulfed the room.

They both nodded.

Dina glanced at the wall clock then rose. "I–I'm not very hungry. I think I'm going to head on out. I want to stop in Farrell to see my mom and then I'd like to get back to Omaha as soon as possible."

Mrs. Martin laid down her spatula and, wiping her hands on her apron, hurried to Dina's side. "You sure, honey? Breakfast is almost ready."

Dina wrapped her arms about the woman and gave her a hug. "I'm sure. Thanks for everything. You've been wonderful to me. I'm so glad I got to know you."

Will stood awkwardly to his feet. "I'll—ah—walk you to your car."

"You needn't. I've already taken everything out. I'm ready to go."

"I'll walk with you anyway."

She answered with a slight shrug. "Suit yourself." After she told his mother good-bye, with Will hobbling beside her the two walked silently to her car. When he opened her door for her, she stuck out her hand. "I'd tell you to take care of yourself but I know you won't. Now that I look back on things, I realize I wasted two weeks of my life by staying here and trying to nurse you back to good health since you're planning to go right back and take a chance on the same thing, or something even worse, happening to you again."

He tried to hold on but she pulled her hand away and hurriedly slipped into the driver's seat, inserted the key in the ignition, and gave it a turn.

"Dina, I wish you'd understand."

She yanked on the handle, shutting the door with a slam. "And I wish you'd understand. I love you, Will. I'll always love you—but not as a bull rider."

"Please, sweetheart, we could have such a good life together."

"Yes, we could, but not under your conditions. Good-bye." Before he could say another word, she pressed down on the gas pedal and took off, scattering rocks and gravel at his feet. The last image she had of the love of her life was when, with tear-filled eyes, she glanced into the rearview mirror.

❧

Heartbroken and discouraged, Will watched through the curl of dust stirred up by Dina's tires until her car disappeared up the road. *God, why? Why, when I've prayed so long for a wife who would accept me the way I am and the pressures of life that have fallen upon my shoulders? Why would You bring such a beautiful, caring, Christian woman into my life, let me fall in love with her, just to have her refuse my proposal? All because I can't quit the rodeo like she asked me to. I don't understand.*

Am I wrong to want to pay off this farm and secure it for my mom? Lord, I'm not a learned man like those doctors Dina works with every day. Other than bull riding, I have no talent, no other means in addition to the small amount this ranch brings in, to earn enough to pay off the mortgage. And I wanted so much to build a house for Dina and me, down by the creek in the area we both love. Was that asking too much? Am I being stubborn, Lord? If I had told her I'd quit bull riding, would You have helped me find another way to pay off the ranch?

Show me, Father. Tell me. I need to hear from You. I need to know Your will for my life.

❧

"He actually asked you to marry him?" Dina's mother gasped as the two sat in the kitchen, sipping freshly made coffee. "I could tell by the way you talked about him when you phoned me that you two had grown close, but I had no idea you had fallen in love with the man."

"I knew it all along, Mom. I just wouldn't admit it to myself. It's hard to explain, but Will was everything I could want in a man, and yet he had the one thing in his life I couldn't tolerate." She glanced into the living room to make sure her father wasn't listening before going on. "What if Will was injured again, maybe even gored by a bull like Dad was? What if he became like Dad, arrogant and demanding, and expected me to wait on him and talked to me like Dad does you? I couldn't take it, and I don't know how you can."

"Mary, come in here!" her father bellowed. "I dropped the *TV Guide*. And bring me a cup of coffee when you come, only this time don't put so much cream in it."

Dina grabbed her mother's arm. "Don't do it, Mom. You're not his maid. His chair is electric. Let him come in and get his own coffee."

Her mother pulled away from her grasp. "I don't mind doing it. He's my husband."

"But he abuses you, both physically and verbally. You don't have to take it from him. I worry about you. He's dangerous with that hot temper of his. Someday, he may actually hurt you."

"Dina, your father may be all the things you say he is, and I admit sometimes I get very irritated and hurt by what he says and does, but we have some good times together, too. Our marriage, before he was injured, was wonderful. Remember when our neighbor led me to the Lord not long after your father was hurt? When I confessed my sins, I realized one of my worst sins was bitterness—bitterness toward your father. I asked God to take my life and make it what He wanted it to be. You know, after I prayed that prayer, my love for my husband became stronger than it had been when we'd first married. When I said 'I do' and vowed to love and care for him until death do us part, I meant it. Now, when the bad times come, I remember the good times. I've never doubted God is the One who brought us together. Taking care of your father is my calling in life."

Her mother's words pierced Dina's heart. She finally understood that the reason for her mother staying and caring for her husband was the same reason Will felt God had called him to love and care for the family his father had deserted and left destitute.

That night, as she knelt by her bed, she asked God for forgiveness for her sins. Not for any dreadful sins she had committed but for not acknowledging God's way was always the best way, even though sometimes she didn't understand it or agree with it.

Forgive me, God. Give me a pure heart, she cried out from the deep inside her. *Show me Your will. I'm so confused. Help me, Father God! Help me!* Sobbing as though her heart would break, she wiped at her tears.

"You call Me Father, but what about your earthly father? Can't you find it in your heart to forgive him, even as you ask Me to forgive you?" a small voice from somewhere inside her seemed to say.

Dina stopped sobbing and listened. *God, is that You?*

"It's time to forgive your father and make things right between the two of you," the small voice continued. *"He, too, is having a rough time. He needs his daughter."*

The rest of that evening and far into the night, Dina thought about the last conversation she'd had with Will, as well as the things God had laid upon her heart. She wanted to accept Will's desire to continue riding bulls, but she just couldn't, even though she knew God *could* protect him. Paying off the rest of the farm's mortgage and having enough money to build a house down by the creek were admirable goals, goals that had kept Will working day and night since he had been twelve years old. There had to be another way, other than his winnings, to do what he felt he had to do. But how? *Please, God, show us a way. Will and I love each other and want to be together. Isn't this what You want, too?*

When her cell phone rang at five the next morning, with Will's number showing on Caller ID, she leaped to answer it.

"I couldn't sleep for thinking about you, sweetheart," he told her with a heavy sigh. "We can't let a love like ours die without at least trying to come up with a solution. I've given our situation some serious thought, Dina. I'm giving up bull riding. I—I don't know how I'll manage to pay off the mortgage without the extra money—but I can't live without you."

"Oh, Will, are you sure? As much as I want to marry you, I wouldn't want you to do something you'll regret later and end up hating me for."

"I could never hate you, Dina, for anything. But I'm serious about giving it up. There's no getting around it; bull riding is a dangerous sport. Who knows? Next time I might get hurt even worse. As I lay in bed last night, I weighed out my options. What was more important to me? Paying off the ranch? Or marrying you, the woman I love, and spending the rest of my life as your husband and, hopefully, the father of our children? When I faced those two choices head-on, the decision was easy."

Tears filled her eyes as she gripped the phone. "Honest? You're not just saying that because it's what you know I want to hear?"

"Dina, I'd do anything to have you by my side. Being here at the ranch without you last night, knowing I may never see you again, hold you in my arms, kiss your sweet face—well, it made me just plain sick. Somehow, I'll figure out a way to earn the extra money. I'm a good worker. I can always hire myself out to other ranchers who need help."

"Will, I've been thinking, too. I really wouldn't mind driving back and forth to McCook. With my background and the glowing recommendation I'm sure my supervisor will give me, I know I can land a well-paying job in their new rehab facility. With what I could make at the McCook hospital and what the ranch would bring in, surely we could pay off the mortgage within a year as you planned."

"Driving back and forth to McCook every day could get mighty tiresome, especially in the winter. Southwest Nebraska winter storms can be pretty bad, with lots of snow."

She let loose a nervous giggle as her excitement grew. "Oh? And you think our winters here in Omaha are like the tropics? I could do it, Will. I know I could. That way we could be together. Besides, I have a little money saved up and I still have the savings account my aunt left me."

"We'd have to live with Mama. It might be years before we could get enough money ahead to build our house."

"I love your mom. We got along great while I was there. It's a big house. There's plenty of room for all three of us."

The sudden silence on the other end frightened her. Now that he had come face-to-face with the decision he would have to live with for the rest of his life, was he having second thoughts?

"I know you want me to give up bull riding, sweetheart, and I'm gladly doing it, but I was wondering how you'd feel about me raising bulls for rodeo stock?"

"Oh, Will, I'd be totally happy to see you raise bulls. I know you love the rodeo and, as long as you aren't riding bulls yourself, I might even get to the point that I loved rodeo, too, just because you do."

"Then it's settled?" he asked brightly. "You're accepting my proposal?"

She could almost see his smiling face. "Oh yes, my love! Yes! Yes! Yes!"

"What are you doing here this time of day?" her mother asked the next morning when Dina walked into her kitchen. "It's nearly noon. I thought you had to be back to work this morning."

"I have been to work, Mom. I turned in my resignation."

"What? You're quitting? Why? I thought you loved that job. What are you going to do?"

Dina couldn't contain her joy. "I'm going back to Will! I've accepted his proposal. He's giving up bull riding!"

"You talked to him?"

She threw back her head with a laugh. "Yes! He phoned early this morning. Everything is settled. I'm going to spend the rest of the day packing up my personal items, everything else the movers can pack. I'm heading back to Belmar first thing in the morning."

Her mother sat down at the table, staring at her with wide eyes. "I—I had no idea—"

"Neither did I when I went to bed last night but, believe me, I really prayed things would work out and they have! God is sooo good!"

Mrs. Spark gave her head a shake. "I can't believe it. My little girl is getting married."

"I'll let you know when we decide on a wedding date. I want us to be married in Belmar since that's where we'll be making our home, and I want you and Dad to be there. I had a long talk with God last night." She gave her mother shy grin. "Or should I say God had a talk with me. Because of that I'm making some radical changes in my life and I couldn't be happier." She gestured toward the living room. "Dad in there?"

Her mother nodded. "I was just about to take his lunch to him."

"Could you hold off for a while? I need to talk to him."

"I guess so." She eyed Dina suspiciously. "You're not going to get into another argument with him, are you?"

"No, just the opposite. I'm going to apologize and ask his forgiveness." She gave her mother a quick peck on the cheek. "Pray for me, okay?"

Her father was sitting in his chair, staring out the window when she walked up behind him. Dina reached out and wrapped her arms around him then kissed his forehead. "Hi, Daddy. How are you feeling today?"

He turned with a look of surprise. "I thought you were at the hospital."

"I was earlier. I'm making some major changes in my life, but I don't want to talk about those. Mom will fill you in on them later. I want to talk about us, you and me." She knelt before him and cupped his hands in hers. "I've wronged you, Daddy, and I'm sorry—so sorry for the disrespectful way I've treated you. I've said things to hurt your feelings and I've gone weeks without even speaking to you. I had no right to behave that way. You're my father and I'm so thankful for you. I know I don't deserve it, but can you find it in your heart to forgive me? I love you and I want you to love me."

Her crusty, vindictive father began to weep. "I love you, too, daughter. I'm the one who should be asking for forgiveness. I've been so caught up in my pitiful physical condition, I haven't been the dad to you I should have been. I've been pretty rotten to your mom, too. I'm surprised she hasn't left me by now."

"We've both been at fault, Daddy. Can we start over? Begin anew?"

He pulled her back up to him then wrapped his arms around her, his tears flowing once again. "I'd like that. I've missed my little girl."

"I'm getting married, Daddy, to the man I've been taking care of for the past two weeks."

He brightened. "Married, huh? I kind of wondered if something more than his physical therapy was keeping you in Belmar. You haven't known him long. Is that man worthy of you? You're pretty special."

"Oh, yes. He's a wonderful man. You'll like him. Our wedding will be in Belmar. I want you and Mom to come. You have to give me away."

"If *you* love him enough to marry him, I'm sure I'll like him, and I'll be proud to give you away."

Dina kissed his cheek once again then rose. "Gotta go, Dad. I've got a full day ahead of me."

"I love you, Dina."

"I love you, Dad."

With a quick good-bye to her mother, Dina rushed out the door, into her car, ready to go back to her apartment to call Will one more time just to hear his voice, and begin packing.

At six the next morning, she headed west on I-70, singing along with the radio and praising God for the two special men in her life. Will, the man she was going to marry, and her father.

Will opened his eyes as the sound of a vehicle came closer and closer. It had to be Dina. As the familiar-looking car came to a stop, he let out a yelp.

Dina was so excited she could barely find the door handle after she turned off the key. Leaping out, she ran to the porch and up the steps, right into Will's arms. "I love, love, love you!" she told him, looping her arms about his neck.

She reached up and, after cupping his face in her hands, gazed into his blue, blue eyes. "I meant every word I said. I love you, my sweet Will, and I want to spend the rest of my life with you."

He bent and kissed her. "I can't believe you're actually here, sweetheart."

"Well, I am and I'm here to stay." She tilted her head and gave him a flirtatious grin. "You do want to marry me, don't you? Or have you changed your mind?"

"Yes, I mean no. I mean yes, I want to marry you and no, I haven't changed my mind." He pulled her close with his good arm and gazed down at her with eyes of love. "I'm the happiest man alive. You have no idea how much I love you, my darling. No more bull riding. You have my word on it and, trust me, I never go back on my word."

"I do trust you, Will, and with God's help, I'll do everything I can to help you."

"If we keep our minds centered on God and live for Him and each other, how can we fail?" He gazed into her eyes for a moment then his lips sought hers and he kissed her again but, this time, with a kiss unlike any of the others they had shared. Though it was as sweet and as loving as any kiss could be, it was also a kiss of promise, of dedication, a bonding kiss, a sealing kiss that promised true love and devotion for the rest of their lives.

"So how soon can we have the wedding?" he asked as their lips parted. "I'd say the sooner the better. I guess you'll want to have it at your church in Omaha."

"No, my darling. I want it here in Belmar, and I want to invite the entire community."

A frown creased his forehead. "But what about your dad? You'll want him there. Will he come all this way?"

A big smile burst forth on her lips. "Yes, and he's already consented to give me away. Oh, Will, I'm so glad that through all of this God revealed to me how I had wronged my dad as much as he had wronged me. And that I should forgive him, apologize to him, and tell him how sorry I am for the way I treated him. We decided to put the past behind us and start all over again with a clean slate. That's why he agreed to come. In fact, he's excited about it, so both of my parents will be here." She gave him a gentle nudge. "You need to forgive your father, too. Carrying that grudge isn't hurting him—it's hurting you."

Will held up his hand between them. "Whoa, let's not get carried away here. At least your dad stayed with you and your mom. Mine walked out on us. There's a big difference."

"You'll never have true peace if you don't—"

"I didn't say I *wouldn't* forgive him. I just said—"

"I know what you said, and I understand why you feel the way you do, but promise me you'll at least think about it, okay?"

He nodded. "Yeah, okay. I promise, but right now we need to set our wedding date."

Dina smiled up at him. He had agreed to think about it. That was a start. "If the pastor is available, and if the church is, too, I was thinking of two weeks from today."

Will let out a loud, "Two weeks? Yee haw!" then gave his fist a victorious thrust into the air.

She chuckled. "I guess that means you're happy with the date."

"I couldn't be happier. I still think I'm dreaming."

Weaving her fingers through his, Dina led him to the glider then snuggled up close to him when they sat down. "I think we should have an old-fashioned, down-home wedding, with even a few fiddlers to entertain our guests before the wedding starts. Maybe even have it in the city park where there will be room for anyone who wants to come."

"You serious? That could be a whole lot of people."

"I know, but Belmar is your home and it's going to be my home, too. I want everyone to share in our happiness."

"How are we going to seat that many people?"

"Maybe we could ask everyone to bring their lawn chairs." Her exhilaration grew with each thought. "We could decorate the gazebo with dozens of pots of red geraniums, maybe hang hundreds of long streamers of red and white crepe paper from the trees and let them dance in the wind. And you and your best man could wear blue jeans and boots."

His eyes grew wide. "You weren't kidding when you said you wanted an old-fashioned, down-home wedding! Blue jeans and boots sound much better to me than a formal tuxedo. I'm sure, if Ben consents to being my best man, he'll like being able to wear jeans."

"Since this is my first—last, and only—wedding I want to wear a white gown, and I'd like you to wear a white shirt."

A slight frown wrinkled his brow.

She treated him to a teasing smile. "A *Western-cut, gripper-fastened* white shirt, with that beautiful silver bolo of yours at the neck. And," she added quickly, "of course you'll want to wear that amazing gold and silver belt buckle you won for being Bull Rider of the Year at the Cheyenne rodeo."

"Now you're talking my language."

"You're not just saying that to please me? You really do like my ideas?"

"Sure I like them. What's not to like?"

"Maybe my attendants can wear boots and red and white gingham square-dance style dresses. Do you think Ben would go along with wearing a gingham shirt to match the girls' dresses?"

"I'm sure he will. He's a city boy now but there's got to be a little bit of rancher left in him."

She clapped her hands with glee. "This is going to be so much fun, a wedding to remember. I'm so anxious to meet your brothers. Do you think both Jason and Ben will be able to come? Teresa, too? I want her to be my bridesmaid."

"No way would they miss their big brother's wedding. Count on it. They'll be here."

Smiling up at him, Dina rested her head on his shoulder. "I love you, my sweet cowboy."

"I love you, too, babe."

"You haven't changed your mind about giving up bull riding? No regrets?"

He gave her a mischievous smile as his hand rose to pat her cheek. "Not a one. You're cuter than any bull I've ever seen."

She jabbed him in his ribs. "Thanks for the compliment."

Seriousness replaced his smile. "All kidding aside, I can honestly say giving up that part of my life was the right decision. God brought us together, dearest, and I know—as long as we keep our marriage centered around Him and His Word—He will keep us together."

"I know He will, too."

"Someday, my precious one, trust me, I *am* going to build a house for us."

"And our kids?"

He chucked her chin playfully. "At least a dozen, but half of them have to be boys. I'm going to need help on this ranch."

She loved his sense of humor and she loved him. "I have a favor to ask."

"Ask away. For you, I'd do anything."

"If I cleaned them up real good, would you wear your spurs to our wedding?"

He frowned. "Why?"

"Remember that day at the hospital when you told me to leave, go back to Omaha?"

"How could I forget? Telling you to leave was the hardest thing I've ever had to do."

"If I hadn't had your spurs in my car, I would have run out of there and never looked back. But I knew how much they meant to you and I couldn't leave without making sure I got them back to you." She lifted her hand and cupped his cheek. "Those spurs and the kiss we shared that day are what brought us together." She laughed. "Besides, I'm marrying a cowboy. Remember what you told me? A cowboy isn't a cowboy without his spurs."

He tapped her nose with the tip of his finger. "Then I'll wear them!"

Chapter 15

A little past nine the next morning, while she and Mrs. Martin were in the living room discussing wedding plans, Dina heard Will's new cell phone ring. She hoped it was Pastor Harris responding to the message about their wedding they had left on his voice mail.

"Dina, sweetheart! You'll never believe what happened! Talk about an answer to prayer!" Will came hobbling into the room, his face blanketed with a broad smile. "Dr. Farha just called from Denver with great news! Both he and Dr. Flaming, as well as Dr. Grimes, have decided not to bill me for their part of my surgery! They're all three doing it pro bono. Isn't that amazing? Now the only cost I'll have to worry about will be the hospital bill!"

Her heart thundering with excitement at his news, Dina's jaw dropped as she stared at him. "He actually said that?"

"Sure did. Now, with what my insurance will pay and the help I'll receive from the Rodeo Contestant Crisis Fund, hopefully, the hospital will let me pay out the remainder in monthly installments."

She ran to him and threw her arms about his neck. "Oh, Will, that's such good news. I know how concerned you've been about paying those doctor and hospital bills. See, God is able to perform miracles. We just have to have faith in Him."

Will cupped her cheek with his hand and smiled down at her. "I shouldn't have been surprised. He's already performed one unbelievable miracle in my life. He brought you back to me."

The next two weeks were a whirlwind of activity as Dina worked to get everything ready for their wedding and still have time for Will's therapy. Fortunately, her mother and father arrived a few days early to help, as well as to get acquainted with their soon-to-be son-in-law and his relatives, and attend the rehearsal dinner.

Finally Dina and Will's big day arrived.

Being careful not to muss her lovely white wedding gown, Dina pulled back the flap on the tent that had been set up to serve as the bride's dressing room and peeked out at the area of Belmar's city park where she and Will would soon be pledging their love and their lives to each other. From the looks of the crowd that had gathered, the entire community had turned out for their wedding as she'd hoped.

Her gaze went to her beloved as he stood at the little altar Brian Canter had made for them, straight and tall in his new blue jeans and white Western-cut shirt, the hammered silver bolo about his neck, and the gold and silver rodeo belt buckle at his waist. Just the sight of him made her heartbeat quicken. How handsome he was, and how different he looked from the man she'd met on the road that day. She loved his short hair and Vandyke beard.

She turned when someone touched her on the arm. "You look beautiful." It was Burgandi. "I'm so happy for you. You and Billy Bob—or should I say *Will*—make the perfect couple."

"She's right," Teresa agreed, smiling as she gave Dina a hug. "You're going to be the sister I always wanted. Welcome to the family."

"And you'll be the sister I never had. Will has told me so much about you." Dina lightly kissed her cheek. "I have a feeling we're going to be great friends."

As the music from the portable keyboard sounded, Burgandi grabbed Teresa's hand. "There's our cue. Time for us to go."

"Ready, daughter?"

Dina smiled down at her father as he moved the little lever, nudging his electric wheelchair closer to her. "Oh, yes, Daddy, more than ready." She bent and kissed the top of his balding head then reached out and grasped his free hand, giving it an affectionate squeeze. "I—I love you, Dad." She nearly cried as tears welled up in his eyes.

By the time she and her father reached the gazebo, she thought her face would crack from smiling. Never had she been so happy.

"And who gives this woman to be married to this man?" Pastor Harris asked after Dina and her father had joined Will, Ben and Teresa, Burgandi, the ring bearer, and the flower girl at the altar.

"Her mother and I," Mr. Spark answered proudly, his voice breaking as tears again trailed down his cheeks. "I'm her father."

Dina swallowed at the gaggle of emotions surging through her as she watched him back his wheelchair away and roll up next to her mother who was seated on the front row opposite Will's mother.

She was grateful when Will, seeming to sense the emotions running through her at that moment, reached out and took her hand in his. And once again, she was filled with happiness. She leaned into him, loving his presence, absorbing his strength. He was everything she could ever want in a husband and, best of all, he loved her with an undying, unselfish love, a love of which she could only try to feel worthy.

She listened intently as the soloist sang one of hers and Will's favorite songs,

"You Are the Wind Beneath My Wings," as well as another of their favorites, then to Pastor Harris as he read several scripture passages. All the while she gazed into the face of her beloved.

When it came time to say their vows, Will went first. Though he hadn't had the kind of education most men had, the words he had written were sweeter than any poem she had ever read or heard, and the way he recited them to her made her know they were coming from his heart. She wanted to etch them on her own heart and remember them forever.

Next, she said hers. When she'd been rehearsing them, they'd been merely words she was trying to memorize. But as she gazed into his eyes and slowly repeated them to the one she loved, the words took on new meaning and became the mantra she knew she would strive to live by for the rest of her life.

After one more song and the exchanging of their rings, Pastor Harris again reminded them of what God expected from them as partners with each other and with Him. Then holding his hands over the pair, he said, "William Robert Martin, you may kiss your bride."

Dina suddenly felt breathless. The man who had been kissing her for the past several weeks had been first a patient, then a friend, next her boyfriend, after that, her fiancé. Now, he would be kissing her as—praise the Lord—her husband. She melded into him as he pulled her into his arms, lifting her face toward his. When she felt his lips touch hers, she threw her arms about his neck, twining her fingers through his short hair, and surrendered herself fully to his kiss. When it finally ended, she drew back, even more breathless, still holding on to him for fear her knees would give way and she would end up crumpled at his feet.

"Now, would you please turn and face those who have come to witness the blending of your two hearts into one," Pastor Harris asked, smiling at the newlyweds after he'd prayed a prayer of dedication.

As Dina started to move, Will tightened his grip on her and nodded toward his feet. She stared down then threw back her head with a boisterous laugh. "You did wear your spurs! I wasn't sure you would."

"Yeah, I might look pretty silly to everyone else but I really liked your idea of wearing them. If it weren't for these old spurs we might not have gotten together."

"You told me a cowboy isn't a cowboy without his spurs. This is one more thing we can tell our grandchildren when we grow old."

Pastor Harris asked their audience to rise. Smiling at the couple, he announced, "By the power vested in me by the State of Nebraska, I now pronounce you husband and wife. Friends and loved ones, it is my privilege to introduce to you—Mr. and Mrs. William Robert Martin. May God bless their union."

THE PREACHER WORE A GUN

Chapter 1

"You didn't."

After switching her cell phone to her other ear, Tassie Springer sat down in the worn floral upholstered chair she had rescued out of a Dumpster eight years ago when she graduated from high school and moved to Omaha to enter college, nearly broke, tired, and discouraged. All she knew back then was that she wanted to leave Grand Island to get as far away as she could from the memory that plagued her day and night. Attending college in Omaha seemed to be the only logical and acceptable excuse she could use to get out of town—and away from *him*.

"Yeah, Mom, I did. I quit. My boss accused me of lying when I stood up for another employee. Considering the six faithful years I had worked for him after dropping out of college, he should have known I'd never lie, so I quit."

"So—what are you going to do now?"

Tassie swung her jean-covered leg atop the footstool then rested her head on the crocheted doily she had placed on the chair's headrest to cover a torn spot in the fabric. "At this point I'm not sure what I'm going to do, although I have come up with several options."

"You could come back to Grand Island."

Tassie patted her knee then waited until Goliath, the big black Lab she had rescued from the Humane Society, rested his big head there, his eyes focusing on her as if she were the queen of his life. "I've considered that. I may live in Omaha but Grand Island has always been my home. I've never wanted to admit it, Mom, but I made a big mistake, dropping out of college after my sophomore year to take that low-paying job. I was just tired of going to school all day and working nights and weekends babysitting my neighbor's three children while she worked. Then, with having to wedge in study time, my grades went into a downward spiral. I guess I was overstressed and suffered a burnout. If I was going to drop out of college, I should have come back home then, instead of taking that dead-end day job at the photo shop. I much preferred the babysitting but, unfortunately, it just didn't pay enough."

"I—I wish your father and I could have paid for your college but the money just wasn't there at that time."

Tassie crinkled up her face. She had only meant to explain, not accuse. "I know,

Mom. I never expected you to pay my way."

"If you really want to finish your education why don't you come back and attend the University of Nebraska in Kearney, live here with your father and me, and drive back and forth? It's only a fifty-mile trip. You might even be able to find a ride. A lot of Grand Island residents go to UN Kearney."

"Funny you should mention that. I've been seriously thinking that very thing. Coming home would solve a lot of my problems."

"Your father and I are in a little better financial position now than we were back then, so we could help with some of your college expenses."

"No, Mom. I'm a big girl. Twenty-six years old to be exact. If I can't make it on my own, I shouldn't even try."

"Just remember, we're here if you need us, financially or in any other way. The spring flowers in the garden are beginning to bloom and you always liked to help with the gardening. Think what fun we could have together."

"You do make moving back sound enticing."

Her mom responded with a laugh. "I hope so. I am trying to entice you, and this time of year would be the perfect time to make a new start. It would be so good to have you home again. Your room is sitting there just like you left it."

"You know, Mom, other than a few friends at the church I attend, I have no real ties to Omaha, especially now that I am out of a job. I've already checked. If I did enroll in the school's Kearny division, all of my credits would transfer. I've always wanted to pursue a career in hospital or healthcare management and the Kearney branch has a Bachelor of Science degree in that field."

Smiling, she clutched the phone even tighter. "Let me reweigh all the options overnight and pray about it again, and if I come to the conclusion I think I will, you can put the light on in my bedroom, Mom. If I decide to come, I'll be there in no more than two days." She could almost see her mother's beaming face on the other end of the line.

"Oh, my precious daughter, you have no idea how happy this makes me. I can't wait to tell your father there's a chance you'll be coming home. He'll be as excited as I am." Her mother's voice fairly chirped with joy, which made Tassie feel absolutely wonderful, a feeling she hadn't had in a long time. It was always nice to know you were loved. Who said you couldn't go home again?

As Tassie stood and told her mother good-bye, Goliath jumped to his feet, eyeing her quizzically.

"If I do decide to go you're going to love Grand Island, Goliath. My parents have a huge fenced-in backyard. You'll be able to run to your heart's content and not be cooped up in this stuffy apartment all day. Wouldn't that be nice?"

Goliath, apparently not understanding her words, walked nonchalantly away.

Chapter 2

"Stop! That's breakable!" Mitchell Drummond grabbed for the lovely crystal vase as it tumbled from the table but he was too late. It hit the floor and shattered into a zillion pieces.

"No, don't step in it, Babette. Sit on the sofa or go to your room. I don't want you to get hurt." He gazed at the broken shards, not exactly sure how to go about cleaning them up. Rather than do as she was told, his four-year-old daughter made straightaway for the pile of broken glass and began to stomp it with her feet.

"Babette, stop!"

When she failed to heed his warning and continued to tromp through the broken glass in her pink ballet slippers, he grabbed onto her arms, lifted her up, and firmly set her on a nearby chair. "Stay there and don't move until I say you can."

She gazed at him for a moment then slid off the chair and once again began to tromp through the glass, pounding her little feet into the shards as if trying to break them into even smaller pieces.

About to explode with anger, Mitchell grabbed at her, tugged her out of the shattered mess, and held her in his arms. "Didn't you hear Daddy? Daddy doesn't want his baby girl to get hurt. You have to stay out of the glass!"

She tried to wiggle free but he held her fast.

"Let me go."

"No, not until you promise to stay out of the glass." *Promise,* he thought. *I'm asking a four-year-old to make a promise when I'm not even sure she knows what the word means.* Turning, he carefully lowered her onto the sofa. "Be a good girl. Sit there, pumpkin, and watch Daddy till he gets all the pieces into the trash can, okay?"

But his pumpkin apparently didn't like the idea of sitting and waiting. Instead, she jumped off the sofa and right into the pile of broken glass again, giving him a defiant look that made him sick to his stomach.

"Dad! You broke that ugly vase?"

Mitch turned as his thirteen-year-old son sauntered into the room, wearing his athletic shoes with the cleats in the soles and swinging his bat. "It wasn't ugly. It was expensive, and don't wear those shoes in the house, Tony. They'll tear up our hardwood floors. And quit swinging that bat before you break something."

Tony pointed to what was left of the vase. "Me break something? Looks like you already did. Don't yell at me!"

"I didn't break it. Babette did."

A smirk crossed the young boy's face. "You're blaming a little girl?"

Babette pointed to her father. "I didn't break it. Daddy did."

"Yes, you did; I saw you!" Mitch felt like a heel when Babette began to cry.

"You're a mean old daddy. I hate you. I don't want you for a daddy!" Crossing her arms over her slim chest, she spun around and headed for her room, wailing all the way.

"Now look, you made her cry."

His anger flaring, Mitch glared at his son and pointed to Tony's feet. "Didn't I tell you not to wear those shoes in the house? That's it, Tony! You're grounded and no TV or baseball games for the next two days!"

Tony huffed then swung the bat over his head, barely missing the ceiling light fixture. "And who is going to be home to make sure I stay grounded? You're always off working on a case, and Grandma lets me do anything I want."

"Not this time, young man. I'll give her specific instructions as to what you can and cannot do!"

Tony let loose a belly laugh. "As long as she has her booze she doesn't care what I do."

"Your grandmother told me she wasn't drinking anymore."

"Oh, yeah, as if you can believe her any more than you could Mom."

"Leave your mother out of this."

"You're the one who always talks about her, not us kids," Tony shot back.

"Go to your room—now!" Mitch gestured toward the stairs, his hand shaking with anger. "And don't come out for the rest of the day, do you hear me?"

Tony shrugged. "Ha! Yes, Father. Anything you say, Father."

Mitch watched as his son headed up the stairs toward his room, swinging his bat from side to side as he walked, banging it into the walls. *I've tried so hard. Where have I gone wrong?*

He cleaned up the remains of the expensive vase he had bought for his wife the last Christmas she had been with them, then moved into the garage where he emptied the shards into the large trash container.

After making sure the floor was squeaky clean, he headed up the stairs to apologize to both Tony and Babette. But when he reached his daughter's room and found her curled up on her bed, fast asleep, her thumb in her mouth, he quietly closed the door.

He moved on down the hall then, ignoring the Do Not Enter sign with its skull and crossbones, and pushed the door open a crack. "Can I come in, son?"

When Tony didn't answer, Mitch rubbed his forehead. Should he go in? Invade the boy's privacy?

"Tony?"

No answer.

"Tony, are you there?" *Maybe he decided to take a shower.* But he hadn't heard the water running when he had passed the hall bathroom the kids shared.

He carefully widened the crack and peered inside.

Tony was gone—probably climbed out his window and headed to a friend's house. If this was the first time he'd done such a thing, Mitch would have been worried. Unfortunately, this disappearing act was nothing new when it came to his son, or his oldest daughter.

Three days later, Tassie threw herself onto her bed and gazed up at the huge poster-sized picture of her and her three best friends taken during their grade school years. She remembered how upset her father had been when he discovered she had thumbtacked it to her bedroom ceiling. Later that day, when her friends had come over, all four had stretched out on her bed, giggling at their images, trying to decide which one was the cutest, which one was the ugliest, and which one had the prettiest teeth. That last question had made them all laugh since all four had been wearing ugly braces at the time.

What dreams and lofty goals she'd had back then. How could she have let those things slip from her fingers like that? If she would have been stronger, able to say no when she should have, would things have been different? But she hadn't been strong. She'd been weak and that weakness would be bothering her the rest of her life.

"Tassie?"

Tassie rubbed at a tear before turning to face her mother. "Yeah, Mom, come in. I was just lying here—reminiscing."

"Supper will be ready in a few minutes. By the way, I got a big bone for Goliath from the butcher when I went to the store this morning. He's out in the backyard, having the time of his life chewing on it."

Tassie pulled herself to a sitting position, folded her legs, then wrapped her arms around her knees. "Thanks, Mom. That was really thoughtful of you. I know you don't like animals in the house but. . ."

Her mom waved a hand at her. "Don't give it another thought. A lot of my ideas have gone by the wayside since you've been away. Times have gotten so much worse, even in a peaceful city like Grand Island. I'd feel much safer with a dog in the house."

"Goliath won't mind staying in the backyard. Maybe Daddy and I can build him a doghouse to sleep in."

"No, he's used to staying inside. Your father and I agree it would be best for all of us if Goliath stayed in the house anytime he wants but especially at night."

Tassie tilted her head in question. "You're not just saying that because you think it will please me?"

Mrs. Springer lifted her hand, witness-style. "Honest, we really do want Goliath inside."

"I had no idea he'd get that big when I got him. He has been terrific company. I don't know what I would have done without him."

"Then it's settled. Goliath comes inside whenever he wants. Come on, let's eat supper. I'm sure your father is already at the table."

Once the three were seated and her father had prayed, he reached across and grasped his daughter's hand. "I can't tell you how happy we are to have you home again. We've missed you."

Tassie swallowed at the emotional lump in her throat. "It's good to be home, Daddy."

Opal Springer picked up the platter of golden pan-fried chicken and handed it to her. "I've fixed your favorites, sweetheart, even lemon meringue pie for dessert."

"Thanks, Mom. Everything looks wonderful, but you shouldn't have gone to so much trouble." She carefully perused the platter then selected a beautifully browned breast, her favorite piece.

Her father speared a pickled beet with his fork. "Have you decided what kind of job you'd like for the summer?"

"Not really, not that I have such terrific skills to offer an employer. I didn't mind my job at the photo shop but I can't say I'd want to do it again. I'd like to get a job at the hospital or a doctor's office, but I doubt they'd want to hire and train me when I'm only going to be there for three months. I'd have to be honest with them. But I am going to apply at those places anyway. I've also thought about maybe a job as a salesclerk at Dillard's or Penney's in the Conestoga Mall. They usually hire summertime help and I might be able to work for them on weekends after school starts."

"What about one of the Wal-Mart stores? They always seem to be hiring."

"I've thought of that. I guess I'll just start making the rounds tomorrow and see what I can find."

They finished their meal with pleasant conversation and then, after helping her mother clear the table and load the dishwasher, Tassie went to her room to unpack the bags and boxes she'd brought in from her car. Later that night, after giving Goliath's head a final pat, she switched off the lamp and lay snuggled up all cozy in her bed, staring at the luminous stars stuck to her ceiling, the ones she had placed there when she was in junior high, and she felt warm and comfy. At long last, she was home again and it felt oh so good.

Unfortunately, some of that feeling of euphoria disappeared the next morning as she left the hospital and walked from store to store in the mall in search of employment. Three hours later, weary in both mind and body and filled with discouragement, she headed for home.

"How'd it go?" her mom asked as Tassie entered the house and tossed her purse onto the kitchen counter.

"Not good. When the lady at the hospital human relations office discovered I'll be starting college in the fall, the only job she offered me was in food preparation in the hospital kitchen, a minimum wage job with crazy hours. I had hoped for more. No one else where I applied or inquired wanted full-time help, especially for only three short months."

"What about Wal-Mart? Did you go there? They may be interested in summer help."

Tassie kicked off her shoes and wiggled her toes. Her feet hurt. "I'm going there first thing in the morning."

"I'm sure you'll find something, dear. You just have to be patient."

"Patient? I don't have time to be patient. By scrimping, I've managed to save almost enough to enroll in college but not nearly enough to stay there." She lifted her hands in frustration. "No full-time job, no school."

"I've told you your father and I will help."

"Thanks for offering, Mom, but no. I have to do this on my own."

"But—"

Tassie lifted her hand. "No, Mom, I mean it. Just letting me stay here at home until I get on my feet is more than enough." She grinned at her mother then bent and kissed her cheek. "Besides, I know you're praying for me. Surely God will answer prayer. Where is your faith?"

By eleven o'clock the next morning, Tassie had already been to Dillard's, Penney's, Wal-Mart, Target, Super Saver, and Skagway, with each manager saying he or she would go over her application then call her, as if all she had to do was wait by the phone. From there she trudged on to Walgreen's, U-Save Foods, Bag 'N Save, and Pump and Pantry, with much the same results, although one of the managers she met with did give her a little hope.

"So how did it go today?" her father asked after the three had gathered around the dinner table and thanked the Lord for their food. "Find anything promising?"

Tassie huffed as she unfolded her napkin and placed it in her lap. "'Promising' isn't exactly the word I would use to describe my day. Grueling would be more like it."

"I take that to mean you didn't have any success."

She felt her mother's hand lovingly circle her forearm. "Perhaps tomorrow will be better, dear."

Tomorrow—how she hated to even think about doing the same thing the next day. "Maybe I made a mistake coming back to Grand Island. Not that living in Omaha was so terrific, but at least there seemed to be more jobs there. But that's hindsight. I've already quit my job and given up my apartment. Don't worry, Mom. God knows I need a job. He won't let me down."

Later, as the two were cleaning the kitchen, her mother received a call on her cell phone from one of her friends at church. Tassie smiled at her then shooed her out of the room, motioning that she would finish the job herself. When the kitchen was finally back to order, she moved into the living room and sat down on the sofa beside her father. "I love you, Daddy," she told him, leaning her head against his shoulder.

He lowered his newspaper and smiled at her. She loved his smile. Why couldn't she have inherited his dimples?

Grinning and excited about something, her mother flitted across the room toward them. "Tassie, guess what! I think I have a job for you!"

Before Tassie could respond, her mother wiggled her way in between the two and sat down. "That was Phyllis Cramer. She said her neighbor is frantic for a babysitter for his three children!"

None too enthused, Tassie screwed up her face. "Thanks, Mom, but I don't think so. I love children, and have had plenty of experience as a babysitter, but I need a full-time job."

"It is full time, actually more than full time. He wants a live-in nanny, and Phyllis says she thinks the pay is pretty good. She's already highly recommended you!"

She frowned. "Why would a man need a live-in nanny? Where's his wife?"

"Gone. Killed in a car wreck a few years ago I think Phyllis said."

"Doesn't the guy spend any time with his kids?"

"Yes, as much as he can, I guess. She said he needs someone there 24/7 because he works odd hours and is sometimes called out on a case for days."

"Case? What's he do?"

"Oh, I guess I didn't mention that. Phyllis said he is a detective. His wife's mother has been living with him and caring for the children but apparently there was some kind of disagreement and she has moved to California. Phyllis has been pinch-hitting and taking care of them until he finds a replacement. I think you should go see him."

Tassie gave her head a slight shake. "I don't know, Mom. He's probably looking for someone on a permanent basis. I doubt he'd want to hire me for just three months then have to find someone to replace me."

"You've always been great with kids. You ought to at least talk to him, find out exactly what he does want." She reached into her apron pocket and pulled out a piece of notepaper. "My friend gave me his number."

Tassie took it and stuck it into her jeans' pocket. "I'll think about it. Meantime, I'm going to go out in the backyard and toss the Frisbee to Goliath."

As she dressed the next morning in preparation for hitting the pavement again in search of a job, she remembered she had left her car keys in the pocket of her jeans and reached into the closet to retrieve them. As she pulled the keys out, a folded piece of paper fell to the floor. But as she picked it up and turned to toss it onto her dresser she stopped. Maybe she should give that man a call; then at least she could tell her mother she had tried. Most retail stores didn't open until ten so she still had plenty of time before slipping on her shoes and heading out. Pulling her cell phone from her pocket, she dialed the number. To her surprise he answered on the first ring.

"Mr. Drummond? This is Tassie Springer. I've just moved back to town and I'm looking for a job. Phyllis Cramer, a friend of my mother, said you were searching for a full-time babysitter. I thought—"

"When can you come for an interview?"

What? I know Mrs. Cramer recommended me but isn't he going to ask about my qualifications? "I—I guess I could come anytime it is convenient for you."

"Where are you now?"

"Now? At—at my parents' home on Wilson Way Road."

"What's the house number?"

"Ten sixteen, but—"

"I'll be there in ten minutes." A click sounded in her ear.

Still holding the phone in her hand, Tassie staggered her way into the kitchen where her mother was preparing the ingredients to go into the bread machine. "He's coming here."

Her mother screwed the lid onto the bottle of ground cinnamon then swung around. "Who's coming here?"

"The guy who needs a babysitter. Mitchell Drummond."

Chapter 3

Mitch double-checked the address then punched the door-bell button with one hand and worked at his tie with the other. This woman—this Tassie Springer, if he liked her and felt she would do a good job—had to say yes. *At this point I'd almost settle for an orangutan as a babysitter if it could keep my kids in line.* He smiled to himself. *Maybe that's not such a bad idea. Wonder where I could get one.*

When a lovely late-fortyish-looking woman answered the door, smiling at him, he thought maybe God had heard his prayers after all. "I'm Mitchell Drummond. I'm the one who needs a babysitter—ah, I guess these days they call them a nanny, someone full time." When she pushed open the screen door he quickly stepped inside.

"Would you like a glass of lemonade? I made it fresh not more than an hour ago."

He sat down as she gestured toward the sofa. "Thank you, no." Then glancing around the room and being pleased with what he saw, he offered, "Lovely place you have here. So homey. Have you had much experience taking care of children?"

Her hand went to her throat as she gasped. "Oh, I'm not the one interested in the job. It's my daughter, Tassie. And as for your question, yes, she has had lots of child-care experience. As a teenager, she babysat for several families on a regular basis. Then when she went off to college she babysat for her neighbor's children while the woman worked nights and weekends. She'll be here in a moment, Mr. Drummond. She went outside to spend a few minutes with her dog."

Both he and the woman turned as an attractive young female came hurrying into the room and extended her hand.

"Hi. I'm Tassie Springer. You're Mr. Drummond?"

"Yes." He rose quickly and shook her hand. "Nice to meet you, Miss Springer."

After motioning him to be seated, she sat down across from him as her mother said a hasty good-bye and scurried from the room. "I hope I haven't wasted your time. I never expected you to rush all the way over here before we'd even had a chance to visit on the phone. You never even asked me about my qualifications."

"Your mom took care of that after I got here. She told me about all the babysitting you've done. And you did come highly recommended."

"Oh? Then you know more about me than I know about you. Tell me about this nanny position of yours, your children, and what is expected of whomever you hire."

This woman sounds perfect for the job. "Well, my wife died a couple of years ago and since then, her mother has been living with us, caring for the children and running the house." He nervously cleared his throat. "I have to be honest with you. Actually, my three children have been running her, and the house has pretty much gone unattended. My kids can be a real handful."

"I was sorry to hear about your wife. Her loss must have really been hard on you and your family."

"It has been hard." *But not as hard as the day she walked out on us to go live with her drunken biker boyfriend.* "We have tried to manage, but now that my mother-in-law has moved to California I'm without a babysitter."

"You have three children?"

"Yes, Babette, she's four. Tony, he's thirteen, and Delana, she'll be sixteen soon. After my wife died I used some of the life insurance money to buy a new minivan, so you'll have dependable transportation to drive the children around to their activities. You'll have a room of your own, of course, up above the garage, but I would expect you to sleep in the house on the nights when I have to be away. On the sofa or maybe in one of the girls' rooms."

"And you expect the person you hire to live at your home seven days a week, with no days off? Not even Sundays?"

"Oh, I'm sure I'll be able to spare you at least one day each week, they just won't be regular. I'm a detective, so my schedule is pretty hectic. I may work fifty hours one week and eighty the next. It depends on what's happening on Grand Island's crime scene. I just need to make sure if I'm out all night, or get a phone call and am called away, someone is there with the children."

"Is there anything else you'd like to know about me? I'm sure it must be difficult even thinking about turning your children and your home over to a complete stranger."

"I should probably ask more questions but I can't think of any right now. I'm not very good at this sort of thing, but one thing I am good at is judging people. In my business you get so you can read 'em like a book, and you have had experience with children. Just meeting you and talking with your mother, I can tell you'll work out fine. It's obvious you've come from a pretty nice family."

She gave him a weak smile. "You—ah—haven't mentioned the pay."

"Oh, I haven't, have I?" He rubbed at his chin and gave it some thought. If he made it too low, she would probably say no without even considering it. And taking care of his kids wasn't going to be any picnic. He threw out a figure he hoped would seem fair. "And, of course, other than your personal items, I'll pay all your expenses while you're there."

He watched while she gave it some thought, hoping and praying she would say yes. He was prepared to go a bit higher in wages if he had to, but not much. He made a decent salary with the Grand Island Police Department but it was never enough to do everything he would like to do for his family. "Well, what's your answer?"

Tassie scrunched up her face in thought. "I'll admit I wasn't too interested in the job when I first heard about it, mainly because I'd be working so many hours, but I could really use the salary you're offering, Mr. Drummond. I've always liked and gotten along well with kids, so I'm not concerned about that part. And, thanks to my mom, I know how to clean. And when I was living at home she turned me into a pretty good cook—but there may be a problem we haven't yet discussed. A problem I would have mentioned on the phone if you'd given me half a chance."

He leaned forward with a reassuring smile, willing to do whatever it took to get her to say yes. "I'm sure we can overcome whatever it is." The more she said, the better he liked her. He had to convince her to accept his offer.

"You said you needed someone full time. Working full time would be fine for me now, but I can only work through the summer. I'm going to go back to college in the fall. I want to get my degree."

Mitch felt as if he had been kicked in the stomach. Tassie had seemed so right for the job. Finding a nanny—one who would live in—was proving to be far more difficult than he had imagined when his mother-in-law just up and walked out on him without notice. "Only through the summer?"

"Yes. I'm sorry but I had to be honest with you. Since that apparently won't work out for you, I do hope you can find someone else. I know how concerned you must be, being without proper child care, especially since your children will soon be out of school for summer break. Couldn't Delana care for her brother and sister until the fall semester begins? You said she was almost sixteen. I started babysitting when I was only twelve."

"Actually, I prefer to have an adult with them." *As disobedient as Delana is, there is no way that would work out. She would have the house filled with her friends the minute I left for work.* He shuddered. *Friends or boyfriends!* Filled with disappointment, he rose and headed toward the door. "You sure I can't change your mind?"

"No, I dropped out of college once and I'm not going to let that happen again. I'm determined to get my degree."

He opened the door then stepped outside. "Keep my number just in case, okay?"

"I will but I won't be changing my mind. Nice to have met you, Mr. Drummond. I wish you the best."

When the door closed behind him, he stood on the porch for a moment, half tempted to ring the doorbell again and beg her to take the job. She had seemed so right. But he didn't. She had said no and he had to accept it. Finishing college and getting her degree was important to her and certainly admirable. It wasn't fair to even tempt her to give up such a noble thing.

But as he climbed into his car and headed for the police station, he couldn't help but compare the excitement he had felt on the way to Tassie's house to how he felt now. Lousy.

Tassie received calls from two prospective employers the next day with each offering no more than minimum wage and less than twenty-five hours per week. As much as she hated to, she turned them down. She filled out applications at several more of the smaller shops in the mall then headed home, discouraged and again second-guessing her move back to Grand Island. Was this God's way of punishing her? Wasn't living with what she had done all those years ago punishment enough? Did He have to heap on more?

"What's wrong, sweetheart?" her father asked that evening. "Your mom told me about the nanny job you turned down. Is that what's upsetting you?"

She sat down next to him and snuggled close. He felt warm, safe, just like he had when she had been a child and had snuggled up to him with a book in her hand, hoping he would read her a story. "Sorta, I guess, that and being rejected by all the places where I've applied for jobs. I feel so low, Dad, like I'm of no value to anyone."

"You are to me, honey, and to your mom. Next to our Lord and each other, we love you more than any person on earth."

"I know, Daddy, and I love you for loving me, but I'm a twenty-six-year-old woman now. Not a child. I should be able to make it on my own. I can't come running to you and Mom all my life."

"We like having you run to us; we just wish we could do more. God knows your needs, Tassie."

"I know, but my need right now is a job, and so far He hasn't given me one."

Off in the distance a phone rang. Tassie leaped to her feet. "Be right back; that's my cell phone. I left it in my room." She hurried down the hall, hoping to get there before her voice mail picked up or the person hung up. "Hello," she answered breathlessly.

"Miss Springer?" said a familiar voice.

"Yes?"

"Hi, Tassie. This is Mitch. Mitch Drummond."

"Oh?" Disappointed it wasn't another job offer, she felt her hopes deflate. "I'm really sorry, Mr. Drummond. I know you need a nanny but I can't change my mind. I *am* going to college in the fall."

"What if I told you I wanted you to work only *until* the fall semester?"

Slightly heartened, Tassie switched the phone to her other ear and sat down on the edge of her bed. "I—I don't understand."

"Look, I need a nanny, babysitter, or whatever you want to call it, and I need one now. You're available now, but only until the fall semester begins. Finding the right person for this job is proving to be much harder than I had anticipated and you seemed so right for it. So I got to thinking. *If* you agree to take the job only until your classes start, that will give me slightly over three months to find your replacement. Surely in that length of time I can find someone competent. It's a win-win situation for both of us. What do you say?"

She hurriedly thought over his offer. He was right, it would be a win-win situation for both of them and she could sure use the kind of money he had offered. "Going to church is important to me. I'd have to have Sundays off." *Lord, if You want me to accept this job, please work things out so I won't have to miss church.*

From the pause on the other end she figured she had blown it, that he wouldn't agree since he had been so adamant about her working a flexible schedule; but that's the way it had to be. He could take it or leave it.

"Having *every* Sunday off might present a problem. The bad guys don't take Sundays off. Crime happens seven days a week and when it occurs I need to be there."

As much as she wanted to take the job, she couldn't. She had to honor God and stand her ground. "Then I'm sorry, really I am, but attending church is important to me."

When he paused again and the connection lay heavy with silence, she thought he had hung up on her. But as she pulled the phone from her ear and started to flip it closed, he said, "I have an idea that may work for both of us, if you're agreeable to it."

Please, Lord, don't let him offer me more money if I work Sundays. I don't want to be tempted to miss church.

"You could take my kids with you."

"To church?" His suggestion was one she should have thought of herself and she almost felt ashamed for not offering to take them. "I'd love to have your children go to church with me." *Thank You, God!*

"I'm afraid I haven't been a very good father. I used to attend but I haven't taken them since my wife—ah—died, and my mother-in-law certainly never took them. I like the idea of my children attending church."

"What if they wouldn't want to go with me?"

"They may rebel at first but I'm sure they'll come around once they get used to it. I might even come with you, too, on the Sundays I don't have to work. Believe it or not, I used to be pretty active in our church, even sang in the choir for a year or two. So will you come to work for me? I'd like you to start as soon as possible."

"Like—how soon?"

"Tomorrow?"

"And you'll pay me what you originally offered?"

"Absolutely, and if things go as well as I hope they will, there may be a small severance bonus for you when your classes start."

The job seemed to be everything she had hoped for and more. "I accept, Mr. Drummond. I'll gather up my things and report to your home in the morning no later than eight o'clock."

"Could you possibly make it by seven? I want to introduce you to my children before the two older ones leave for school, and I have to be at the courthouse by eight."

She glanced at her watch. Seven was less than thirteen hours away. She'd have to pack, load her car, take a shower—

"But if seven is a problem, I could—"

"Seven will be fine, Mr. Drummond. I'll see you in the morning."

Another thought occurred to her, an important one. "Oh, I have another problem, one I haven't mentioned. I have a dog. I can't leave Goliath here and expect my parents to take care of him."

"Goliath? He's not a Great Dane, is he?"

She chuckled. "No, but he's a big dog. A black Lab."

A sigh of relief sounded on the other end. "Bring him. My backyard is fenced in and my son has always wanted a dog. Besides, I've heard black Labs make great family pets."

"They do."

"Is he an outdoor dog or used to staying in the house?"

"He stayed in my apartment most of the time when I was in Omaha but—"

"Don't worry about it. He can stay in the house if he wants. I'm sure my kids will like him."

"That's very kind of you, Mr. Drummond."

"Then I'll see you—and Goliath—at seven. The address is—"

"Just a moment, let me get a pen," she said as she grabbed a pen and paper from her nightstand. "Okay, I'm ready."

"It's 2442 East Windmill Lane. It's the only quad-level in the block. My red car will be parked in the driveway."

"I'm sure I can find it. I'll see you at seven."

Early the next morning, Mitch glanced at the clock on the range, gulped down the final swig of coffee, then hurried to the bottom of the steps leading to the upstairs bedrooms. "Tony! Delana! I need you downstairs now. We need to talk. Your new nanny will be here in fifteen minutes," he hollered, cupping his hands to his mouth.

No response.

He brought his hands together in a loud clap. "Delana, Tony. Did you hear me? I said now. It's six forty-five. You need to at least eat a bowl of cereal before leaving for school."

Still no response.

"Am I going to have to come up there and get you? Because if I do, I'll guarantee you it won't be pleasant. Come down here right now! That's an order."

The only sound in response was the loud slamming of a door.

Mitch grabbed the handrail and, taking two steps at a time, rushed up to the landing. "Last call. I mean it. I want both of you out here right now!"

The bathroom door opened and Tony, sending his father a look of disgust, emerged in a pair of baggy jeans, his underwear sticking out over the top, and a shirt with the words SCHOOL IS FOR IDIOTS AND LOSERS emblazoned across the front, his hair in a feeble attempt at a spiked-up Mohawk.

"Quit yer dreamin', Dad. That woman won't last a day."

Mitch wanted to grab his son, order him to get rid of the weird hairdo, and shove him back into the bathroom, but he didn't. The last thing he needed was a scene when Tassie arrived. "She'd better last more than a day or you'll have me to answer to. I expect the three of you to be on your best behavior."

With a snort Tony pushed his way past Mitch and headed downstairs to the kitchen. Mitch walked the few steps to Delana's door and rapped softly. "Delana, come on out, sweetheart. It's nearly time for Tassie to arrive."

When Delana didn't respond, Mitch turned the knob and, knowing how angry his daughter got when he invaded her privacy, pushed the door open only a slight crack. "Honey, did you hear Daddy?"

When she didn't answer, he pushed the door fully open and stepped inside. To his dismay the room was empty. Mitch's heart sank as he saw the open window. He hurriedly walked over and closed it, making sure to hook the latch. If his daughter had climbed out the window, as she had done several times before to spend the night with one of her girlfriends, when she came back home she'd have to come through the door. But what was he going to tell Tassie? If he told her the truth, that his daughter was nothing more than a rebel teenager who constantly disobeyed his orders, she'd probably walk out and he'd be back to square one—without a nanny.

Struggling to set his anger over Delana aside he moved down the hall and, ignoring the KEEP OUT sign his four-year-old had taped to her door, he turned the knob, entered her room, bent over the sleeping child, and gently placed a loving kiss on her pink cheek.

Without even opening her eyes, Babette pushed him away. "Leave me alone!"

"Daddy was just trying to wake you up, baby. Your new babysitter will be here. . ."

He stopped mid-sentence at the ringing of the doorbell. *Oh, no. She's early!* "Get your clothes on, pumpkin, then come downstairs, okay?"

Babette flipped onto her side and yanked the covers over her head. "Don't want to."

"Please. For Daddy?"

The doorbell sounded a second time. Mitch swallowed hard then went to answer it.

Tassie stepped back from the door and surveyed her surroundings. The house was nice. Well painted and, except for two pairs of muddy running shoes and an equally muddy skateboard lying on the porch, it was fairly neat. The grass had been recently mowed but not edged, and the flower beds boasted no flowers, only weeds, but Mitchell Drummond was a single, apparently overworked father. More than likely, planting flowers and making sure his lawn was edged wasn't in the top ten on his priority list. She pressed the button again and waited. Finally, the door opened and Mr. Drummond's smiling face appeared.

"Sorry, I was—my daughter Babette and I were—ah—talking." He motioned her inside.

She nodded then stepped into the foyer, which was nothing more than a closet door on one side and on the other, a chest with a mirror—desperately in need of a good washing—above it. She followed him into the living room.

"The kids are—ah—getting ready for school. Well, Tony is, or was, now he's in the kitchen having breakfast." His gaze went to the stairway, which was directly behind the sofa. "Since Babette is only four, she doesn't go to school. She's—ah—sleeping. I'm sure she'll wake up in a little while." He gestured toward the stairway. "The kids' bedrooms are upstairs. They share the hall bathroom." He pointed to a set of stairs leading to a lower level. "A second bathroom is down there and so is the family room. It has a fireplace. My bedroom is on the lowest level."

Tassie nodded. "What about the laundry room?"

He pointed toward an archway on his left. "By the back door."

"No dining room?"

"Not really, but the kitchen has space for an oblong table and six chairs."

"And I'm to sleep above the garage?"

"Yes. Sorry about the inconvenience. The stairway to the garage room is on the outside. But," he hastened to add, "there is an intercom so when I have to leave during the night, I'll be able wake you up without coming to your room. I'd show it to you now but I want you to meet Tony before his ride comes to pick him up."

"Before I do anything, I need to get Goliath out of my car."

"Oh, yes, Goliath. I nearly forgot about him." Mr. Drummond took the small suitcase from her hand and placed it on the floor. But as he reached for the doorknob the front door opened and a teenage girl, her hair a tangled mess, mascara smeared on her upper cheeks, wearing too-red lipstick and long earrings that dangled precariously to her slim shoulders, entered.

Tassie took one look at the girl's belligerent expression as she glared at her father, then at the teen's skimpy attire, and shuddered. Surely this wasn't Delana—but deep down inside she knew it was. And if it was, and Tony was even half as rebellious as his sister appeared to be, Tassie's work was cut out for her. She could hardly wait to meet Babette. Surely, being only four, she wouldn't yet have had a chance to be tainted by the world—and her siblings.

From the way Mitchell's face reddened and the way he clenched his fists at his sides, Tassie knew the girl was in trouble. "Go wash all that stuff off your face," he told her in an almost monotone. Although Tassie couldn't see his face, she was sure he was gritting his teeth. "I'll deal with you later, Delana. I have to be at the courthouse by eight."

Without a word, Delana gave him a flip of her shoulders and headed up the stairs.

"Better hurry!" he called up after her. "Your friend's mom will be here any minute to take you to school and I want you to meet Tassie." Mitchell raised his brow and gave Tassie a sheepish grin. "That girl has no sense of time."

Tassie felt her eyes widen. How dumb did he think she was? It was obvious the girl had been out all night! Hadn't he been aware she'd been gone?

Both she and Mitchell turned as Tony waddled into the room. Tassie had never been able to figure out why a guy would want to wear pants hung so low they impeded his walking. And his hair! What a mess.

"Hey, is somebody going to drive me to school? I think my ride forgot to pick me up."

"Drive you to school? No, it's only a couple of blocks away. Walk. The walk will be good for you."

Trying to be friendly, Tassie sent Tony a smile. "Hi. You must be Tony. I'm Tassie. I'll walk out with you. I want to introduce you to Goliath."

The boy wrinkled up his nose. "Who is Goliath?"

Tassie crooked her finger in his direction. "Come with me and I'll show you."

Without even a good-bye to his dad, Tony followed her as she walked out the front door toward her car.

"Wow! Goliath is a dog!"

The smile on his face warmed Tassie's heart. Every boy she had ever known had been crazy about dogs. Maybe Goliath would be the very thing she needed to establish some sort of common ground with Tony. "You like dogs?"

He reached inside and stroked Goliath's head. "Yeah, I always wanted a dog, but Dad said no." Then turning to her he asked, "Is he going to let you keep him here? In the house?"

"Yes, he said it was fine with him."

Tony reared back, his eyes rounded. "*My* dad said that?"

"Sure did." She pointed toward Goliath. "He likes you. I can tell."

"I like him, too. Wow, Dad said a dog could stay here. Wait'll I tell Delana. She'll never believe it. He must have been pretty desperate for a babysitter to hire one with a dog."

"Your big sister likes dogs?"

Tony cautiously leaned into the open door. "Yeah. She kept one of those fancy little dogs in her closet for three days before my dad found out. Boy, did she get in trouble for that one."

"You think she'll like Goliath? He's a lot bigger than one of those fancy little dogs."

The boy stroked the dog's ears. "Yeah, she'll like him. Who wouldn't? He's a great dog. Babette'll like him, too."

Tassie suddenly felt a warm burst of satisfaction. Thanks to Goliath, maybe living with the Drummond kids wouldn't be so bad after all; but of course she still hadn't yet met the third child. She'd have to wait and see what Babette was like.

At only four years old, she couldn't be too bad. Could she?

Chapter 4

After a few final words with Mr. Drummond, he unceremoniously handed her a house key as he headed out the door, Delana on his heels, ignoring Tassie's good-bye as the girl rushed out to meet her ride. She closed and locked the front door. Then, after checking to make sure Babette was still asleep, Tassie made a second trip out to her car, filled her arms with a few of the remaining items, then led Goliath back into the house.

"The situation here is a little different than at Mom and Dad's," she told him as the two moved through the house and up the outside stairway to her room.

"Um, not bad," she said aloud after glancing round the small room that was to be hers for the next three months. "You and I are going to have to be patient. I have a feeling these kids are going to try to walk all over us." Once everything had been placed on her bed or on the floor for sorting out later, Tassie, leaving Goliath behind, moved back downstairs to check on Babette and establish her presence in the Drummond home. If she demonstrated her authority right from the beginning, perhaps the children would be more cooperative. Even though she would do it in a pleasant manner, she would let them know right up front what she expected of them.

Ignoring the KEEP OUT sign, although just the sight of it infuriated her that a four-year-old child could have such dominion over a household, Tassie tapped on Babette's door. "Hi, Babette. It's me—Tassie. Are you awake? Can I come in?"

"No! Stay out! This is my room!" came back the answer. "I don't like you and I don't want you here!"

The voice was that of a near baby but the words definitely conveyed her meaning. Little Miss Babette wasn't about to accept the newest addition to her home. Turning, Tassie hurried through the house and up the stairs to her room to get Goliath. "Come on, Goliath, I've got a job for you."

With the dog at her heels, she climbed down the outside stairway and back through the house to the bedroom wing. "Someone wants to meet you, Babette. Come and see who it is."

"Don't want to. Go away."

Tassie gave Goliath's head a pat. "I think you're going to like this new friend." Although it took a great deal of effort on her part, she tried to keep her words sweet and not show the impatience that was building inside her.

No response. She pushed the door open a little farther and stuck her head inside, only to be pelted by a flying pink flip-flop. Her impatience turned to anger. Holding her hands in front of her face to ward off any other objects that might come flying her way, she pushed the door fully open and entered the room. There, standing on the bed in the middle of a jumbled combination of dirty clothes and rumpled sheets, stood the young girl, still in her cute little Barbie jammies, her hands on her hips, her chin jutted out defiantly. "Get out!"

Undaunted, Tassie grabbed Goliath's collar and tugged him toward her. "See, I told you someone wanted to meet you. This is Goliath. He's going to be living with you this summer."

"Don't like dogs!"

"But Goliath is such a nice dog. He wants to be your friend."

Babette stomped her little foot, pointed a finger toward the door, and screamed at the top of her lungs, "I hate you! Get out!"

Tassie edged closer. "Now you know that's not true, Babette. You don't even know me, so how can you hate me? I want to be your friend, too."

Babette leaped off the bed, barely landing on her feet, and grabbed a cell phone from her nightstand. "My daddy is a policeman. I'm going to call and tell him to take you to jail!"

The child had her own cell phone? Tassie could only imagine what would happen if Babette did call 911 and told them some awful tale, which she wouldn't put past the belligerent child. Struggling to keep her voice even, she moved quickly forward and took the phone from the little girl's hand. "You don't really want to call the police. Besides, your daddy wants me here. Wouldn't you rather pet Goliath's head? He wants someone to play ball with him."

Babette narrowed her eyes, then folding her arms across her slim chest, glared at Tassie. "Don't want to play ball."

"Then how about coming downstairs and letting me fix you some breakfast? Maybe some nicely browned bacon and french toast? Do you like french toast? With maple syrup on it?"

The child's lower lip curled down. "Don't want no breakfast."

It was obvious she wasn't getting anywhere with the stubborn little girl. "Well, Goliath and I are hungry. I guess, since you don't want any breakfast, I'll go downstairs and fix bacon and french toast for the two of us. If you change your mind, come on down."

As promised, Tassie fixed the bacon and french toast in hopes Babette would relent and join them, but by the time she had finished the plateful she had made for herself, Babette still hadn't appeared on the scene.

"What do I do now?" Tassie asked her mom in desperation after she had dialed her number and described Mr. Drummond's children's behavior. "I've never seen such rebellious children."

"The best thing you can do: Pray for them, ask God for wisdom and strength, and be a shining witness to them."

"Thanks, Mom. You always know the right words to say. From now on, I'm going to look at my position here as a ministry, the ministry God has called me to. But please pray He will make me love these children because, to be honest, they are not very lovable."

"You know I will. Just remember each time they're giving you fits, you're not alone; I'm praying for you *and* for them. Hang in there, sweetheart. Things are bound to get better once they know you. Just love them, Tassie. That's all God requires of you."

With her mother's encouraging words ringing in her ears like a melodious sonnet, Tassie set about cleaning the kitchen and sorting the clothing and other soiled items that had accumulated on the laundry room floor. After that she worked at running the sweeper and dusting everything on the main level. Next, she moved upstairs, deciding first to work on Tony's room.

Until she opened the door and stepped inside.

The place was a shambles with the bedding half pulled off the bed onto the floor. Underwear, T-shirts, and socks were scattered everywhere. There were even drink glasses and ice-cream bowls with mold growing in them, green as grass. The room smelled bad. Determined to get it organized, and with plans of making sure it stayed that way, she dove into the mess with a vengeance.

"Tony is going to be mad at you."

Tassie spun around to find Babette standing in the open door, a ragged teddy bear cuddled in her arms, and she was still dressed in her jammies. And on the front of her shirt was a stain—a stain that looked remarkably like maple syrup. Had the child slipped downstairs and enjoyed breakfast while Tassie was cleaning her brother's room? Ignoring the stain, she continued working.

"Tony may not like it when he realizes I've been in his room, but I'll bet he'll be glad to find everything put away and his bed made. Most boys don't like to make their bed."

"I'm going to tell my daddy you were in Tony's room."

"You can tell him if you like. He hired me to take care of his family. Cooking, doing laundry, and cleaning are part of that job. I have a feeling your father, too, will be glad I did it." Then making sure her smile was pleasant and friendly, she added, "I was going to work on your sister's room next but I can do yours first, if you like."

Babette's face took on a scowl. "No! Don't want you in my room. Stay out!"

Tassie watched as the girl darted out of the room then flinched when she heard Babette's door slam. That little girl was going to be a real challenge, but she'd be patient, just like her mother had said she should; and hopefully, by the time her three-plus months were up, they'd all be friends.

She was still standing in the middle of the room, trying to figure out her next step, when the phone rang. It was Mr. Drummond, checking to see how things were going. Deciding she really hadn't been on the job long enough to honestly evaluate the situation, she dodged his question by turning the tables and asking how his day was going.

"Not too great," he answered with a heavy sigh. "This case we're working on really has me baffled. Looks like I won't make it home for supper like I'd planned, maybe not even until morning. I might be involved in an important all-night stakeout. I hate it that this is happening on your first day. Is everything going okay with Babette?"

"I—think so."

"Good. You have the number. Remember, you can always call me on my cell phone if you have questions or any problems."

"Thank you. I will. You have a good day," she told him before cutting the connection.

"Well," she told Goliath as she hung up the phone, "Mr. Drummond isn't going to make it home for supper. That means I'll be dealing with his children by myself tonight. I was hoping he'd be here to help get things off to a good start, but that isn't going to happen."

Goliath met her words with a cock of his head.

"And if he is involved in that stakeout I'll be spending my first night on the sofa instead of the bed in my room." She smiled at the dog. "Guess where you'll be sleeping. On the floor right next to me."

At noon Tassie fixed two peanut butter and lettuce sandwiches. One she ate, the other she placed on a plate on a pretty placemat and added carrot and celery sticks, in hopes that Babette would come into the kitchen when she wasn't looking and eat like she had done with her breakfast plate. By one o'clock, the sandwich lay exactly where she had placed it. But the next time she passed through the kitchen the plate was empty.

After checking the refrigerator to make sure she had everything she would need to prepare supper, she made her way back upstairs to Delana's room to work on the trash that was strewn all over the furniture and carpet. How anyone could live in such filth and enjoy it was beyond her.

Like most young girls, she herself had been rebellious as a teenager, but even with that she had kept her room in fairly decent order. Not as neat as her mother would have preferred, but decent. Not Delana's. Her room was knee-deep with discarded clothing, hats, purses, scarves, shoes, hair clips, perfume bottles, shopping bags, empty hair spray cans, wadded up paper, fast-food wrappers and

Styrofoam containers, napkins, and drinking straws. There were also textbooks, spiral notebooks, jewel cases from both computer software and music CDs, discarded posters, numerous partially used bottles of nail polish, playbills, receipts—you name it and it was probably there. Tassie stood in the middle of the muddle staring at it. The job looked impossible. She hardly knew where to begin.

"*What* are you doing in my room?" a stern voice asked from behind her.

She turned and found two dark-rimmed eyes glaring at her from beneath heavily darkened eyebrows and a head of hair boasting a broad streak of green running through her bangs. It wasn't time for school to be out. Had this girl actually gone to school or had she skipped classes? Maybe spent the day with friends? She hadn't had that streak of green when she'd left the house this morning.

"I'm cleaning your room but now that you're here you can help me," she answered, forcing a smile and trying to sound nonchalant.

"I don't want my room cleaned. I liked it the way it was. You have no right to be in here." The girl pointed a long fake nail painted with shiny black polish toward the door. "Get out!"

"Look, Delana, I know life hasn't been easy for you. Your father hired me to take care of you and your brother and sister because he loves you and is concerned about you. All I'm doing is making sure the trash is sorted from your personal belongings, throwing it away, and placing your clothing and shoes in their proper places. If you want to finish the job yourself, that's fine with me. I'll even help if you'll let me, but you have to stop throwing everything on the floor. Believe it or not, I was your age once myself and not so long ago. I liked my privacy, too, and my mother let me have it—so long as I did my part and kept my room halfway neat and orderly. That's all I'm asking of you."

Delana's fists went to her hips. "Who do you think you are? God?"

"Of course not, but I did pray about coming here before I took the job."

The girl glared at her. "And you think because you prayed you can come into our home and upset it like this?"

Tassie's eyes scanned the cluttered room.

"This is my space, not yours," Delana snarled. "You have no right to order me around. I'm going to call my dad!"

Giving her a gentle smile, Tassie pulled her cell phone from the side pocket of her jeans and held it out toward the girl. "Here, you can use my phone. I've already put his number on speed dial."

Delana let out a snort, then, ignoring the phone, threw herself onto the bed and kicked off her shoes, letting them thud to the floor. Without another word, Tassie gathered up an armload of the strewn clothing and shoes and placed them in the trash container.

Delana quickly sat straight up, her eyes bugging wide open, her face red and distorted with anger. "How dare you put my things in the wastebasket! I've had those shoes barely a week and that shirt was practically new! I'm going to tell my dad to fire you!"

Tassie picked up several more items and added them to the trash container. "I just supposed since they were on the floor they were trash." She picked up the container and headed toward the door. "If you don't want your precious things thrown away, it might be a good idea to put them where they belong. Because anything I find on the floor I will assume is trash, and it will end up in the Dumpster." She paused in the doorway. "Oh, and I want to remind you, supper will be ready at six."

A heavy object of some sort hit the door as Tassie closed it behind her and she sucked in a deep breath. *Whew, that was close. This tough love thing is even harder than I imagined it would be, and I still have Tony to contend with when he gets home. I just hope Mr. Drummond will go along with me. Because if he doesn't, and if he can't understand that my heart is in the right place and I'm doing my best to help his kids, I may be quitting this job before my second day even gets here.*

But things didn't go any better. In fact, they got worse. When she walked into the kitchen to prepare the taco salad she had planned to serve for supper, the room looked vandalized. Cupboard doors were standing open with grape jelly smeared on both the doors and the brass handles. More jelly was smeared across the countertops, with at least half the slices from a loaf of bread scattered haphazardly on the table and floor. The refrigerator door was standing open, and on the floor was an overturned carton with the full half-gallon of milk running in a trail across the floor. And, if that wasn't enough, two ice-cream cartons lay open and melting on the table.

Tassie wanted to cry. Tony! It had to be Tony who had done this horrible thing while she was upstairs with Delana, but why? Had he come home early, too? Surely expecting him to keep his room clean wasn't enough to cause him to do such a violent, destructive act. But when she discovered the words *GO HOME* spelled out in red lipstick on the tile above the sink, she knew Tony hadn't done it alone. He'd had an accomplice. A green-streak-in-her-hair accomplice who had probably added her touch before coming upstairs and going into a tirade. It was obvious those kids were trying to get her to leave.

She did the best she could to clean up the mess; after that, she prepared the taco salad. When the children showed up at the supper table, she wanted to personally strangle them with her bare hands, but instead she went through the entire meal without even mentioning the damage they had done to her clean kitchen. Since this was probably the last supper they would be having together, she decided to fake her way through the evening and leave them with a good taste in their mouths. Either that or they'd think her a bigger fool than ever for not wanting to retaliate. But regardless of what they thought, this would be her first and final evening in this house. She was going to quit. Maybe she had misunderstood when she thought God had called her to this family as a ministry. There were plenty of other places she could serve to honor Him, places where her efforts would be appreciated.

By the time their father phoned at nine o'clock to say he wasn't going to make it home until morning because he definitely was going to do the all-night stakeout, not only was Tassie ready to give her notice that she was leaving the next day, but she had begun to pack up the few things she had unpacked.

"I'm really sorry about this, Tassie. Knowing firsthand how uncooperative my children can be, I had hoped to be there early this evening to relieve you, definitely before the children went to bed, but this case I'm working on really has me stymied. It's about a missing child and this is the first real lead I've had. I could ask one of the other guys to fill in for me, but I really want to be there myself in case anything goes down. The guy we're after is a real sleazeball. We have to get him off the streets before he harms another child."

"I—"

"I—I really hope you don't mind having to spend your first night sleeping on the sofa or in one of the girls' rooms," he went on, not giving her a chance to interrupt. "I'd sure like to be sleeping in my own bed tonight. This has been a really rough day. I'm beat, but I need to be here. Maybe I can catch a couple hours' sleep tomorrow."

"But, Mr. Drummond, I—"

"Call me Mitch. Everyone does. I can't tell you how relieved I am to know that both you and your dog are there. I worry about my kids. I want them to grow into loving, responsible adults, so I'm glad you'll be taking them to church with you. I'm definitely planning to go along myself the next time I can wangle a Sunday off." He paused. "Oh, I'm sorry, you started to say something and I interrupted you."

Tassie blew out her cheeks in frustration. From the sound of it, he'd had a really rough day, too, maybe even rougher than hers, and he was going to have to stay awake all night. How could she add to his troubles by announcing that she was quitting and moving out the first thing in the morning?

"You already have too much to think about. We can discuss it tomorrow."

"How did your day go with Tony and Delana? Did they give you any more grief?"

Tassie huffed inwardly. *Mr. Drummond, you don't know the half of it. If what I saw today was their best behavior, I'd never want to be around to witness their worst!* Deciding whatever complaining about the day's happenings could wait until morning, she dodged the question as best she could. "I think you'd better ask Delana, Tony, and Babette. Their take on things might be a little different than mine."

"Hang on a sec."

She could hear mumbling, like he was talking to someone with his hand over the mouthpiece.

"Sorry, my partner is ready to leave. Gotta go. I'll be home sometime in the morning to try to catch a little shut-eye. We'll talk more then. But, Tassie, I want you to know how much I appreciate all you're doing for my family. Thank you for being there."

She swallowed hard. "I–I'll see you in the morning, Mr.—Mitch. Stay safe."

"Stay safe?" He chuckled. "No one has told me that since my mom passed away. She always worried about me. It's nice to hear those words again. You stay safe, too. Good night."

"Good night."

Although Mitch had said he would be home in the morning and he did phone twice the next day, it was nearly six o'clock before he walked through the front door, face drawn, shoulders slumped, and in clothing that looked as if he had spent the night in the car, which he said he had. Tassie had never seen a man look so beat.

She was tired, too—dead tired—from the day spent running the sweeper in rooms that looked as if they hadn't been swept in months, washing windows both inside and out, cleaning bathtubs and showers until they sparkled, and completing a myriad of other household tasks that should have been done on a regular basis. Had Mitch and his children gotten so used to living in such disarray they hadn't even noticed how bad things had become? The only decent and organized room in the house was Mitch's room, and even that had needed a good dusting. She had decided early that morning, since she was going to quit, she was going to leave things in the best possible condition. Maybe that way, whoever replaced her could at least start out with a clean house.

Mitch placed his briefcase on the hall closet floor then dragged himself into the living room. "Wow! Sure looks nice in here. Where'd you put all the stuff?"

She smiled. "In the closets and desk drawers where it belonged."

"Where are the kids?"

She motioned toward the stairs. "Delana and Tony are *supposed* to be in their rooms, doing their homework. Babette is watching a VeggieTales video and playing with her teddy bear."

"VeggieTales?"

"It's a terrific animated series designed for kids, fun for them to watch but with a great message. I picked up the DVD at the Christian bookstore today when I talked Babette into going with me. I bought her a book, too, and she actually let me read it to her."

"That's terrific." His brows rose. "And the other two are doing their homework? That's a first."

"I said *supposed* to be doing their homework. At least they were the last time I looked in on them."

Mitch wandered into the kitchen, Tassie following, and sat down before leaning his elbows on the table and cupping his face in his hands. "Thanks for taking this job, Tassie. I know it's not easy. My kids are a handful. Even though you haven't said much about it, I'm sure they have given you all kinds of trouble both yesterday *and* today. I don't know how to thank you for putting up with them."

"Your children *are* a handful, Mr. Drummond." Somehow, since she was going to complain about his children, it seemed improper to call him by his first name. "I wanted to tell you this yesterday but when you called and said you wouldn't be home at all last night, you had sounded so frustrated and tired that I decided to wait until now. I worked all day yesterday at getting Tony's, Delana's, and Babette's rooms in order, and today at giving the rest of the house a good cleaning. Each of your children's rooms was an absolute catastrophe."

Mitch hung his head. "I know. I'm sorry you had to see them that way. I never expected you to clean them up for them. Cleaning those rooms should be their responsibility."

"You're right. That should be their responsibility but I didn't mind cleaning them. In fact, I had hoped that by seeing them clean they would want to keep them that way. But apparently it didn't work."

"I guess that means things didn't go so well."

"Not well at all. My first real episode yesterday was with Babette and the second with Delana when she came home and found me cleaning her room. After that was with Tony, when he came home from school and saw what I had done to his room. I had half expected your older children to explode when they found I had been in their rooms, but Tony called me names I wouldn't want to repeat. Delana didn't call me names but she made it pretty clear she didn't want me in her room. So did Babette. I was shocked when a four-year-old actually ordered me out of her room and threatened to call the police! I'm sorry to say it because I don't want to hurt you, but your children's behavior has been deplorable. And I haven't even told you about the horrible mess Tony and Delana deliberately made of my clean kitchen by smearing the cabinets, countertops, and floor with grape jelly. Not to mention leaving cartons of ice cream out to melt, the refrigerator door standing open, and a milk carton turned on its side, spilling milk onto the floor I had just mopped."

Mitch gave his head a sad shake. "I'm sorry, Tassie. I don't know what else to say. No one deserves to be treated that way."

"After the day I'd had with them, despite my resolve to stay, I came to the conclusion it might be better if I moved on, looked for another job, and forgot all about your family. But being an old softie, and feeling sorry for running out on you without notice, when all three children showed up for dinner right at six o'clock last night and consumed every bite of the taco salad I had fixed, and you weren't able to make it home all night, I decided I would give things another day, hoping to see improvement. But I wasn't staying today for them, Mr. Drummond, I was staying for you. Unfortunately, I'm sorry to say, today hasn't been any better."

He gazed at her with tired eyes. "I wish I could say I'm surprised by their abhorrent behavior but I'm not. The decent thing would have been to have given you more of a warning before you took the job but I couldn't. I was desperate for someone to stay with them and at my wits' end. As much as I had hoped you'd stay I can't blame you wanting to quit."

"My heart goes out to you because I know you love those kids and want the very best for them, but unfortunately, your children don't think I'm the best. They see me as an enemy."

"They treat everyone as their enemy—me included—and I have no idea what to do about it. I've tried everything from grounding them to taking away their allowance. I've even taken them to a psychiatrist. Nothing works." He shrugged. "I'll pay you for the entire week and I'm sure that doesn't begin to be enough, considering all they have put you through."

"No, I can't let you do that. All I expect to be paid for is the two days I've been here. Of course, since I'll be leaving first thing in the morning, you'll have to make some kind of arrangements for Babette."

"I'll call our neighbor. She won't be too happy about it but after a little persuasion I'm sure she'll agree to help me out again, at least for a day or two."

"Then I guess I'll say good night."

"Yeah, good night. Thanks again, Tassie. You're a terrific person. I wish you only the best."

"Thanks, Mi—Mr. Drummond. I wish things could have worked out differently."

His heavy sigh broke her heart.

"Me, too, Tassie. Me, too."

It was nearly ten o'clock by the time Tassie finished her daily Bible reading and enjoyed a long, hot, relaxing shower. But as she turned off her hair dryer and slipped it into her overnight bag, she remembered she had forgotten to start the dishwasher after loading it with the supper dishes. She would need the stainless steel frying pan to cook the bacon she planned to prepare for breakfast before leaving the next morning.

Quickly pulling on her robe over her pajamas, she made her way down the outside stairs and into the kitchen. But as she crossed the room toward the dishwasher, she heard voices coming from upstairs. It was Tony and Delana having some sort of heated discussion on the upstairs landing. Her first reaction was to remind them to go to bed because they had school the next morning, but telling them what to do and when to do it was no longer her responsibility; it was their father's. But knowing how tired and worn-out he was, he was probably already downstairs in bed sound asleep and didn't even hear them.

Determined to stay out of whatever was going on, she headed back across the kitchen, stopping mid-step when she heard her name mentioned rather loudly.

Unable to resist listening to what they were saying about her, she softly padded her way through the darkened living room and crouched beside the stairway.

Chapter 5

"If you would have put that dead mouse in her bed like I told you to," Delana was saying, nose to nose with her brother, "she would have been out of here by now, but no—you wouldn't listen to me. You had a better idea."

"She'd know in a minute it was me who put it there and go running to Dad. I think we had better just keep messing up the things she cleans, argue with her, be brats, call her names, that kind of stuff. You should have seen the look on her face when I called her a—" His voice fell to a whisper.

Delana let loose a belly laugh. "You actually called her that? What did she do?"

"Just acted like she was all upset and told me no one ever talked to her that way before."

"Do you think she told Dad?"

Tony snorted. "I dunno. But I thought for sure she'd quit after we smeared jelly all over the kitchen cabinets and did that other stuff. I kinda felt sorry about it, knowing how hard she worked to get it clean."

"I didn't feel sorry about it. I want things back like they were when Grandma was here. That old lady was so drunk all day she didn't have any idea what we were doing and she sure didn't care. She might as well have crawled into that bottle of hers for all the good she was around here. I don't know why I bothered going in and out of my window when I wanted to leave. I could have walked right over her and out the front door and she wouldn't have known the difference."

"So what do we do next? Doing all this other stuff sure hasn't made her leave."

"Maybe we could take money out of Dad's billfold while he's asleep then tell him that we saw Tassie take it."

"You think he'd believe us? If we both told the same story and didn't slip up?"

"Probably. We could plant the money in her room. That'd be even more convincing," Delana added, lowering her voice a notch.

"Oh, I like that idea. What else?"

"I don't know. I'll have to think about it but we can't let up. We have to keep pushing her. No stranger is going to come in *my* home and tell *me* what to do. I want my freedom back. I can't stand having someone breathing down my neck."

"Yeah, me neither."

"Well, go on to bed, Tony, there's nothing else we can do tonight. But don't forget to mess up your room really bad before you leave for school in the morning. I'll make sure the bathroom is a total disaster before I leave. That'll tick her off. And let's hang out with our friends until about the time Dad gets home so she'll be worried about us. We'll show up just in time for supper."

"Good thinking."

Tassie stayed crouched until she heard both bedroom doors click shut, so upset by what she heard she could barely stand it. *They're actually working together to run me off? Maybe I should stay after all. What those kids need is a dose of good old-fashioned discipline administered in Christian love, and it appears I'm the one God has sent into this home to give it to them. At least for the next three months.*

When she reached her room, the first thing she took note of was her Bible lying open on the table. Placing both hands on it and bowing her head, she began to pray aloud. "Lord, You sent me to this home to be a witness for You. Please, I don't want to just put in my time until the three months are up—I truly want to win the Drummond family into Your kingdom. Even when the children are giving me fits and I want to turn tail and run, give me strength and make me remember that this is where You want me to be. I don't want to simply tolerate Tony and Delana and Babette; I want to love them as You would have me love them, but I can't do it alone. Sometimes—most of the time—those kids have been just plain unlovable. I need Your help, Father God. Mr. Drummond needs You, too. From the few things he has said, I get the feeling at one time he may have been close to You. Speak to his heart and bring him back into Your fold, please."

Tassie awoke a full half hour before her alarm went off the next morning and was in the kitchen, stirring the scrambled eggs, when Mitch came into the room, still looking tired and haggard.

"Good morning," he greeted her, none too enthusiastically. "I've already made out your check. It's downstairs in my room."

"Forget about the check." She took on a smile. "I've changed my mind. If you'll have me, I'm staying."

His expression brightened. "Really? You're staying? That's the best news I've had in a long time. You were so determined to leave. Did something happen to make you change your mind?"

"Umm, let's just say after our talk last night, I began to see things differently."

"Differently?"

"Yes. I'm staying for you, Mis—Mitch. You're a good man. I know your heart is in the right place when it comes to your family. Even though your children have made it perfectly clear they don't want me here, I've decided it really isn't *me* they don't want, it's *anyone* who would come into their home, invade their privacy, and attempt to discipline them. But I'm willing to give it my best shot *if* you're willing to back me up—when discipline becomes necessary," she added quickly. Having his support was paramount. No way were his children going to listen to and obey her without it.

"You will back me up, won't you?" Having said all she had to say, Tassie pulled a mug from an upper cabinet and poured him a cup of the freshly perked coffee. The ball was in his court now.

He nodded his thanks then took a slow, careful sip. "Of course I'll back you up. I hate to admit it, but I know my kids are monsters. I've let them go way too far and for far too long, because I felt sorry for them having their mother walk out on them like she did, and then losing her in that accident."

"She walked out on you?"

"Yes, I should have told you up front. If I had, maybe you'd better understand my children's attitudes. Babette doesn't remember much about her leaving, but Delana and Tony do. June ran away with her biker boyfriend. Apparently they had been having an affair for months and I hadn't even realized it. And once she left, even though we always hoped she'd come back, we never saw her again. Less than a year later, they both died when a car hit them on a mountain road."

Tassie gasped. "How awful for all of you."

"And since I'm being honest about my wife, I'll admit I went into a depression when she left me. I know that's no excuse. I'm those children's father, but despite the way she treated us, I still loved her. Regardless of what I was going through, I should have been there for them. Instead, I backed away and threw myself into my work, letting my mother-in-law move in and take over. During the few years she was with us and I left them in her care, there were weeks at a time when I barely even saw my kids. If I got home at all, it was usually after they were in bed and I left before they got up in the morning. I'm not proud of what I did. I realize it was a mistake, but I can't go back and undo it. I remember someone saying you can't unring a bell, and I can't get back those years I lost with my children."

He looked so pitiful Tassie wanted to throw her arms about his neck and give him a hug. But she didn't. He was her employer and it wouldn't be right. Instead she simply said, "I'm sorry. I know it hasn't been easy, Mr. Drummond, and I'll do everything I can to help you get your children on the right track."

He reached across and patted her hand. "Mitch, Tassie. Call me Mitch. I feel like an old man when you call me Mr. Drummond. We are in this thing together."

She felt a flush rise to her cheeks. "Mitch."

"That's better." He took another sip then rose and placed the mug on the counter, taking time to bend and pat Goliath's head before speaking. "Don't let the rest of that coffee get away. I'll be back after another cup. But right now I want to go up and see my kids."

"Good idea." Tassie watched until he disappeared through the kitchen door. *Those children are lucky to have a man like Mitch for a father. A man who is willing to admit he's made mistakes and wants to rectify them. I just hope they realize it.*

Mitch. The word played on her tongue. She liked his name. It had a strong sound to it. "Come on, Goliath," she told the dog who lay at her feet half asleep. "We've fooled around long enough; it's time to get busy. The kids will be down for breakfast any minute now."

Goliath eyed his mistress then rose, and after arching his back and stretching first his front legs then his hind, ambled toward the door and whined to get out.

"Some help you are." She let the big dog out then closed the door and leaned against it. "Like it or not, I'm staying. For the next three months the Drummond home is going to be our home, too."

She filled the juice glasses, added the butter container and a plate of bread slices to the table, and was about to pull the milk carton from the fridge when Mitch, with one arm around Delana and the other around Tony, sauntered into the kitchen, a big smile on his face. "Breakfast ready?"

Tassie smiled back then gestured to the table. "Sure is. I've been keeping it hot for you."

"You'd better save some for Babette. She was sleeping so soundly I didn't have the heart to waken her. I was just telling the kids. . ." He paused long enough to pull out a chair for his daughter and seat himself. "That from now on I'm planning on being home by six each night so we can all have dinner together."

Tony huffed. "You've told us that before but you never made it."

Mitch covered the boy's hand with his. "I know, and I'm sorry. And I may not make it every night, even though I'd like to, but I am going to try. I love you kids and I want to be with you."

Delana responded with an indifferent shrug of her shoulders. "It's okay if you don't make it. We're used to you making promises you don't keep."

Their father's eyes narrowed. "Seems to me you kids also make quite a few promises you don't keep. At least I try to keep mine."

"Oh, yeah?" Delana challenged. "What about my birthday, when you promised you'd take all my friends out for pizza?"

"I told you I was sorry about that but it couldn't be helped."

"That's what you always say when you break your promises," Tony added, siding with his sister. "Your job always comes ahead of us."

"I don't have a choice, Tony," Mitch answered almost angrily. "That job is what puts food on this table, a roof over your heads, and clothing on your back. And money in your pockets to buy all the electronic and computer gadgets you seem to require, plus all the jewelry and doodads Delana needs to keep up with her friends. Not to mention the fancy cell phones I've purchased for each of you and the extra fees for your text messaging. Even your four-year-old sister has a cell phone. You kids must think I'm made of money. You have no idea what it takes to keep this family going." He turned toward his daughter. "Since you're going to be sixteen soon, maybe you should think about getting a summer job and start paying for some of those doodads yourself."

The young girl rolled her eyes in disgust. "You expect me to give up my summer and *work*?"

"Why not? I worked when I was in high school. I'll bet Tassie did, too. A lot of high school students work during summer vacation."

Delana crossed her arms over her chest. "Well, none of my friends work and I'm not going to, either. You're mean!"

She threw her spoon on the table then quickly rose, knocking her chair over with a loud thud, and stomped out of the room.

Mitch picked up the platter of eggs and handed it to Tony. "I know I've let you down in the past, son, and I'll probably let you down in the future, but from now on I'm going to do everything in my power to try to spend more time with you three kids. Meantime, Tassie is my representative in this home and I want you children to respect her and do what she says, because if you don't—you'll have me to answer to. Understand?"

Tony answered with a ridiculing snort.

Mitch reached across the table and grabbed hold of his son's wrist. "I mean it, Tony."

The boy gave his head a slight nod then yanked his arm away from his father's grasp and bolted out of the kitchen.

Mitch leaned back in his chair with a look of defeat. "Did I win that battle or did they? Maybe I was too harsh with them."

Tassie gazed at him for a moment before answering. "I'm not sure any of you *won* the battle but at least you're taking command. That's what's important. They may not be happy about it but as long as you let them know you love them, given time, they'll respect you for it."

"I hope you're right."

"So do I. You are going to make it for supper?"

"Yes, regardless of what's going on in Grand Island's crime world, I'll be here. It's time I started doling out some of my work to others instead of taking it all on myself."

❧

As promised, Mitch arrived home as he'd said with even enough time to take a quick shower before supper. After donning a clean T-shirt and pair of jeans, he hurried to Babette's room and tapped on the door. "Babette? It's Daddy. Can I come in?"

Within seconds the door swung open and Babette's smiling face appeared. "Hi, Daddy."

He lifted the girl in his arms and held her close. She smelled like lilacs. "You smell good. Did you just have a bath?"

She nodded. "I used some of Tassie's bubble bath."

Mitch glanced about the room. Everything was in its place, without a single shoe or article of clothing lying about. "You ready to go downstairs? I'll bet Tassie has a good supper waiting for us." When the child nodded he carried her downstairs. How long had it been since he had cuddled her in his arms like that?

"Tony! Delana! Supper time!" he called out over his shoulder as they reached the kitchen. "Tassie has everything on table." To his surprise both children came bolting down the stairs. Once they were all seated around the table, he motioned for Tassie to join them.

At first, she declined, but he kept insisting until she finally sat down. "I want you kids to realize Tassie is not our servant. For the next three months she is a full-fledged member of this household and we are each going to treat her with the respect she deserves." Then turning to her he smiled. "Tassie, the fried chicken smells wonderful. Would you please ask the blessing?"

Although she seemed surprised by his request, without missing a beat she prayed. How good it felt to hear someone pray who seemed to have a close relationship with God and could talk to Him in such a personal way. Other than a few desperate words sent heavenward now and then when troubles came his way, Mitch hadn't prayed, honestly prayed, in years.

"Can we eat now?" Using her fingers Delana snatched one of the two chicken breasts from the platter, barely beating her brother who hurriedly took the other.

Mitch rolled his eyes. "Did the thought ever occur to either of you that there are others at the table who might also prefer white meat?"

Delana peeled off the skin, took a big bite, and snickered. "First come, first serve," she mumbled, her mouth still full.

Tassie frowned. "Next time, instead of getting a whole fryer, maybe I should get just chicken breasts."

It was obvious to Mitch she was trying to avoid controversy over such a trivial thing. Maybe he should, too.

"Maybe that would be best, so long as you also purchase a leg or two." He nodded toward Delana. "Why don't you share that breast with your sister? Babette likes white meat, too."

Delana complied begrudgingly.

He picked up the serving fork, and speared a leg. "I'm a dark meat man myself. How about you, Tassie? Which piece do you prefer?"

He was relieved when she said she also liked the breast but liked a leg or the thigh almost as well. He feared, just to keep the peace, she was settling for a thigh when she would rather have had a portion of a breast.

Tassie smiled then reached for the bowl of mashed potatoes. "I made gravy, too."

"Mmm, homemade gravy. My mom used to make gravy," Mitch said. "I haven't had homemade gravy since she passed away."

"I hope you like it. I made it the way my mom taught me."

He bit into the chicken leg. "Mmm, this is good. I like that crunchy coating."

Delana wrinkled up her nose. "What's that? In that bowl?"

Tassie pushed the bowl toward her. "At our house, for lack of a better name, we always called them chicken crumbs."

The girl turned her head away and made a face. "Yuk! That sounds awful."

Mitch took hold of the bowl and spooned out several of the largest crumbs then popped one into his mouth. "These are great! How did you make them?"

"They're pretty simple. After I flour the chicken and place it in the hot oil in the skillet, I take the leftover flour and add salt, pepper, and just enough water to make it like a thick paste. Then I drop it by scant teaspoonfuls into the skillet, filling all the empty spaces and let them cook and brown right along with the chicken."

Mitch passed the bowl to Tony. "You gotta try these, son. They're amazing."

Tony hesitated then slowly slipped one into his mouth and began to chew.

"So, whatcha think?"

After a mischievous grin, Tony pulled the bowl closer and scooted four or five of the beautifully browned crumbs onto his plate. "They're pretty good."

Mitch gestured toward the bowl. "How about you, Delana? Want to give them a try?"

"Never! Those things are disgusting!"

"I want one."

Mitch smiled at Babette. "Sure, honey. Here's a nice big one for you. If you like it, you can have more." After placing the golden crumb on her plate, he handed the bowl to Tassie. "If you want any of these you'd better get them now. I love these things."

She took two of the smaller ones. "I'm glad. I wasn't sure you would."

"Hey, those chicken crumbs are almost as good as the chicken! Promise every time you make fried chicken you'll make crumbs."

Delana rolled her eyes. "Do you have any idea how many grams of fat and how many calories you're consuming by eating those—things?"

Mitch chuckled. "Surely you didn't think about fat and calories when you grabbed that chicken breast off the plate."

"I pulled the skin off. I'm only eating the white meat and I'm not eating any of that fattening gravy."

He paused, then smiling, ladled a generous serving of gravy onto his mound of mashed potatoes. "Good, that means more for the rest of us!"

"Go ahead. Eat that awful stuff and get fat. See if I care!"

"Come on, Delana, I was only teasing. Maybe, since you're really into this nutrition thing, you could help Tassie plan the meals."

"That's a wonderful idea," Tassie responded with enthusiasm. "She could even help me with the shopping."

"No way! I have better things to do with my time than spend it with our servant!" Delana rose then wadded up her paper napkin, tossed it onto her plate, and hurried out of the room.

Embarrassed by his daughter's behavior, he turned toward Tassie with a shrug. "Sorry, I guess that didn't go so well."

"You tried and at least you all gathered together for dinner. That's a start."

Tony glanced around the kitchen. "Any dessert?"

Tassie grinned. "How about Twinkies?"

The boy wrinkled up his face. "I had those at school. Two packages."

Smiling, she pushed back her chair and walked toward the refrigerator. "Then how about a nice big wedge of butterscotch meringue pie?"

Tony's face lit up. "Are you kidding? That's my favorite kind!"

She pulled the door open and reached inside, pulling out a beautifully browned meringue pie. "Then you're in luck! That's the kind I baked. I was only kidding about the Twinkies."

Mitch frowned. "How did you know that was his favorite? I didn't tell you."

She cut a liberal wedge, placed it on a clean plate, then set it down in front of Tony. "Lucky guess. I figured every boy likes butterscotch meringue pie."

Mitch eyed the luscious-looking pie as she cut another wedge, hoping it was for him. "You're going to have all of us spoiled."

Using the spatula, she placed some pie on a plate and handed it to him. "That's my intent. I love to cook and it's fun to cook when people appreciate it."

Babette took a final bite of the small piece of chicken breast Delana had given her then pushed her plate toward Tassie. "I like pie."

Mitch watched with delight as his two children devoured their pie. Maybe Tassie's good cooking would be the way for her to win the hearts of his children. "Their mother rarely cooked. She said it was a waste of time. When she was alive, most of our meals were either eaten at a restaurant or delivered to our home." He smiled at her. Having such good home-cooked meals was one of the fringe benefits he hadn't expected when he'd hired Tassie to care for his family. How lucky could they be?

"A lot of women don't like to cook, but my mom always loved it. I guess I inherited my love of cooking from her."

"I'll help clear the table," he told her when they had finished their pie and both Tony and Babette had gone to their rooms, "just as soon as I finish the rest of this delicious coffee." He waved his hand toward the pie pan. "I'll eat that last piece later—unless you want it."

"No, it's all yours."

He emptied his cup, all the while gazing at her, then gathered the dishes from the table, rinsed them, and arranged them in the dishwasher while she put things in the refrigerator and wiped off the counter. In no time at all, the kitchen was spotless.

"I don't know what to think about Delana," he told her as they made their way into the living room. "Nothing makes that girl happy. It's like she goes through life looking for something to complain about."

He waited until Tassie sat down in one of the chairs then seated himself on the sofa.

"You need to spend more one-on-one time with her, Mitch."

"I know but she never seems to have time for me."

"Maybe she thinks you don't have time for her. You yourself said you're never home. What about Tony? Have you ever made time for that boy? Like daughters, sons need their fathers."

"Are you saying I'm the one responsible for my children's outlandish behavioral problems?"

She shrugged. "You're their father. Have you made any real effort to get to know them—or Babette? She had to have been a baby when your wife left. That little girl needs her daddy. Can you honestly say you've been there for her? Just making sure a reliable babysitter is with your children isn't enough. They need you."

He leaned back and spread his arms across the back of the sofa and deeply exhaled. "What is this? Stack it on Mitchell Drummond night? Is everyone against me?"

"I'm for you, Mitch, but I've been doing a lot of thinking since you told me about your wife. Maybe more of the responsibility for their bad behavior belongs to you than you're willing to admit."

"Me?" His anger rose to the boiling point. "You've got a lot of nerve blaming me. I've worked my fingers to the bone to provide for this family."

"I'm sure you have, but the one thing they need most you haven't provided. A father who is always there for them! I know one thing for sure, when and if I ever marry, it won't be to a detective. Not if his job always comes before me and any children we may have. I'd rather be married to a ditchdigger. At least he would have regular hours."

"Look, lady, you can't march in here, spend a few days in my home, and tell me how to run my life. You've never even been married! What makes you an authority?"

"I'm far from an authority, Mitch. I'm merely stating my observations as one who is genuinely concerned about you and your family. I hope you'll take it that way. I'm simply trying to remind you that time is slipping by. Delana is nearly sixteen. Before long, she'll be gone, either to college or out on her own, and Tony is but a few years behind her. Unless you establish a good relationship with them now, while they're under your roof, you may never have one with them. A good relationship means having respect for one another. Just ask yourself, do your children have respect for you, or are you only the person who pays the bills, comes home occasionally when you're not tied up on some case, and lets them get by with their inexcusable behavior?"

He started to speak but stopped when she held up her hand to silence him, deciding to let her have her say before defending himself.

"And do you respect them?" she went on. "Those children aren't just disobedient leftovers from a failed marriage. They're your flesh and blood. You say you love them, but do you really? Because, from my vantage point, if you loved them as you say you do, you'd be with them more, even if it meant cutting down on the hours you work. You yourself told me you could have asked one of the other men to cover that all-night stakeout for you but you didn't, because you wanted to be there."

Mitch fumed as he listened to her accusatory words, but she was right. He had said that very thing. "You just don't get it, Tassie," he told her, gritting his teeth and trying to keep control. "Someone else could have taken my place, but no one can do my job like I can!"

She rose and stood staring at him for a moment. "You are so right about that, Mitch. No one can do your job like you can—especially your job as a father. I rest my case."

He lifted his hands in the air in frustration. "Okay, you're right. Everything you've said is true. I've known it all along. I just don't like hearing it from someone else! Does that make you feel better?"

"Not at all. My intent was not to hurt you, Mitch; it was to help you." With a roll of her eyes, she moved away from him.

"Listen to me. I sound just like my kids. Or maybe they sound just like me. I haven't exactly been a shining example for them. Their behavior does have a lot to do with mine, doesn't it?"

Her expression softened. "You said it, I didn't. Think my words over carefully. I'm going to bed."

He watched as she quickly moved into the kitchen then listened until he heard the outside door close. As his anger lessened and he calmed down, he began to rationally mull over the things she had said. Everything she had accused him of and everything she had said about him and his family was true. He had given his children everything he could except for the one thing they needed most. Himself.

Deciding there was no better time to start than right now, he tamped down what little anger remained inside him, forced a smile, and headed upstairs to tell each of his children good night and remind them how much he loved them—and that he would always be there for them.

Babette was already dressed in her Barbie jammies and sitting cross-legged in the center of her bed, the clothing and shoes she had worn that day scattered over the floor amid dolls and toys. Rather than scold her or leave them on the floor for Tassie to clean up, he picked them up and neatly stacked them on a chair. "So you liked Tassie's butterscotch pie?"

She nodded. "Uh-huh, I liked the chicken, too, and those funny-looking things."

He frowned. "Oh! You mean the chicken crumbs. Yeah, those were pretty good."

"Would you read me a story?"

Mitch gazed at his daughter for a moment before answering, Tassie's words ringing in his ears. He couldn't remember the last time he had read a story to Babette and he felt ashamed. "Sure, sweetie. Why don't you pick out the book while I go tell your sister and brother good night, okay?"

Babette let out a childish giggle of delight then leaped off the bed and began running her little finger along the spines of the books Tassie had organized on the shelf in her nightstand. "Hurry, Daddy."

He assured her he would then moved on to Tony's room and was shocked when he found the boy propped up against his headboard, hovering over a big thick book.

Tony gave him a startled look as he entered. "Ah—hey, Dad. You—ah—know anything about history?"

Both pleased and surprised to see Tony actually studying, Mitch pulled a stool up next to the bed and sat down. "I used to love history, why? Do you have a question about something?"

"Yeah, kinda. Did George Washington really cut down a cherry tree and then confess he did it or did someone dream up that story to make him look good?"

"Do you doubt he did it?"

"Yeah, I saw this thing on YouTube—a video a guy had made showing some other dude cutting down the tree and then blaming it on Washington, and when George denied he had done it his father whipped him really bad. That guy said a lot of the stuff we read in history books isn't true."

Mitch couldn't help but smile. "YouTube, huh? I don't think I'd take the word of some stranger on YouTube for what George Washington did or didn't do. I'd rather believe the history books. George Washington was a great president. We, as citizens of this country, owe him a debt of gratitude." Mitch wanted to shout with joy when his son looked up at him with eyes of admiration; usually they were filled with contempt.

"Thanks, Dad. I knew you'd know the answer."

"No problem. Maybe we can talk about this some more tomorrow night but right now you and I have something else to discuss. Tassie was reluctant to talk about it when I asked her how her day went, but she finally admitted you behaved in an extremely ungentlemanly manner toward her. Did you?"

"Yeah, sorta, I guess. But she's always messing around with my stuff. Nobody touches my stuff and gets away with it."

Mitch did an exaggerated glance about the room. "You mean the *stuff* that used to cover the furniture and floor in here? The *stuff* I no longer see because Tassie went to all the trouble to put it away for you? Something you should have done yourself? That the *stuff* you mean?"

Tony crinkled up his face. "Yeah, but that stuff was mine. She's got no business snooping around in here."

"She wasn't snooping. What she did took work, hard work, work you should have done yourself. Besides, you don't have anything in your room you wouldn't want found, do you?"

Tony growled, "No, of course not."

"Good, I'd hoped not, but I am interested in hearing whatever you said to her. It seems she was hurt and offended by it. I'd like to hear those comments from you."

The boy shrugged. "Aw, Dad, it wasn't such a big deal. She's making too much of it."

"*If* the things you said were as common as you imply, then I'm sure you'll have no trouble telling me what they were."

His head lowered, Tony pursed his lips tightly together.

"Tony, I have no intention of going out of this room until you tell me, and don't leave anything out. I want to hear every word."

"All I said was she was a nosy old witch and had no business being in our home, that you would never have hired her if you hadn't been desperate."

"That's all you said?"

"Yeah—well maybe a little bit more."

"How could you say something like that to someone who was trying to help you? No wonder she was hurt! She had every right to be. I—I don't know what to do with you, Tony. Because of you children's outrageous behavior, Tassie decided to quit after being here only two days!"

"Quit? She's leaving?"

The weird smile of satisfaction that broke across his son's face ripped at Mitch's heart. It was as if Tony was proud of his part in getting Tassie to quit.

"Wouldn't you quit? If someone treated you as badly as you've treated her?"

"I—I dunno. Maybe."

"Well, fortunately, for some unknown reason, she changed her mind and decided to stay. She's not leaving after all." *Unless she got so upset with me and the way I talked to her tonight that she changed her mind again.*

His intention when he had come into this room had been to tear down fences, but he had to stand up for Tassie. He couldn't let Tony's words of criticism go unheeded. He had been ignoring things too long. "Well, you'd better get to bed. Want me to put that book on your desk for you?"

"No. I want to finish this chapter first."

Hoping to show an interest in his son and his schoolwork, Mitch leaned over, intending to simply see what period of history his son was studying, but what he found folded into the page was a nude picture torn from a girly magazine.

"Tony!" he railed at his son, yanking the picture from the book and ripping it to shreds.

"It's not mine, Dad. It belongs to a friend. I was just keeping it for him."

"Surely you don't think I'm dumb enough to believe that old line." Deciding he'd had about all the confrontation he could take for one night and not sure if he should lecture the boy, take away his allowance, or punish him in some other way, he simply stared at Tony for a moment then walked toward the door before turning back to the boy. "I'm disgusted by this, Tony, and believe me, this incident is going to be dealt with as soon as I decide how to punish you. There is no place for porn in this house. If you have any more of it hidden away, I suggest you get rid of it immediately because from now on your room is subject to search at any time. If it is here—I'll find it and you'll wish you'd never heard of that filthy stuff. What you see and read in those magazines is nothing but trash and not at all like real life. Understand?"

His eyes as wide as saucers, Tony nodded.

"Nodding isn't good enough. I want to hear you say it."

"Okay, yes, I understand."

"Good. Now get to bed."

Mitch closed the door behind him then leaned against it, his heart pounding wildly in his chest. He knew from experience most adolescent boys were filled with curiosity about the opposite sex. He just hadn't realized his son would be one of them, and so soon.

Hoping to do better than he had with Tony, he moved on to Delana's room, only to find her pulling things from her closet and her drawers and throwing them onto the floor in a fit of rage.

"Do you know what that woman has done? I can't find a thing!" she yelled at him when he entered. "I hate her, Daddy! If you don't fire her I'm going to run away! I can't stand her touching my things and spying on me! She's evil!"

Mitch hurried to her, throwing his arms around her and pulling her to him. "Now, Delana, aren't you overreacting a bit? All Tassie has done is try to help you."

Placing her hands on his chest, she angrily shoved him away. "Help me? She threw my things in the trash! Good shoes and good clothes I had barely worn. She even took them out to the Dumpster!"

Since he was reasonably sure Tassie had simply put his children's items in one of the big empty boxes in the garage and not the Dumpster cart, he smiled to himself. "Come on now, I doubt she would throw those things away without good cause. Did she tell you *why* she was throwing them away?"

Delana sat down on the edge of her bed, her lower lip rolled down in a pout. "She said it was because she found them on the floor after she had warned—"

"Had you left them on the floor?" he asked, knowing full well she had. His daughter never put anything away.

A huff and a haughty toss of her head was his answer.

"She did the same thing to your brother's and your sister's rooms. She only did it to help you, Delana. Those clothing items cost money. Money I work hard for. I want you to have nice things but—"

"Then you should tell her to keep her hands off my stuff. She's the one who threw them away. Not me!"

"But if you toss them haphazardly on the floor—"

The tip of Delana's finger pointed angrily toward the door. "Are you saying it's okay for *that woman* to throw *my* things away? Just because I'd rather leave them lying around on the floor than hang them up or put them in drawers? I happen to like a messy room!"

Mitch cleared his throat with agitation. There seemed to be no way to answer that would appease his daughter. "I'm saying, my dear daughter, if you have any respect for me and the hard-earned money I spend on you, you would take care of your things to make them last. Throwing clothing on the floor and then walking all over it has to be hard on those garments. Is it asking too much of you to expect you to be careful with them?"

Delana avoided his eyes by pinning her gaze to the floor. "I'm tired. I want to go to bed."

"Did you finish your homework?"

"No, and I'm not going to. I'm sleepy."

Mitch shot a glance toward her cell phone when it rang. "If you're too tired to do your homework, you're too tired talk on the phone. I suggest you tell whoever is calling you'll see them tomorrow." He stepped into the doorway and listened until she begrudgingly relayed his message to the person on the other end then hung up. "For your information, Delana, Tassie quit over you kids' bad behavior. But she—"

"She quit? Good! I'm glad. I did everything I could to make her know she wasn't wanted here."

"She *quit*—but after she quit she changed her mind. She's staying!"

The girl's face took on an intense scowl. "She's staying? Oh, terrific."

"Yes, and I expect you to make sure she continues to stay. From now on things around here are going to be different. I'm going. . ."

The girl screwed up her face even more. "Yeah, sure they will. Don't you ever get tired of singing that old song?"

Mitch released a breath of frustration. "Look, Delana, Tassie is the best thing that has happened to this family in a long time. We're—"

"She's nosy, Dad. She's always into my stuff! Why are you yelling at me? I can't believe you are taking that woman's side when I'm your very own daughter."

"I'm not taking anyone's side, Delana."

"Oh no?"

"Look. Having to adjust to someone new living in our home was bound to put a strain on all of us, Tassie included. But we each need to put our hurt feelings and pettiness aside and try to live together in harmony."

Remembering his resolve to be a better father, he smiled at his daughter. "Now go to bed, honey, and get a good night's sleep. We're all tired. Things will look better in the morning. Just promise you'll try to work with Tassie. If you think *she's* bad, try to imagine what the next nanny might be like. Take it from me, a good live-in nanny is hard to find. Especially one I can afford." He blew her a kiss then gently backed out the door, closing it softly behind him before lingering in the hall.

He was worried about Delana. She had been such a good kid before her mother walked out on them. Since that day it was as if she was out to make as many people as possible as miserable as she could, and he had no idea what to do about it. His shoulders lifted and fell in a despondent shrug. After taking several deep cleansing breaths and pasting on a happy face, he headed for Babette's room to read the story he had promised her.

But when he entered her room the child was already fast asleep, her bear cuddled in one arm, a book in the other.

As with so many things in his life, once again he was too late.

Chapter 6

Tassie was pulling a pan full of beautifully browned pancakes from the oven when Mitch entered the kitchen the next morning with a cheerful, "Hello." She placed them on the table.

"Good morning, Mitch. I've been keeping your breakfast warm for you."

"The kids up yet?"

"Not yet. Since it's Saturday, I thought I'd let them sleep until you came up. I hope you slept well."

"I'd like to say I did, but I didn't. I. . ." He paused and cast his gaze to the floor, avoiding her eyes. "Everything you said about me was true, Tassie, but I should never have responded like I did. The truth is hard to face. I hadn't cared to admit it until I heard it come from your lips. I—" Mitch lifted his face to hers, a faint smile of contrition tilting his lips. "I'm asking you to accept my apology and I'm begging you to stay."

"Even if your children are doing everything they can to get rid of me?"

His eyes widened in surprise. "You knew Delana was doing all she could to get you to leave?"

"Yes, both she *and* Tony. They had not only proved it by their actions since I've been here, I actually overheard them making plans on how to accomplish it right after I had given you my notice and you'd gone to bed. I'm sure they thought I was up in my room. That's the reason I decided to stay. I couldn't stand the idea of letting a thirteen- and a near sixteen-year-old run me off, especially since I had prayed about coming here even before I told you I would take the job. Did you tell her I'm staying?"

Mitch took hold of both her hands and smiled at her. He loved her fragrance. "I sure did. I made that part perfectly clear and I also reminded both her and Tony that I expect them to treat you with respect. I—I just wish I could guarantee they would do it."

She lifted misty eyes to his. "I do, too. It would sure make things a lot less complicated."

He freed one hand and pulled a paper napkin from the metal holder on the counter then gently blotted it to her eyes. "You have every right to be upset but please promise you'll hang in there. Don't let them get you down. I can't bear the thought of losing you—as a nanny," he hastened to add. "With your sweet smile and your desire to make things work. . ." He tacked on with a chuckle, "Not to mention your great cooking, they're bound to come around eventually."

"I'll only be here three months. That's not a lot of time."

"I know, and I'm going to do my part, I promise you. I may not make it home for dinner every night but I'm going to give it a royal try, honest I am."

She smiled up at him. "No one can take your place, Mitch. Only you can be their father."

"I know, and I'm going to be here for them—and for you. I mean—I don't want you to have to shoulder the responsibility alone." *What is that fragrance? Honeysuckle? Roses?*

"I can't tell you how much it means to know I have your support."

"I'll be here to back you up, Tassie, you can count on it. The kids need to see us as a united front."

Feeling the need to break whatever spell her presence was casting over him, he sat down and watched as she busied herself with the hot syrup that was simmering on the range. "Want me to call the kids to breakfast?"

"Yes, everything is ready."

To his surprise, even though all three children looked as if they had just crawled out of bed when they'd heard his voice, they came on the first call, but only Babette wore a smile.

Delana took one look at the plate containing the pancakes and sausage and crinkled up her face. "More fat and cholesterol? I'm not eating those things. Didn't anyone ever tell you fat and cholesterol are bad for you?"

Tassie pointed to a clear plastic container on the counter. "I eliminated half of the egg yolks when I made the pancakes and I drained the sausage on paper towels."

"But they're fried. Can't you fix anything that doesn't have to be cooked in a frying pan?"

Mitch frowned at his daughter. "I will not have you talking to Tassie like that, young lady. Apparently you've forgotten the little talk we had last night. Apologize right now or go to your room and stay there until you're ready to apologize."

"Yeah, and what if I refuse to apologize?" Delana shot back with even more determination in her voice.

"Fine. Don't do it. It's your choice. I don't care if you have to stay in there until the snow flies, and you're not going to spend the day talking to your friends. Give me your cell phone."

Reluctantly the girl pulled her cell phone from her pocket and handed it to him. "You're being mean to me. I just might call Child Protective Services and file a complaint!"

"Look, Delana, I've let you get by with just about anything you've wanted since your mother left us because I felt sorry for you, but no more! Either apologize to Tassie or—"

"Never!" Her face filled with anger, she spun around and raced through the living room and back up the stairs.

⁂

They all jumped in reflex when Delana's door slammed with a bang, but Tassie had to smile when Babette held out her plate and calmly said, "Pancakes, please." She placed one big lacy pancake on the girl's plate then added some of the hot syrup and grinned at her. "There you go, sweetie."

Tony picked up his plate. "I'll take some, too. I don't mind fat and cholesterol." Although Tassie had to smile, not wanting to embarrass the boy, this time she kept it to a minimum.

Mitch nodded toward the platter then sat down in his chair. "Nothing is better for breakfast than a big plateful of sausage and homemade pancakes."

Once breakfast was over and Tony had gone back to his room and Babette to the backyard to play with Goliath, Mitch poured both himself and Tassie another cup of coffee then scooted his chair closer to hers. "I have to work today, but I already told the guys down at the station that short of a national disaster, I'm not working tomorrow. You should have heard them hoot when I said it was because I was going to church."

"You actually told them that?"

"Hey, don't look at me like that. I may not be as close to the Lord as I once was, but I am a Christian. I gave my heart to God when I was about Tony's age, at our church's summer camp. I wish I could say I've always been a good person like you, but I haven't been."

"What makes you think I've always been a good person? I've done things to separate myself from Him, too." The words slipped out before she could stop them. Even though God had forgiven her for her sin, she hadn't—and couldn't—forgive herself.

"Come on. Don't put yourself down to make me feel better. I'll bet the worst sin you have ever committed was being late to church."

Tassie felt her heartbeat quicken. "No, I've done something much worse than that, but I'd rather not talk about it."

He took hold of her hand and cradled it in his. "Whatever it was, I know God has forgiven you."

"Yes, He has." *Now if only I could forgive myself.*

"I'm glad you're going to be taking my kids to church." He turned loose her hand then gave her a smile. "I just hope when I walk in the door with you, God doesn't say, 'Who are you?'"

"I'm sure God will remember you. Have you told the children yet? That you're all going to church with me tomorrow?"

"I was going to tell them at the breakfast table, until Delana threw her little temper tantrum. I'll do it later on when she comes out of her room. Or should I say *if* she comes out of her room? But right now I have to go up and have a little talk with Tony."

She gave him a quizzical look.

"Nothing you need be concerned about. It's a man-to-son thing."

Man-to-son thing? What does that mean? Did something happen I don't know about? But since he didn't seem to want to elaborate, she decided to put his strange remark aside.

"Delana can be pretty stubborn. She may not want to go with us."

He shrugged. "I guess we'll have to pray that she will."

She frowned. "*We'll* have to pray that she will?"

He met her frown with a teasing chuckle. "Where's your faith, woman? You do believe in answered prayer, don't you?"

"Of course I do."

Mitch rose then extended his hand and pulled her to her feet beside him. "Then I guess Delana will be going to church with the rest of us."

Tassie rolled her eyes. "You're incorrigible."

He gave her a teasing smile. "And you're beautiful, you smell nice, and you're fun to have around."

Not sure how to respond, she returned his smile then moved to the sink and began scraping out the frying pan. Finally, without turning to face him, she said in a soft low voice, "You're fun to be around, too."

His laughter rang throughout the kitchen. "Are you saying *I'm* not handsome and *I* don't smell good? I used my best aftershave this morning."

"That's not what I meant and you know it. I'm just not used to kind, handsome men giving me compliments."

He sidled up close behind her. "You deserve those compliments and more. Want some help with the dishes?"

Tassie's heart thundered against her chest as she stepped to one side and began to wipe the counter. When he backed away, she turned to look at him, not sure if she should laugh, say something witty, or just ignore what she didn't understand.

He lifted his hand surrender style. "Sorry, I didn't mean to crowd you. Ah, maybe I'd better be going." As if embarrassed, he grabbed up his briefcase from where he had placed it on one of the chairs and moved quickly toward the living room.

"I'll be home in time for dinner. I'd planned to have a talk with Tony this morning. . . ." He paused mid-sentence. "I'll do it later."

She eyed him suspiciously. Had something happened with Tony he hadn't told her about?

"If Delana tries to leave her room without apologizing, call me."

"I—I will." Tassie remained standing by the counter, her heart racing. *Father God, what is going on between the two of us? I've liked Mitch—a lot—since the day I met him and have had strange feelings every time I'm around him. Surely he's not having strange feelings about me.*

She fingered her hair. *He said I was beautiful. Only one other man told me I was beautiful, and that man hurt me terribly. I can't let Mitch hurt me, too. I'm sure his actions were nothing more than an attempt at being friendly.*

At exactly six o'clock that evening, just after her father entered the front door, Delana came out of her room and peered down over the railing at Mitch and Tassie. After placing his briefcase in the hall closet, Mitch strode up the stairs and stood before her. "Did you clean your room?"

She huffed. "Yes."

"Everything is hung up or put away?"

"Yes."

"Nothing on the floor that shouldn't be?"

"No. If you're through with your questions, I'd like to get something to eat. I'm hungry."

Mitch smiled, then stood back and gave his arm a wide swing toward the stairway. "Sure, but don't forget apologizing to Tassie is a part of this deal."

"Da–ad!" she strung out, her lower lip turning down. "I cleaned my room. Isn't that enough?"

"No, that's not enough. Either apologize or go back into your room."

Even from the bottom of the stairs Tassie could tell the girl's face had turned red with anger.

"Can't I get a sandwich and some pop first?" she whined. It was obvious the girl was used to having her way and this was a whole new experience for her.

Mitch shrugged. "Nope. Not even a bread crumb until you apologize."

Rolling her eyes, Delana stormed past her father, down the stairs, and stopped directly in front of Tassie. "I'm sorry," she spat out angrily.

He leaned over the handrail. "With a little more sincerity, please."

Delana, her eyes filled with fire, visibly sucked in a deep breath and let it out slowly. "I'm sorry, Tassie," she said, her voice dripping with an exaggerated sweetness that was almost sickening, her head turned so her father couldn't see the vengeful expression on her face and the way her eyes narrowed as she spoke.

Tassie gladly accepted the girl's apology. The last thing she wanted was to upset everyone so that none of them would go to church with her without Mitch having to drag them there.

He hurried down the stairs to join them. "That's better. By the way, sweetie, we're all going to church together in the morning. You included."

"Dad! I don't want—"

He raised his hand to stop her. "Come on, Delana, you might actually like it. You and Tony had better set your alarms before you go to bed tonight. Church starts at eleven and I want us to be there on time." He paused, then gestured in the direction of the kitchen. "I'm sure Tassie has supper ready. Let's all go eat. I'm starving."

Chapter 7

Tassie wakened even before her alarm went off the next morning, surprised she had slept so soundly. *No wonder I slept,* she told herself as she stepped into the shower and let the delicious, warm water sweep over her face. *I put in a pretty grueling day yesterday. Today has got to be better. I just hope the kids don't throw a fit about having to go to church.*

She hurriedly toweled off and dressed, making sure to add a bit of lipstick and mascara, then headed down the stairs and into the kitchen to fix her specialty—eggs in a basket. She had gotten the recipe from a romance novel she had read, titled *With a Mother's Heart*, where the heroine fixed eggs in a basket for the hero and his invalid daughter. She was certain the Drummond family would love them as much as she did.

The house was eerily quiet when she entered, so quiet she found herself tiptoeing around as she put the coffee on to perk and loaded the grill with long strips of bacon. Soon the aromas of both hot coffee and sizzling bacon filled the house. Hopefully, the enticing aroma would make it easier for the Drummond children to crawl out of bed and the day wouldn't start with another scene. She had no more than had the thought when, to her surprise, an alarm sounded in one of the upstairs bedrooms. *Good. I was dreading having to wake them up!*

But the ringing alarm was soon followed by the solid beat of some rock and roll tune, a beat so heavy and pronounced it vibrated through the walls. Tassie's hands instinctively went to her ears. Then from somewhere else upstairs a second rock and roll number began to play, even louder than the first. The sound of a door banging against the wall and a few unsavory words from both Delana and Tony as they confronted each other in the hallway, with each screaming at the other to turn down their respective radios, and the war between the Drummond children was on.

What a way to start our Sunday! Tassie bolted up the stairs and stepped in between them. "Enough! If you want to play that ridiculous music in your rooms, that's your privilege, but you simply cannot play it loud enough to intrude on the privacy of others."

Almost instantly, she felt a sharp sting on her cheek as Delana slapped her. Caught off guard, Tassie spun around and connected with Tony who immediately pushed her back toward his sister.

When Delana grabbed onto Tassie's arms she found herself staring at the girl, nose to nose.

"Don't you ever tell me what I can and cannot do! You're nothing but a maid in this house and don't you forget it!" Turning her loose, the girl whirled quickly around and disappeared into her room, banging the door behind her. A second later, her radio blared even louder—so loud it nearly drowned out Tony's music that was still booming in the background.

Tony, obviously surprised by what had happened to Tassie, stared at her for a moment then went back into his room, leaving her standing alone in the hallway. With her heart pounding in her chest and not sure what to do next, she simply cradled her throbbing cheek with her palm and walked back downstairs and into the kitchen. She turned the strips of bacon over and then, almost robotically, began cutting big circles out of bread slices, neatly stacking them beside the grill. In all her life, no one had ever slapped her. Should she go downstairs to the lower level, knock on Mitch's door, and tell him so he could deal with his daughter? He'd said he would back her up.

She pulled the egg carton from the refrigerator then stood staring at it as it lay on the counter. No, that would make her look weak, like a tattletale who couldn't handle the situation and had to run for help. *Running to Mitch will never do.*

It seemed she had only two choices. Turn tail and run, get out of the Drummond home, and never look back, or take charge herself, handling things the way she felt the Lord would have her do it. After lowering the setting on the grill, Tassie bowed her head in a quick prayer then lifted her head high and marched up the stairs directly to Delana's room. After a quick rap on the door, she pushed it open and faced the girl head-on, gently taking hold of her arm. "Delana, I know you have had a hard time of it since losing your mother and I am so sorry you had to go through that, but you need to understand something. I am *not* your servant. In some ways, I am now a part of this family. So for the next three months we will all be living under the same roof. You can accept the fact that I am here to stay until then and work with me, or you can continue to make things miserable for all of us."

Although surprised when the girl remained silent she continued on. "Every home has to have rules. This one is no exception."

When Delana rolled her eyes and tried to yank her arm away, Tassie slightly tightened her hold. "My rules are few but each one is important if we are all to dwell together in harmony. Number one. Don't ever hit or even think about hitting me again! And no swear words are to be uttered in this house at any time. No TV, music, Internet, or phone calls until your homework is done, and absolutely no music played loud enough to disturb others. Your room must have a semblance of order at all times. I don't expect it to look perfect, but no more clothes on the floor or draped on furniture, and your shoes at least should be tossed onto your closet floor. If you need help organizing your drawers or closets I'll be happy to assist. I'd love to be able to spend some time with you and get to know you better. I'd like us to be friends."

Delana responded with, "In your dreams."

Choosing to ignore her remark, Tassie continued. "The rest of my rules are quite simple but equally important. Curfew times will be met exactly, unless later times are preapproved before you leave for the evening. No boys in your room—ever. And don't even think about crawling out your window and shinnying down that tree again because if I find you even trying to get out that way, I'll have to have someone come and cut down the tree. And lastly, breakfast will be at seven each morning, at least until school is out for the summer, and dinner at six each night. I am counting on you to be there on time both times, even if your father isn't."

"But—"

Tassie lifted her free hand. "Hold it a minute. In addition to helping around the house with a few tasks now and then, you will be expected to babysit your little sister occasionally, when needed. And you may be asked to help in the kitchen and with other things from time to time, like helping me plan the menu, which I hope you will do cheerfully."

Delana glared at her for a moment then spit in her face. "Forget it, lady. No one tells me what to do!"

Stunned when the spittle hit her cheek, Tassie released her hold on the girl just long enough to allow Delana a chance to give her a hard shove, sending her flying through the doorway and into the hall. Before she had time to regain her balance, the door slammed and the click of the lock sounded. Heartbroken and discouraged, Tassie leaned against the wall and, using the tip of her shirttail, wiped at her cheek. *Well, that didn't go as I'd hoped. Now what do I do, Lord?*

"Tassie?" Although she could barely hear with Delana's music blaring from her room, she turned at the sound of Mitch's voice.

"I–I'm upstairs!"

"Did you know the bacon is burning?"

She rushed down the stairs and into the kitchen to find him pulling slightly burned bacon strips from the grill and placing them on the platter she had set on the counter earlier. "I'm so sorry. I—I got sidetracked upstairs."

He grinned. "No problem. I like my bacon well done."

She glanced at the deeply browned strips on the platter. "I'll do better next time."

His grin broadened as he moved toward the coffeepot and poured himself a cup. "Mmm, nothing like a good hot cup of coffee to start a guy's day. From the sound of that loud music I guess the kids are up."

"Yes, they are." She busied herself by adding the bread slices to the grill then breaking an egg into each of the holes she had cut, watching intently as the clear whites of the eggs began to cook.

Mitch walked up close behind her and peered over her shoulder. "Ah, now I see. I wondered why you had cut the centers out of that stack of bread slices. I've never seen eggs cooked that way before. Looks good! I'll bet the kids will love them. And I like the way you're browning the cut-out bread circles on the grill. Those will be great with jam."

Tassie nervously nibbled on her lower lip. *If they'll even come down to breakfast. And if they do, they'll probably complain to him how I got after them, especially Delana. By the time she tells the story her way, I'll probably end up looking like a monster and he'll fire me on the spot. He said he'd back me up, but blood is thicker than water, especially when it comes to one's own children.* "I—I hope they'll love them."

He nodded his head toward the stairs. "I think I'll go and hurry them up. We don't want to be late for church, and we sure don't want those—what do you call them?"

"Eggs in a basket."

"Oh, yeah, eggs in a basket. We don't want them getting cold."

She watched as he left the kitchen then waited with bated breath for the explosion she was certain would come as Delana and Tony gave their father their version of the fracas that had gone on earlier. But it didn't happen. Instead, the foursome entered and sat down at the table as casually as if the whole incident hadn't even occurred.

Still shaking from her bout with the girl, Tassie removed the cooked egg concoctions from the grill, placed them on the platter with the bacon, and carried them to the table.

Mitch looked up, brows raised. "You've only set the table for four. You are going to eat with us, aren't you? You're a part of this family now, at least until September." He grabbed hold of the empty chair beside him. "Please, Tassie, get yourself a plate and sit down."

"But I need to get the juice and the milk from the refrigerator."

He gestured toward Delana. "She can get it. You sit down."

Prepared for an angry reaction, yelling out how Tassie was nothing more than a servant and had no business joining the family at the table, she shot a glance toward the girl. But instead of responding in a negative, hateful way, Delana simply walked to the refrigerator, took out the juice and milk, and placed them on the table.

"You kids have to try these," Mitch told his children while using the spatula to place bread slices on each plate.

Delana wrinkled her nose and stared at her plate. "What are those things?"

"Eggs in a basket." Mitch smiled as he answered. "That's what Tassie called them. Now let's ask her to pray."

Grateful for being asked but deciding the fewer words the better at this point, Tassie bowed her head and said a simple prayer.

Mitch added a quick "Amen," then sliced off a big bite with his fork and popped it into his mouth. "Mmm, delicious. From now on, I want all my eggs fixed this way." He waved his empty fork toward his oldest daughter. "Taste it, Delana. Go on, take a bite."

He waited until she had placed a tiny bite in her mouth and began to chew. "Okay, what's the verdict? Thumbs-up or thumbs-down?"

The girl lifted a feeble thumb. "They're okay, I guess."

Tassie felt relief. She had expected a thumbs-down just for spite.

"I like them. They're good." Tony pushed his plate toward his father. "Can I have another one? Give me a couple of those bread things, too, and some more bacon."

Tassie couldn't believe it when not one person complained about the bacon being too done, but she had noticed Mitch had taken the worst ones and placed them on his own plate before giving the least burned ones to his children.

After filling his son's dish, he reached the platter toward the sleepy little girl sitting in the junior chair, her chin braced against her palm as her elbow leaned on the table. "What about you, my baby girl? Aren't you going to try Tassie's eggs in a basket? They're good."

Without lifting her face, she sighed. "I'm too sleepy. I wanna go back to bed."

"Sorry, you can't go back to bed. Remember? We're all going to church together this morning! Now eat your breakfast, pumpkin. You need to eat it while it is hot." Using his knife, he cut a small portion from her egg, forked it, then held it close to her mouth. "Come on, take a bite for Daddy." She slowly opened her mouth and unenthusiastically allowed him to slip it between her lips. "Now isn't that good?"

The child's eyes grew wider as she chewed. "Can I have one of those bread things like Tony has?"

"With jam on it?"

"Uh-huh." Without using her fork, the little girl picked up the slice of bread circling the egg and began nibbling on it, her eyes brightening and widening a bit more with each bite.

Tassie hurriedly pulled two bread circles from the platter and slathered them with the delicious peach jam then handed them to her. Babette took one small bite from each of them then placed them on her plate before taking up a piece of bacon. She didn't say thank you, Tassie noted, but at least she was pleasant. That was good.

Soon they had finished their breakfast and the platter lay empty in the middle of the table. As everyone rose, Mitch suggested they each carry their dishes to the sink before going to their rooms. Although his suggestion was met with narrowed eyes and a shrug on Delana's part, each person complied without a word.

Mitch turned and gave Tassie a wink as he left the kitchen. "Great breakfast! By the way, I heard some ruckus going on upstairs a while ago, especially the yelling between you and Delana. I almost rushed to your rescue but I liked the way you managed things. You're exactly what my children have needed. What I've needed. This household craves order and structure and, like I've already told you, I'm 100 percent behind you. Every rule you gave Delana is a rule I should have set and enforced long ago. If I had, perhaps we wouldn't be in this mess."

"Thank you, Mitch." His words of support and reassurance were just what she needed to hear.

He let out a sigh. "I know she spat on you. Most people probably would have either choked her or quit right on the spot. All I can do is apologize for her. No one should have to endure such a distasteful experience. I can't believe how well you handled it."

"Handled it? She shoved me into the hall and locked her door before I could say a word. That isn't exactly what I'd call handling it."

"You handled it by staying. I'm sure my daughter thought you would pack up and leave after that but you didn't—you stayed and you even told her you wanted to be her friend. And when she saw you here in this kitchen, preparing breakfast, she must have realized you had no intention of leaving, that it was a waste of her time and energy to even try to run you off. Not that she won't continue to try your patience—she will—so will Tony and so will Babette—but please, Tassie, don't let them get to you. Those kids need the stability in their life that you're bringing to them."

"I want so much to help them, Mitch."

"And you are. Up until you came the only two women they were ever around was a mother who made no pretense at caring for them, who never once told them she loved them, and their grandmother, who was not much better to them than her daughter. Please don't give up on them. Think about where they're coming from. I'm finally beginning to realize how much losing their mother has affected them, and I didn't help any when I went into my own funk. Especially Delana. Being the oldest I'm sure she felt abandoned by her mother. Not once, but twice. When she left us and when she died. I know, because of their outlandish behavior toward you, they don't deserve it, but please—when you feel like you've had enough and can't stand being here one more minute, take a breath and remember what those children have gone through. You're a Christian, Tassie. Let your light shine before them. Let them see God's love through you."

His words humbled her. When she had accepted this job, especially when he had asked her to take his kids to church with her, she had felt God had called her to work in the Drummond home. Yet she'd been sworn at, slapped, and spit upon. Like Mitch had said, no one deserved to be treated like that, especially if she had done nothing to deserve it. Yet, inside, deep down in the recesses of her heart, a small voice seemed to say, *"Someone else was treated like that, Tassie, was sworn at, slapped, even beaten, and spat upon when He had done nothing to deserve it. Jesus, your Lord and Savior,"* and she wanted to cry. What she was going through was totally insignificant compared to what He had gone through. Her misery could never even compare to His.

Mitch walked toward her and wrapped a comforting arm about her shoulders. "Promise you won't give up on us. I—I don't know what we'd—what I'd do without you."

With the still small voice still ringing in her ears, Tassie lifted misty eyes and smiled at him. "I know God loves your children, Mitch, and He wants me to love them, too. No matter how bad things get, as long as you back me up and want me to stay, I'll be right here, doing my best to help your family in any and every way I can. I know from experience love can speak volumes when words alone fail us. I am going to love your children, pray for them, and be there for them, no matter what."

Mitch gazed at her for a moment before speaking. "No one could ask for more." Then lifting his face heavenward, he added, "Thank You, God, for sending Tassie to us. Having her here is like breath of heaven itself to this family."

As he removed his hand from her shoulder and headed back downstairs to take his shower, she let out a long slow breath. *I, too, thank You, God. Now, please, give me the strength to face whatever this day may bring. Amen.*

She'd barely said the words when angry voices drifted down from upstairs. Tony and Delana were at it again. Yanking off her apron, she bolted up the stairs just in time to hear each one call the other by names that really upset her and made her want to wash their mouths out with soap.

Dodging flying hands and fists she wedged her way between them. "Stop it! Now! One more word and I'll take your computers out of your rooms!"

Delana's chin jutted out defiantly. "You wouldn't dare!"

Though her heart was racing, Tassie kept her face even, not about to show her whirling emotions to this girl who was just aching to challenge her.

"You do that and my father will fire you!" the girl shouted angrily.

"Your father has given me carte blanche to run this house and care for you children. If you don't believe me, you can ask him as soon as he gets out of the shower," she explained, trying to maintain an evenness to her voice.

Turning slowly, Tassie focused her attention on Tony. "Why can't you children follow my rules? I was hoping by making them it would help us avoid confrontations like this."

He gave her a blank stare. "I—I didn't know you had rules."

Suddenly she felt bad. She hadn't given him her rules, only Delana, and even then she had blurted them out with no real thought as to what the consequences would be if they were violated.

"You're right. I'll tell you what I'll do. I'll type them, print them, then post them on the bulletin board in the kitchen, and I'll make sure I leave at least one copy on your and your sister's beds. It would be a good idea to tape them inside your closet door or somewhere you can refer to them. If you need an extra copy just let me know." She pasted on a smile. "Now, go back into your rooms and get ready for church. I'm going to go help Babette."

As Tassie moved toward Babette's room she heard a sudden crash.

Chapter 8

Turning and rushing into the room, Tassie found Babette sprawled on the floor next to her desk amid a sea of scattered books, broken glass, and a crumpled lamp shade. The child was crying and her arm was bleeding. She hurried to Babette and gathered her in her arms.

"I fell!" the girl uttered between sobs as she pointed her finger in an upward manner. "I was trying to get my kitty."

Tassie's gaze went to the series of shelves mounted above the child's desk. The very first time she had entered Babette's room, she had noticed the big white shaggy stuffed kitten reclining lazily on the top shelf because it had looked so real. "You climbed up on your desk?"

With tears rolling down her cheeks, the girl simply nodded.

"Babette, you should have told me you wanted your kitty. I could have gotten it for you." She paused long enough to press a tissue from the box on the desk to Babette's cut. "That shelf was much too high for a little girl like you to reach. Promise me you won't try that again. I don't want you to get hurt." Satisfied that, other than the superficial cut on her arm, the child was all right, she carefully lifted her from the floor and sat down on the side of the bed, cradling the shaking little body in her arms.

Babette cowered against her, hiding her face in Tassie's shirt. "Don't hit me! I didn't mean to break the lamp!"

"Hit you? Why would I hit you? I know you didn't mean to break it. You were only after your kitty." Why would the child think she would hit her? Was that the way her grandmother had punished her when she didn't behave? Tassie gently tugged Babette away from her shirt and smiled down at her. "I don't think your cut is very bad. Would you let me put some medicine on it and bandage it up? Then I'll kiss it and make it all well!"

Babette, still sobbing, nodded.

Tassie stood and lowered the child onto her bed. "You wait right there. I'm going into the bathroom to get the tube of medicine and some gauze and tape and I'll be right back." She hurried into the hall bathroom and much to her surprise found everything she needed, even a small pair of scissors, and then hurried back.

Although the little girl said nothing the entire time Tassie was cleaning and dressing her wound, she sat perfectly still, her gaze pinned on Tassie's every move. After Tassie finished she kissed the boo-boo, returned each item to where she had found it, then lifted Babette in her arms and carried her to the rocking chair sitting in the corner of the room. "Would you like me to rock you? That's what my mom always did when I had a boo-boo. And you know what? It always made me feel better."

When Babette tilted her head and eyed her suspiciously, Tassie smiled at her, hoping to convey an element of trust. "We have a little time before leaving for church, so maybe we could read a book. Which book would you like?"

Babette pointed to one of the books scattered across her floor and seemed to perk up. "That one, about the baby."

Being careful not to drop her precious cargo, Tassie leaned over and picked up the book. Once Babette was seated comfortably on her lap with her arm resting on a toss pillow, Tassie opened the book and began to read.

"We need to leave in half an hour, and I know how long it takes women to decide what to wear! Are you guys about ready?" Mitch called up to them.

"Babette and I are up here in her room!" she called out, pleased he was eager to get to church on time. "She had a slight accident but she's okay."

Concerned, Mitch climbed the stairs two at a time and stopped short as he entered his daughter's room. He took one look at the broken lamp then hurried to the rocker and knelt beside it, gazing with concern at Babette's bandaged arm. "You cut yourself on the glass?"

"She's fine, Mitch. It's just a surface cut. I think the fall scared her more than it hurt her. From what she said, I guess she tried to climb up on the shelf to get her kitty, lost her balance, and fell. Don't worry. Her arm will be good as new in a few days."

He rose and began pacing about the room as pangs of guilt assaulted him. "It's my fault. I'm the one who put that silly stuffed cat on that top shelf. I got tired of tripping over it every time I came into her room. If I hadn't put it there, she wouldn't have gotten hurt."

"You can't blame yourself. Accidents and falls are a part of every child's life. That's why God made them so durable."

Babette held out her arm. "Tassie kissed my boo-boo and made it all better, Daddy. Look, she drew a smiley face on the tape."

Mitch breathed a sigh of relief then gave Tassie a smile of gratitude. "I see, pumpkin. That was really nice of Tassie."

"Babette got ready for church all by herself. Doesn't she look pretty? And she didn't get one drop of blood on her dress."

He smiled proudly. "She's beautiful."

"Tassie was reading me a story. Do you want to hear a story, Daddy? It's about a baby."

He shook his head. "I'd love to hear the story, sweetie, but I have to make sure your brother and sister are getting dressed for church. Maybe you and I can read a book together tonight. Would you like that?"

She nodded then once again snuggled up against Tassie. "Okay."

He smiled at Tassie as he backed toward the door. "Thanks for taking such good care of my family."

"You're welcome. It's always nice to know you're appreciated."

He paused in the doorway and stood listening as she lifted the book and began to read. What a beautiful sight. His regret was that as long as that rocking chair had been in the house, he couldn't remember ever seeing his wife hold and rock one of their children in it. June simply hadn't been a demonstrative person. She required her space and resented anyone or anything that infringed upon it, especially him. Looking back, he wondered how they had ever come together often enough to even have children.

Oh, how he thanked God for sending Tassie into his life—even if only for three months.

"Smile," Mitch told his oldest daughter as he and Tassie and the three children seated themselves in a pew at Linwood Community Church. "I don't want everyone thinking I dragged you here."

"That's exactly what you did. I sure didn't come because I wanted to," Delana snapped back with a snarl.

"I didn't want to come, either," Tony added. "Only sissies go to church."

Mitch gave Tony a gentle nudge. "Make the best of it, kids. From now on, you're going to be here every Sunday."

Delana started to make a comment but stopped when her dad tilted his head in a warning manner and narrowed his eyes.

Although the children didn't cause a commotion during the service, it was obvious they weren't listening to a word the pastor said.

"Maybe next Sunday they'll feel more comfortable," Mitch reminded Tassie as the family made their way through the line at the local buffet restaurant after church.

Tassie nodded in agreement. "I wish we could get them in Sunday school so they could meet some kids their own age."

"Yeah, that would be nice but just getting them to church is a real accomplishment."

Later that afternoon while Babette was napping, Tassie typed her rule list on the computer then printed out one copy each for Delana, Tony, and Babette, even though the little girl couldn't read it for herself, and one to post in the kitchen. She even printed one for Mitch so he would know what she expected of the children, and then she printed a few extra copies as well.

When Tony came home from school the next afternoon, she led him into the kitchen and gave him the snack she had earlier prepared then sat down at the table and quickly went over her copy of the rules with him. He didn't say much but she could tell by the way he fidgeted and narrowed his eyes he wasn't too happy about them.

"Gonna go play some ball with my friends," he told her after stuffing the rule list into his pocket.

"*After* you've straightened your room, Tony. You left it in quite a mess this morning."

He scowled. "That's not fair."

"All I'm asking is that you hang up your clothes and clean up the mess on your floor like you should have done this morning. If you knuckle down it will only take you a few minutes."

"Then I can go outside?"

"Yes, but please, no TV after supper until you have finished your homework." She grinned at him. "Smile. Only five more days and you'll be out of school for the summer."

Snarling something under his breath he snatched up his backpack and stomped up the stairs to his room, slamming the door with a loud bang. Ten minutes later she heard the front door close behind him.

Delana came into the kitchen more than a half hour later, definitely not wearing the clothes she had been dressed in this morning. Tassie looked first at Delana's bare navel, then at the pleated skirt that barely covered her behind, then at the low cut of the flimsy see-through blouse she was wearing. "What happened to the clothes you had on when you left this morning?"

After raising one arm high in the air and striking a pose much like the models on the cover of the latest issue of some teen fashion magazine, she gave Tassie a sardonic smile that conveyed more than words could ever say.

"I asked what happened to your clothes."

Delana flipped her shoulder in response. "I traded with one of my friends."

Tassie's jaw dropped. "You traded them? Permanently, or just until tomorrow?"

This time Delana shrugged both shoulders. "Haven't decided yet. Might keep them. Might not." She did a mock pirouette. "They look good on me, don't they?"

"Delana, the attention girls get from dressing like that is the kind of attention you really don't want. You're not quite sixteen. What kind of a message do you think you're sending by exposing yourself that way?"

She shrugged again. "Who cares as long as the boys look at me?"

"I hate to put it so bluntly, but wearing clothing like that is the same as asking for trouble. I'm not saying that to scare you, I'm concerned about you, Delana. I don't want to see you get hurt."

The girl let out a snort. "The best thing you can do for me is leave me alone. I don't have to take orders from you; you're a nobody. If you are so smart and claim to know everything, why aren't you out working at a real job instead of being a babysitter? Anyone can be a babysitter. It takes no talent whatsoever."

Tassie wanted to grab the girl, throw her over her knee, and give her a good spanking—not because she had made fun of Tassie but because she was genuinely concerned about her. Somehow she had to reach her. There were men out there just waiting for girls like Delana. She didn't want her to end up as someone's play toy or victim. Deciding to put an end to their conversation, she reached for Delana's copy of the rules and handed it to her. "By the way, here's a printed copy of the rules we discussed earlier. Read them over and I'll be happy to discuss any of it with you."

"This is what I think of your rules." The girl ripped the paper into shreds then tossed them in the air and watched with satisfaction as the pieces fluttered to the floor.

"There's another copy on your nightstand. Probably be a good idea to keep them; otherwise you won't have any idea why you're being punished when you disobey one of them."

Delana's face contorted with anger. "You were in my room again?"

"Yes. Why? Is there something in there you'd prefer I didn't see?"

"No, but it's my room! You have no business going in there! Ever!"

"Delana, I don't want to go into your room. Like you, I wanted my privacy as a teenager. And you'll get it—just as soon as you show me you are a team player and can be trusted. With trust comes freedom. All your father and I ask is that you show us you can be responsible and that you are trustworthy."

"All you ask? Forget it, lady. My dad may be taken with you, but to me and my brother you're nothing. A big fat zero."

"Delana, as much as I'd like to have value in your sight, what you think of me really doesn't concern me as much as what God thinks of me. As long as my heart and actions are right with God, it makes very little difference what anyone else thinks. I am here at your father's request, to care for you and make sure your home runs smoothly. You can cooperate or you can fight me on every move, but I *am* here to stay."

Tassie paused, leaving time for her words to sink in. "So if you are as smart as I think you are, I'm sure you'll decide to go with the flow and cooperate."

After a loud "Ha!" that seemed to come from the pit of her stomach, Delana whirled around and left the room.

Chapter 9

Her knees so weak from the confrontation with Delana that she could barely stand, Tassie lowered herself onto the sofa. So far, even though she had made a bit of headway with Babette, she had alienated herself from both Tony and Delana. She hoped she had done the right thing by being so firm with them. If not, she'd really blown it. She considered going to her room to have a good cry when Babette wandered into the living room and scooted up close to her on the sofa.

"My boo-boo feels all better," she told Tassie, giving her a little grin.

"Well, then, let's kiss it again. Kisses always make a boo-boo heal faster." Tassie bent and kissed the child's arm just above the bandage then gazed at her. "I was just about to fix Goliath's supper and take it out to him. Would you like to help me?" When Babette smiled and nodded, Tassie rose, took her hand, and led her into the kitchen. The little girl held Goliath's dish while Tassie carefully filled it with the big dog's food. Then, with both of them holding on to the dish, they walked outdoors onto the patio where Goliath lay stretched out on his side under a tree, sleeping peacefully. He leaped to his feet when he heard their voices.

"I'll hold the dish if you want to pet him before he eats. It's always best to pet him when he isn't eating. Sometimes dogs get upset and nip if people bother them while they're enjoying their meal."

She watched as Babette placed her small hand on his head. "Goliath likes it when you scratch his ears."

Babette grinned up at her. "I wish I had a dog."

"You do? Well, I have an idea. As long as Goliath and I are living here with you, why don't you pretend he is your dog, too? I'd be happy to share him with you and I know Goliath likes being your friend."

Babette grinned then hugged the big dog around his neck. "Okay."

"But right now, I think we'd better give Goliath his supper so I can go back inside and cook supper for you and your family. Your father is going to try to make it home in time to eat with us. Won't that be nice?"

Babette nodded her head enthusiastically. "Maybe he'll read me a story."

"Your daddy loves you. You do know that, don't you?"

"Uh-huh, but I don't have a mommy. She went away with a man."

Her words broke Tassie's heart. Babette couldn't have been more than two at the time, maybe not even that old. Mitch hadn't been very specific about the timing. Did she remember seeing her mother leave that last time? How sad if she did. Not sure if she should make a comment or ignore Babette's words, she simply asked, "Would you like to set the table?"

Babette shrugged. "I don't know how."

After helping the child wash her hands, Tassie pulled a stack of five place mats from the pantry shelf and laid them on the table. "It's easy. Just place one of these on the table in front of each chair. Add a plate, one knife, one spoon, one fork, and a napkin." She glanced around the kitchen then grabbed up a candle from the built-in hutch. "To make our dinner really special we'll light a candle. Doesn't that sound like fun?"

Babette clapped her hands with glee then set about her assigned task, all the while smiling. "What are we having for supper, Tassie?" she asked when the last spoon had been placed and she sat down at the table.

"I put a nice roast in the oven a few hours ago. Can't you smell it? I think it smells delicious."

The girl sniffed the air. "I do smell it. Are we going to have mashed potatoes? I love mashed potatoes."

"I was going to butter them and add a carton of sour cream and chives but if you'd rather have them mashed, then mashed they'll be. If you'll help me, we'll add a nice big pat of butter on top and a good sprinkle of black pepper just before we serve them. That makes them look real pretty."

Again, Babette clapped her hands. "This is fun. I never cooked before."

"Well, I can always use help in the kitchen. You're more than welcome to join me anytime. In fact, if you like, you can be our table captain."

Babette puckered up her face. "What's a table captain?"

"Oh, being a table captain is a very important job. No one is allowed to set the place mats, dishes, and silverware on the table except the table captain."

"I want to be the table captain."

Tassie wrinkled her forehead and took on a serious expression. "Are you sure? Like I said, it's a very important job. You'll have to do it every night. That's a lot of responsibility for a little girl."

"I can do it. Please let me, please, please, please."

"All right, if you insist. I'll expect you to be here in the kitchen with me while I'm putting the final touches on our meals. Is that okay with you?"

"Yes, oh yes." Babette leaped from her chair and began marching around the kitchen, singing, "I am a table captain; I am a table captain," over and over, making up the tune as she skipped and jumped along.

As promised, Mitch arrived home in time for dinner and was ecstatic when

Babette rushed into his arms as he opened the door. He had never seen her so happy. She kept muttering something about being a table captain, which he didn't understand at all, but as long as she was happy, he was happy.

The wonderful aroma of roast beef drifted in from the kitchen. To a man used to eating in restaurants or having nothing more than frozen TV dinners or an occasional frozen lasagna served on paper plate, the thought of another home-cooked meal was almost more than he could handle. "Is that roast beef I smell?" he called out.

"Yes," came a voice from the kitchen. "I hope you're hungry!"

"I'm famished!" he called back in reply as he lifted his daughter and hurried into the room.

"We're having mashed potatoes. Tassie said we could. I get to put the butter on top," Babette said proudly, using her little hands to turn his face in her direction. "I set the table. I'm the table captain!"

"That's wonderful, honey." Then turning to Tassie he asked, "Want me to tell Tony and Delana supper is ready?"

"Yes, good idea. Everything is on the table."

Still cradling Babette in his arms, with a smile of contentment he headed toward the stairs.

To Tassie's surprise, neither Tony nor Delana mentioned anything about the rule list or the run-ins they'd had with her. Instead they both sat quietly through supper, even bowing their heads when she prayed. Both even nodded their agreement when Mitch complimented her on the great roast and how he loved the way she had cooked the vegetables along with it.

"I'm the table captain," Babette stated proudly around her mouth full of potatoes.

Her sister leaned back in her chair and rolled her eyes. "Table captain, huh? Is that the way Tassie is getting you to do her job for her? By giving you a fancy title?"

Mitch let out a deep sigh. "Delana, why can't you be civil? That remark was uncalled for. I think you should apologize to Tassie."

Delana jutted her chin out defiantly. "Apologize? No way. Forget it!"

His eyes narrowed. "Now, Delana. I mean it."

"And what will you do if I don't?" she shot back, meeting his intense gaze with one of her own.

Mitch looked quickly to Tassie, as if he needed guidance for an answer, but she held her peace. As far as she was concerned, it was about time he began to take a stand and now was as good a time as any.

"Or—or—I'll cut your allowance in half this week."

Again, the girl huffed. "Sure. As if you'd actually do it. That's what you told me last week but you gave it all to me anyway."

"I might have done that last week but things around here have changed. From now on—"

Her eyes flashing, Delana leaped to her feet. "They've changed all right. You don't care anything about us kids, your own flesh and blood." She paused long enough to fling her finger toward Tassie. "All you can think about is *that* woman. What is it, Dad? Are you so hungry for a woman to take to bed, you'll let her get by with anything?"

That comment was the last straw. Tassie jumped to her feet, grabbed Delana by both shoulders, and stood toe to toe with her. "You have no business talking about me that way, Delana, and I refuse to sit here and let you talk disrespectfully to your father. It's about time you learned the world doesn't revolve around you and your wants."

Mitch tugged at Tassie's hand then stepped between them, his full attention focused on his daughter. "Tassie is right, Delana. You and your siblings have become spoiled little tyrants and it's my fault. I've been so concerned about giving you kids the material things in life I've forgotten what you need most—a parent who loves you unconditionally and loves you enough to discipline you and train you in the way you should go. You may not like Tassie, but having her here has shown me what the four of us are missing in life is a good stable home, where each of us loves and respects the other and where each contributes to our everyday life. Even though your mother isn't here, we're still a family and we need to act like one."

"But you're never home," Tony inserted.

"You're right, son, but I'm changing that. I've already let it be known at the station that I'm cutting down on my hours. I want and need to be home with you children." He lovingly slipped an arm around his daughter as he nodded toward Tassie. "Like we are tonight, all sitting around the table, having dinner together."

"And arguing!" Delana yanked away from his grasp. "How exciting. Maybe tomorrow evening we can all wear boxing gloves and duke it out."

Mitch's jaw dropped. "Delana! What in the world is the matter with you?"

Delana headed for the stairs. "What's the matter with you, Dad? Why all this sudden interest in your family? You've never cared about us before. Is this all *her* idea?"

He started after her but Tassie grabbed on to his arm. "I'm the cause of this. Let me go."

"But. . ."

Before he could stop her, she turned and ran up the stairs, sticking her foot in

Delana's door before she had a chance to close it.

"Look, Delana, I don't know if it's me you don't like or if it would be any woman who intruded on this household, but I want to assure you of one thing. If I didn't personally care about you and Tony and Babette, I would have been out of here long ago. I can only imagine how hard it was to see your mother walk out on you and then lose her in that accident, but life goes on. Your father suffered a loss, too, a loss as great, or even greater, than yours, but being your father he's had to go on and try to make the best of things."

Delana plunked herself onto her bed, kicked off her shoes, and crossed her arms. "So what are you saying? That you want to marry my dad and be our mother? 'Cause if that's what you have in mind, forget it. I can assure you it's not going to happen."

"No, that's not what I have in mind at all. You know I'm going back to college in the fall."

"Unless you can snag him!"

Tassie had to work hard at controlling her anger. "To be real honest with you, Delana, no sane woman would want to marry your father and come into this home with the kinds of attitudes you children have."

"Yeah? And we're going to continue to have that *attitude*, as you call it. We don't need a woman coming in here, making ridiculous rules and telling us what to do. You'll be here for a while and then you'll leave us, too, just like my mother did, my grandmother did, and even Mrs. Cramer!"

Was that a tear Tassie saw in Delana's eye? "Oh, honey, is that what you think? That those women have all abandoned you? No wonder you feel like you do." She tried to slip her arm around the girl's shoulders but Delana shied away. "Is that why you're so upset about me being here with you? Because I'll only be here for three months? But don't you see? I'm not abandoning you like you feel the others did. I'm going back to college."

"But you're leaving!"

"Yes, you're right, I am. But we all knew that up front. I've never deceived you."

"My dad should never have hired you! I don't want you here."

Tassie realized she wasn't getting anywhere. Their conversation was going in circles. "Look, Delana, you're right. We're only going to be together three months but I have no intention of leaving until my time is up. I want you to know I'm here for you. You can come to me at any time, for any reason. I want to be your friend."

"I have all the friends I need," the girl spat out.

"Just remember what I said. The time may come when you need help from someone you can trust. I'm that person." Tassie turned and, even though tumultuous emotions were raging inside her, walked calmly out the door, closing it securely behind her. *I've done all I can, God. I'm out of ideas. I just don't seem to be able to reach her. The rest is up to You.*

As she moved back downstairs she could hear voices coming from the living room.

"Tassie!" Mitch called out. "Come here. There's someone I want you to meet."

She smoothed her hair as she hurried into the living room.

"Tassie, this is my coworker and my best friend, Chaplain Dale Lewis. The two of us started out as beat officers and then we were both promoted to detective. Dale left the force about four years ago to attend Bible college. Now he's the police chaplain."

Chaplain Lewis, a pleasant-looking man with an oversized sincere smile, held out his hand. "Nice to meet you, Miss. . ."

"Tassie Springer. Please call me Tassie, Chaplain Lewis."

"Only if you'll call me Dale."

She smiled her agreement. "So you're a chaplain with the police department?"

"Sure am and I love it."

Mitch chuckled. "But he still carries his gun. Show it to her, Dale."

Tassie reared back. "That's okay. I'm not really interested in guns."

Dale smiled as he reached into the shoulder holster under his jacket. "You might be in this one. It belonged to my great-grandfather who was a sheriff over in Missouri in the late 1880s."

Mitch gestured toward the gun. "Look at the pearl set into the handle, Tassie. It even has his great-grandfather's initials and the year he got the gun etched into it."

She moved closer for a better look. "It's beautiful. I didn't know they made guns like that."

Dale smiled proudly. "There aren't many like this around anymore. It's a real keepsake and one of the most dependable guns I've ever used."

"And he needs that gun. As a chaplain, Dale deals with a number of seedy characters," Mitch explained as Dale slipped the gun back into its holster.

Dale gave his jacket a pat. "Mitch is right. This gun goes with me everywhere I go. I'm never without it. I also respond to a number of domestic violence calls. Those are the worst kind. I pray I'll never have to use it, but it's wise to be prepared." As if wanting to change the subject, he turned to Tassie. "Mitch tells me you're a believer."

"Yes, I am."

He nodded toward the stairs. "Sounded like you and Delana were having a difference of opinion when I arrived."

"Tassie is trying so hard to reach my daughter," Mitch explained. "That girl shuts everyone out. Even me. I have no idea what to do with her. It's like she's mad at the world and everyone in it."

"She's had a rough time of it, but I don't have to remind you of what she's gone through. You've gone through it, too."

"And I wouldn't have made it if it weren't for you and your wonderful counseling. The many times we prayed together helped, too."

"You are praying for Delana, aren't you? Prayer is a powerful tool."

Mitch bobbed his head. "Yes, both Tassie and I are praying for her, but sometimes it seems as if God isn't listening."

The chaplain chuckled. "Oh, He's listening all right, but never forget: God does things in His own way, in His own time—but that doesn't mean He doesn't use people to accomplish His will. That's why He made parents. Just hang in there, pray, and show her your love even when she seems not to want it. Prayer is powerful and so is love. Team those two together and you can't miss." He sent a smile Tassie's way. "Maybe the three of us can get together soon and talk about it."

She nodded. "I'd like that. I really want to help Mitch win his children to our Lord."

"Good. I wish I could stay longer but, if you'll both excuse me, I really need to be going." Then, turning to Mitch he added, "I knew you'd want that report about Jeff Clarkson's family. They're going through a rough time right now with their son in custody."

Mitch followed him to the door. "Thanks, Dale. I'll give them a call. By the way, plan on having dinner with us sometime soon. Tassie is a great cook."

"You name the night and I'll be here."

Mitch told him good-bye then turned to Tassie with a look of concern. "So how did you make out with Delana?"

Her shoulders rose in a shrug. "I have no idea. At least she listened to most of what I had to say. I guess that's progress."

He moved close to her. "You're not leaving us, are you?"

She mustered up a smile. "No, I couldn't leave if I wanted to. I told Delana I was staying. Leaving would admit defeat."

Mitch reached for her hand, then cradling it in his, brought it to his lips. "Delana didn't mean what she said. She was only spouting off. I'm with you on this. You do know that, don't you?"

She nodded. "Yes, I know, and I'm counting on it."

"I'm still amazed at how sweet and loving Babette is," he told Tassie one evening as they sat on the sofa, watching the evening news on TV. How did you ever get her to do such a turnaround?"

"I guess by just giving her the attention every little girl craves. I wish the attention I try to give Delana would work that well."

He shamefully hung his head. "That attention should have come from me. How could I have been so blind? I put my baby girl's material needs above her emotional needs."

The pitiful look on his face broke Tassie's heart. She turned and laid her hand on his shoulder. "You were hurting, too, Mitch. When your wife left you, you had to have felt rejection. Then—even though the two of you were no longer together—you lost her in such a horrible way. Granted, those children lost their mother, but you lost your wife."

"But I was adult. I should have. . ."

She met his gaze. "Don't do that to yourself. What is past is past. You can't change any of it. All you can do is move forward."

"What would I have done if you hadn't come along?"

"Me? All I've done is alienate your older children and cause an even bigger rift between you and them."

"No! That's not what you've done at all. I don't want my kids to be juvenile delinquents and I'm afraid that's the way they are headed. What you've done is given me the courage to take charge and let them know who is in control around here. To stand up and become the father they deserve."

"It's not going to happen overnight," she said honestly.

"I know."

When he scooted closer and put his arm around her shoulders, she didn't resist. She loved being near him. In fact, the time they had begun to spend together each evening, cleaning the kitchen after dinner, had become her favorite time of day. She loved the way they could laugh and talk together about the things that happened to him on his shift as a detective.

"I can't do it alone. I need you by my side in this, Tassie."

"I am with you, Mitch, but what you really need is to rededicate yourself to God. I can help, but as the spiritual leader and head of this household, it's your responsibility to make sure your family attends church and is taught the Word of God."

"I know, but sometimes my job. . ."

She frowned at him. "Come on, be honest. Did you really have to work all those Sundays in the past or was it because you were so dedicated to getting the bad guys off the street you let your job take over your life? Mitch, what you do is admirable. The streets of Grand Island are safer because of you, but your children are a gift from God. If He didn't expect you to be there for them He would never have given them to you. You owe them your time."

He gazed at her for a moment as if thinking over her words.

"I don't mean to offend you by speaking so bluntly, but no one else can take your place."

"Okay, message received. If I'm to be the good daddy I want to be I'd better go up and read that story to Babette before she goes to sleep."

"Good idea. I think I'll go to my room, call Mom and Dad, read awhile after I take my shower, then get to bed early. See you in the morning. Did you remind Tony and Delana that since tomorrow is Sunday, they'll need to set their alarms?"

"I'll remind them after I read that story to Babette." He leaned toward her and gently planted a kiss on her forehead. "Good night, Tassie."

"Good night, Mitch."

The next morning, much to her surprise, all four members of the Drummond family were dressed and ready for church when she called them to breakfast. Even the ride to church was pleasant. Mitch looked good sitting behind the steering wheel, smiling and joking with her and his family. And rather than make their usual disturbance during the service, both Delana and Tony sat quietly beside their father and listened, or at least gave the appearance of listening.

"I really admire the way you openly worship the Lord," Mitch told Tassie when they arrived home after the family had enjoyed lunch at an Italian restaurant. "You know, it feels good being back in church again. I've always felt guilty for not taking my kids and making sure they knew the Bible, but not guilty enough to do anything about it—until you came along."

She gave him a shy grin. "And bugged you about it?"

He smiled back. "Yeah, I guess you could call it that, but it worked. Maybe there's hope for me yet."

"Of course there is. God never gives up on anyone. We may leave Him but He never leaves us. I'm sure He rejoices each time He sees you back in His house."

"The kids behaved pretty well today, didn't they?"

"Yes, I was quite proud of them."

"Me, too. Who knows? They may even be enjoying it."

The next four weeks went by with reasonably few confrontations, which both Tassie and Mitch attributed to putting Dale's wise advice into action. Tassie hoped the calm meant Mitch's older children were finally beginning to accept her. At least they were tolerating her presence in their home.

"Can you believe Tony and Delana are no longer complaining about going to church?" Mitch asked her one Sunday afternoon as he helped Tassie finish loading the dishwasher.

She closed the dishwasher's door, started it, then turned to face him. "And they've almost stopped harassing me. Probably because they see so little of me since they're out with their friends every day, enjoying their summer vacation. Mitch, I'm trying so hard to reach Delana, but she still shuts me out."

Their conversation was brought to a halt by the doorbell. "That's probably Dale." Mitch reached for her hand; then the two of them hurried to the door. "Good, you made it," he told his friend as he pushed open the storm door to allow him entrance.

"Hey, I'd never turn down an invitation to visit with friends." Dale paused and grinned at Tassie. "Especially since Tassie told me she'd save me a piece of her famous pineapple Bundt cake."

She smiled at him as she gestured toward the sofa. "You two go ahead and sit down while I get the coffee and cake."

She liked Dale. He was a good man, but more importantly he loved the Lord. Although she and Mitch hadn't invited him over specifically for a counseling session, they did plan to take advantage of his being there to ask a few questions and beg for some much needed advice.

By the time she'd filled the tray and headed back into the living room, the two men were deeply engaged in conversation.

"Mitch tells me little Babette has adjusted well to having you in her home." Dale stopped long enough to nod a thank-you when she placed his coffee and cake plate on the end table beside him. "But the older two are still not accepting you as part of this household."

"Unfortunately, that's true, Dale. I tried everything I can think of to reach them. I think Tony is slowly, but surely, coming around, but Delana is. . ."

"She's jealous of you, you know."

Tassie gasped. "Jealous? Of me? Why? She looks at me as nothing more than a servant. She even insinuated I had only taken this babysitting job—as she calls it—because I couldn't get a real job!"

Chaplain Lewis looked from Tassie to Mitch and back again. "Not the envious kind of jealousy. She is jealous of you as a woman—the woman she fears might take her father away from her."

Tassie felt a flush rise to her cheeks. "I—I don't know what you mean."

Mitch gave Dale a puzzled look.

"Oh, come on, you two. Don't try to tell me you aren't attracted to each other. You maybe have tried to hide it, but it's been pretty obvious. I've known it for weeks."

Tassie's hand went to her throat. *He noticed?*

"I'm sure, with all of you living under one roof, the children noticed it, too."

Mitch set his cup on the table with a thud. "Whoa, Dale. Tassie and I have never done anything improper. I've barely even held her hand."

"Knowing you both like I do, I'm sure that's true, but you have to look at it from your daughters' and your son's perspectives. First their mother abandoned them; then she died. That was like losing her twice. Next Grandma moved in and, although she was here physically, to be frank, we both know she was in a drunken stupor most of the time; then she abruptly moved out. Again, double abandonment. That would have been bad enough, but you abandoned them, too, Mitch. You literally turned your back on your kids and let your work take over as a way of dealing with your grief."

"I didn't mean to abandon them," Mitch said quickly in his defense. "I guess I just couldn't face reality."

Dale reached across and gave his hand a reassuring pat. "I know, old friend. Most men would have reacted the same way. Not only was your heart broken, your ego suffered a tremendous blow. But I'm proud of you. You've come out of it, you're doing all you can to be the father you should be, and you're taking your kids to church."

"I couldn't have done it if it weren't for you, Dale, and for Tassie's encouraging me to get the kids to church."

Dale gestured toward Tassie. "One of the smartest things you've done is bring Tassie into this home to help you. Having her here has to be a God thing. To be able to find a fine Christian woman willing to come into this home under those circumstances was nothing short of a miracle."

Tassie, not sure how she should respond, said a simple, "Thank you."

Mitch leaned back against the sofa and stared off into space for a moment before speaking. "You're right, you know."

She froze.

Dale gave him a shy grin. "About your and Tassie's attraction toward one another?"

Mitch swallowed hard. "Yes. I can't speak for Tassie, but I've been attracted to her since the first day she came to us. I know I shouldn't. . ."

Dale shrugged. "Shouldn't what? Be attracted to a pretty young woman like her? Why not? There's nothing wrong with two people who are not committed to someone else to develop a fondness for each other. I like the idea. It looks to me like the two of you belong together. That's part of the problem. Your children feel the same way. They probably noticed the attraction long before you two were willing to admit it. That's what scares them. They're afraid—if you and Tassie do get together—she'll abandon them like every other person they have ever loved and trusted has done."

Mitch gazed at him with a look of bewilderment. "So what should we do?"

"First and foremost—continue to pray. Fall on your face before God and ask Him to guide your every action, your every word. Next, be honest with them.

Believe me, they already know what is going on in your hearts. Don't keep them in the dark. They may not like the idea of the two of you getting together, but they'll be more receptive to it if they feel like they are a part of it, rather than thinking you're trying to hide it from them."

Mitch rubbed at his forehead. "Are you saying we should tell—"

"Not *we*, Mitch. You. You're their father. At this point, Tassie should not be included. They need to hear it from you and you alone. Once you've told them, you need to sit back and listen to them, hear their viewpoint, let them know their opinions are valuable to you."

"So if they say they don't want Tassie and me together, we end our relationship?"

"No, not at all. That decision is up to you, but at least your children will feel like you were listening to what they had to say, that they had a part in whatever decision you make. But remember this. . ." He paused and looked at Tassie before turning back to Mitch. "It's what God wants that counts. Seek His will in this. If He wants the two of you together, He'll allow a love to develop between the two of you, a love that refuses to be denied."

"Even if my children—"

"Look, Babette has already become Tassie's shadow. It's obvious that little girl already loves her. You said Tony seems to be coming around. Do you doubt God can change Delana's heart, too?"

Frowning, Tassie said, "I don't want to be the cause of—"

Again Dale interrupted. "Tassie, this family was dysfunctional long before you came, so don't try to take on any of the blame. You told me you prayed about taking this job before you accepted it, and I know both you and Mitch are in continual prayer for his children. Plus, I know you are both children of faith. You have to do all you can to show them how much you love them, but more importantly, you have to turn it all over to God and trust Him. He is able to move mountains."

Mitch reached for his cup then motioned toward Dale's uneaten cake. "Thanks, Dale. We'll try to take your advice. But right now, you'd better let Tassie pour you a fresh hot cup of coffee so you can enjoy that cake."

Later that evening as the two sat on the sofa, discussing their conversation with Dale, Mitch gave Tassie a shy grin as he reached for her hand. "I'm more than attracted to you, Tassie. It may be premature for me to mention it, but I think I'm falling in love with you."

Awestruck by his words, she simply stared at him.

"I know I'm a bit older than you and come with a ready-made family, but do you think you could ever love me?"

"L–love you?" she managed to utter as her heart fluttered within her chest. "I—I think I already do."

He scooted closer and slipped his arm around her shoulders. "You have no idea how happy that makes me. Even though I didn't want to admit it, I've been attracted to you since the first day you came into our home."

She felt as if she should pinch herself. Was this really happening? "But—what about the children?"

He lifted his shoulders in a shrug. "Like Dale said, we have to turn everything over to God. If He wants us together, it will all work out."

They discussed their newly admitted situation for some time and the effects it would have on all of them. Then Mitch gave his fingers a snap and reached for his billfold. "I nearly forgot. I need to give you some money. Tony said you were driving him and a couple of his friends up to Wayman's Lake tomorrow so they could go swimming. Maybe you could take them to lunch at some hamburger joint when they get through. Knowing how boys can eat, I'm sure they'll be famished. You don't mind, do you?"

She took the bills and slipped them into her purse. "Mind? Not at all; it'll be fun, and I'm sure Tony will appreciate it."

"I heard Delana say she is going to spend the day at her friend's house, so I guess she won't be going."

"Too bad. Tomorrow promises to be a beautiful day. I guess it will be just Babette and me."

"Are you and Babette going to swim?"

Tassie let out a snort. "And embarrass Tony? I don't think that's such a good idea. Babette and I will be there to watch them but we'll do our best to stay out of sight."

"Just the same, I'm glad you'll be there. Did you ever swim at Wayman's Lake?"

"Yeah, I used to swim there all the time when I was kid. I was even a lifeguard there the summer before I went off to college."

"Lifeguard, huh? You never told me."

Tassie grinned. "There are a lot of things you don't know about me, and I'm sure there are quite a few things I don't know about you."

He gave her a coy grin. "I'd like to know every little detail about you."

"Dad!" Delana's voice shrieked from somewhere upstairs. "I can't find my cell phone. Did you hide it from me?"

Tassie pointed to the pink cell phone lying on the coffee table then picked it up and held it out toward Mitch. "You want to take it to her or do you want me to?"

"I'll take it. Maybe if I start spending more time with her she won't be so jealous of you."

"You really think she's jealous of me, like Dale said?"

"What he said certainly made sense. I know I need to let the kids know what is going on between us, but maybe I should hold off for a few days. . .let things calm down a bit first."

She nodded in agreement.

"Dad! Did you hear me?" the voice from upstairs rang out again. "Did you hide my cell phone?"

Mitch gave Tassie's hand a hurried squeeze. "We'll talk later, okay?"

She nodded. "Yeah, sure."

"It's pretty crowded out here today. You sure it's safe for you guys to swim?" Tassie asked Tony as his friends began piling out of the minivan the next morning when they reached the lake.

He gave her a fierce glare. "Safe? You've got to be kidding. What do you think we are? Babies? You don't have to stick around. Why don't you leave and come back for us later?"

"No, we're staying. Your father will expect me to keep an eye on you."

"That's the lifeguard's job," he shot back. "Not yours."

Tassie took hold of Babette's hand and the two backed away, ignoring his disgruntled remark. "By the way, in case you and your friends got thirsty, I placed the ice chest in the back and filled it with soft drinks. There's also a bag of chips."

"We won't need them. Eric brought a bunch of stuff in his backpack."

"They'll be there if you change your mind, but please, Tony, keep an eye on one another and be careful." Determined to stay out of his way, she took Babette for a leisurely stroll along the water's edge, stopping often to admire the wildflowers and the natural greenery. Eventually, when Babette tired of walking, Tassie pulled out the old blanket she had brought along, spread it under a tree, and the two stretched out.

"This is fun," the child told her, smiling. "Can we come again sometime?"

"Sure, sweetie. Maybe next time you and I will go swimming. Would you like that?"

Babette lay down, flipped onto her side, curled up close, and yawned. "Yes, I'd like that."

"So would I." She began to gently stroke the little girl's back and soon Babette was fast asleep. Tassie gazed at the child, now so peaceful and lovable, and not at all like the raving little tyrant who had ordered her out of her room that first day. She turned her attention to where Tony and his friends were jostling out at the end of the long dock, and trying to shove one another into the water.

Tassie laughed at their antics until Tim, a boy much larger in stature than the others, the apparent bully of the group, began struggling with Tony. The boy was being far too aggressive and Tony appeared to be wearing out. She wished he would just jump in and get it over with before someone got hurt. The big kid's playfulness was getting out of hand. Finally, after one mighty shove, both Tony and the boy fell off. The other boys continued to jostle with one another, but as she watched, she realized Tony wasn't anywhere in sight. Was he simply treading water on the opposite side, or was he in trouble?

Unable to stand it any longer, Tassie leaped to her feet and, while both calling out Tony's name and praying, ran the length of the dock. When he didn't answer, instinctively, Tassie leaped into the water and began franticly searching the area in hopes of finding him. But Tony wasn't there! And he wasn't with the other boys. After sucking in a big breath, she dove under the murky water, flailing her arms and hands in search of him. When at last she surfaced, she screamed out for help, but both the crowd and Tony's friends were yelling and being so rowdy they didn't hear her, and the lifeguard was down the beach, breaking up a fight going on between another group of boys.

She dove again, screaming for help each time before she sucked in another breath and dove down, but no one was paying any attention to her. She couldn't waste precious time. It was up to her to find him.

For a brief moment, she thought she felt something brush against her arm.

But her air was gone.

She had no choice but to resurface or risk drowning, herself.

Chapter 10

With both her energy and her air nearly spent, Tassie gasped for air as her face hit the surface. "Help! Someone help!" *God, please! Please, oh please, help me find Tony!*

Sucking in the biggest breath her lungs would allow, she dove again. She was about to resurface when her fingers came in contact with his face. Grabbing hold of his arm, she used her free hand to fight her way to the surface and screamed out again for help. This time her shrill cry caught the attention of three of Tony's friends who immediately jumped into the water and helped her pull his limp body to the shore.

Tassie moved into position over Tony and, using the skills she had learned in lifeguard training, began CPR. In between breaths she glanced in Babette's direction and mercifully found the child still sound asleep, totally unaware of her brother's plight. "You, Jimmy," she told the third boy, "go to the car, get my cell phone, call 911, and tell them we need an ambulance and a rescue team!"

In desperation, she kept working on Tony, all the while praying. When a noise, an almost guttural sound, came from Tony's throat, his head gave a slight jerk to the left, and he gasped for air, she shouted a loud, "Hallelujah, praise the Lord!"

As Tony's breathing evened out, she lifted his slim frame and cradled him in her arms. "Relax, Tony. You're okay now. You have a cut on your cheek that will probably need stitches but, thank God, it looks like you're going to be all right."

The boy stared up at her with glassy eyes then glanced around. "What happened?"

"You must have hit your head when you fell off the dock."

"Tassie pulled you out," one of Tony's friends explained with widened eyes.

"Tassie!" Babette screamed out as she wakened from her nap and began to cry.

Another of Tony's friends brought Babette to Tassie, who then explained to her as best she could what had happened to her brother. "But don't worry. He's going to be fine."

Suddenly, off in the distance, she heard the wail of a siren. By the time the ambulance and rescue crew roared into the parking area, Tony's breathing had returned to near normal and he was sitting up on his own.

One of the EMTs quickly knelt beside him, and after asking a few questions and checking him out, gave him a thumbs-up. "Everything seems okay, but since that gash on your cheek will require a few stitches, we'll take you to St. Francis Med Center and let them have a look at you."

"Is Tony going to ride in the am-a-lance?" Babette asked, wide-eyed.

Tassie gave her a reassuring smile. "Yes, the doctor needs to take care of that cut."

"Can I ride in the am-a-lance with him? I never went in an am-a-lance."

"No, honey, you have to ride home with me. You wouldn't want me getting lonely, would you? Besides, we have to take Tony's friends to their homes and tell their parents what happened."

Babette smiled up at her. "Okay. I'll ride with you."

Knowing Mitch had to be told about Tony's accident, as soon as the ambulance pulled out of the parking lot, Tassie dialed his cell phone only to get his voice mail. She certainly didn't want to leave bad news like that in a message. Mitch would freak out, so she simply told him to call her as soon as he got her message. After that she called the station and was told he was out on a case and currently unreachable.

She had barely broken the connection when her phone rang and Mitch's number came up on the ID. "Oh, Mitch, Tony had an accident at Wayman's Lake, but he's okay. The am—"

"Accident? What kind of accident? What happened?"

"He and his friends were at the end of that long dock, trying to shove one another into the water. That big kid, you know the one I mean, the Grisham boy—he got pretty rough with Tony and when he shoved him in, Tony either hit his head on the dock or one of the pilings and it knocked him out."

"But he's okay? Someone got to him in time to pull him out?"

"Yes. The EMTs checked him over and they said he looked fine but they took him to St. Francis to make sure and to have his cheek looked at. It'll require stitches. I wanted to go with him but Babette is with me and someone has to take his friends home. Oh, Mitch, I've never been so scared."

"I need to get to him. You and Babette go ahead and take the boys home. I'll stay with Tony until they release him. And, sweetheart, thanks for being there for him. I'll see you as soon as we get home." He paused. "Tassie?"

He called me sweetheart! "Yes?"

"I—I love you."

Her heart reeling at his unexpected words, she found herself almost unable to speak. "I—I think I love you, too."

"Thanks for being there for my boy, and for being with Babette."

"You're welcome. I–I'm glad I was there."

Once her mind began to settle down again, a wave of thankfulness washed over her as she gave in to reality. Tony could have died if she hadn't gotten to him in time. But praise the Lord, God had answered her prayers. What an awesome

God she served. And if that wasn't enough, the man of her dreams had declared his love for her.

Delana sauntered into the living room when Tassie and Babette entered the house. "It's about time you got home. I was beginning to wonder if we were going to have to go without supper."

"Tony had an accident while he was swimming. He nearly drowned," she explained. "The EMT said he thought he was going to be okay, but they took him to the hospital. He sustained a nasty cut on his cheek that probably required stitches, and they wanted to check him out. Your father went to the hospital to be with him."

The girl rolled her eyes. "That sounds like something my klutzy brother would do. He's always doing something stupid."

It upset Tassie to see how unconcerned the girl was about her brother, especially when she simply shrugged and went to her room without asking any more questions. How could she be so heartless?

It was nearly eight before Mitch arrived home, and Tony was with him, the side of his face covered by a big white bandage. Tassie nearly went into shock when Tony hurried to her and gave her a feeble hug. "Dad said I should thank you for jumping in after me."

Mitch rushed to the pair and circled them with his long arms. "The EMT told us it was you who saved my son's life, Tassie. Why didn't you tell me you were the one who found him and pulled him out?"

As he pressed his head against hers she felt tears fall onto her cheek.

"All I did was jump in the water and search for him. It was God who led me to him. You wouldn't believe how hard I prayed."

Tony gave her a shy smile. "I'm glad you found me."

She placed a gentle hand on his shoulder. "I'm sorry about your cheek. Does it hurt very much?"

"It's okay. Good thing you stayed at the lake when I told you to go home."

Mitch pulled back and stared at Tony. "You told her to leave? Why?"

"Because all the guys made fun of me, Dad. They called her my babysitter."

"I'm glad you realize your *babysitter* is the one who saved your life while your so-called friends were all too busy having fun to realize you were in trouble. Tassie was pretty brave to leap into that water and search for you like she did. Especially after the way you've treated her. Maybe now you two can become friends."

Mitch gave Tassie a wink, and wrapping an arm about his son, tugged Tony toward the stairway. "But right now off to bed with you, kiddo. You've had a busy day. I'm sure you're exhausted."

"I could fix you both a sandwich," Tassie volunteered, gesturing toward the kitchen.

"Thanks, but we went through the drive-through on the way home and picked up a hamburger."

She fought back tears as she watched them walk away. Realizing Tony was missing and then diving into that water, not knowing if she would find him or not, had taken its toll on her, too. Now that they were all safely back home and things had nearly returned to normal, every bone and muscle in her body ached. All she wanted was to finish loading the dishwasher then get a cool drink of water and head for her warm, comfy bed. But as she finished and turned off the light before heading to her room, in the darkness an arm circled her waist and pulled her close. From the scent of aftershave that filled the air she knew it was Mitch.

"Marry me, Tassie," he breathed into her ear. "I've loved you from the moment you set foot in my house. It just didn't feel right to admit it until we talked to Dale."

She swallowed hard then held her breath. Was she hallucinating? Had she been underwater too long? Her brain been deprived of its much needed oxygen?

"I know my proposal is unexpected and I have no right to ask you this soon," he went on, "and I wouldn't be surprised if you slapped me. I'm not asking because you saved my son's life—it's because I love you. I—I want to spend the rest of my life with you."

"Marry—you?" she squeaked out, still in shock.

"We've spent many hours together these past couple of months, you and I. We probably know each other better than many couples do after a long engagement. I know I don't have much to offer you, a worn-out cop who works long hours with kids who are enough to drive any sane woman away, but I—"

"But your kids would never want you to marry me! They hate me."

"I've finally realized it's not you they hate. Like Dale said, it would be the same for any woman who came into our home. They'll come around once they realize I love you. Look at Tony. He's bound to accept you after what you just did for him, and Babette's already crazy about you."

"You really think so?"

"I know so." His cheek lightly caressed hers.

"But what about Delana?"

"Where's your faith? If God wants us together, can't He change her mind, too? Look, Tassie dear, I don't have a mansion or unlimited funds to lavish upon you, and I'm not only a failure as a father but as a husband and as a Christian, as well, so I wouldn't blame you if you walked out that door come September and never looked back. But I can promise you one thing: If you say yes and marry me, I'll love you until death us do part and I'll try my best to be the God-fearing, God-serving, God-loving husband you deserve."

"I—I. . ."

"Shh, don't answer now. Before you say no, I want you to think about it. Like I said, I don't feel this way about you because you saved my son, and not because Babette loves you, and certainly not because of the wonderful way you keep this house and this family going, or the way you cook. I love you for you, sweet Tassie, and I want to love you as my wife." With that he gathered her in his arms and kissed her.

She thought she was going to melt right there in his arms from the sheer wisps of delight that coursed through her body. Mitch, the man who had been the center of her wishful dreams, was there in the darkness, holding her, kissing her, declaring his love.

Finally, when their lips parted and he released her, all she could do was sigh in contentment. Never had she been so happy and yet at the same time, so confused.

"See you in the morning, my love," he whispered and then he was gone, having disappeared into the darkness of the house.

Tassie felt as if her feet never touched the floor as she made her way to her room. After kicking off her shoes and preparing for bed, she picked up the phone and dialed a number. "Hi, Mom," she said, trying to keep her voice calm. "I know it's your bedtime, but I had to call you. I—I have good news. Mitch just asked me to marry him!"

"Tassie? Is—is that you? We must have a bad connection. I thought you said something about marriage."

"Yes, Mom, it's me, and I did say something about marriage. Mitch proposed to me!"

"Proposed to you? Why? You hardly know each other. Why would he do such a thing?"

"I know it sounds crazy, but I love him, Mom. I think I've loved him since the first day I came to work here. We've spent a lot of time together. He's never been anything but kind to me. He's a wonderful man. He—"

"Tassie, even if that were so and you two *were* in love, think about it. Do you really want to marry a man who already has three children? I know Mitch is good-looking and seems quite nice, but to marry him?"

She gazed at the third finger on her left hand, trying to imagine what it would be like to wear Mitch's wedding ring. "But, Mom, Mitch shares my faith and you know how important that is to me."

"But I thought you said he hadn't been attending church for several years before he started going with you."

"He hadn't been but he had accepted Christ as his Savior when he was a boy."

"I can't imagine a Christian not wanting to go to church."

"It wasn't that he didn't want to go. He's been so busy with work and his family, he's gotten away from the Lord. But he's a new man now, Mom. He's doing a turnaround. He wants to be close to the Lord. He loves going to church with me."

"Maybe he's just doing that to win you over. And what about his children? Wouldn't you rather have children of your own?"

Tassie searched her heart. "Of course I want children of my own, but I love Mitch's children." *Or at least I'm trying to.* "We could always have children if we decided we wanted more. And, Mom, you're wrong about him lying to me to win me over. You don't know him like I do. He'd never do that."

"He mustn't have been much of a husband to his first wife. Didn't you say she left him?"

"Yes. But she's the one who left, not Mitch. Left not only her husband but her three children. She couldn't have been much of a wife or mother to be able to walk away like that."

"Well, I'd certainly want to know more about their breakup before committing to him if I were you."

"I do know, Mom. He told me all about it."

"Oh, sweetheart, I don't know about this," her mother said with concern. "Take your time. Don't do something rash. You haven't told him yes already, have you?"

"No, but I want to. He told me to think about it."

"Smart man. I'll give him that much credit. Every girl should think long and hard before accepting a marriage proposal, but it's your life. You've always been levelheaded and made wise decisions. Whatever choice you make, I'm sure it will be the right one. But first pray about it. Let God lead you."

"Thanks, Mom. I didn't want to upset you, but I had to call you. I was so excited I was about to burst."

"I'm not upset, dear, just a little shocked. By the way, I called you this afternoon just to visit, but no one answered the phone."

"I drove Tony and his friends out to the lake."

"Oh? Did you swim? I know how you love the water."

Not wanting to go into detail, Tassie bit at her lip. "Sorta. I'll tell you all about it later. Good night, Mom. I love you. Don't forget to pray for me."

"I won't forget, sweetheart. I'm confident God will lead you to do whatever is in His perfect will as long as you remain open to it. I love you, too. Sweet dreams."

Totally worn-out after her unusual and busy day, Tassie yawned as she hung up the phone. *My dreams will be sweet, all right, and all about Mitch.*

Mitch was already dressed and waiting for her, drinking a cup of coffee at the table, when she entered the kitchen the next day. "Morning."

She grinned. "Good morning to you. You already made the coffee?"

After placing his cup on the table, he rose and sauntered over to her. "Yeah, I'll pour you a cup, but first. . ." He paused and gave her a bashful grin that made her heart sing. "First, I'd like to hold you in my arms and give you a good-morning kiss—if you'll let me."

Not sure how she should respond, Tassie simply stared at him.

"You're not upset with me, are you—about last night?"

She shook her head.

He extended his arms toward her then opened them wide. "Then come to me, Tassie."

His words were all it took. Without pondering his invitation or wondering if she should or should not, she leaped into his arms, lifted her face to his, and welcomed his kisses.

"Does this mean you'll marry me?" he asked when he finally allowed her to pull away.

"I think so, but I still need time, Mitch—just a few days. I won't take long. To me, as I'm sure it is to you, marriage is a lifetime commitment. We both need to pray about it. We want to be sure this is God's will for our lives."

Mitch dramatically wiped at his brow. "Whew, you scared me. There for a moment I thought you were going to say no, mainly because I'm still not sure you could ever love me."

"Ever love you? Mitch! I think I've loved you since the day I came to work for you!" Her words plummeted out before she could stop them. Not that she really wanted to stop them; she just hadn't planned on voicing them quite that way or at this moment.

He grabbed her up and whirled her about the room. "You do? You actually love me? Wow!"

"Of course, you silly! How else could I have put up with all the trauma you and your children have put me through?" she teased.

"I hate to admit it, but there may be more traumas in the future—before we get this thing licked."

"I know."

"And I want you to finish your education, Tassie. I'd never want marriage to me to stand in your way. I know how important it is to you."

"I've been thinking," she stated, grinning with a mischievous lilt to her voice. "Maybe I should delay it for another year. Somehow, finishing my education doesn't seem nearly as important now as it did when you hired me." Her grin faded. "Mitch, if we do marry I want to be a full-time mother to your children, not just a caretaker. I don't mean as a replacement for their own mother but as a second mother, one who loves them as her own and wants them to love her. Is that asking too much?"

"Not at all. In fact, that is exactly what I had hoped you would do. My children need a mother figure in their life. Just look what you've accomplished with Babette. That child has done a complete turnaround."

"Babette is a beautiful child, Mitch. All she needed was love."

"Tony was already coming around, and after what you did for him yesterday, I have a feeling he, too, is going to change." He paused thoughtfully. "It's Delana I'm worried about. To be honest, I have no idea how she will respond if you accept my proposal."

"I know. Rather than make any headway with Delana, I'm afraid all I've done is cause more problems. If I do accept your proposal, please don't get me an engagement ring. Seeing me wearing your ring would upset her even more."

Mitch lovingly gazed into her eyes and stroked her cheek with his finger. "As much as I'd want you to wear my ring, I know you're right."

"I want so much to get along with your daughter. I wish she wasn't so angry all the time."

"Everything you've done, you've done to help her. I think her mother's leaving us for another man hit her much harder than I realized."

"Mitch, tell me about June. If I'm to even consider being your wife, I need to know everything. You said she left you for another man. Was that the only reason she left? Had you two been having marital problems?"

He lowered her to her feet and motioned toward a chair at the kitchen table. "Yeah, I guess you could say we'd always had marital problems. June's beauty, her free spirit, her carefree zest for life, her impulsiveness—all the things that had drawn me to her in the first place—became the things that separated us once we became husband and wife. She loved bragging to her friends that she was a cop's wife, but she hated that it took up so much of my time. She spent money—money we didn't have—without a thought to living on a budget but wouldn't even consider going to work to help pay for those things. I shouldn't be talking this way about her. I'm sure she had legitimate complaints about me, too."

"Yes, Mitch, you should. I need to know. Surely there was some love between the two of you during your married years. You had three children."

Rubbing his forehead, he began to pace about the kitchen. "I did love her, and I wanted to have children with her. She didn't. But her girlfriends were all having babies, so she decided she would, too. She loved being pregnant with Delana and strutting around in her maternity clothes, and she was a fairly good mother at first. Then Tony came along. Caring for two children was way more than she could handle."

"What about Babette?"

"June left me the first time several years before Babette was born. About a year later she appeared at the door and begged my forgiveness and I took her back. The next few months were like a second honeymoon—until the doctor told her she was pregnant again. She was determined to have an abortion but I told her if she did, it was all over between the two of us. From that day on, it was like I was her enemy. She couldn't say a civil word to me and she turned her back on Delana and Tony."

"But surely when she saw Babette's sweet little face and held her in her arms she—"

"No, she barely paid any attention to Babette, and she was gone all the time. We went through babysitter after babysitter because she would never come home at the time she said she would. I tried to reason with her but she wouldn't listen."

Tassie reached out to him. "Oh, Mitch, how awful that must have been for all of you."

He sat down beside her and cradled her hand in his. "It was an awful time. It sounds mean-spirited for me to say it, but after finding out she'd been cheating behind my back with her lover again, I was almost glad when she left us that second time. I'm sorry to say it, but I'd had about all I could take—we all had; and after what she had done, I'd never have been able to trust her again."

"Mitch, I'm so sorry. I know it has been hard for you—telling me all of this—but knowing what you and the children have gone through gives me a better understanding of so many things. Not only of you, but of Tony's and Delana's attitudes, especially Delana's. Being the oldest she probably remembers more of what happened than the other children do."

"I'm sure she does, but sweetheart, we can't let her keep us apart. Delana is almost sixteen. In a few years, even if she doesn't go to college, she probably won't be living at home. Once most girls graduate from high school all they can think about is getting out on their own. I doubt Delana will be an exception."

"You're probably right. I love my parents dearly, and have always gotten along with them fabulously well, but I, too, wanted to get out on my own. Moving out of your parents' house is like announcing to the world you have arrived, that you are now an adult."

"And it seems to me the best thing I can do for her while she is still with me is to keep her under the influence of a positive, cheerful, godly woman. You, my love."

"She doesn't want my influence. She can barely stand the sight of me."

"I know. She doesn't want my influence, either. I won't try to deceive you by telling you it will be easy—I'm sure it won't. And I can't say she won't break your heart with her hateful words and her uncalled-for actions—because I'm sure that will happen." His shoulders rose and fell in a shrug. "I'm selfish for even asking you to share your life with my dysfunctional family."

"But I *want* to share my life with your family. I not only want to share it, I want to be an active and accepted part of it. I love your children, Mitch, and while I hate what she does and the way she behaves toward others—especially you and me—I love Delana because she is a part of you and because God loves her."

"Then you might say yes?"

"I want to say yes, but first I have something I must tell you, something that has been weighing on my mind for nearly ten years. Something I have to tell you before I accept your proposal."

Mitch raised a brow. "Uh-oh. That sounds ominous."

Tassie blinked hard. "I–I'm not the unblemished, squeaky-clean person you think I am."

A frown clouded his face. "What do you mean?"

"It'll be easier to tell you if I start at the beginning." She pulled away from the shelter of his arms and began to pace about the room. "When I was a sophomore in high school one of the senior boys, the star quarterback on our football team, asked me for a date. I was afraid, since he was older than me, my parents wouldn't let me go, so I never told them. Rather than letting him pick me up at my house I asked him to meet me at the mall. I thought we were going to a movie, but instead, he took me to his friend's house where there was a party and a lot of drinking going on. I had never even tasted liquor before that night. But everyone was drinking. So, even though I knew it was wrong, trying to be like them, I drank, too. I really didn't like the stuff, but my date kept filling my glass, so I kept chugging it down. Next thing I knew, we were in his car and—"

"He raped you?"

Her heart thundered in her ears. She had never voiced her experience to another living soul, not even her mother and especially not her dad.

"I know it sounds crazy, but I'm really not sure. I was so drunk by that time I was totally out of it, but he said I went along willingly. And he told me to keep my mouth shut or he'd tell everyone in school what we did. After that night he never looked my way again, acted as if he didn't even know me."

Mitch gazed at her as if spellbound, as if he couldn't believe what he was hearing. "That's terrible. What did you do?"

Tassie had tried so hard to put that fateful night out of her mind and here she was reliving it again. Voicing that horrid experience was making her sick to her stomach and she wanted to throw up.

"What could I do?" she asked with a shrug. "Nothing, absolutely nothing. I wanted to tell my mother but I couldn't. She thought I was her perfect little girl. The knowledge of what I had done would destroy her. And I was so naive. I thought every time someone had intimate relations with a person they automatically became pregnant. For the next five months I lived in dread and fear. My grades went down. I was queasy all the time. I thought for sure I was having a baby. Until I checked some books out of the library and read about a home pregnancy test and found out I wasn't. But I'll tell you one thing. I did a lot of praying. What I had done was sin and I knew it. Even though I didn't deserve forgiveness, I asked God to forgive me and dedicated my life to serving Him. I've been walking with Him ever since."

"Oh, Tassie, I wish I'd been there to protect you."

"I'm so ashamed of what I did, Mitch. I know God forgave me for my stupidity but He never promised I'd forget. That awful time in my life haunts me every day."

"What happened to the guy?"

She shrugged her shoulders sadly. "I have no idea, and I hope I never see him again. What happened to me is in the past. I want to keep it that way. God forgave me. That's the important thing." Her eyes filled with tears of shame. "If you've changed your mind and don't want to marry me, I'll understand."

Mitch leaped to his feet and gathered her up in his arms, holding her close. "Change my mind? Why would I want to do such a thing? You must have been about Delana's age. You thought you could trust the guy. He knew what he was doing when he plied you with alcohol."

"But I—"

He put a finger to her lips to silence her. "My dearest, like God's Word says, we've all sinned, every one of us, certainly me included. No one is less deserving of His forgiveness than I am, but He has promised to forgive us our sins if we but ask. You asked Him and He's forgiven you. How could I even begin to hold anything against you for being naive and becoming that man's victim?"

"You're not upset with me about it?"

"Of course not, sweetheart. I'm just thankful you came out of it as well as you did. Things could have been a lot worse. But, my dear Tassie, you need to forgive yourself."

"I know, and I'm going to. I can't believe I've been stupid enough to carry this burden for so long."

"Let's you and me forget about the whole thing and never speak of it again."

Tassie stood on tiptoe and kissed Mitch on the cheek. "I love you."

He gave her a shy grin. "I love you more, my darling. Just think, if you say yes, you'll be Mrs. Mitchell Drummond."

"Then, knowing this about me, you still want me to marry you?"

"Of course I do. I love you!"

Tassie gazed into the eyes of the only man she'd ever loved then threw her arms about his neck. "Then, yes, Mitch, my darling. Yes, yes, yes! I'll marry you!"

"Really? When?"

"Whenever you say. I want so much to be your wife. Oh, Mitch, this is so exciting. I love you. I love you. I love you!"

"What do you think about having the wedding at your church but having our friend, Dale Lewis, perform the ceremony instead of your pastor?"

"I think it's a wonderful idea."

"I've got to tell the kids!"

"You know they're going to be upset."

"But Dale said we should be honest with them. Besides, we can't wait too long, sweetheart. The college fall semester will be starting in a few weeks. I'd like for us to be married before then. How about two weeks from today?"

"Two weeks from today for what?" Delana asked as she entered the kitchen, her eyes narrowing suspiciously. "You hugging our servant because she saved your son, or is something else going on?"

Scowling, Mitch let go of Tassie and hurried toward his daughter. "How many times do I have to remind you? Tassie is not our servant; she is our nanny. Tassie and I had decided we would tell you three children at the same time but since you're here and questioning our relationship, I guess you should be the first to know. I've asked her to marry me and she said yes."

Her eyes blazing, Delana glared at her father. "You're going to marry our maid? You've got to be kidding."

"Look, Delana, I love Tassie and I hope you will learn to love her, too. She's—"

"Love her? The way she treats me? Forget it, Dad! And don't count on me being at your wedding, 'cause I won't be there!" With that she turned and bolted out of the room. Moments later, she slammed her bedroom door hard enough to knock it off its hinges.

With a look of defeat, Mitch turned back to Tassie. "Now she's really upset."

"Don't beat yourself up. No matter when you told her it wouldn't have made any difference. She's determined to hate me."

He reached for her hands then gripped them tightly in his. "Her tirade hasn't made you change your mind, has it?"

"No, I still want to be your wife. Hopefully, with much prayer on our part, eventually she'll come around like Dale Lewis said she would and realize I want only the best for her."

He kissed her on the forehead then let his kisses slowly drift down her cheek to her lips. "So what do you think about having our wedding in two weeks?"

"It's a little fast, but I love the idea. Like you said, we probably know each other better than many couples do who have been dating for a long time. But I think a small wedding of just friends and family, and maybe those you have worked with over the years, would be best. Maybe if we keep it limited to just a few people, Delana will decide to come. A small wedding shouldn't take too much planning."

"But you will wear a white gown, won't you?"

"Oh, yes. This may be your second wedding, but it's my first."

They parted quickly as Tony and Babette came into the room. "Hey, what's going on with Delana? It felt like an earthquake when she slammed her door. She mad or somethin'?"

Mitch shot a quick glance at Tassie. "I guess now is as good a time as any to tell you. I've asked Tassie to marry me and she said yes!"

Tony grinned. "Now I know why Delana slammed her door."

Mitch did a double take. "You're not upset about it?"

"Naw, I knew you guys were getting along pretty well."

"Daddy, what does married mean?"

Mitch bent quickly and lifted Babette in his arms. "Oh, honey, I'm sorry. I should have done a better job of telling you kids. Married means Tassie won't be our nanny anymore, she—"

"But I want her to be my nanny. I love Tassie!" Babette began to cry.

Tassie quickly pulled the girl from Mitch's arms and held her close. "Oh, honey, I'm not leaving. I'll still be living here and taking care of you. Things will just be a little bit different."

"I guess that means you'll be our mom," Tony said matter-of-factly.

She whirled around to face him. "No, Tony! No one can ever take your mother's place, but I would like to be like a second mom to you. I love you kids."

"So when is the wedding?"

"Two weeks," Mitch said proudly. "In two weeks Tassie will be Mrs. Mitchell Drummond."

"Since it's a warm day, I thought we'd pick up some chocolate-chip ice cream," Tassie told Babette the next afternoon after they had visited the library and she pulled the car into the grocery store's parking lot. "Would you like that?"

Babette's eyes sparkled. "Yummy. I love ice cream."

"Me, too."

"I like going to the store with you, Tassie."

"And I like going to the store with you!"

They purchased their ice cream then headed for home, only to be surprised when they saw Dale Lewis coming out their front door with Delana a few steps behind him. *Oh, please, God, don't let Delana be in any trouble,* Tassie breathed in prayer as she pulled in beside them. But Dale was smiling. That had to be good sign.

"Hi," he told her with a friendly wave. "I saw Delana walking home from the mall, so I stopped to give her a ride."

When Tassie turned to smile at Delana she found the girl's mascara smeared, as if she had been crying. "You could have called me, Delana. I would have been happy to pick you up."

Dale grinned. "Naw, it worked out better this way. It gave me and Delana a chance to have a chat. Gotta go. See you all later."

Tassie watched until his car disappeared down the street. When she turned around, Delana had already gone back into the house.

"Did either of them say what they chatted about?" Mitch asked her after he got home. "Did she seem mad at him or upset?"

"If she would have been mad at him, I doubt she would have walked him to his car, but she did sort of look like she had been crying. Maybe you should ask him."

He shrugged. "I know it sounds silly, but I'm not real sure he'd tell me. He's pretty tight-lipped when it comes to counseling someone."

Her eyes widened. "You think that's what he was doing? Counseling her?"

Again he shrugged. "Who knows? Maybe. I doubt Delana will tell us and if I ask her she'll probably get mad and tell me it's none of my business. I guess if he did counsel her, we'll have to pray she pays attention to him. I know it won't be easy, but let's try to put all this out of our minds for now and think of something pleasant. We have a wedding to plan."

Tassie gazed lovingly into his eyes. "I need to talk to you about something."

"Oh no. Don't tell me you've changed your mind about marrying me."

"Oh, no, nothing like that, but I've been thinking. Now that we're engaged and I'm no longer simply an employee in your house, it seems improper for us to be living under the same roof."

"But I need you with the kids."

"I know, and I have a plan. I was thinking I could move back to my parents' home and come to work every morning at six to prepare breakfast and be here with the kids all day. Then I'd leave as soon as Babette goes to bed and—"

"But what if I get home late or am called out during the night?"

"I haven't asked Mom yet, but I think she would be willing to come and spend the nights at your house until we're married."

Mitch wrinkled up his face. "That seems kinda silly."

"Maybe, but I think it would set a good example for the children."

"I'm sure you're right. As Christians we don't want any appearance of impropriety."

"Good, I was hoping you'd agree with me. I'll call Mom in the morning."

Although the next few days were filled with a flurry of activity and more happiness than Tassie had ever before experienced, there was still a constant strain between

Tassie and Delana. It wasn't that the girl was rude or said or did anything out of the ordinary; instead it was as if a heavy gray cloud hung between them.

"Delana, dear, I wish you wouldn't treat Tassie the way you do," Tassie overheard her mother saying in a sweet voice. "Tassie loves you."

Tassie's mother had stayed at the house this morning to help with some final details, and Tassie—just coming out of the kitchen—stopped short, not wanting to interrupt.

The girl responded with a loud huff. "Loves me? If she loves me why is she so mean to me?"

"Come on now, sweetheart. What has my daughter ever done to you that was mean?"

"She's always messing in my stuff and spying on me."

"It may seem that way to you but all she's doing is trying to help you."

"I don't need her help. I just want to be left alone."

"Please, Delana," Mrs. Springer pleaded with her, "this isn't just Tassie's wedding; it's your father's, too. He loves you, and despite what you may believe, we all love you. Nothing would make him any happier than to have you attend their wedding. Promise you'll think long and hard before doing something foolish enough to break his heart."

Delana huffed. "His heart is already broken. My mom took care of that a long time ago."

"Believe me, Tassie isn't going to run out on you, sweetie. She isn't just marrying your father, she's marrying his family. She wants so much to be a second mother to you kids. And. . ."

When she paused, Tassie backed away a bit.

"And she wants so much for you to be her maid of honor."

"Her maid of honor? No way!"

Tassie listened as a noise sounded, like a plastic bag tearing or a box being pulled open.

"Look, I've brought her prom dress," her mother said kindly. "It's your size. I know it will fit you."

"Since I'm not going to the wedding, I won't be needing it."

"I'll leave it here, in case you change your mind. You'd look so pretty in pink. Just imagine how happy your father would be if you walked up that aisle toward him, wearing that dress."

As the two moved toward the doorway, Tassie rushed back into the kitchen, lest she be discovered. *Oh, Mom, if anyone can reach Delana it will be you with your sweet spirit. If only I were more like you.*

Despite Delana's absence, the dinner and wedding rehearsal went well that evening.

Tassie was glad Mitch had asked Chaplain Lewis to perform their ceremony. She liked him. He was one of the strongest Christians she had ever met and just the kind of man Mitch needed at this time of his life. His wise counseling was exactly what they'd both needed.

Although both Tassie and Mitch were concerned about his daughter's reluctance to attend their wedding, once they reached home they spent a pleasant hour holding hands and cuddling on the sofa, declaring their love for each other.

About eleven, she gave Mitch a final kiss and hug then excused herself, with plans to go to her parents' home and get a good night's sleep.

The ringing of her cell phone wakened Tassie a little before two. After flipping on the light she answered with a sleepy, "Hullo," but the sobs and the upset voice she heard in response made her eyes open wide and her heart quiver with fear.

Chapter 11

"Tassie, I need your help."

Tassie gripped the phone tighter. "Delana?" There was a pause but she could still hear sobbing.

"I've done something terrible." The words came out between sniffles.

Tassie sat straight up in bed. "Where are you? It's after midnight. I thought you'd be in bed by now!"

"I—I snuck out my window and climbed down the tree right after my dad went to bed."

"Why? Why would you do such a thing and where are you? I hear music."

"At the Wal-Mart store over on Locust."

"What are you doing there?"

"I don't want to call my dad. Can you come and get me?"

Tassie glanced at the clock. "Of course I can, but why can't you call your father?"

"Just come, please," the anxious voice pleaded amid sobs.

Tassie glanced at the clock again. "You still haven't told me what you're doing at Wal-Mart this time of night."

"I'll tell you when you get here, I promise."

"Wait for me inside, by the customer service counter. Don't, under any circumstances, go outside until I get there, you hear me?"

"Okay, but please hurry!"

Tassie's heart pounded in her ears as loud as a kettledrum as she hurriedly slipped into her jeans and T-shirt and headed for the Wal-Mart store.

But when she reached the store, before entering, she paused long enough to dial a familiar number on her cell phone.

When she finally made her way through the big glass doors she found Delana waiting right where she had told her. Wrapping an arm about the girl she led her toward her car. Once they were safely inside with the door locks engaged, she turned to her with a look of concern. "Delana, please tell me why you were here instead of at home in bed. I need to know."

Delana wiped at her heavily mascaraed eyes and swallowed hard. "I was mad at Daddy for getting married, so I decided to run away from home. My boyfriend was going to go with me, but neither of us had a car—so—I took Daddy's keys off of the hall table after he went downstairs and—"

"You took your Dad's car?"

"No, I took the minivan. I had to have it to run away."

"What did you plan to do for money? Gas is expensive and you'd have to eat and have a place to stay."

The girl hung her head. "I took Daddy's billfold and his credit cards. I took the money from his desk, too."

"How much was that?"

"About a thousand dollars."

"You knew your dad was saving that money for emergencies. If you and your boyfriend were running away and you had the minivan and that money, why did you call me?" She glanced around the parking lot. "By the way, where is he?" *And the minivan.*

"He got scared when I wrecked the—"

"You wrecked the van?"

"I couldn't help it, Tassie. Some guy stopped real quick in front of me, and I ran off the road to keep from hitting him!"

"Were either of you hurt?"

"Not really, just shook-up a bit, but it scared me really bad. We ended up in a deep ditch about four blocks from here."

"Did you call the police and report your accident?"

"No. I was afraid they'd call Daddy."

"You mean the minivan is still there?"

"Yes. I sorta hit a tree."

"Oh, my." Tassie rubbed her forehead. "You're going to have to tell him what happened, you know. We can't just let the van stay down in that ditch overnight. When did your boyfriend leave you?"

Delana winced at the question. "Right after it happened."

"Just took off and left you?"

She nodded.

"And you walked to Wal-Mart by yourself? It would have been much safer if you'd locked yourself in the car. Why didn't you call me then instead of risking your life by walking alone in the dark?"

"Because I was afraid you'd call Daddy."

Stricken with fear over what might have happened to the girl, Tassie reached across and placed her hand on Delana's arm. "God must have had His hand of protection on you, Delana; otherwise some guy might have come along and tried to get you into his car."

Delana covered her face with her hands. "A man in a car did offer me a ride, but I told him no."

Tassie scooted closer and gathered the quivering girl in her arms. "But he didn't try to get you into the car?"

"No, he just drove off. Daddy's going to kill me for taking the minivan and his money. I hated to call you, but I was afraid to call him."

She stroked the girl's hair. "Didn't I tell you I'd be there for you if you ever needed me?"

"Yes, but I've done some things—"

"The things you've done have upset me but they didn't keep me from loving you. But I still don't understand why you would try to run away, especially without leaving a note so your father wouldn't worry about you."

"I—I didn't think he'd care that I was gone. Even though Mr. Lewis said he did, I never thought my dad loved me. He's never treated me as nice as he treats you."

"Oh, honey, he's always loved you. You're his daughter. Besides, the love your dad and I share is a totally different kind of love than the love he has for you. You're his baby, his Delana." Tassie gently ran a finger down the girl's cheek. "No one could ever take your place in his heart, not me, not anyone. It's important that you know that. Oh, sweetie, I'm so sorry you felt that way. No matter what you do, your father will always love you. You're his flesh and blood. His precious child."

"I guess what I did *was* pretty stupid."

"Yes, it was, but you're not the first girl to do something really dumb. I—"

Both Tassie and Delana startled as a rap sounded on the girl's window and Mitch's face appeared.

Delana swung around angrily as Tassie hurriedly lifted the door's lock to allow him entrance. "You called him?"

"I had to, sweetie. He's your father. He deserved to know."

"What's going on, and why are you at Wal-Mart this time of night?" Mitch asked, an angry tinge to his voice.

Delana dipped her head and cowered beneath his penetrating gaze. "I'm sorry, Daddy, but as much trouble as I've caused you, I thought you'd be glad I was gone," she explained between sobs.

"Gone? What do you mean *gone*?"

"I—I was running away."

"Running away? How could you even think of running away?"

When she sent a glance for help toward Tassie, Tassie answered for her. "She took the minivan, Mitch."

"Delana, how could you?" Mitch glanced around the parking lot. "Surely you weren't running away alone. Was someone else with you? Where is the minivan?"

Again, Delana winced. "My boyfriend was going with me but he got scared when I. . ."

His eyes widened. "When you what?"

"It wasn't my fault, Daddy. Someone made me run off the road!"

"You had a wreck?" He gave her a frantic once-over. "Are you okay?"

"Uh-huh, I'm okay but—but the minivan is in a ditch."

"About four blocks from here," Tassie inserted then watched with a broken heart as Mitch, a big, strong man who had faced many a hardened criminal, buried his face in his daughter's hair and began to weep.

"Where is your boyfriend? Was he hurt?"

"He left right after the accident happened. I—I guess he went back home."

A scowl dented Mitch's forehead. "Good thing. If I had him here I'd want to wring his neck. Was this running away thing his idea or yours?"

Tassie grabbed hold of Mitch's wrist. "The important thing is that Delana is safe and uninjured."

He stared at his daughter for a moment then wrapped his arms around her. "Tassie's right. I love you, Delana, you have to believe that. I don't know what I would have done if anything had happened to you. You and your brother and sister are the most important things in my life. Without the three of you, life wouldn't be worth living. You three and Tassie *are* my life!"

"But, Daddy, how can you say that? You're never home, and when you are—you're always yelling at me."

"I know and I'm sorry, Delana, so sorry. I've been a terrible father to you three kids. It nearly killed me when your mother left. I guess I never fully realized how much it hurt you, too. Instead of worrying about how her leaving affected you kids, I wallowed in my own self-pity. I guess I tried to forget about her and the rejection *I* felt by throwing myself into my work. How can I even begin to ask you to forgive me? If I had been the father I should have been, you wouldn't have felt the need to run away from me."

"I'm sorry, Daddy. I didn't mean to scare you."

Mitch pulled her close, sheltering her in his arms. "Please, baby, promise me you won't leave me again."

"I won't. I promise." Pressing her face into his chest, Delana sobbed like a baby.

Tears trailed down Tassie's cheeks as she watched the scene playing out before her. It was a tender moment she would never forget.

Mitch planted a kiss on his daughter's forehead then lifted her face to his. "I've been a miserable example to you children, but I'm trying to change. I want us to be a real family, Delana, the kind of family God intended us to be, and you are such an important part of it." He let out a sigh that seemed to come from the pit of his stomach. "I should have taken you children to church when you were little, even though your mom refused to go."

"You're taking us now."

"And I plan to continue taking you, but we can talk about that later. Right now, Tassie needs to head back to her mother's house and I want you to show me where the minivan is so I can call a wrecker."

❦

The fact that the house was quiet the next morning when Tassie entered didn't surprise her. The children were being allowed to sleep late since they were on summer break. She found Mitch and her mother sitting at the kitchen table, engaged in conversation.

"Morning, sweetheart." Mitch rose, kissed her cheek, and pulled out a chair for her. "Sit down. I'll pour you a cup of coffee."

She thanked him then glanced toward her mother. "I guess Mitch told you what happened last night after you'd gone to bed."

"Yes, he did. It must have been a pretty harrowing experience for all of you. I'm sorry I didn't hear Delana leave. Maybe if I had, this whole thing could have been avoided."

Tassie hurriedly gave her mother's hand a pat. "Don't blame yourself, Mom. You couldn't possibly have heard her from where you were sleeping in my room above the garage. Besides, she knew her father was downstairs in his room. I'm sure she went out of her way to be quiet."

Mitch placed Tassie's cup of coffee on the table then nodded in agreement as he sat down beside her. "She's right, Mrs. Springer, and you couldn't have stopped her even if you'd tried. There is no one to blame for this fiasco but me."

Tassie quickly leaned toward him and cupped his hand in hers. "Don't be so hard on yourself. She's talked about running away several times, but neither of us ever thought she would go through with it."

"I sure didn't. I figured her threats were nothing more than a means of getting her way."

"Whatever her reason, at least she's home now and not off in some stranger's hands who could do her harm."

"Yes, praise the Lord for watching over her." He gave Tassie a half smile. "I'm glad, since she was afraid to call me, she called you. I wouldn't have handled things nearly as well."

Tassie swallowed at the lump that had suddenly risen in her throat. "I was afraid she'd be furious with me for calling you, but once she realized you weren't going to be too angry with her, she seemed to have forgotten it."

Scooting his chair even closer, he wrapped his arm about her shoulders. "You did the right thing, sweetheart; you had to let me know. Surely, she realized you had no choice but to call me."

"Mitch is right," her mother offered. "I'm sure Delana is glad you called her father. Once that boyfriend of hers took off and left her alone, she knew she was in trouble and the only people who could help her were the ones who loved her. And she did tell Mitch she was sorry. Shower her with love and understanding, give her a little time and space, pray for her like you've never prayed for her before, and let God handle things. After all, isn't He the God of love?"

Tassie blinked back tears, tears of love and appreciation for her mother and her valuable insight. "Thanks, Mom. You always have the right answer."

"I agree." Mitch smiled at Tassie. "I'm sure glad I'm marrying a woman with such a smart mom."

A sweet expression blanketed Mrs. Springer's countenance. "And I'm glad my daughter is marrying a man who is big enough to admit his mistakes, and with God's leading, willing to work to make changes." She rose, and after placing her cup in the dishwasher, turned to face them. "Now if you'll excuse me, I'll leave you two lovebirds alone and go home to my husband. I'll see you both at the church."

Once they heard the front door close, Mitch pulled Tassie close and leaned his head against hers. "Know what day this is?"

She gave him a coy smile. "Friday?"

"Yeah, Friday, but that's not what I mean."

She pursed her lips thoughtfully. "Umm, it isn't a special holiday, is it?"

"It is for me. I'm getting married today."

She lifted her face toward his with a mischievous smile. "You're getting married? And you didn't invite me to your wedding? I don't remember receiving an invitation."

He playfully brushed his lips across hers. "I'm inviting you now. Not only to come to my wedding but to spend the rest of your life with me."

She pulled away and glanced up at him. "Your life? Oh, my. What will your new bride think about that?"

"Since you, my beloved Tassie, are the new bride I will be marrying in a few hours, I'm hoping you'll be as excited about spending the rest of your life with me as I am about spending my life with you." He lovingly stroked her hair. "This is the best day of my life."

"It's my very best day, too. I'm marrying the man I love and I'm gaining three wonderful children."

He tossed his head back with a laugh. "*Wonderful* children? I wouldn't exactly call them wonderful, considering all the mean, hateful things they've done to you. And surely you're not forgetting that because of Tony's reckless behavior you had to jump in the lake and save his life. And what about having to rescue Delana?"

"But, Mitch, don't you see? At the time those things seemed like terrible experiences, but I think God is using them for good. Tony and I are finally becoming friends and Delana set her pride aside and called *me*, of all people, to come after her. I just know that, eventually, she will accept me. And hopefully she'll accept God, too."

He grinned. "You know, you're absolutely right. I hadn't thought of it that way. God does work in mysterious ways, His wonders to perform." He pulled her close again. "So does that mean you still want to go through with this wedding?"

"Yes, my love, more than ever." Tassie stood and kissed Mitch on the cheek. "I love you."

His lips tilted up in a smile. "I love you more, my darling. Tonight, you'll be Mrs. Mitchell Drummond."

She wrapped her arms about his neck and lovingly gazed into his eyes as she twined her fingers through his hair. "I know, and I can hardly wait."

"I know we haven't had much of a courtship, and I'm not a man of flowery words or a man of means, but I promise to spend the rest of my life doing everything I can to make you happy."

Lifting her hands she cupped his face between her palms. "And I love you, my precious one. You're the man of my dreams in every way."

He harrumphed. "Man of your dreams? A father with children who have given you more grief than any person should have to endure in a lifetime?"

"But, Mitch, once we say 'I do,' those children will become my children as well. I will share equally in the responsibility of bringing them up to be caring, productive, God-loving adults, a responsibility I gladly and joyfully accept."

The smile he gave her touched her heart. "You're crazy; you know that, don't you?"

She nodded. "Crazy about you! Oh, Mitch, I can hardly wait to be your wife."

"And I'll be the proudest man alive." After nuzzling his chin in her hair, he bent and kissed her with a kiss that made her heart thunder and her head reel.

When they finally parted, he backed away. "I hate to leave you but I'd better get out of here. I know you have a million things to do before our wedding and so do I."

Her lower lip took on a pout. "You mean I won't see you again until our wedding?"

Smiling, he shrugged. "I guess not, unless you want to slip off and have lunch with me."

She snickered. "Is that an invitation?"

"Sure."

"At that little Italian place in the strip mall down the street?"

"If that's where you want to go."

"At straight-up noon?"

"Yep, straight-up noon."

"I'll be there. Mom is coming over in a few minutes. I'm sure she won't mind staying with the children until I get back."

She giggled like a schoolgirl. "See you at noon, my love!"

The rest of morning flew by as Tassie worked on countless tasks she was determined to complete before leaving for their wedding.

By eleven forty-five, when she left to meet Mitch for lunch, Delana still hadn't come out of her room.

"How's the lasagna?" he asked as they sat in a corner table in the little Italian restaurant, fondly gazing across the table at each other.

"It's wonderful but I'm too nervous to eat," she confessed, her mind still on Delana.

"You're still worried about her, aren't you?"

She nodded.

"I'm worried about Delana, too, sweetheart. But this is our day, Tassie. We can't let her ruin what should be the happiest day of our lives."

She blinked at a tear. "I know but I so want her at our wedding and I know you do, too."

He reached across the table and took both her hands in his. "She knows it, too, sweetheart. We've got to leave it in God's hands."

"I'm trying. I not only wanted her to be there, I wanted her to be my maid of honor. I know I could have asked one of the ladies at the church, but if I can't have Delana I don't want anyone."

Mitch's thumb rubbed at her ring finger. "I wish I'd gotten you an engagement ring."

She gave her head a vigorous shake. "No, Mitch, an engagement ring on my finger would have only added to Delana's anger."

"Well, like it or not, as my wife you are going to wear a wedding ring." His expression softened as he gazed into her eyes. "A quite pretty wedding ring, if I do say so myself."

"Oh, Mitch, I hope you didn't spend more than you should have. A simple gold band is all I need."

They discussed the minor redecorating they planned to do to the house, the shrubs they wanted to plant in the front yard, and several other non-children subjects, then walked to their cars holding hands.

"You *will* show up at the church, won't you?" Mitch teased as he closed her car door and leaned into the open window.

She turned the key in the ignition then grinned up at him. "Absolutely. No way am I going to miss a chance to become Mrs. Mitchell Drummond." After blowing him a kiss, with a little wave she drove away.

Delana was standing in the middle of the living room when Tassie entered the house. "I've been waiting for you. Your mom said you wanted to ask me something. I hope it's not about that bridesmaid thing."

"Sweetheart, I really want you to be my maid of honor at our wedding. Won't you please reconsider?"

Delana quirked up her face. "Why would you want me to be your maid of honor?"

"Because I love you, Delana. Mom said she showed you my prom dress. It may not be the kind of dress you'd pick to wear, but I'm sure it will fit you. We can even take the bow off. And your father and I both so want you at our wedding."

"I haven't even decided yet if I'm going."

Tassie reached for Delana's hand and was pleased when she didn't pull away. "Look, sweetie, I understand where you're coming from. With the exception of your father, the people you have loved the most are the ones who let you down and walked out of your life." She paused and with her free hand lifted the girl's face to meet hers. "I promise you on my word of honor, my precious Delana, I will never leave you. I'm here to stay. I've told you several times I wanted to be your friend and I still do. But more than that, I want us to share our lives together much like a mother and her natural daughter would. I want to be there proudly watching you when you graduate high school and when you walk down the aisle and pledge your life to the wonderful man you will one day meet and marry. I want to be there when you have children and be a grandmother to them. I want to share in your joys and sorrows, to be there for you whenever and wherever you need me. And most importantly, I want you to let me love you and for you to love me. I know it will take time but. . ." She stopped mid-sentence when tears began to trickle down Delana's cheeks.

"You're not just saying those things so I won't be mad about you marrying my dad?"

"Oh, honey, no! I mean every word! I can't tell you how much I want you there. Your father does, too!"

"Then—I guess I'll go."

"To our wedding?" Tassie felt her eyes widen. This was almost too good to be true.

"Yes, but I don't want to be your bridesmaid or whatever you called it."

"I'd really like to have you as my maid of honor but just knowing you will be at our wedding is a wonderful answer to prayer." Cautiously wrapping her arms about the girl, Tassie couldn't help but sob. God was answering her prayer, their prayer.

"Couldn't you get one of your friends at church to be your maid of honor?"

She shook her head. "No. I told your father if I couldn't have you I didn't want anyone."

Delana gazed up at her. "You really said that?"

"Yes, and I meant every word. I want you, sweetie. Only you. No one else."

"So if I don't do it you won't have one?"

"That's right."

The girl gave her a sheepish grin. "Then I guess I'll do it."

Tassie's heart nearly exploded with joy. "You will? Really?"

"Yeah, I guess so." She paused with a grin. "If your dress doesn't make me look stupid."

She glanced at her watch. "We still have a couple of hours. If you don't like it we'll make a quick run to the bridal shop. I can hardly wait to tell your dad! He'll be so pleased."

Delana shook her head. "No, don't. I want to surprise him."

"You mean we should keep it from him until he sees you come up the aisle?"

She nodded. "Yes. I think he'd like to be surprised."

After planting a quick kiss on the girl's cheek, she smiled. "Let's go take a look at that dress to see if it will work."

Delana smiled back. "I've already tried it on. If you take that stupid big bow off the back it will do just fine. In fact, I kinda liked it."

As the two ascended the stairs arm in arm, Tassie lifted her eyes heavenward. *Oh, God, my Father, how could I have doubted You?*

Chapter 12

Mitch smiled at Dale Lewis as the two stood at the altar. "Surely you didn't wear that gun to our wedding."

Dale patted his coat. "Of course I did. Didn't I tell you and Tassie that gun goes with me everywhere I go?"

"This isn't a shotgun wedding," he responded with a grin. "No one is forcing me to marry this little gal. I'm doing it quite willingly."

Dale laughed, then his face sobered. "All kidding aside, Mitch, I hope you'll both remember the things the three of us talked about before the wedding rehearsal. Blending families is a tough job. You're going to have some rough times ahead, but God is faithful. He'll never fail you, and don't you fail Him. Take any differences you have to the Lord and leave them there for Him to handle and all will be well with you."

"I will, Dale. I've learned a lot these past three months. I won't make the same mistakes again; I promise."

"Just remember, I'm always here any time you need to talk."

"I will, old friend, and thanks."

He glanced toward Tony, who had agreed to be his best man, next at the doors at the back of the sanctuary, then at his watch. In a few minutes his bride would be coming through those doors.

He'd no more than had the thought when the organ began to play, the double doors opened, and their flower girl appeared—his adorable daughter, Babette, wearing the pretty pink dress Tassie had picked out for her. And her lips were turned up in a cute little smile that made his heart sing as she began to drop rose petals from her basket onto the floor.

Mitch felt as if he were going to explode with happiness. The only thing that could have made this day any better was if his oldest daughter would have agreed to attend the wedding instead of staying home by herself. But, to his joy, Tony and Babette were not only there, Tony had agreed to be his best man. At least that part of his and Tassie's prayers had been answered. Hopefully, now that they were being married, and since Tassie had been willing to rush to Delana's aid when she had needed her, the girl would begin to accept her as his new wife and give up on her crusade to get rid of her. *God,* he said in his heart, *if You could bring Tony and Babette around, then there has to be hope for Delana.*

Tassie's mother dabbed at her eyes with her hanky as she stood in the bride's room off the sanctuary, smiling at her. "You've never looked more beautiful, my precious daughter. You make a lovely bride. I knew that dress was the perfect one for you the moment we saw it in that bridal shop window."

"I just hope Mitch likes it."

Her mother sent her an adoring smile. "How could he not like it?"

Tassie checked to make sure the little diamond stud earrings were in place—the something old she had borrowed from her mother. "You are happy for me, aren't you?"

"Oh, yes. Staying nights in Mitch's home to be with his children has made me see why you love him. He's a fine man, Tassie. He's made mistakes but he honestly loves his kids and wants to do the right thing. He's determined to make sure they have a Christian upbringing, and with you there to help him, I'll know he'll succeed."

Mrs. Springer turned to Delana. "You look pretty, too, young lady. That dress fits you like it was made for you. And your hair looks beautiful pulled up that way."

Delana fingered one of the long tendrils falling softly at her neckline. "Tassie did it."

"I'm so glad you decided to be Tassie's maid of honor, dear."

Delana smiled at Mrs. Springer then at Tassie. "I'm glad, too."

A chill coursed through Tassie as she gazed at Mitch's daughter. She hadn't won her to the Lord yet, but by showering the girl with love and prayer, she knew it would happen. "Your father is going to be so proud," she told her as she lovingly cradled the girl's cheek in her palm. "Now each one of his children—our children—will be taking part in our wedding. What a blessing!"

Tassie's dad grinned at the three as he pushed open the door a crack and pointed to the clock on the wall. "You ladies about ready? The groom and the best man are gettin' a little antsy out there waiting for you."

"Oh, my! I should be in my seat." Her mother shook a cautioning finger at both Tassie and Delana. "Remember, you girls, step, together, step, together, step, together. I know you're both going to be in a hurry to get to Mitch but take your time. Enjoy every moment of your walk up that aisle." She blew an air kiss toward her daughter. "Especially you, my baby girl. This is your wedding day, the day every girl dreams of. Make it special."

Tassie leaned forward and placed a gentle, loving kiss on her mother's cheek. "I will, Mom. I'm going to remember this day forever." She smiled toward Delana. "And having Delana here with me is truly making this day special."

Mrs. Springer motioned at Delana as she opened the door and the organ music sounded. "There's your cue. You'd better come with me. It's time for you to make your appearance."

With a final glance at Tassie, Delana followed her step-grandmother-to-be out the door.

"You're beautiful," Tassie's father told her when her mother and Delana had gone and they headed down the hall toward the sanctuary. "I can't tell you how proud I am of you. You've grown into a lovely young woman. You're going to make a wonderful wife."

Her emotions suddenly taking over, Tassie felt like crying. "I want to be a good wife, Daddy, and a good mother to his children. I so want Delana to give her life to God."

"Don't you worry about that girl. She's come a long way in the past twenty-four hours. With all of us praying for her, I have a feeling she'll soon be accepting our Lord. She's young and she's been hurt. Being rejected by her mother like she was had to have left deep scars. They take time to heal. But God is still our Great Physician and always will be. Healing that girl's heart is child's play for Him. Have faith, sweetheart. God is able and He wants to answer your prayer."

"Thanks, Daddy. You always know the right thing to say."

Taking hold of Tassie's hand, he slipped it into the crook of his arm. "Ready?"

She smiled up at him through tears of joy. "Oh, yes, Daddy. I'm ready!"

As Babette reached the front of the church, Mitch glanced back toward the double doors. *Hurry, my love, please hurry.*

But the next person to enter wasn't Tassie; it was someone else. Had she asked one of the young women at the church to be her maid of honor and forgotten to tell him? He narrowed his eyes for a better look. *No, it can't be!*

But it was. It was Delana! Delana was here! Delana had come to their wedding after all—and she was Tassie's maid of honor! *Oh, Father God, how good You are!*

Mitch's heart nearly melted when his daughter drew nearer—a vision of loveliness in a pink gown, her hair all piled on top her head—and she was wearing so little makeup he could barely see it. *God, You did this for me? When I'm so unworthy? I don't know how You did it but I praise You for it. You are truly an awesome God. Thank You! Thank You! Thank You!*

"I love you, my darling daughter," Mitch whispered to her when she reached the altar as he drew her into his arms and hugged her close.

"I love you, too, Daddy."

All rose as the strains of the wedding march filled the sanctuary and Tassie appeared in her glorious gown of white. Her eyes sparkled as she walked slowly toward the front of the sanctuary, pausing only long enough beside the front pew to present a single red rose to her mother.

"Who gives this woman in marriage to this man?" Chaplain Dale asked as she and her father stepped before him at the altar.

"Her mother and I do."

Tassie smiled as her dad kissed her cheek then placed her hand into Mitch's before turning to take his place by her mother.

"You're here! You're actually here and you're going to be my wife! And all three of my children are here. Is God good or what?" Mitch whispered as she stepped up beside him.

"Dearly beloved," Chaplain Dale began in his deep, rich voice. "We are gathered today to bear witness as this man and this woman are joined in the holy state of matrimony. Their marriage is being entered into with reverence. For there is no greater joy than for two like-minded souls who love each other and love God to be joined together. To strengthen each other in all ways, to support each other through all sorrow, and to share with each other in the gladness of life."

Mitch cast an adoring glance at Tassie and then at the beautiful young woman at her side.

"Marriage in itself is an act of faith," Dale continued, "an ever-deepening commitment. It is a loving union between a man and a woman. Marriage between two people who love each other has been described as the very best and most important relationship two people can share. Marriage was ordained by God Himself and it should never be entered into lightly. The apostle Paul compared the relationship between husband and wife to that between Christ and the church. Marriage is a decision of two individuals to share the same type of pure, Christian love described by Paul."

Although Mitch listened carefully to Chaplain Dale's words, he couldn't help thinking about God's miraculous answer to prayer.

"Mitch, Tassie, would you please hold hands and face each other?"

Tassie handed her bouquet to Delana then turned to Mitch. He eagerly took hold of both her hands. They felt warm, soft to the touch. Just holding her hands sent chills through his body.

"Mitch, repeat after me." Dale paused. "I take you, Tassie Springer, as my wife. To laugh with in joy, to grieve with in sorrow, and to grow more in love with each day as we serve God together."

His heart thundering against his chest, Mitch repeated the words with great sincerity and dedication. Loving Tassie was going to be the easy part. Being worthy of her love was what worried him.

"Now, Tassie, repeat after me." Again, Dale paused. "I take you, Mitchell Drummond, as my husband. To laugh with in joy, to grieve with in sorrow, and to grow more in love with each day as we serve God together."

Mitch couldn't remember a more happy time in his life as he listened to Tassie repeat her vows.

"And I know you both intend to keep your vows. Trust each other and trust God and all will be well with you." Turning to Tony, Dale asked, "Do you have the rings?"

His lips tilted upward in a nervous grin, Tony reached into his pocket and pulled out two rings.

Mitch took the one with the small diamond solitaire and lovingly placed it on Tassie's finger. "This, my love, is a small token to remind you of my love and the pledge I've made to you this day."

The look of adoration on his beloved's face was almost more than he could bear. Although he had loved his first wife, the love he felt for Tassie was nothing like that love. This love felt permanent, fulfilling, satisfying, and, yes, challenging. With God's help he would do everything in his power to be the husband she deserved.

For a moment, Tassie gazed at the ring he'd placed on her finger then took the other ring from Tony and slipped it onto Mitch's finger.

"This ring, my precious one, is a small token of my love. May it symbolize the unending love I have for you. I commit my life to you, Mitch. May our love last a lifetime and may God grant us many years together as husband and wife."

Dale nodded toward Mitch. "You may kiss your bride."

Without a moment's hesitation, wrapping Tassie tightly in his arms, he complied.

Tassie felt giddy with happiness as Mitch's lips pressed against hers. Never in her wildest dreams the day she quit her job and decided to move back to Grand Island did she imagine she would be marrying a wonderful man like Mitch and become the stepmother of three children. How good God had been to her, and she knew He would be good to her in the future as she took on the daunting task ahead of her and worked to deserve the love of his children.

"Let us pray." The chaplain bowed his head. "Oh eternal God, You have heard the words of promise these two have just spoken. May the Holy Spirit speak to this man and this woman and give them a sense of the sacred and binding power of their vows. May they be a blessing to each other, and to those about them, as they enjoy the blessedness of a home life together, and may they cling to each other and to You. We ask these things in the name of Jesus Christ our Lord. Amen."

Tassie leaned into the strength of Mitch's arms. Never had she felt so exhilarated, so safe, and so loved.

"Tassie Springer and Mitchell Drummond, you have exchanged your promises and given and received your rings in my presence and in the presence of family and friends. By these acts and declarations you have become husband and wife. According to the power vested in me and the laws of the state of Nebraska, I hereby pronounce you husband and wife."

Tassie couldn't help but let out a little squeak. *Husband and wife! Mitch and I are officially married!*

"Now if you would turn and face your audience of well-wishers, I would like to introduce you." With a dramatic wave of his arm and smile of sincerity, Chaplain Dale said, "Friends, loved ones, it is my pleasure to introduce Mr. and Mrs. Mitchell Drummond. May God bless their union and bless them as they become a family."

As the strains of the wedding march sounded from the organ, the two made their way out into the foyer, headed toward the life they had just dedicated themselves to—a life centered around their family and God.

A Letter to Our Readers

Dear Readers:

In order that we might better contribute to your reading enjoyment, we would appreciate you taking a few minutes to respond to the following questions. When completed, please return to the following: Fiction Editor, Barbour Publishing, Inc., P.O. Box 719, Uhrichsville, OH 44683.

1. Did you enjoy reading *Rodeo Hearts* by Joyce Livingston?
   - ❑ Very much. I would like to see more books like this.
   - ❑ Moderately—I would have enjoyed it more if ________________

____

____

2. What influenced your decision to purchase this book? (Check those that apply.)
   ❑ Cover ❑ Back cover copy ❑ Title ❑ Price
   ❑ Friends ❑ Publicity ❑ Other

3. Which story was your favorite?
   ❑ *The Bride Wore Boots* ❑ *The Preacher Wore a Gun*
   ❑ *The Groom Wore Spurs*

4. Please check your age range:
   ❑ Under 18 ❑ 18–24 ❑ 25–34
   ❑ 35–45 ❑ 46–55 ❑ Over 55

5. How many hours per week do you read? ________________

Name ________________________________

Occupation ____________________________

Address ______________________________

City________________ State__________ Zip__________

E-mail _______________________________